I0606593

Jack wanted to help people, but he didn't want to be a patsy.

Jack felt guilty. It'd been almost three weeks since he'd gone back to see Ethel and pick up his stuff. He knew he couldn't stay, but he wanted to talk to her and see if she was all right. He still had his key, which he needed to return to her. He also wanted to take care of her. Other than Mary, Ethel was his only real friend, especially over the last six months. Debbie didn't call him once even, though he'd called her time and again. He spoke to Mark now and again, but Jack knew that Mark was on his own and really didn't care if Jack called or not. Mark sided with his mother, so that told Jack a lot. He was going to call Ethel's son to see if he'd pick up the slack with Jack's needing to leave. He'd visit her a lot after everything died down and he wasn't harassed like he knew he'd be over the next several months. Everyone would want a piece of him, but that would go with the territory. Everybody had money problems. If you had a family, you couldn't escape it. However, he'd formulated some plans in his head for all those who asked him for money. He didn't mind. Hell, he had plenty, but he wanted to separate the wheat from the chaff.

Jack thought of a simple formula for giving away money to others for projects or funding that he wasn't a part of. Whatever was asked of him, that person would have to match his or her request one hundred percent, either in money or in volunteer time to the project that Jack wanted done. If they weren't willing to do that, then their request would fall on deaf ears, unless they were so poor and sick that they couldn't comply with Jack's request. If someone needed money to pay their mortgage so they could keep the house, Jack would give them half and make a deal with the bank that the person would do work for the nonprofit at a rate of twenty dollar per hour, which was, on the average, above what most people in Troy made per hour. They'd have a time card and would do work either cleaning up the career center, helping tutor the children of those getting an education at the center, babysitting their children while they went through the program, or a hundred different jobs they could do to earn their money. They could help hand out flyers on the weekend, instead of just Jack, week in and week out. Jack would hire a volunteer coordinator who'd keep track of what was owed and what was earned back. Anyone who paid up in full would receive a certificate that he'd offer with pride for a job well done.

Fired at age fifty, dumped by his wife and grown, college-age children—his wife moved her lover, a UPS delivery-man, into the house as soon as Jack left—Jack Manning is humbled beyond words. Six months later, he's down and out, living in a rented room in the Burgh, cooking meals for his eighty-year-old landlady, while walking to work at the corner convenience store. No car. The only job he could get was for $12.00 an hour for the night shift, six days a week.

He bought a Powerball ticket, using the birthdays of all the people who hated him, woke up, turned on the news, and found out that he'd split 990 million dollars with two others across the country. Taking a cash payout, he would net $198 million. What would he do now that he was rich with no support payments or any family who cared about him? He was sure he would make a lot of friends real soon. But, like a lot of folks, he'd divvied up his winnings a long time ago in his daydreams when he was bored. This could be very interesting. Maybe he could right some wrongs, change lives, payback through kindness not revenge, help those who want to help themselves. Will it work? Will a lot of money make a difference? Maybe…

KUDOS for *You Don't Know Jack*

In *You Don't Know Jack* by Daniel J. Barrett, Jack Manning has had a really bad day at the office. He gets fired from the nonprofit agency where he works. And when he goes home to tell his wife, she informs him that she has someone new and wants a divorce. She kicks him out of the house and takes everything he owns. It gets worse, and six months later, Jack is reduced to working in a local convenience store and living with an old woman whom he takes care of for a break on his room and board. Then Jack wins the lottery, and suddenly he's wealthy. His divorce was final several months ago, so no one has a claim on his $330 million but him. However, that doesn't stop them all from trying. But Jack has wised up in the last six months, and he's not the same pushover he once was—as people are about to find out. Cute, clever, and emotionally satisfying, this one will make you laugh, sigh, and warm your heart—a feel good book if there ever was one. ~ *Taylor Jones, The Review Team of Taylor Jones & Regan Murphy*

You Don't Know Jack by Daniel J. Barrett is the story of Jack Manning—a fifty-year-old pushover, who can't say no, and teacher for a nonprofit organization in Troy, New York. Jack has spent the last several years helping underprivileged youth train for high-tech jobs in the local job market. But leaders of the organization where he works want to shut down his program and focus on serving Medicaid clients because they think they can make more money. So Jack gets fired, as do many of his coworkers. When Jack tells his wife what happened, she kicks him out of the house, saying that she's seeing someone else and wants a divorce. She gets everything in the divorce and leaves Jack with nothing. Even his car is repossessed.

But six months later Jack wins the Powerball Lottery for $330,000,000. Now it's time for a little payback, and he's going to have a lot of fun doing it, as people are going to discover they really didn't know Jack. Giving us a glimpse into the life of a lottery winner and the world of nonprofits, *You Don't Know Jack* both educates and entertains, along with making you dream about "what if…"
~ Regan Muprhy, The Review Team of Taylor Jones & Regan Murphy

Books by Daniel J. Barrett

Conch Town Girl series
Death But No Taxes (Prequel)
Conch Town Girl
Can't Sing or Dance
Taking Care of Your Own
Never Say Never

Other Novels
You Don't Know Jack

ACKNOWLEDGMENTS

Once again, I would like to thank everyone at Black Opal Books, including Lauri Wellington, Faith, and Jack for their dedication to their authors. It is appreciated.

You Don't Know Jack

Daniel J. Barrett

A Black Opal Books Publication

GENRE: WOMEN'S FICTION/HUMOR/FAMILY RELATIONSHIPS

This is a work of fiction. Names, places, characters and incidents are either the product of the author's imagination or are used fictitiously, and any resemblance to any actual persons, living or dead, businesses, organizations, events or locales is entirely coincidental. All trademarks, service marks, registered trademarks, and registered service marks are the property of their respective owners and are used herein for identification purposes only. The publisher does not have any control over or assume any responsibility for author or third-party websites or their contents.

YOU DON'T KNOW JACK
Copyright © 2018 by Daniel J. Barrett
Cover Design by Daniel J. Barrett
All cover art copyright © 2018
All Rights Reserved
Print ISBN: 978-1626949-37-9

First Publication: JUNE 2018

All rights reserved under the International and Pan-American Copyright Conventions. No part of this book may be reproduced or transmitted in any form or by any means, electronic or mechanical, including photocopying, recording, or by any information storage and retrieval system, without permission in writing from the publisher.

WARNING: The unauthorized reproduction or distribution of this copyrighted work is illegal. Criminal copyright infringement, including infringement without monetary gain, is investigated by the FBI and is punishable by up to 5 years in federal prison and a fine of $250,000. Anyone pirating our ebooks will be prosecuted to the fullest extent of the law and may be liable for each individual download resulting therefrom.

ABOUT THE PRINT VERSION: If you purchased a print version of this book without a cover, you should be aware that the book is stolen property. It was reported as "unsold and destroyed" to the publisher, and neither the author nor the publisher has received any payment for this "stripped book."

IF YOU FIND AN EBOOK OR PRINT VERSION OF THIS BOOK BEING SOLD OR SHARED ILLEGALLY, PLEASE REPORT IT TO: lpn@blackopalbooks.com

Published by Black Opal Books **http://www.blackopalbooks.com**

DEDICATION

I would like to, once again, dedicate this book to my wife, Sandy, whom I love dearly.

I would also like to dedicate this book to my friend, Missi Stockwell, and thank her for her dedication, friendship, and assistance as my primary reader and inspiration in completing You Don't Know Jack.

CHAPTER 1

Friday afternoon. It was getting late, around four p.m. Jack Manning was just finishing up the last class before the weekend. Thirty-eight young adults couldn't wait to leave for the weekend. This was week twenty-eight of the thirty weeks needed for certification for a job in the construction and energy efficiency trades. Most had passed their TASC—Test Assessing Secondary Completion—test with flying colors. TASC was almost impossible, compared to the old GED standards. Most current high school graduates couldn't pass the TASC exam. Jack paid high school graduates to take the test just to prove his point. They didn't pass without TCC intervention. Jack's non-profit, the Troy Community Council, had won over a million dollars to educate, train, and obtain jobs for the most needy youth in the community.

This was the last group before a new grant had to be written and won. Everyone was confident that with its track record, TCC would get refunded for another three years. They were now in their twelfth year, and going on their fifth award. TCC was recognized across the country as one of the top youth training programs that successfully placed young people into solid, good paying jobs that would turn their family's future around. As the program director, from the start, Jack was extremely proud of his team and what they'd accomplished. Over 300 young adults have gone through the program. Not all succeeded but a vast majority did and came back to thank everyone for their success. In two weeks, there would be another graduation ceremony, right near Thanksgiving, topped off by a banquet. Local educators would attend along with the board of directors of TCC, local politicians, friends, and family. Many had re-marked that Jack and his team remembered every student's name and the names of all their family members. Jack and the team were fully invested in the lives of those under their care.

This last group was a truly amazing conglomeration of young people, male and female, mostly minority from the inner city. When they arrived last summer, most hated school. That's why they dropped out as soon as they could. They couldn't see the relevance.

The teachers in the high schools they attended didn't re-flect the culture of their own students. At two p.m., the teacher parking lot would empty, and within minutes after the bell, the only adults left were those involved in sports. These kids didn't have time for sports. They were out hus-tling for their lives, selling dope, while joining gangs for protection, mostly in the north central part of the city. The only hope most of them had was to not be dead by age twenty-one, whose odds weren't in their favor based on ex-perience. A high school degree for what? To live in contin-ued poverty? To beat the same streets until they were dead? Who cared?

Jack and his team cared. They were on the streets every day and night. They talked to these kids. They made a dif-ference in their lives. Jack didn't preach. Neither did the team. They spoke in the youth's own vernacular. "We'll pay you to come get your degree and certification. We'll help you succeed. We'll give you the tools you need. We aren't bullshitting you. You'll see—if you give us a chance."

It worked. There was success, and the community im-proved. These graduates bought homes. They cleaned up the neighborhood. This program rehabbed houses right in the community and sold at cost to low-income families residing there. It was a win-win.

Before leaving, Jack made it a point to make sure that the students were back on Monday. He looked everyone in the eye and shook their hands before they left. Mary, Joan, Fred, and Tim all did the same. The team was there, day in and day out, leading by example. Everyone, including the students, the counselors, the TASC teachers, construction team, and Jack left with homework. Jack's included walking the neighborhood every Saturday morning until noon to meet and greet the kids and let them know he was there and committed. This had also caused some problems in Jack's personal life. His wife worked as a local bank branch manager, and their kids were finishing college. They hardly ever saw Jack, except on Sunday. Jack had some fence mending to do this weekend. He knew it. He couldn't avoid it any longer.

CHAPTER 2

As Jack was walking up the stairs to his office, his boss, the president of TCC, Howard Singer, stopped him. "Jack, can I see you for a minute before you leave for the night?"

"Sure, Howard. Let me get my things from the office, and I'll be with you in a minute."

"Fine, take your time. I'll be in my office with Marvin."

Marvin Manville was the treasurer and vice president for human resources and, like a lot of HR people, a pain in the ass. Howard Singer, age fifty-five, had been president of TCC for the last three years and came from another nonprofit in Albany. He was a little uptight but an okay guy. He didn't make any waves and did exactly what the board of directors wanted him to do. He didn't have a lot of imagination but always treated Jack respectfully and complimented him on his program on a number of occasions. Marvin, on the other hand, was also in charge of the finance department and continually bitched, moaned, and complained about petty issues, including the cash flow problems created by Jack's workforce development program.

The nonprofit was a good size, almost ten million dollars a year in annual budget with almost 200 employees. Marvin was a welfare guy. He only wanted to do work with the New York State Medicaid system and not worry about processing grants and waiting sixty days to collect. Marvin was a dream killer, as far as Jack was concerned. He was constantly hounding him. It didn't matter that this youth jobs program put TCC on the map and got them a lot more additional funding across the board because everyone knew, that whatever they did, they'd be successful. Jack's dream was not Marvin's. Howard never had a dream in his life, or so Jack thought.

Jack went to his office and put on his hat and coat. He grabbed his bag and turned off the lights. Friday night. *Couldn't he wait until Monday? Christ, the only thing I want to worry about is keeping Maureen happy.* It was two weeks to Thanksgiving and graduation for his students. The kids could wait as well over the weekend. He went down the stairs and turned left to Howard's office.

"Yes, Howard. Hi, Marvin. What's up?"

"Jack, please sit down. We need to talk to you about your program."

"What about it, Howard? Graduation is in two weeks, and we need to file our next grant for the incoming class. You know we have over one hundred kids signed up and waiting," Jack said.

Marvin chipped in, "Well, that's all going to change."

"What do you mean? Why?" asked Jack.

Howard said to Marvin and Jack, "Let me explain what's going on in layman's terms. Jack, we're getting out of the workforce development business for kids for many reasons, but the main reason is that we're losing money."

"That's not true," said. Jack. "Just because Marvin wants it to be so, it's not true. His cash flow is always caught up. We've never had a deficit at the end of a contract. We've never lost a dime. Just because it takes sixty days to get paid, doesn't mean we don't collect. His two hundred thousand dollar loss is a fallacy, and you know it."

"Be that as it may, Jack, we're closing down your program for good as soon as your last class graduates," said Marvin. "We may need you for a month or two once we close it down but then you better start looking for another job." Marvin had a smirk that Jack wanted to smack right off his face.

Howard noticed that this was going badly and stared at Marvin as if to say "shut up you asshole." But it was too late.

"What about my team? What happens to them? They put their heart and soul into this program. You know that. What happens next?" said Jack.

"They'll receive their benefits until the end of the month and any vacation pay owed. That's it," said Marvin. "You as well."

Howard then said, "As you know Jack, we've been talking about this for a while. This shouldn't be a surprise to you. You attended most of the director meetings. We're moving in the direction that New York State wants us to move. Starting soon, New York State will implement the Medicaid Redesign Team (MRT) Waiver Amendment.

He continued, "The DSRIP's purpose is to fundamentally restructure the health care delivery system by reinvesting in the Medicaid program, with the primary goal of reducing avoidable hospital use by twenty-five percent over five years. Over six billion dollars are allocated to this program with payouts based upon achieving predefined results in system transformation, clinical management, and population health. There's no money for jobs for youth, but there's six billion allocated to changing Medicaid, and we want that money. There's no discussion. The board has spoken, and we're closing your program."

"Who tells my staff, the students and the community about this and when?"

Marvin said, "If you want to get paid for the next two months, you'll tell everyone, and fully support it, or we don't need you."

Howard didn't say a word. Jack had been there for the entire twelve plus years of the program and never received less than an excellent review. Howard just hoped that Jack would accept his fate and if not, he'd be escorted off the premises.

"Good luck to you. You can tell everyone how you screwed everyone over and how three-hundred-plus jobs were meaningless to the community. Get your eighteen hundred dollars a day per person under Medicaid and screw all of us, huh? Well, Howard and Marvin, you can tell them yourselves. I'll have no part of this. I won't do this to those counting on us."

"Well, today, right now, is your last moment of employment. Clean out your desk. You're done," said Marvin. Howard never said a word.

With that, Jack could barely contain himself, but he kept his dignity, at least he tried. He went back to his office, unlocked the door and filled up his wastebasket with a decade of awards and memorabilia. He walked down the flight of stairs and saluted both Marvin and Howard on his way out. Unemployed at age fifty.

There were no other workforce development programs like theirs in the entire region. Jack and his family would have to move or figure something out. His two weeks' vacation pay wouldn't last very long. He needed to get home and tell Maureen what happened. She was already mad at him because of the time her spent here every day, day in and day out. Maybe this could help renew their relationship. He could only hope.

What about the kids? Mark was twenty-two and a senior at U Albany. He could make it to graduation. Debbie was twenty and a junior at Siena College. This would be harder but filling out the financial aid forms just got easier. He'd have no income and not much savings. The kids and college took most of it. He had to get home before he burst into tears. He went downstairs to talk to his team before they left.

Mary and Joan were still there. Fred and Tim had left for the evening. Linda was on vacation. Marvin was right behind him and walked into the career center and told Jack that he couldn't be on the premises any longer. Mary and Joan looked at Jack wondering what was going on. Jack waved to them and made an "I'll call you" sign next to his ear. Marvin was talking to Mary and Joan, and Jack heard, "Please sit down. I've something to tell you." Howard K. Singer, MSW was nowhere to be seen.

CHAPTER 3

Jack lived in the Town of Brunswick just a few miles northeast of Troy. Troy was close to the Vermont border but only ten miles north of Albany. He lived right over the city line just a few miles from Tamarac High School. Maureen, his wife of twenty-five years, was a bank branch manager for Bank of America in downtown Troy, only a few blocks from Jack's office. On the way home, Jack was trying to figure out what to say to Maureen. He was sure she'd take it well even though she'd been mad at him for a while.

At least now, he could tell her it was for the best, it would help them become closer since he'd be able to spend more time helping her around the house, doing things that she wanted him to do forever but always failed to accomplish anything at home. They could take a vacation now and at least go to Cape Cod for a week. It was nice around late fall at the Cape. No one was around. They could walk the Dennis Beach like they did when they were first married, almost twenty-five years ago. Dennisport was Maureen's favorite place in the world. Just suggesting a short trip would put her in a better mood, he thought.

He hit Hoosick Street, right over the bridge and stayed in the left lane to hit Oakwood Avenue, heading home to Brunswick. Friday night traffic was terrible coming off the bridge. It was the direct route up Route 7 to Vermont, bumper to bumper. The late fall leaves were thinning and tourists from New York City and New Jersey were doing their last cleanups of their winter condos before ski season began.

Jack started to think about his long marriage to Maureen Bauer. It would be their silver anniversary this year. Their son, Mark, age twenty-two, would be graduating in May from Albany and Debbie, age twenty-one, would only have one year left at Siena College. Mark was an accounting major and already had a job lined up. He had a steady girlfriend, Cara, for the last two years, and it looked like she could be the one. Maybe there would be a wedding coming up soon or they'd probably just live together like every other couple these days. Debbie was a psychology major and wanted to go on and get her master's in counseling at U Albany after graduation. She'd be home for a while, and the bills would still be coming in. As Jack thought about his situation, which only began less than an hour ago, he was starting to feel the pressure.

Jack, now fifty, and Maureen, age forty-eight, met at Siena College when Jack was a junior and Maureen was a freshman. They went to different high schools in the capital region. Jack was a Troy boy through and through, graduating from Troy High with honors. He was a social worker at heart and got his BS from Siena. Maureen was a business major who lived in Latham with her family and commuted every day to Siena, which was only two miles away.

She'd worked for a bank during her time at Shaker High School and would continue after she graduated from college. Her career was pretty well mapped out for her. She'd wind up in the bank's training program after a few years as a customer service rep and then would become a bank branch manager as she was now. Jack bounced around for a few years until he wound up at the Troy nonprofit. He was ready for a change and put his heart and soul into this new job. He'd become the first director for the career development center that he started and hand picked his own staff that stayed right with him, right up to today.

Jack got home by five-thirty p.m. He opened the door and saw Debbie sitting in the living room watching television. Mark worked until eight p.m. at the accounting firm and would probably head out with his girlfriend after that. Jack wouldn't see him until the next day, Saturday.

"Hi, Debbie, how are you?"

"Good, Dad. Mom called and said she'd be a little later than seven p.m. She said she had a few items to pick up. She said to go ahead and get something to eat, and she'd get something later."

"Great," he muttered to himself. "Just what I need the day I get fired. I've such pent up emotion. I just want to talk to her, but I guess it'll have to wait."

"I'm going out with my friends in a few minutes. There's some cold cuts in the refrigerator, if you want, or order a pizza," she said.

"I'm fine. I'll get something in a little while." He went to the refrigerator and got a beer. He drank right from the ice-cold bottle. At least something was right tonight, taking another sip. He sat on the couch and watched Debbie go to her room to get ready to leave. He just shook his head. He wanted to call everyone to see if they got the ax as well, but he had to wait for Maureen. He had to tell her first, or she'd never forgive him if she found out she wasn't the first to receive the bad news. Debbie said goodbye and that she'd be back by eleven p.m. or would call if she stayed over in the dorm at Siena with one of her friends. He was now officially alone. Little did he know how alone he'd eventually be.

CHAPTER 4

Maureen didn't make it home until close to ten p.m. Jack heard the key go into the lock and watched Maureen come in through the back door.

"Where have you been? I was worried," he said.

"Out," she said.

A woman of many words, he thought. "Out where?" he asked.

"I stopped at the Price Chopper for a few items and ran into an old friend. So after shopping, we went for a quick drink. Okay?" she said somewhat belligerently.

"Okay. I've been waiting here since five-thirty p.m. to talk to you. Do you have a minute now?" He was really steamed but kept it under control as best he could.

"Can I put my coat away and take off my shoes? It's been a long day for me too, you know? Fridays at the bank aren't such a fun time either," she said.

"Sure." Could their answers back and forth be any shorter? he wondered.

Maureen walked back into the kitchen after hanging up her coat and putting on her slippers. "What's up?"

Jack wanted to break the news to Maureen much more gently, but at this minute, he was really pissed. "I was fired today."

"What do you mean, fired?" she said.

Her face was screwed up, and Jack couldn't tell if it was fear, anxiety or hatred. Maybe a little of all three. "Yes, I was fired today. Can you come over here so we can talk?" he asked.

She moved to the couch and looked him in the eyes. He explained the entire situation to her and told her not to worry, that it was for the best and that it would be good for them to become closer to each other. He told her about taking a trip to Cape Cod, and she was shaking her head from side to side like she was a contortionist from *Rosemary's Baby*.

"That's great," she said. "We've got two kids in college. Where's the money going to come from, especially for Debbie's last year and then her master's degree? Where? A vacation to Cape Cod? Are you nuts? Are you serious? Am I going to have to support all of us now? You gave up two months' pay because of pride? Do you know by doing that you couldn't even get unemployment? You quit. Do you realize that? What the hell is wrong with you?" She was going ballistic.

"Well, I could have told you earlier before you had a few drinks, and maybe we could've had a more reasonable conversation. Did you drive home like this?"

"You asshole," she said. "I've been pissed at you for months, and now you go and do this to me. To us? To your family? I guess this is as good a time as any, Jack. I don't love you anymore, and I want a divorce. Because of your 'responsibilities to your youth,' unable to couldn't spend even one day a week with me, I found someone else. I want you to leave this house right now. I don't want to see you again. You'll hear from my attorney. I'm not supporting you, Jack. Is that clear? Sorry you lost your job. You lost your family and me long before this. Hope you're happy. I didn't know how I was going to tell you about leaving you, but you just made it simple. Thank you, Jack, and now get out."

"Are you serious? I know you're mad. It's not my fault I lost my job. I can't believe you. Twenty-five years and this is what you have to say to me? You've been seeing someone behind my back? I've never cheated on you, not once, ever. Who's going to tell the kids? You? That's great. Thank you, Maureen. Well, I guess this was the only way I'd ever find out about your infidelity, huh? I'll leave, and I hope you'll be happy."

Jack went to their room and pulled out a suitcase. He had no idea where he'd go. He'd probably go to the Hilton Garden Inn on Hoosick Street, at least for tonight until he could figure out what to do. *Cheating on me all this time. I know I spent too much time at work, but this is ridiculous.* He didn't even have a cellphone now. It was his business phone, supplied by TCC. They took it before he left the building.

Maureen was standing by the door with a drink in her hand. "Goodbye, Jack. I'll have the kids call you tomorrow. Oh, that's right. You don't even have a phone. Bye."

"No, I don't have a phone. I'll call them with a new number after I get one. I can't believe you, Maureen. I really can't believe this. After all these years, it's come to this? Thanks." He grabbed his suitcase and slammed the door.

He opened the car door and threw his suitcase in the backseat. He got behind the wheel, was shaking like a leaf. He had to calm down, or he'd be a disaster on the road. *How does that song go? "If it weren't for bad luck, I'd have no luck at all."*

With that, he left and headed to the hotel. He'd check in with his credit card and go to the Recovery Room restaurant at the hotel and drown his sorrows. He couldn't even call anyone until he got to his room. He'd stop at Walmart in the morning, get a phone, and call the kids. Both Mark and Debbie had a cell phone. He'd try to meet both of them for lunch and talk to them about their future. He didn't want them to worry. He could only imagine what Maureen would say to them first. He had to set the record straight.

Jack checked in at the Hilton. Room 403. He got his key card and went to the elevator and up to his room. He thought he'd call the kids first before Maureen got to them. He dialed both their numbers but got no answer. He left messages for them to call him at the hotel. He waited a while but no one called, so he went downstairs to the restaurant. It was a local sports bar chain with lots of TVs on the wall and a big bar with lots of local sports memorabilia from local colleges and high schools.

He decided to sit at the bar, have a few beers, and think about his next steps. He couldn't believe Maureen. *Cheating on me all this time? With whom? Why?*

He knew why, but he was seriously pissed. No explanation. No chance to talk about it. He just gave her the opportunity of a lifetime to walk away from him and their marriage with it all being his fault. He knew he was a complete idiot.

CHAPTER 5

Jack always slept until nine a.m. at home on Saturday before heading out to the neighborhoods he covered for his job. This morning, he just couldn't sleep and got up at six-thirty a.m. He showered, shaved, and dressed. He decided to stay one more night at the hotel as a release valve. Maybe he'd go see Maureen on Sunday to see if she'd calmed down or wanted to talk. He wanted to talk to the kids, but it was too early. He went downstairs to the breakfast bar to eat. He'd call them afterward. He'd head out, get a new phone, and put their numbers in it. He'd call his coworkers after breakfast to see what happened after he left.

He picked up the *Times Union* at the front desk, an apple, and a few cookies and headed to his room. As soon as he opened the door, he headed to the phone and started calling his friends. He'd call Mary Evans, the recruiter and job counselor, first, followed by Joan Angley, the TASC teacher. Both of them had been with him from the start, twelve years ago. He'd then call Fred Comstock, the construction coordinator, and his assistant, Tim Canton. One of them would have to talk to Linda Franklin, his administrative assistant, if she called in from the road.

"Mary, it's Jack. Are you okay?"

"Not really. After I found out you got fired, I exploded and was asked to leave as well. Evidently, Joan and Fred took it differently. They said they'd continue for the next two months to help out. I'm not sure what Tim said. Linda's away."

"God, I'm sorry, Mary. I never saw this coming."

"It's not your fault, Jack. It's that jerk, Marvin's fault, followed by that incompetent twit, Howard Singer. I'll be fine, Jack." Mary always kept her emotions to herself. Jack was always surprised that she never married. She was beautiful, fun, and very bright. She'd joined the Sisters of St. Joseph, right out of high school, and got her degree from The College of Saint Rose. She left the convent and had an interview with Jack, who gave her the job that was hers to this day. Mary was three years younger than Jack.

"Well, it's you and me against the world, Mary. I can't be mad at Joan or Fred. They've their own crosses to bear, so to speak. Fred doesn't even have a degree, and his daughter is starting college in the fall. I'm surprised at Joan because if she thinks she can hook on with another job in the organization, she's sadly mistaken. She's the TASC teacher, and there are no openings around. She could be in trouble shortly."

Mary sighed. "What about you, Jack? I noticed the phone number isn't your cell number or home phone. Where are you?

"I'm at the Hilton Hotel on Hoosick Street. Let's just say it didn't go so well at home." He hesitated for a moment. "After I told Maureen that I was fired, she asked me for a divorce. Evidently, I wasn't the only one in her life."

"Jack, I'm really sorry. I didn't think things were going well with you two, but I certainly didn't expect that, you know? How are your kids?"

"I didn't expect it either, and I tried calling the kids, but maybe they didn't recognize the number at the hotel. I left a message, but I'm afraid Maureen has already gotten to them by now. We'll see."

"Jack, stay in touch. When a door closes, a window opens, as they say."

"I'll call you when I get a new phone and leave you the number if you ever want to call me. Thanks, Mary. I guess you might be my only friend at this point."

"Stay in touch, Jack. I'll say a prayer. You know I used to be really good at it until I gave it up, being a nun and all." She laughed and then said goodbye.

Jack left the hotel and headed up to Walmart on Hoosick Road. He got a temporary TracFone because he was sure he'd hook up somewhere else and they'd give him a phone. He got the double 400-minute plan and a cheap flip phone. It was charged already, and he had the store add the minutes to the phone and set it up while he waited right there. He'd rather make a hundred dollar mistake rather than sign up for Verizon plan that costs a fortune.

From the parking lot, he called Mark first, him being the oldest. It was about ten a.m. as Mark answered his cell.

"Hello," Mark said into the phone like he was barely awake.

"Mark, it's Dad."

"What the hell happened? Mom has been going bird shit. You lost your job?"

"Yes, I did. What else did she say?"

"Nothing. She said you left and weren't coming back. She's blaming you for everything, is that right? I don't know if I believe it, but she said if I wanted a roof over my head I was to take her side. Dad, I've got until May to graduate. The timing couldn't be worse."

"Someday, not today, I'll sit down with you and explain things to you. How's your sister?"

"You don't want to talk to her. She's a mamma's girl, in case you don't know that. She's as bat shit crazy as Mom. She's worried about college, graduating, and her masters. I don't blame her but what the hell did you do?"

"Should I call her?"

"You can try, but I think Mom has her completely wound up, and I doubt she'll talk to you. Mom said you abandoned us. I don't know if that's true or not, but I wouldn't come home for a while. Mom said she's seeing a lawyer tomorrow, on Sunday."

Well, there goes my Sunday visit. I wonder if I'm going to need a lawyer. All we have is the house and a few thousand saved and Maureen's retirement. Jack hadn't been able to save anything due to paying the college tuition payments. He doubted that he even had enough for a lawyer. At least he had a $10,000 line of credit on his Visa to get him through. So much for today's visit. He tried to call Debbie, but she hung up on him after she screamed at him on the phone. He called Maureen. She picked up, said hello, and, when he spoke, she hung up as well. Jack seemed to have hit the trifecta today of bad calls.

☙❧

He was still at the Hilton on Monday. He thought he'd get a weekly plan at the hotel for two weeks and then make permanent arrangements if needed. He really couldn't use his cell phone because the minutes were expensive and limited. So, he stayed in his room and started sending out resumes to his friends at local nonprofits in the region. Most of those that he sent were to friends, who were polite but said they too were going in the Medicaid direction, just like the Troy Community Council, and they were getting out of the job training business as well. None were even close to the size of Jack's program, but by the end of the year, over 500 young people would no longer be receiving training for high tech jobs in the region. Getting Medicaid funds was a higher priority than jobs for the future of young people.

As he was leaving his room, there was a knock on the door. He opened it, and a young man asked if he was Jack Manning. He said he was. He was served with legal papers, and Jack signed for the package. He went back to his room and opened it. Jack was served with divorce papers. In three days, his entire life had turned to crap. He had no home, no wife or family, at this point, and a credit card with a $10,000 limit. That was his legacy that he'd leave to the world.

He called an attorney that he knew and made an appointment to see him on Wednesday. Jack decided he'd better make living arrangements until he got back on his feet.

Little did he know how long that would be.

CHAPTER 6

Six Months Later:

Jack had been living in a house in Lansingburgh, on 6th Avenue near 122nd Street, with an eighty-year-old woman. He rented a room for fifty dollars a week, as long as he cooked her dinner every night. Meals were included, and he was grateful. He'd run out of money trying to get a job, any job that would get him back in the good graces with his wife and kids. At age fifty, he made too much, was overqualified, or didn't have the right credentials to work in the nonprofit world anymore. Medicaid dictated who went where and for how much. There's no such thing as non-discrimination for older workers. It's a fallacy. Companies can hire anyone they want and especially didn't have to hire older workers, regardless of race, creed, color, religion, or sexual preference. They worried about those people under age forty.

Jack spent his birthday at home, in his room. Ethel Rounds, his landlady, made him a cake and they celebrated before he went to his job at the convenience store right around the corner. That's how he found out about the room for rent when he went into the store for coffee and the paper on his way by. He also saw the sign that they were paying twelve dollars an hour for the night shift that included closing up the store six nights a week. His life was complete.

He slept, made dinner, and went to work. On Sunday, he went over to the ten-thirty Mass at St. Augustine's and that was the culmination of his week. He walked everywhere.

He saw Mary Evans at church almost every Sunday. She lived in the Burgh as well with two roommates who were also former nuns who taught at Catholic High. She didn't need a lot of money, so she became a teacher's aide at St. Augustine's Elementary School and taught a few classes at Catholic High, which got her by. At least she was better off than Jack. They'd go to Duncan Donuts after Mass and talk. They were really good friends, still. His other co-workers all moved on and never called Jack back. What was the point? He used to say, "Don't let the door hit you in the ass on the way out." His expectations of people, other than Mary, were extremely low and right on target.

He explained to Mary, a few months after the divorce that he'd found out from a work associate of his ex-wife what really went on behind his back. Evidently, Maureen didn't really work late on Fridays. She met her boyfriend, Chuck Falcone, for drinks on Friday nights right at five p.m. and then went for a quickie to his place in Green Island, before heading home by seven-thirty p.m. Maybe that's why she was usually smiling when she got home he told Mary. They laughed. He could laugh now that he realized what a fool he was. However, the joke seemed to be on Maureen as well. Mr. Falcone, the UPS route driver for their Brunswick neighborhood, seemed to be servicing several unhappy housewives in the area. Mr. Falcone, age forty-two built like a brick, because of his heavy package lifting, was not only good looking but evidently had a line of shit a mile long and a smile to go with it. He drove a 2012 BMW and looked like a million dollars. He made good money but was broke most of the time.

As soon as Jack and Maureen's divorce became final, Chuck officially moved into Jack's old Brunswick house and took his place. He had been unofficially there, anyway. Jack got all this information about Chuck from his good friend and old next-door neighbor. Evidently, the love fest may have lost its luster because the cops had come over to keep the peace a few times over the last month.

Mark had moved out before graduation and moved in with his girlfriend in Albany. Debbie was still home. He wondered how that worked. Jack also found out that Chuck started living there off and on only two weeks after Jack was asked to leave. The neighbor also told Jack that Maureen had asked his wife if she knew anything about Chuck around the neighborhood. The neighbor's wife knew a lot that was going on. She knew that Maureen was being used, just like a few other women in the area. She never told Maureen a thing because she liked Jack and thought Maureen was a slut.

This information made Jack disgusted, to say the least.

Mary smiled and never said anything. Jack continued to look for career development jobs but the closest one he could find, for which he was qualified, was in Baltimore, Maryland. He was tempted to take the job and ask Mary if she wanted to go along for the ride. He knew she was quite content doing what she was doing. He'd ride this out and would never give up, so he thought…

It was Thursday night, like every Thursday night. Jack had a few dollars on him and thought he'd buy a few Powerball tickets. He asked the other night clerk to give him four quick picks and then he thought that he'd pick his old address number and the birthdays of everyone who hated him. At least five of them. He used his ex-wife's birthday, his son, his daughter, Marvin's, and Howard Singer's. He took the quick picks, folded the tickets in half, and put them in his wallet. He took his personalized ticket and put it in a separate section.

The Powerball this week was for $990,000,000, the biggest of the year with fifteen weeks straight of no winners. He'd no idea how many tickets he sold that night. There were hundreds of receipts, and it took an extra hour just to cash out. He closed up and said good night to his coworker. He walked home like every night. His car had been repossessed a few months earlier, but walking was good for him. He had actually lost twenty pounds over the last six months and seemed to be in better shape than ever. Mary even commented on it. Working for a nonprofit, sitting down all day, was a killer if you never exercised. Jack moved around but ate up a storm as well. He'd cut down on his eating as well.

At least, after Maureen took him for every penny he had, he had no more bills. He couldn't pay any bills anyway. Maureen got the house and Debbie's student loan payments. Mark was on his own now and seemed to be living a separate life. Jack ran up his Visa bill with the divorce but was only paying the minimum. For what, the next thirty years at eighteen percent? *Great*, he thought.

Mark never called his father. Jack left messages but never got a response. No calls from Debbie either. He saw Maureen one day during the week, a few weeks ago. She was in his Burgh bank branch for the day, doing training. She looked up and saw him as he waited in the teller line to cash his measly check. He nodded and said hello. She turned around and walked away.

How mad can somebody be? God, he thought. She also looked as though she had aged a little since the last time he saw her at the attorney's office, signing the final papers. She used to pride herself on her appearance, especially as a bank branch manager, but there seemed to be a disconnect, or she didn't seem to care. Maybe Chuck drained her dry? *Who knows?* Wasn't Jack's problem.

This was what she wanted, and she got it.

CHAPTER 7

Jack usually slept in every morning since he worked the late afternoon to midnight shift. He got up around ten a.m. and hit the head. He brushed his teeth, showered, shaved, and went down stairs to have breakfast. Ethel usually waited for Jack to eat, and he'd fix her tea and toast, every day like clockwork.

"What's for dinner?" she asked.

Jack smiled. "Ethel, it's ten-thirty a.m. Do you have anything, in particular, that you would like?"

"How about pork chops, apple sauce, home fries, and peas?"

"Do we have any of those items, Ethel?"

"I don't know. Isn't that your job, Jack?" she said as she laughed.

"Yes, ma'am. I'll get right on it after breakfast. I do believe that you looked in the refrigerator and the pantry and already knew that we had those items. Am I right, Ethel?"

"I believe you're right, sir."

Jack actually got along better with Ethel than almost everyone. His parents were deceased, and Maureen's never liked him much, anyway. No big loss. He had no brothers or sisters and a few cousins in Vermont that he never saw but still liked. He needed to get up there to see them before long. Maybe he'd ask Mary to use her car and take her along for a ride on a Sunday, his only day off. Maybe they could head out after Mass, and he could show her where his family was from. He'd ask her on Sunday if she'd like to go in a few weeks. He had nothing better to do.

Jack really needed a car if he wanted more out of life. His only problem would be financing, and his credit rating was in the toilet with the repossession of his car and minimum payments on his Visa. He was taken off the mortgage when Maureen took over the house, but he still cosigned for the student loans. As long as Maureen kept the payments up for Debbie and Mark did the same for himself, Jack would be okay. Only time would tell.

The noon news came on the TV, as Jack was finishing up his laundry. He didn't get the paper, except occasionally on Sunday.

"Jack, didn't you buy tickets for the Powerball?" Ethel asked. "They're reading the winning numbers, but I can't see them. Can you come in and tell me what the numbers are?"

The lead story was that someone locally, in the capital region, was a winner in last night's Powerball. The weather and sports highlights were on, and then it was "stay tuned for the news." Jack sat on the couch next to Ethel with a pad and pen in hand.

As the reporter came back on, she said, "Last night's Powerball numbers were four, eight, nineteen, twenty-seven, thirty-four, and the Powerball number was ten. The winners beat the one in two-hundred-ninety-two-point-two-million odds by picking that combination. The winner can opt for annual payments over decades or an immediate lump sum. There were three winners nationally, one in California, one in Florida, and one in New York. We now go to the Lansingburgh convenience store that sold the lottery ticket. The convenience store owners must be thrilled. They get one hundred thousand dollars for selling the winning ticket."

Jack looked at Ethel stunned. "Ethel, the numbers were four, eight, nineteen, twenty-seven, thirty-four, and the

Powerball number was ten. Do you have any?"

"No, of course not, Jack. I only buy one ticket. I gave you my dollar, and as usual, I'll die broke," she said as she ripped up her ticket.

Jack excused himself and said he had to go out for a while. He went to his room to get his jacket and looked down at the piece of paper with the numbers written on it. He pulled out his hand-selected ticket and looked at each number. Every one matched. He started to shake. Then he smiled, and his life flashed before his eyes. He was dumbfounded. He took the other tickets and put them in his drawer just to be sure he didn't make a mistake or throw out the wrong ticket. He put his winning ticket into his wallet and left the house.

He wasn't sure exactly what to do, and he felt vulnerable and paranoid. So he walked to Mary's house six blocks away. It was early Friday afternoon, and she got out of Saint Augustine's at noon so she might be home. He had to see her. She was his only friend in the world next to Ethel. Yeah, he had friends and acquaintances at work but nothing like Mary Evans, ex-Sister Mary Evans. She lived right near Catholic High. He went down six blocks, crossed over to 7th Avenue, hopped up the three steps, and rang the bell. Mary's car was outside. Thank God.

"Mary, hi. I really have to talk to you. Do you have time right now?"

"Jack, are you all right? You're shaking like a leaf. Please come in. Jane and Martha are working, so we'll be alone. What's wrong?"

"Wrong? Nothing's wrong. Except, I may jump right out of my skin if I don't talk to you. Do you have your iPad handy?"

"Sure, come on in and sit at the kitchen table. I've got coffee on or do you want something stronger?"

"Stronger."

A man of many words. Mary got her iPad from her room, turned it on, and connected to the Wi-Fi in the living room. "Tell me what you want to look up, Jack."

"Last night's Powerball numbers."

She went to the site, and it came onto the screen. The immediate headline was that three people would be splitting $990,000,000, one from Florida, one from California, and one from New York.

She looked at Jack. "And? Are you telling me something?"

"Yes," he said as he handed her his winning ticket.

She looked at the numbers on Jack's ticket and matched them to the Powerball site. Her eyes filled up, and she started to cry. So did Jack. "For real?" she said.

"For real," he said.

She gave him a huge hug and a kiss. "My God. Oh my God. You have to be kidding me. What do you want to do now? Seriously, you have over three hundred million dollars in your hand right now. Oh, my God."

"Mary, that's why I'm here. I've absolutely no idea what to do. I don't want to screw it up. You're my best friend and the nicest person I've ever met. Please help me."

She looked him in the eye. "Of course, I'll help you, but I want you to know that I don't want anything. My life is fine as is. I don't want anything to change. Jack, your life can be a living hell or something great to help a lot of people. Who the hell needs three hundred million dollars? Nobody, right?"

"Nobody. That's right. But I need you to help me figure out what to do with it, so I can help others and help myself as well. What do we do?"

"First, let's go and find a website that tells winners what to do if they win big. There must be something online. Hell, there's everything online. Let me get a pad and pen for both of us. Do you have an attorney?"

"Only the one from my divorce that I'm still paying, and he calls me every month looking for the balance."

"Well, we don't need him. I've got a very good friend who's an attorney. Honest as the day is long, and we can see the attorney today if you want."

"Of course, I want. He won't charge me three hundred million, will he? You know how attorneys are," he asked as he smiled from ear to ear.

"Probably slightly less but you'll still have more than you had this morning. You can now buy that pot to piss in, Jack," she said as tears came to her eyes laughing.

"Thanks, just what I need."

They sat next to each other and downloaded several sites explaining what to do as soon as you hit the big one. The first site—and Mary was right—was *Things to do when you win the Powerball jackpot*. They read them in order: *Don't tell a soul and change your phone number. Review your family history.* Jack stopped and laughed, "That's easy. I don't seem to have a family anymore, none that care, anyway."

Mary smiled. "They will."

They went on. *Hold off counting your money.* Evidently, taxes took a large chunk, and if you wanted it in a cash payout instead of installments over decades, you immediately lost forty percent of what you won. Next, *Google other winners and see where they went wrong. Sign your ticket immediately and make a photocopy, send it to yourself and mail a copy to yourself. Just in case.*

"Shouldn't that have been number one? Sign the ticket?"

"Yes," she said. "Sign it right now, and I'll call my attorney friend. It's a woman by the way. An ex-nun. You don't mind, do you? We seem to get along okay," she said. "Sister Evangeline is now the high-powered Albany attorney, Kristen Sanderson, same age as me, married with three children and a wonderful husband. Is that okay?"

"Do you think I'm going to complain? How did Sister Evangeline become Kristen Sanderson?"

"Long story. I'll tell you on the way down to Albany if we can get in."

Mary called her friend and set up an appointment for two-thirty p.m. in downtown Albany, right at 69 State Street at the corner of State and Pearl. It was a bank building with law offices on the top floors. Kristen said to park in the lot and come in the back way, off Maiden Lane. Her office was 1212. She told Mary to have Jack sign the ticket immediately and make copies to keep and mail one to Jack. They put on their coats, and as they did, Mary scanned the signed lottery ticket, put it into her computer and saved it as a PDF, emailed one to Kristen and printed out two copies which would be more than enough. Jack had a lot to do before handing in his ticket. He needed to call in sick to work and call Ethel and tell her that he'd order her a pizza with mushrooms to be delivered exactly at five p.m. just like he did when he cooked her meals every day. Dinner was exactly at five p.m.

They stopped at the post office at 114th Street, went in, and had the envelope hand-cancelled stamped to make sure it went out that day, return receipt requested.

Jack whispered quietly in Mary's ear, "Should I insure this letter for three hundred million or so?"

She chuckled, punched him in the side, and smiled.

They hopped back in the car and headed down 787 to Albany and a life of riches.

CHAPTER 8

Jack and Mary got out of the car and went to the booth to check in. Jack told the guard where they were headed, and he called up to the office. He got off the phone, nodded to Jack and Mary, and handed the parking ticket to Jack. They walked across Maiden Lane into the rear entrance and got on the elevator for the twelfth floor. They walked up to the front desk and told the receptionist that they had an appointment with Kristen.

"She's expecting you. Please follow me. Would you like something to drink?"

Jack said, "A bottle of water would be great," and Mary nodded "yes" as well. They walked down the hall to room 1212.

Kristen got out of her chair and came to greet them. "Mary, how are you?" She turned to Jack. "Mr. Manning, it's nice to meet you."

"Please call me Jack," he said.

"Jack it is. Please take a seat. Congratulations, Jack. I believe congratulations are in order, according to Mary," Kristen said as she turned and smiled at her.

Jack smiled at Mary, turned to Kristen, and simply handed her the signed ticket. She looked it over, looked at the Powerball numbers, and the numbers matched. "It looks like we have a winner." Kristen smiled. "I've never seen a winning lottery ticket, let alone one worth over three hundred million dollars."

"Neither have we," said Jack. "What do we do?"

"First, you did the right thing. Mary said you also made copies of the ticket, front and back, and mailed them to yourself, return receipt requested. Correct?"

"Yes, that's exactly what we did. Now, what do we do?"

"Jack, it's very important to have all your ducks lined up as they say. Do you mind if I call a few partners in to discuss your next steps? But before that, I want you to sign an agreement with us that we're representing you in this matter."

"I don't have any money, honestly."

"Do you have a dollar on you?"

"Yes."

"Good enough. Give me the dollar. I'll give you a receipt after you sign the representation document. Mary, please read it as well. I know you trust me, but this is a life-changing matter."

Jack read the document, got out his dollar, handed the document to Mary to read, signed it, and then handed it back to Kristen. She called her senior partners to the conference room right next to her office and herded Jack and Mary into the room. Kristen introduced all the players around the table. They were senior tax attorneys and accountants, an estate planning lawyer who was an expert on wills.

"Jack, once we discuss everything with you, we'll call the New York State Lottery Commission in Schenectady and tell them that we represent the winner from New York State. We won't give out any names, but, according to the lottery rules and regulations, you have to appear before the commission and accept a blown-up poster-size check for publicity purposes. It's in the fine print. My partner, Frank Smith, our chief accountant and CPA, will now tell you about the actual payout you'll receive if you choose the cash payment rather than the annual, thirty-year payment. Frank, go ahead, please."

"Jack before you do anything, between now and when we show up, we need a quick will, just in case. Do you have one?"

"You know, we did, my ex-wife and me, but since the divorce, I've been broke and didn't see the need. She took everything I owned."

"So your divorce has been settled?"

"Yes, I signed an agreement where she got everything I owned. I thought it was going to the kids, but I was sadly mistaken. However, I've got no further financial obligation to her. Now, my kids are ages twenty-two and twenty-one, with birthdays coming up. What happens to them? I'd like to settle up their student loans, but they walked out on me too, so that's as far as I'm willing to go for now unless something changes. I'd like to set up a trust for all three, now, so at age sixty-two, Maureen gets a million dollars, and at age thirty-five, each of my kids gets two million. Is that reasonable? And by the way, I want a new will with Mary as the only executor of my estate from now on."

Mary looked at him wide eyed. "Why?"

"Because you're my best friend. You stuck by me. You might be my only friend, and you're the best person that I know. I know that if something happened to me, you'll do your very best to put the money to a good cause. And you're getting a chunk, whether you want it or not." Then he smiled at her and gave her a hug and a kiss.

Kristen smiled. "Well, Mary, you might just be my second largest client next to Jack."

"Jack, the Powerball for nine hundred ninety million dollars was split three ways," Frank continued. "Your share before any deductions is three hundred thirty million dollars. If you decide to take all of it up front, you'll receive approximately sixty percent of the total of three hundred thirty million or one hundred ninety-eight million."

Jack laughed. "Not a bad day's pay."

Mary punched him.

"Now, you can immediately declare a portion to go to charity, and we can set up a tax free trust for that purpose, depending on how you want to work the trust. Anything outside the trust is taxable at a federal rate of thirty-nine-point-six percent the top bracket and nine percent for New York State."

"I make up my mind quickly. I want to immediately contribute fifty million dollars to a charity trust, mostly to build a facility and fund a new career development center for youth, just like what we were running when we were so rudely fired. I also want to build the facility right next door to the Troy Community Council building. In addition, I want to support the program for up to five hundred youth over the next ten years. I also understand that the TCC building is owned by another for-profit entity. I want you to quietly find the owners and make them a deal they can't refuse.

"In addition to the fifty million, and I don't want you to say a thing, Mary, but I want a trust set up in the name of Mary Evans for fifteen million. If she wants to give it away, that's fine. If not, she'll have half left after paying both federal and New York State taxes." Jack went on, "The rest is mine after taxes, and I don't know what I want to do with it, yet. Just pay the taxes and put ninety percent of the proceeds into tax-exempt, grade-triple-A municipal bonds that are now paying two-point-eighty-eight percent. I make quick decisions and live with those decisions. Oh, by the way, I don't have a car, which I'll need, and I need you to clean up my credit rating." Jack paused for a breath. "How much will this cost?"

Frank grinned. "For everything, we charge one percent of the value of the funds. For that, we do estate planning, your taxes, any attorney or legal issues, the buying and selling of stocks, bonds or any other issues that may come up, including banking."

"Do I get a free checking account?" Jack said with a

snicker. "That's fine, but you aren't to include Mary's trust value. That's a freebie to you from her."

Kristen smiled. "How do you rate, Mary?"

"I've no idea," Mary answered.

Frank brought out his calculator and took the $330 million, subtracted the sixty percent for the cash discount, arriving at $198 million. From there, he subtracted the fifty million for the charity trust and wound up at $148 million approximately. He subtracted the thirty-nine-point-six federal taxes and nine percent for New York State tax, and the fifteen million for Mary and said to Jack, "After the discount, charity donations, Mary, and taxes, you'll receive sixty-eight million, three-hundred-sixty-two hundred thousand dollars."

"I can live with that."

"Jack, I'll need to keep your lottery ticket in our safe, and I'll give you a receipt. I know our firm isn't worth three hundred thirty-three million, but you'll have to trust us."

"Done." And then Jack said, "As of now, I'll pay you an annual fee of one percent on the fifty million-dollar trust and my sixty-eight million three-hundred-sixty-two hundred thousand dollar estate after taxes. Is that correct?"

"I guess you're quite quick, Jack. The fee for the first year is based on one hundred-eighteen million, three-hundred-sixty-two hundred thousand dollar times one percent or one million, one hundred eighty-three thousand, six hundred twenty dollars, with no additional fees for anything, including any financial transactions. Mary saves one hundred fifty thousand dollars a year in fees."

"Do we get free parking along with free checking?"

"I'll pick you at your door wherever you're living at the time," Kristen said. "Mary and Jack, you need to immediately get away for two weeks. Jack, here is a checking account with a balance of ten thousand dollars as a thank you present. I already opened your checking account downstairs at the bank after Mary called me. Here are your forms to fill out, a new Visa card, and a debit card. The Visa also has a ten thousand dollar limit. We'll meet both you and Mary back here in two weeks from today and then head out to the New York State Lottery headquarters in Schenectady. We'll pick you up in a town car if you don't have a car when you get back. We can help you with that also and deliver it to your house when you get home. Any particular car you want?"

"I always wanted a Ford Explorer, especially now that I can afford the gas. How about you Mary?

"I'm good," she said.

"Well, that's settled. I want a black Ford Explorer just like the FBI. That would be cool, pulling up to my new building, next to the TCC."

"Since no one knows you hit the big one Jack, there won't be any need for security for now, but when you get back, both of you'll need at least one full time bodyguard each, around the clock. You can afford it and don't tell me you don't want it. There are a lot of crazies that'll be coming out of the woodwork. You need to be secure. Jack and Mary, if you can wait one hour, we'll type up a new will for both of you. Mary do you have one?"

"Yes, everything goes to my mother first and then to my two ex-Sister roommates. Jack, can I leave everything to them if something happens before I get to select what I want to do with the money? They'd do the same as I would."

"I doubt they would, Mary, but you can do anything you want. Let's get the wills done and then head out to the airport. I need to go downstairs and get a few grand in cash and call Ethel and tell her I won't be home for a few weeks and not to worry. By the way, I'm going to take care of her as well. The two of you, and now Kristen, are the only friends I have. I'll bet we get new ones rather quickly. Don't you think?"

"I think so, Jack. Where do want to go for two weeks?" she asked.

"First, I want to go to Key West for a few days and then

hop on a cruise ship for a week. Do you have a passport? I actually have mine on me because I didn't know what ID I'd need."

Mary smiled, opened her pocketbook, and pulled out her passport. "Great minds think alike. Let's leave right after we sign our wills. We can buy clothes anywhere. I need a new wardrobe anyway and a swimsuit."

CHAPTER 9

Kristen drove them to the airport in Mary's car. She'd bring it back to the bank parking lot and leave it there for two weeks until they returned. The attorneys were the only people to know where they went, hopefully. Jack and Mary walked up to the Southwest booth; showed them identification, including their passports; and bought tickets to fly to Key West through Tampa. The last flight was to Baltimore with a transfer to Tampa arriving at eleven p.m. Mary booked two rooms at the Grand Hyatt for the night. They'd catch an American Airlines flight to Key West the next day at five forty-five p.m. arriving in Key West at six fifty-seven p.m. They'd buy clothes and suitcases, at the Westshore Plaza Mall in Tampa before leaving for Key West. Just in case, Mary and Jack had their wills and passports on them at all times. They'd put the wills in their luggage when they got to Tampa. They still needed to show identification from Tampa to Key West.

Kristen called the lottery commissioner in Schenectady and told them that they represented the New York winning ticket. They made arrangements for the lottery security staff to go to the law offices to verify the ticket. Kristen made the lottery staff sign a confidentiality agreement until Jack and Mary got back from their imposed vacation. Kristen wasn't positive that the information about Jack Manning being the

Powerball winner from New York State would be held back. She could probably hold the lottery people's feet to the fire and get a date for the announcement at least two weeks out, if not a little longer. So, in three weeks, the entire world would know that Jack Manning was a multimillionaire, if they didn't spill the beans before that. When announced, everyone would believe that Jack was worth $330 million dollars. Nobody considered all the deductions and what he was going to do with the money.

Kristen thought Jack was a good guy. She had no idea why his wife left him. She couldn't imagine that he'd be a bad guy if he were Mary Evans's best friend. He ended up with sixty-eight million out of $330 million and was pleased. She wondered about Jack and Mary's relationship. The previous Sister Evangeline, now a married mother of three and an attorney at the largest law firm in Albany, knew what changes were in store for both of them. She was pleased that Mary trusted her so much. It was an honor and moved Kristen up the pecking order at her own firm. She was a partner before, but she was now a "rainmaker."

❧

Jack and Mary arrived at the Tampa airport right on schedule and took a shuttle to the hotel. They were both exhausted. They said goodnight to each other with a hug and said they'd meet for breakfast at the hotel for eight a.m. Jack used his phone to call the convenience store before they closed to let them know that he wouldn't be back for a while. He told them it was an out of town emergency and had to leave immediately. He didn't tell them where they went. Mary did the same, catching her roommates watching Jimmy Fallon. She told them that she was called away and couldn't talk about it, but when she got to her final destination, she'd text them and let them know where she was. She texted Kristen as well, who texted back that everything they talked about was under way and all the paperwork would be ready when they got back. Kristen told her to enjoy herself and to say hello to Jack.

The next morning, they went to the front desk and kept one room until their five forty-five p.m. flight to Key West. Jack checked out of his. They didn't have to worry about leaving anything in the room because they came to Tampa with nothing. Jack hoped that they could buy what they needed in the morning, come back, pack their suitcases and get ready to leave the hotel by shuttle for their flight. They'd get room service for lunch so they wouldn't waste any time.

They took a taxi to the Westshore Plaza Mall and got everything they needed. They went their separate ways with Jack handing Mary $1,000 in cash. She went to The Loft, Macy's, and J. C. Penney for a bathing suit. He got his at Men's Fashion House, Macy's, and J. C. Penney as well. They met back up at Macy's at the luggage department and compared purchases to see what size they needed. Jack bought half as much as Mary and got the carry-on and Mary needed a full size suitcase. They'd check the luggage in, anyway, since the American Airlines flight was a smaller plane. Jack didn't have to worry about jamming his in the overhead compartment. They'd do the same on the way home.

Their flight left right at five forty-five p.m., and they could see Key West as they landed northwest of town, at the Key West International Airport. Before they left, Mary went online using the hotel's Wi-Fi and booked rooms for a few nights at the Southernmost Beach Resort, right in the heart of Key West. It was located at 508 South Street and close to everything. Since this was their first time to Key West, and as Jack said "money doesn't seem to be a problem," with a smile, they decided to go first class with rooms in the $400 range, right on the beach in the heart of town. They also had a town car pick them up as soon as they arrived, which made quite an impression on Jack and Mary.

After getting their luggage, they couldn't help but notice a young man holding a sign for MARY EVANS. She smiled and waved. Jack got both suitcases off the carousel. He came over and met Mary standing next to the young man. The driver got Mary's bag, and Jack took his to the front door where the car was parked. Evidently, the Southernmost Beach Resort had a lot of pull at the airport to be sitting right outside the front door, with it running and with the blinker lights on. Mary was asking questions a mile a minute on the way to the hotel. Jack knew she was happy and excited. Mary had never been any place before, even as a child. From high school, to the convent, to the TCC, she never really got a vacation. Her family was blue collar all the way. A trip to Lake George or Saratoga Springs, during the summer, was the best they could do. Mary's parents were thrilled when she told them she wanted to be a Sister of Saint Joseph. They didn't have to pay for her college, which was a double Godsend.

They pulled up to the hotel and got out and went to the front desk. Their rooms were on the second floor, away from the noise but right on the ocean a foot away. They checked in and went to their rooms, next to each other, and Mary was grinning ear to ear. Jack was pleased that she was so happy. They left their luggage in their rooms and went to the Pineapple Bar tucked around the corner on Duval Street, the main drag. They ordered their house special drinks, a few snacks to hold them over until later, and watched the people and traffic. Jack thought he was in Provincetown, Cape Cod—same crowds, same traffic, and same eclectic people walking around. They decided to go back to their rooms, shower, unpack, and then ask the concierge to recommend places to go after nine p.m.

CHAPTER 10

Andrea Hooley answered the phone at the convenience store. She was wondering who was calling near midnight. She never expected Jack's call. She was wondering what happened to him. He said he was called out of town on an emergency. The place was going nuts since everyone knew that someone bought the Powerball ticket at this store. She asked him if he knew anything about it.

"The owners showed up and had pictures taken," she said to Jack. "You'd think they'd share with the staff some of their hundred thousand dollars they'd be getting for selling the ticket. I doubt it, though."

When Jack hung up, she remembered that Jack never answered her question if he knew anything about the lottery winner. "Can you imagine if it's him?" she mused.

He was a very nice man, and it couldn't happen to a better person, but it would have been better if she'd bought a ticket. But she'd have never wasted her money on the lottery. She had better things to do with it.

All the media was camped outside, all day along until a few hours ago. They'd be reporting that no one claimed the ticket. She wondered how that would work. Would someone call the lottery or what?

She'd been left alone until almost nine p.m. when the manager filled in for Jack. He was not a happy man. The manager was not the owner, so he got the short end of the stick and no money as well. Jack had been there for almost six months, and the manager thought he found a valued employee. This emergency better be true, or Jack would be gone when he got back. Never for a minute did he think Jack was the winner.

ℤℤℤ

When Jane got back to their apartment, she read Mary's note. It said that she had a meeting in Albany with Kristen and would be home late. When their other roommate, Martha, came home, Jane showed her the note, and they didn't have a clue why she went to Albany. They knew it was her half-day on Friday at Saint Augustine's and only taught a few classes at Catholic High during the week. They were surprised when the phone rang late that night, and it was Mary telling them that she wouldn't be back for two weeks due to an emergency. They tried pumping her, but Mary said she couldn't tell them but she was safe and was in good hands. They wondered what possessed her to leave without any notice at all. They'd already checked her room, and she took nothing with her except her pocketbook and her iPad. Mary asked both Jane and Martha to tell the staff at both schools that she was called out of town and would call them during the week. They'd call Kristen at her office on Monday morning, since this was Friday night, if Mary didn't call by then to let them know where she was. It wasn't like Mary to be so cryptic.

ℤℤℤ

Jack's ex-wife was back in Lansingburgh, training new tellers on Friday, and there was a buzz in the air. The scuttlebutt was that someone had the winning lottery ticket from last night's Powerball drawing, and they bought the ticket only a few blocks away at the convenience store. The store banked at this branch, and they hadn't been in yet. Whenever the Powerball hit record numbers, they needed additional staff to count the cash from the ticket purchases. No one had called yet to tell them when they'd be in. She knew Jack worked at that store, but he was lucky enough to have a roof over his head by this time, let alone have money for lottery tickets. She knew that when the divorce was finalized, she got everything he had, and she was pleased. She could pay down Mark and Debbie's student loans and keep the house, which was almost paid for. She made good money but never bought lottery tickets. The lottery was for suckers and for people desperate for a last chance before circling the drain.

The news stations were non-stop all day, telling the public that they had a Powerball winner right in the region. They showed pictures of the convenience store and interviewed people walking in and out of the store asking them if they knew who the winner was. Nobody knew. There was total bedlam all day right up until the early evening when the news trucks pulled out and left. One smart ass went into the store and bought a lottery ticket with the exact winning numbers from yesterday to see if he could fool the reporters. It didn't work, but he got his minute of fame. The news went national that three winners—one from New York, one from California, and one from Florida—would split the winning $990,000,000 jackpot. The father of the family with the winning ticket from California came in as soon as the numbers were drawn. They didn't know who won the lottery from the grocery store in Lake Worth, Florida, just west of Palm Beach.

Mark called his mother about the lottery winner. He'd heard at work that someone at his father's store won the Powerball. He was just curious if anyone claimed the ticket. Maureen told him she hadn't heard a thing and that Debbie called as well. She didn't tell him that her live-in lover, Chuck, called her several times as well to see if there was any news. Mark said he called his father's house, but no one picked up. He knew that his landlady was hard of hearing and that he'd jot down any calls for her from the answering machine when he got home. Mark never called him unless there was something he wanted. Jack had mentioned it a few times, but it fell on deaf ears. Debbie hadn't spoken to her father since that night he lost his job. Mark told his mother that he'd drop by his father's place over the weekend with his girlfriend if he were around. He didn't hate his father. He thought his mother was nasty for what she did to him. He thought that Chuck Falcone was a loser, sucking money out of his mother, but she didn't want to hear it. So, he didn't talk to anybody. He graduated and was on his own, except for the student loans. He still had to be nice to his mother, or he'd be stuck with the bill. He knew his mother very well. If he ever did get married, he could only imagine the seating arrangement for his parents, if he invited his father.

෧ඥඥ

Jack had called Ethel early Saturday morning before breakfast and told her that he wouldn't be back for two weeks that he was called out of town on an emergency. He had to shout to her over the phone. Thank God she picked it up. She thought it was Jack calling anyway. She wanted to know where he was. She said she was worried about him. He told her not to be, that he was fine but out of town. He left it at that.

He called her son as well and told him that he needed to look in on his mother while Jack was away. Of course, he'd told him that a hundred times, but that was the role Jack was supposed to play since he moved in. It relieved the son's duties concerning his mother, and that's the way he liked it. Ethel had told Jack that many times. She said he was more of a son to her than her own son.

The man was even older than Jack with no responsibilities. He thought Jack should be grateful to get a room for next to nothing.

Jack was.

CHAPTER 11

Right at nine p.m., Jack knocked on Mary's door, and she opened it immediately. She was ready. It was breezy but warm, so she took a light sweater that she bought in Tampa and wrapped it around her shoulders. They went down to the concierge and asked for some tips on a few nightspots. He said that the food at their own restaurant was excellent and usually crowded like some of the other restaurants in town on a Saturday night. He then mentioned several bars and restaurants for dessert, great drinks, and music. He said that they had to go to Sloppy Joe's on the other end of Duval Street to soak in the Key West ambiance. It was a good mile from one end of Duval to the other but walking was the best way to get there on a Saturday night. Traffic was always horrendous, but on Saturday, it didn't move at all. He said it was worth the walk to see everyone out on the streets and the shops and the music emanating from the bars.

Jack asked the concierge if he'd check their restaurant for an opening. He did, and the concierge said they were lucky because they just opened a table for two and he booked it for them if they wanted it. They went around the corner at got the table with an ocean view. The concierge was right. It was a lovely spot at they were lucky to be seated at nine p.m. Jack ordered the conch chowder and drunken scallops cooked in duck fat, pale ale, shallots, bacon, and lobster mash with baby carrots. Mary ordered the grouper with seasoned vegetables and jasmine rice. The grouper was macadamia crusted with mango salsa. Their eyes lit up when they were served. Mary said it was the best dinner she'd ever eaten. Jack concurred.

At the end of dinner, Jack whispered to Mary, "You know, we can stay here at this hotel for the rest of our lives and not make a financial dent in what we'll receive when we get back."

She looked at him. "I know, Jack, but, is that what you want? This is great, but I never want to forget where I came from, you know? I'm still a nun at heart, but I gave up my vows because those vows didn't fit me anymore. Do you know what we can accomplish with what's been given to you?"

"Of course. But, Mary, it's been given to you as well. Don't think I gave you the money because of a debt I owed you. It's purely out my friendship with you and what you mean to me. I think we should go back, just to right the wrongs that we saw, fix everything if we can, and then bring something really meaningful to the community. However, I'm not crazy, and neither are you. I'm willing to give it ten years, see what happens, see what changes and see what we accomplished. But at age sixty, I'm retiring and keeping a big chunk so I can see the world and do things I never thought possible. You can join me in my quest anytime. Whatever is left over will be given away at that time for the things we know will work. Sound like a plan?"

"When did you have time to think about this? Did we even sleep yet since Friday afternoon? I know my head is spinning. I can't imagine what my mother and roommates must think is going on. When they find out that we're together, all hell will break loose, you know? It's a sound plan, though, and we can do some good."

They sat around for a while and had dessert and coffee and decided to head out to Duval Street and see what the night would bring. Jack signed the check, with a very large tip, to be billed to his room, and then thanked everyone for a great meal.

Walking down Duval at ten-thirty p.m., after living in Troy for all those years, seemed like a dream to both of them. They were simply smiling from ear to ear. Jack thought~ this is Provincetown South. They looked in the shop windows, stopped and listened to a few musicians on the street, and meandered their way down to Sloppy Joe's.

By this time, the bar was jammed packed. The band was playing. All the doors were wide open with a breeze coming in off the ocean. They looked around, and Jack was ready to head to the bar for a beer and a wine for Mary when he spotted a high-top table near the back that had two tall pub stools open. He grabbed Mary's hand and asked the people sitting on the other side of the table if it was all right if they sat there. The man said, "Sure."

Jack raised his hand to a waitress going by to signal that they'd like drinks. He turned to the man and woman sitting opposite of them. "Can I buy you two a drink for letting us sit here? It's the least we can do for you being so nice."

"No need, we're fine," the man said.

"Sure," the lady said.

Jack and Mary smiled, and Mary said to the man, "Please let us treat you. We're on vacation, and this is our first trip to Sloppy Joe's. Help us make it memorable."

The man nodded, turned to his wife, and shook his head. "First time for everything, Julie."

Julie smiled at Jack. "Just a little white wine. I'm driving. My husband likes to unwind here once in a while. He'll have a Sam Adams, if that's okay?"

"Coming right up." Jack turned to the waitress, gave the order, and asked if they'd any chips or peanuts. She nodded and came back with their order, including a big basket of salted peanuts.

Jack turned to the couple. "This is great. Thanks."

The man introduced himself as Joe Traynor and introduced his wife as Julie. Jack did likewise, introducing himself as Jack Manning and his friend as Mary Evans. The other couple was obviously much younger than Jack and Mary. Joe's wife was beautiful, and Joe seemed to be outgoing and friendly.

"So you're on vacation?" Joe said. "Where're you from?"

"We're from upstate New York. It's our first trip to the Keys and, boy, what a difference from where we live."

"Where in upstate?" Joe asked.

"We're both from Troy, New York, the north end, called Lansingburgh."

Joe looked like he was in shock. "You have to be kidding me. Really? No shit?"

"Really. No, shit," Jack said. "Why?"

Julie laughed. "You aren't going to believe this, but Joe is from Lansingburgh."

"I grew up in the Burgh and went to Saint Augustine's and Catholic High. I took the long way around. I joined the Coast Guard at eighteen and was in for ten years. I went back to Troy to get my MBA from RPI and then wound back up in the Coast Guard after a brief stay at a nonprofit in Albany. Julie is what they call a 'Conch,' born and raised in Key Largo."

"Well, I'll be damned. It really is a small world."

Mary said, "To add to the amazement of the moment, I'm a teacher's aide at Saint Augustine's and a part time teacher at Catholic High. I live around the corner with two other former nuns. Yes, I'm a former nun."

"Sorry about the 'No shit' comment," Joe said with a grin.

"That's fine. I've heard worse. Both Jack and I worked for a nonprofit in Troy. Maybe you heard of it, Troy Community Council or TCC? We were both let go six months ago after they did away with our department, that we started over twelve years ago helping kids get their high school equivalencies and jobs.

"Sorry to hear that. Are you looking to move down here? We've got a lot of teaching jobs, and we need help," said Julie.

"No, we're going back," Jack said. "We had some problems getting back into the swing of things, but as of Friday, we no longer have any problems unless we create them ourselves."

Both Joe and Julie looked quizzically at Jack.

"I probably shouldn't say anything, but I'm dying to tell someone other than Mary and our attorneys. On Friday, we were the New York State winners of the Powerball. We had to get away before anyone found out and so we could get our team in place to receive the money."

Julie looked at Joe, and they both laughed. Julie said, "That's the best thing we've heard in some time. That's great. So what're you going to do?"

"We're going back to build a brand new career center for young people, right next door to the place that fired us."

Joe almost spit up his beer, laughing so hard. "Really. You must be Irish. Both of you?"

"Yes, and yes," Jack said. "How could you tell?"

Julie told them why they had to be Irish. She relayed several of Joe's stories and what he did to get here. She told them about their recently adopted now-six-year-old daughter and that they lived in Tavernier where Julie's grandmother was watching Bella for the weekend. She mentioned that Joe was still a lieutenant in the Coast Guard and stationed as vice president of the military wing of the Florida Keys Community College. She explained how he was getting his doctorate and eventually planned on moving to the Coast Guard Academy up in Connecticut.

Mary fell in love with Julie. She actually knew about Julie's story and the trials and tribulations she faced growing up. Mary had purchased Julie's trilogy for her Catholic High classes. Julie was astounded about the many coincidences. Jack told Joe and Julie of their plans for the new center. Joe told him that his father and brother owned Traynor Electrical Construction Company out of Troy, and he wrote their phone numbers down with the address of his brother.

"Have you ever been in the Burgh Tavern? My brother used to live there until he met Tanya Fields, hopefully his soon-to-be wife. It only took him thirty-six, going on thirty-seven years to find someone to actually like him enough to go out with him, let alone marry him."

Jack and Mary laughed, and Julie gave him the *look*. "Older brother," she said to them.

Time went by so quickly. Both couples hit it off royally and laughed until after one a.m. Jack told them that they were staying at the Southernmost Resort and so were Joe and Julie, leaving later on Sunday. After Jack told them their plans for the next two weeks, Joe mentioned that instead of a cruise on one of the huge Cruise Ships that they'd be better off chartering a sailboat that could take them all around the Keys and then drop them off at the Port of Tampa the following week. Jack and Mary thought that would be a great idea. In fact, it was solidified when Joe mentioned that a close friend, Skip Lennon, ran a sailboat charter out of Key West. Joe would call Skip in the morning to see if he was available for the week. He told Jack that it wasn't cheap, but Jack laughed and said he didn't see a problem.

Skip Lennon kept the cost down by employing his own family, which kept them close and allowed them the lifestyle that they wanted. His crew consisted of his two mid-twenty-year-old adult children and his wife. He and his wife were about Jack and Mary's age. Skip was a retired Master Chief Petty Officer and Commander of a Coast Guard Sentinel-class cutter out of Key West. At 154 feet, the USCGC Matagorda was the state-of-the-art cutter under his command. There was nothing he didn't know about the Florida Keys. He was born and raised here, and he and his wife were life-long Conch people. That's why they loved Julie as well since she was cut from the same cloth. Since he and his wife owned a home in Key West, when he retired, he bought a fifty-foot Marlow Hunter 50 Aft Cockpit sailboat, that cost him almost $400,000 to start his charter business. The fees for a week were over $4,000 but Joe knew Skip would give them a break but really didn't need to. Joe would call him before Mass and ask to meet them for lunch.

It was late, and they all took the same cab back to the hotel. The roads were thinning out as the partiers stayed in the bars and the not quite so fun lovers went home or back to their hotels for the night. Joe, Julie, Jack, and Mary planned to meet up in front of the hotel and walk over to the Basilica of Saint Mary Star of the Sea for ten-thirty a.m. Mass. They'd meet up with Skip at noon at the Beach Café.

Mary said, "I want to try the specialty Key Lime Margarita."

Julie said, "I've had plenty of those and worth every penny. Also, try the Lobster Benedict if in season or the Crab. I love the lobster."

ຂວຂວ

After Mass, they went to the restaurant and met both Skip and his wife, Linda. Joe was right. Jack and Mary and Skip and Linda were almost the same age and seemed to get along famously. What Jack liked especially that if anyone found out about the winnings, at least Skip could call the Coast Guard quickly, or even Joe, for that matter, if there was a problem. They couldn't leave until Tuesday because they had two-day trips planned for groups. They could sail Tuesday to the following Tuesday and Skip would drop them off at the Port of Tampa where they could rent a car and head to Walt Disney World before heading home. Jack asked if he could book it on his credit card and there was no problem. Skip gave them a rate of $500 a day instead of $650 so it would only cost him $3,500 for the week including drinks, meals and the trip. Jack and Mary put their heads together and said that would be great. Neither Joe nor Julie mentioned the Powerball, so neither did they. Joe mentioned their connections to his hometown and schools, so that was key to the meeting as well.

"Well, we have to head back to our little one. We barely get two days away now since Bella came into our lives. But, we wouldn't change a thing. Would we, Joe?"

"Of course not. You also picked up Spanish as well, which is great down here."

Jack and Mary gave them both hugs and thanked them profusely for being so kind to strangers.

"What else can I do? You're from Troy. That doesn't happen often."

"I'll definitely call your father and brother when we get back after the fiasco with the publicity. We need to go hide somewhere else as well when we get back. We haven't figured that out yet."

With that, Joe and Julie gave hugs to Skip and Linda and hopped in their car to heads home to Tavernier and their own complicated lives. Joe had to stop at the college on the way home to pick up some work. They left the other four to plan out an itinerary. The ship had Wi-Fi so they could make all their arrangements for Walt Disney World while at sea.

CHAPTER 12

Jack and Mary met Skip and his family on Tuesday morning at nine a.m. at the Williams Street historic seaport, E-Dock slips number E-6. They boarded the sailboat and Mary was smiling from ear to ear. Jack smiled. "I think this will work out very nicely."

"Me too. What's not to like?"

Skip introduced them to their son and daughter, Tom and Jamie, who'd be working on the boat all week. As Skip told them, this was a family affair. They went down to their separate cabins and dropped off their belongings. There wasn't much to carry, but on a sailboat, you didn't need much. As Skip said, they'd make several stops on the ocean side in Bermuda, then the eastern Caribbean. When they hit the Gulf of Mexico to bring them back to the Port of Tampa, they'd stop at Marco Island, Venice, Sarasota, and then Tampa, to refuel and they could shop at any stop. All their provisions for the week were on board already.

The week went well, and Mary said she never felt so relaxed and could imagine winding up down in the Keys when they retired, about ten years from now. Jack said that they should have Kristen look into real estate in Key West or near it so they could have a getaway every now and then. They had plenty of money. A cottage could cost them a million dollars but so what, Jack thought, even if they only used it for a few weeks a year. He told Mary that they could buy a boat or even just continue to take day trips with Skip. Mary kept reminding Jack that their dream was still at home and not to get sucked into the life of leisure. A lot of young adults were going to be counting on them, once they were up and running. He needed a plan to spend fifty million dollars on charity, let alone add another fifteen million of hers to the pot. Jack could also drop a few million of his own that he was keeping.

At the end of the week, the following Tuesday, they said their goodbyes to the Lennon family at the dock. Jack had his new checkbook and credit card with him. He'd already paid the fee on the first day of the trip. Being Irish, he knew that you got more bees with honey than with vinegar. As they were leaving, after hugs and kisses, Jack gave both the kids a check each for $500 as a tip. They were shocked, and it brought a smile to Skip and Linda. They thanked them profusely. Jack was never sure if you tipped the owner of the company unless it was a barber or a beauty salon. This tip was accepted with grace since it was out of friendship rather than expectation.

During the week, Mary booked rooms at Walt Disney World for Tuesday night through Sunday. Julie and Joe were close friends with Claire Murphy, the assistant to Marshall Tillman, the president of Hollywood Studios. Julie had called Claire and mentioned that some new friends were headed to Walt Disney World and to keep an eye on them if they would. She alluded that they might need some protection once they arrived. Julie promised to tell her what was about to happen once the news broke. When Mary booked the rooms, they immediately notified Claire who in turn called Mary back and explained who she was and how she was close friends with the Traynors. Mary told Jack that this trip was just getting better and better. Claire told her to check in at the corporate offices at the Hollywood Studios as soon as they got situated and she'd give them the grand tour that the public never saw. Most of it was underground.

They'd stay at the Disney's Beach Club Resort, a short walk or boat ride to all the venues.

Instead of picking up their rental car at the Tampa docks to drive to Orlando, Mary cancelled her rental and called a limousine service to pick them up instead. The costs were about equal since the car rental was for five days. They both agreed that they wouldn't need a car once there. And why bother returning it at the Orlando International Airport once they were leaving? They didn't want to refill the tank after only going seventy miles. As rich as they'd be, they weren't wasteful people and would feel bad, no matter how much they thought would be wasted.

The drive took a little over an hour, and they were dropped at the door of the Disney Beach Club Resort. It was closing in on five p.m., and they were tired. Instead of meeting Claire and keeping her after hours, Mary called her to tell her that they arrived and had checked in to the hotel. They made plans to meet at Claire's office at nine-thirty a.m., the next day. Claire said she'd have a full breakfast ready for them in her conference room.

"Can't beat that," said Jack after Mary relayed the message.

So instead, they stayed at the hotel for dinner, went back to their rooms for a little rest and to make a few calls. They hadn't called anyone in almost a week. They needed to call Kristen to let them know where they were and ask if there was any leak about the winner or where they were. They met up later and walked over to Epcot for a little while to watch the fireworks, which happened every night. Mary wanted to go to Downtown Disney, which was now officially called Disney Springs, with an abundance of souvenir shops and restaurants. She didn't want to drag presents home for her family or roommates, but she wanted to buy something nice for each one and have the presents shipped. Jack felt a little sheepish. The only presents he'd have purchased were for his ex-wife, son, and daughter who were no longer speaking to him. He asked Mary if she'd get something for Kristen and his landlady, Ethel.

"Mary, I was thinking of a name for our new fifty-million-dollar trust. How about The Evangeline Trust. I was also thinking about the new building. It will cost around four million dollars, once complete. I don't want to hand that to a nonprofit company, who could then vote us out as officers and take over the building and sell it. I believe we were already screwed over once. We don't want to be twice. I want to set up a simple real estate corporation called Evangeline Realty, Inc. that would be one hundred percent owned by me, and you if you want, and it will be the holding company for our new career center and maybe even a house down in Key West.

"The reason I mentioned this is because when we start buying up properties right next to the TCC, the first response will be that another nonprofit's taking over Troy buildings and paying no taxes. It's bad enough with RPI, Sage, Hudson Valley, and all the other non-payers. I'd like to pay more than the taxes that were paid by the derelict houses that'll be demolished. I believe on four million in valuation, we'll pay around one hundred thousand dollars in annual taxes that were never paid before-new money to the city.

"Also, I want to run a for-profit not a non-profit. That way, we can run it anyway we want because we're going to use our own money anyway. Later, we'll start a non-profit after everything is up and running. We can use our own cash as matching funds which should make us more desirable for the New York State grants that we'll eventually apply for, along with federal and foundations grants. I guess I'm getting ahead of myself."

"No, that's the frame of mind we need to get back to," said Mary.

The next morning, they arrived at the Hollywood Studio headquarters and met Claire whom they liked very much. Claire had a buffet breakfast spread for them, and Marshall

Tillman walked in and joined them. They were very gracious and spoke highly of Joe and Julie. Claire told them what lengths Joe went to clear her father's name and how Disney would eventually be making a movie out of Julie's trilogy, *A Girl's Life*.

"We had no idea," said Mary. "We just met them last week, and we feel like we've known them all our lives. Do you know that we're from Troy, New York, just like Joe?"

"Julie mentioned it when she called me," said Claire.

For the rest of the day, Claire carted them around all the theme parks so they could get an overview. Then, when they were on their own, they'd know where they were going and what rides and features they should see. They were given a quick-pass bracelet and were good to go after that.

Tuesday through Sunday went quickly. They saw as much as they could. Jack was down to his last few thousand dollars but had several thousand still left on his credit card. Mary blew a bunch at Disney Springs and shipping probably cost as much as what she paid, but it was worth it. They booked a direct flight from Orlando to Albany, but they were leaving late and arriving near midnight. Mary called Kristen and told her not to bother picking them up that they'd stay at the Desmond overnight and would meet her for a late breakfast. They were tired but happy, and their world was about to change.

Jack muttered to himself, "I love the kids, still do, and maybe we'll regain our father-daughter-son status once again." He hoped it wouldn't be because of the money. He looked at Mary several times and thought, *Why couldn't I have met Mary before Maureen? Of course, she was in the convent.*

After these two weeks, he was half in love with her, even though nothing came of it. He'd liked Mary the day she came in for her interview to work at the TCC. Jack couldn't imagine how he could have achieved any success without her. He really did need her for the next ten years if they were to change lives in any meaningful way. Maybe it would lead to something else. She was the only woman that he fully trusted. He liked Kristen, but she was not Mary. *There's something about Mary*. Wasn't that a movie title?

CHAPTER 13

After a quick breakfast at the Desmond, they checked out and were met at the front door by the law firm's town car. The driver got out and put their luggage in the trunk. They made it out of the hotel parking lot and took the first right turn to the on-ramp of I-87 South. They proceeded to downtown Albany on I-90 South to the Clinton Street exit. From there they made it quickly to their parking lot off Maiden Lane. When they got out, Mary's car was still there parked next to a new black Ford Explorer. The parking lot attendant, who appeared to have worked there for forty years, greeted both Mary and Jack and the town car driver. He gave Mary her keys to her car so she could put her suitcase in the truck. He turned and gave Jack the keys to the Explorer.

"Mine?" asked Jack.

"Yes, sir. Here is the registration and insurance card to put in your glove compartment. The Explorer's tank is full, as well as yours, ma'am," he said.

"Nice. I could get used to this, Mary."

Jack put his carry-on in the back of the vehicle. He locked it and played with the keys and the key fob set off all the emergency lights, and it started beeping. Jack sheepishly handed the keys to the attendant who showed Jack how to stop the commotion and relock the vehicle without a problem.

"Thanks," he said. "Never had one of these."

"No problem. Kristen said that you'd be here by now, so she and the staff are waiting for you upstairs."

"Thanks again," they both said to the driver and the attendant. They walked across Maiden Lane to the back door of the bank building, up to the twelfth floor for the law offices of Miller, Reynolds, Coleman, and Straus. Kristen was too young to have her name on the door. She was only named a partner last year, after many years of service.

They got off the elevator and stopped at the receptionist who greeted them with a pleasant smile, "Welcome back. Mrs. Sanderson is waiting for you in the conference room with your team. Would you like anything to drink or eat?"

"Water, please," said Mary. Jack nodded as well.

They walked down the hall and went through the conference room door where everyone greeted them. "I feel like Norm on *Cheers*," said Jack. Mary smiled.

Kristen said, "Welcome back. Have fun?"

"Great time," said Mary. "You'll be getting your gift in the mail. We couldn't carry everything," she whispered.

As soon as they sat down, Kristen began to speak. She went over everything that they'd done while they were away and continued with what needed to be done to secure the funds and have the money wired to their bank account. Jack would receive everything less twenty-five percent federal tax to be withheld and then the accountant and lawyers together would do their thing.

"Thanks for the Explorer," Jack said. "I was hoping, but it was unexpected, knowing that you had to pay for it up-front."

"No problem. Get used to it. We now have power of attorney but—of course—only when you clear it."

"On our trip, Mary and I discussed the name of our trust for the fifty million dollars." Jack smiled. "How do you like the name "The Evangeline Trust Fund'?

"Really?" Kristen said. "I'm honored."

"Couldn't think of a better name after Jack mentioned it.

It's kind of cool and non-descriptive but does have that non-profit religious kind of feel. You know?"

"Well, as I said, I'm honored." The rest of the team kind of stared at each other. The senior members knew of her former life as a Sister of Saint Joseph. The newer members had no idea. "For those who don't know, I was a former nun called Sister Evangeline."

Many in the room were dumbfounded but smiled and said to each other that it was cool and they liked the name anyway, regardless of the connection.

"So," Jack said, "You have the trust name, and I want a corporation, for-profit, for any real estate that we'll own in the future. If the property is in the City of Troy, I want to pay real estate taxes. None of the non-profits in Troy pay much, including RPI. Also, I want to build a brand new career center, in downtown Troy, right next to the Troy Community Council's building. I want the building to be part of my estate. However, I want to be one-hundred-percent owner, in case there are any operating issues down the road."

Jack went on to explain that if a non-profit owned the building, the officers of the nonprofit controlled the real estate and could sell the building right out from under them. So, he wanted to go "for-profit," including the operation. He'd fund the career center operations at one million dollars per year to start and continue for ten years. If it was successful and they produced the results they anticipated, they might go for matching grants. However, in the meantime, Jack said he wanted no issues related to the property or the operation that could be construed as getting back at his old TCC organization. "I believe the new building that I'll be looking at is about thirty-thousand square feet, and three floors at ten thousand feet per floor. This should run around four million dollars, and the property taxes will be in the neighborhood of one hundred thousand dollars per year. I'm looking at several parcels, about three to four acres of derelict buildings, right next door to the TCC. Those buildings are off the tax rolls, and it will cost the city money to knock them down. I want you, Kristen, to quietly pick up the parcels, for next to nothing, with a guarantee that the property to be developed will pay taxes as a for-profit for a minimum of ten years."

"We'll make that priority number one, as soon as the funds arrive," said Kristen.

"Next, as I said before, I believe that the property that houses the Troy Community Council isn't owned by TCC but by an individual who lives in the city of Troy. I've no idea what the rent is that they pay, but if you run a federal nine-ninety form on them, it will tell you what they paid for rent over the last several years. Also, check the records with the city and see how much the taxes are and the valuation of the building. Also, if you can, please find out when their lease is up."

Kristen smiled. "Is this revenge, Jack? You said that you'd kill everyone with kindness."

Mary looked at Jack because she never heard this from him before. "Just what're you planning, Jack?"

"Nothing, I swear to God. But I think it would be nice to be their new landlord. As the landlord, I could never be on their board, but I could certainly persuade them in the proper vision for the organization. I believe the building, being old and needing repairs, could be had for a half million dollars. We could get it for under a million and put the necessary repairs into it. All I'd charge them for was the property taxes and closing costs. If they keep their nose clean for ten years, under new management and a new board, I'll give them the building as a donation. By that time, my fifty-million-dollar trust should be gone, and I'll be retiring at age sixty. I want to walk away with about sixty million dollars of my own and whatever Mary wants to keep.

"By the way, after buying their building, I do plan on pulling up in front of it in my FBI Explorer, wearing a black suit, black glasses, and a black baseball hat, and scare the crap out of them. I'm hoping they'll try to ban me from the building, especially with my bodyguard. A call from our attorneys to theirs should prove to be effective, you think?"

Everyone started to laugh. Mary and Kristen had a smile a mile wide. "Can we go with you when it happens?" said Kristen.

"Sure, the more, the merrier."

Jack then said, "Mary, you're up. I'm done for now. Trust me, I've other plans to incentivize people and organizations, but it can wait until after the center is built. Mary, please go ahead. Sorry. I'm kind of giddy."

"According to Jack, and I don't know why, I'm getting fifteen million dollars to do with what I want. If I want the money for myself, half goes for taxes leaving me with about seven and a half million dollars for myself. Is that right?" she asked as she looked at the accountants.

"Right around there, give or take a few hundred thousand."

Mary nodded. "My trust will be called 'Theresa's Trust,' after Mother Theresa. As an ex-nun, I'll bet she could have used the money, and I'd have given it to her. However, as Jack said, I'm not stupid either. I want to keep three million for myself, and for my estate, so I'll need to keep about six million dollars before taxes. I also want to endow my two roommates, so they don't have to worry about a thing when they decide to retire. I also want to discuss the closing of Saint Augustine's School and Catholic High, and if Saint Augustine's does close, what can we do with it, and the gymnasium. Maybe we can donate it to the school district or the Boys and Girls Club down the street. I'd donate a one-hundred-percent match to everything they could raise to keep the school open, but with only a hundred kids, I don't believe it's viable. If they could turn it into a charter school and hold religious education for those who want it in the gymnasium as a separate entity, I'd consider it. Let's get Jack's stuff done first, and then we can work on my plans."

Jack said, "Mary, that's a great idea. We should talk more about joint plans. I don't need what I have, and I don't want you harassed by everyone if they find out what you're going to be worth."

Mary nodded. "Got it, Jack. It won't happen. I won't let it happen."

Kristen cleared her throat. "Did we cover enough you guys for the moment? I want to talk about your appearance at the lottery commission, Jack. Mary, are you going?"

"I don't think it's wise to drag her into this at this time. When word gets out, then she can represent her own interests, but for now, I should be the only one taking the heat. Trust me, it's the last thing I want to do."

"I hear you," said Kristen. "You may not know it, since you were away for two weeks, but I talked to the lottery commissioner and told him that we represented the winner. They came to our office and verified that, in fact, Jack, you're one of only three holders of the winning Powerball lottery for nine hundred ninety million dollars, split three ways. They thoroughly examined the ticket, did their verification tests, and concurred that it was a winner. They glanced at the back for your name as signed, only after they signed the confidentiality agreement. We're scheduled to appear at the New York State Lottery headquarters in Schenectady, tomorrow. Sorry to spring it on you, but I thought you might like to get that out of the way and not have it hang over your head. As I told you, it's been in our safe since you left but we certainly aren't worth three hundred thirty million dollars, so we want it in the hands of the lottery commission as well. Sound like a plan?"

"Sounds like a plan, and thank you for everything. I know you'll be paid quite handsomely, but I expect that. You can't pay for your friendship, kindness, and honesty and, for that, we're both eternally grateful."

Kristen, Mary, and the entire team were emotionally moved, and they believed that this was a team effort. "Everyone here should feel good that we're doing something positive for the future of the region and all our kids," Jack said. "I hope that's self-evident."

He was told that he'd be picked up in the town car at nine a.m., the next day, wherever he wanted. Since he had his suitcase with him, he decided to stay at the hotel across the street for the night. It was getting late, and Mary, Kristen, and Jack would have a small victory dinner. Then Mary would go home to meet her roommates. She hoped that her presents arrived first to ease the discussion she'd be having with them. She had to leave Catholic High and Saint Augustine's to continue her new life, or was that the continuation of her old life with a six-month blip?

CHAPTER 14

Jack got his suite at the Albany Hilton, right downtown. He asked Kristen if he could get a law office cell phone to use so he wouldn't be hassled by a lot of well wishers. By the end of the day, she gave him one that was left over from an attorney who left. It wasn't new but did the trick. He threw out his prepaid cell phone that he'd been using for the last six months since he never got a job that would give him a cell as part of his work duties. After dinner, Kristen and Mary went home. Jack went to his room, leaving his car at the bank lot. He didn't need it or feel like moving it. They gave him a card for the gate if he wanted to get in and out, so he was set.

Back at his room at the hotel, Jack got out his personal phone numbers and called Joe Traynor. On the way out of the office, Jack had told Mary and Kristen that he'd handle the bodyguards that they'd need soon. He could go under the radar for a few days but not for long. He dialed the home phone for Joe and Julie Traynor in Tavernier, Florida.

"Hello, may I help you?" Julie asked.

"Julie, it's Jack Manning back in Troy. I hope I didn't disturb you. I was looking for Joe."

"Jack, how are you and Mary? Did you have a good trip? It was very nice meeting you down in Key West. Joe spoke to Skip just yesterday, and he said he thought you had fun. Did you?"

"Of course. We had a great time, thanks to you, and we won't forget it."

"By the way, we just got a package from Disney Springs for Bella. She just loved her Cinderella outfit and accessories. I don't suppose you picked the dress out?"

Jack laughed. "Hardly. Mary, all the way. But I'm glad that Bella likes it. She's six now?"

"Just turned. Here's Joe. Thanks again. Say hi to Mary for us. See you when you get back here. Call us."

"Will do, thanks again."

Julie handed the phone to Joe. "It's Jack Manning. They just got back to Troy."

"Jack, how are you and Mary? Hope you had a good time. Skip and Linda thought you did. That was also nice what you did for their kids and for Bella. You're good people. What can I do for you?"

"The announcement by the New York State Lottery Commissioner is taking place tomorrow, and I am sure to be inundated by the press and everyone else I know," Jack explained. "I've heard from others that it could be dangerous. Do you know of any ex-policemen or FBI agents who'd like to be bodyguards for the next few months at least? I'll pay whatever you recommended and give a bonus at the end for the help."

"I have the home number of Tom Matthews up in Albany," Joe said. "He was the director of the Albany FBI office. I'll ask him for recommendations and have him get back to you. When do you need them?"

"Nobody knows about Mary's connection to the Powerball winning numbers. So, she won't need anything for a while or until she becomes known. I'll need at least two for several weeks, twenty-four/seven, and then maybe one during the day after that, when I'm out setting everything up. I'm going to stay at the Albany Hilton, at State and North Pearl, right across the street from the attorneys at Sixty-Nine State Street. I'll pay for two separate rooms for them on either side of me until the thrill wears off. What do you think?"

"I'll call Tom right now, and if he's in, I'd expect him to call you within the hour. We're very good friends, and I'll tell you the story someday how we took down the Mexican Mafia in Albany."

"Is there anybody you don't know, Joe?"

"I never knew anyone filthy rich before, so that's a first."

"Me either." Jack laughed. He hung up after thanking Joe once again for his assistance. "It pays to be a nice guy sometimes because it comes around every now and then," Jack mused.

By nine p.m., Jack was settling into his room. He called down and got a six-pack to go with his room snacks. His new cell phone rang and promptly displayed "private caller." *Must be Tom*, Jack thought. It was, and they spoke for a long time. Tom explained that mandatory retirement age for field agents was fifty-seven, still a youthful age in everyday life. "I have five retirees this year, and most are taking time before they think about restarting another career until they're age sixty-five. I know two who are available. What are your needs?"

"The big event begins tomorrow when they're picking me up at nine to take me to Schenectady for ten a.m. for the big announcement."

"Two retired agents will be at your door at seven-thirty a.m. to introduce themselves to you. They'll follow you in their car together and meet you before you went upstairs to the lottery office. Ex-FBI agents still carry 'FBI on-duty' placards and weapons until they die. So parking is no problem."

"Thank you so much, Tom."

"You've no idea what the FBI and Homeland Security both owe Joe Traynor. He probably didn't tell you, but he has credentials as a lieutenant—in charge of all investigations for the Coast Guard for all of south Florida—as well as badges for Homeland Security and the FBI, which he uses interchangeably, depending on the situation."

"Wow. I guess I hit the jackpot. Thank you. Thank you. Thank you. I'm also worried about Mary, so we can move someone to her if she gets on the radar."

"Sounds like a plan. They'll be there in the morning. They're agents, John Jefferson and Fred Tucker. Make sure you mention Joe's name to them," Tom said. "Also they handed Joe the Coast Guard Commendation Medal with a Ribbon. It's the highest award issued for heroism, not in-volving combat with an enemy outside the country, by the United States Coast Guard."

"Unbelievable. He must be on the side of the angels."

"He is."

With that, they hung up. Jack called Mary to make sure she got home all right. She did and said she was in a very long conversation with Jane and Martha about her wherea-bouts over the last two weeks. "They think we ran away together and we're lovers."

"Let them think what they want. Did they get their pre-sents?"

"Yes. They liked those at least. I'll see you in the funny papers tomorrow or on the news around ten a.m."

"I'll call you later after the announcement. By the way, we're getting two retired FBI agents to follow me around and then you if you need it."

"Hope not. Say a prayer that this will work out well."

Jack couldn't sleep. He knew what was coming and didn't know how to prepare. He needed to keep his mouth shut forever or at least until the money was wired to his ac-count and everything got jump-started. His life would change, but, hopefully, he could roll with the punches. Or not.

CHAPTER 15

Jack was up by six-thirty a.m. At exactly seven-thirty a.m., there was a knock on the door. Jack looked through the peephole and saw two older men, dressed in black suits, red ties, and polished shoes. Jack opened the door with the chain still attached, and the two men identified themselves and showed Jack their identification. Retired FBI agents, John Jefferson and Fred Tucker, shook Jack's hand and asked him if he was ready to go. They'd follow Jack rather than be in the same car so they couldn't be conspicuous to others. Jack told them to meet him right at Maiden Lane at the entrance of the bank parking lot, and from there they'd leave for Schenectady. Jack was meeting Kristen, and they'd be leaving in the company town car.

Jack asked her, "Am I ever going to get to use my new Explorer?"

"When the dust settles," she said.

They headed toward I-787 South toward I-90 West where it ran into the New York State Thruway. John and Fred were right behind them in an obvious FBI vehicle that they must have borrowed for this occasion. They told Jack to have their driver pull up right in front of the lottery building, and they'd head right into the front door. Once in, they'd already cased the building, and they'd park, with the town car, immediately at the back door of the building, near the parking lot, so that Jack could make a quick escape after the short ceremony. They went through the tolls for Exit 24 and continued to Schenectady, Interchange Exit 25 to I-290 West. They'd exit at Broadway and go the short distance to 1 Broadway Center, Suite 700, on the seventh floor where lottery headquarters were located. By the time they got to the front door, it was less than a half hour door to door.

Jack and Kristen got out of the car and headed to the elevator for the seventh floor. Once on, John Jefferson stayed with Jack and Kristen while Fred moved the car to the back entrance with the town car. They said that they'd be as quick as possible, maybe a half-hour to forty-five minutes, at the most.

As Jack, John, and Kristen got off the elevator, there was a bank of cameras and a flock of news people, in the hallway, including local and national television, along with reporters from the *Albany Times Union, Daily Gazette* from Schenectady and *The Record* from Troy. Jack and Kristen walked into the office and asked for the lottery commissioner. Kristen met the security team a while ago when they declared Jack's ticket officially valid but never met the commissioner. Kristen took the lead as Jack's attorney and quietly spoke to the commissioner and his staff and then introduced Jack. John stood quietly by Jack's side. She told everyone that the ceremony shouldn't be dragged out and that Jack was there to fulfill his obligations as a lottery winner and to be officially introduced to the public. He handed his signed ticket to the commissioner.

A podium was set up for the occasion, and the commissioner moved all the media into the boardroom where the ceremony was to take place. He spoke on behalf of the New York State Lottery Commission, and, as a faithfully appointed official by the current administration, he glowingly told the public that New York State was honored to have one of the Powerball winners come from the New York State capital region. He then introduced Jack Manning, from Troy, New York, as New York State's official winner, who'd be splitting $990 million with two other individuals from Florida and California. It was almost three weeks since the numbers were drawn, and the winners were known, not by name, but by where they bought their ticket. The winners from California and Florida had already come forward to claim their prizes.

The commissioner asked Jack to speak, and he simply said, "I'm very pleased to be one of the winners of the Powerball drawing. I'm in the process of developing a plan for the money, so at this time, I'm unable to tell you what I'll be doing with the proceeds, obviously after taxes are taken out. However, I'll be taking the lump sum cash plan as opposed to the thirty-year payout. Thank you for coming today, but that's all I have to say at the present time."

As Jack was speaking, the flashes from the cameras were blinding him. Reporters were shouting out questions. "Where do you live? What do you have planned for the money? Do you have any family here? Can we talk to you afterward? What do you do for a living? How old are you? Are you married? Who's the woman with you? Is she your wife?"

As soon as the questions arose and became a little over-whelming, Kristen took the mike from Jack and told the crowd that Jack wouldn't be speaking any more today. She said that, as time went on, he'd contact the press and news outlets if he had anything further to say. She thanked them for coming, took Jack by the elbow, and turned. Both shook the commissioner's hand as well as those of the staff as-sembled for the meeting. They both followed John, a very large individual by the way, out the office door toward the elevator. Jack pressed the down button and, after what seemed like an eternity but only lasted less than a minute, the door opened, and the three got on. John politely blocked the door from anyone else trying to enter the elevator.

As they rode down, Jack said, "Well, that went well, don't you think? What was it about twenty minutes in to-tal?" as he smiled from ear to ear.

"Less than," said Kristen.

As the door opened, all three fled to the rear exit where Fred was waiting, holding the town car back door open for Jack and Kristen. He tapped on the back as if to say, "Follow me."

Fred and John hopped into the running SUV, pulled around the town car, and went out the driveway and back to where they originally came from.

"Jack, if you don't mind, we've got a little celebration set up back at my office for you. I invited Mary to attend as well. Hope you don't mind."

"Mind? Of course not. I want her to be there. Other than you, I've no one else to celebrate with. Thank you. Thank you. Thank you. Thank you. I couldn't have done this without you, Kristen. And your team."

They made it back to Albany by the same way but traffic to Albany was a lot heavier, and it took a good forty-five minutes to get back. When they pulled into the Maiden Lane parking lot, Jack invited John and Fred in for the celebration. John said he needed to return the FBI vehicle to Albany headquarters, which was only a few blocks away and would return in his own car. Fred left his car in the FBI lot as well and would get it later.

As they walked into the office, there was clapping and cheering, for both Kristen and Jack. Kristen took a bow, all smiles. Jack felt sheepish and simply waved to everyone. Fred looked around to make sure they were all friendly faces. After all, his job, and John's, was just beginning. They'd follow Jack everywhere for at least the next several weeks. If Mary Evans were harassed, one of them would shadow her as well. They'd had a lot of experience in crowd control and shadowing well-known politicians and celebrities, so this was no different.

Mary was in the back of the room, and Jack spotted her. He went over and gave her a big hug and a kiss on the cheek.

One of the accountants said, "Jack, it was all over the news. All three main stations and Time Warner picked up the ceremony, and it just came on CNN, MSNBC, and FOX News at the top of the hour. You guys were great. It was short, to the point, and then you got out of there."

Mary said, "How are we going to deal with this, Jack? After all, we'll be erecting a new building, starting soon, hiring staff, recruiting kids and their families. I hope this doesn't interfere with what we need to do. Will John and Fred be enough protection?"

"If not, we'll hire more. For now, I'm staying at the Hilton with Fred and John, on both sides of my room. I think we need to look at renting a house, maybe out of town but near our work. I don't want to buy anything until we know we can get the property and build. I also want to immediately get the building that houses the TCC so we can have the ability to move forward without a lot of hassle. What do you think? I'll never tell you what to do, Mary."

"Where do you want to move to for now?" Mary said.

"I don't know. Let's talk about it later. Let's celebrate. I can't believe this has all happened. Can you?"

With a smile, Mary said, "No, Jack. I can't."

"Mom, have you been watching the news today?" asked Debbie. She just called her from school and was shaking like a leaf. "We're rich, Mom. We're rich!"

Maureen just heard about the news a few minutes earlier. Chuck just called her from his UPS truck. Someone called him on his cell from the UPS office and asked him if it was Maureen's ex-husband who hit the big one. "You're going to be rich, Maureen," he said. He meant, "We're going to be rich, Maureen."

"Mom, did Dad call you yet?" asked her son, Mark. "Did you hear what happened? Son of a bitch. He's splitting nine hundred ninety million dollars, three ways. That's three hundred thirty million dollars, Mom. I dreamed it was Dad who hit it big. I called him, but he never picked up. What do you think, Mom? Are we getting anything? What do you think?" Mark was so excited that he kept asking her the same questions again and again. "Can you call him and ask him to come see us. Please?"

"I'll try to get a hold of him at the house in the Burgh tonight, Mark. Other than that, I don't know his cell number. He never gave it to me."

They didn't know he dumped the other pre-paid cell phone.

"I have it, Mom. He gave it to Debbie and me when he left the house. Do you think he's pissed at us, Mom? He can't be mad now, can he?"

Maureen was beside herself. She didn't want to admit it, but she'd treated Jack like a piece of crap and threw him out of the house. She was with Chuck now, and Jack knew it. She even threw it in his face one time when he tried to talk to her. The divorce was final. According to the settlement papers, she got everything he had. She signed off on no child support. The kids were now over twenty-one and Mark didn't even live at home now that he graduated from college and was living with his girlfriend, Cara, in Albany. Debbie just became twenty-one a short while ago. Maureen knew that Jack didn't owe her a dime. She also knew that Chuck would be pumping her every day to get money from Jack and that Jack hated Chuck for screwing around with her while they were still married. If she'd any chance of getting any money from Jack, she had to make a decision about Chuck. Should she dump him now or would it be too obvious? Should she go crawling back to Jack after the way she treated him? Did he still love her? Was there any hope for them to get back together now that he owned the world? She started to get depressed, knowing pretty well what her future would be like. At least he should help pay off the rest of the kid's student loans and Debbie's master degree coming up after she got her undergraduate degree.

Maureen would try to get him tonight at Ethel's house. Maybe it wouldn't be so bad.

CHAPTER 16

Jack felt guilty. It'd been almost three weeks since he'd gone back to see Ethel and pick up his stuff. He knew he couldn't stay, but he wanted to talk to her and see if she was all right. And he still had his key, which he needed to return to her. He also wanted to take care of her. Other than Mary, Ethel was his only real friend, especially over the last six months. Debbie didn't call him once even, though he'd called her time and again. He spoke to Mark now and again, but Jack knew that Mark was on his own and really didn't care if Jack called or not. Mark sided with his mother, so that told Jack a lot. He was going to call Ethel's son to see if he'd pick up the slack with Jack's needing to leave. He'd visit her a lot after everything died down and he wasn't harassed like he knew he'd be over the next several months. Everyone would want a piece of him, but that would go with the territory. Everybody had money problems. If you had a family, you couldn't escape it. However, he'd formulated some plans in his head for all those who asked him for money. He didn't mind. Hell, he had plenty, but he wanted to separate the wheat from the chaff.

Jack thought of a simple formula for giving away money to others for projects or funding that he wasn't a part of. Whatever was asked of him, that person would have to match his or her request one hundred percent, either in money or in volunteer time to the project that Jack wanted done. If they weren't willing to do that, then their request would fall on deaf ears, unless they were so poor and sick that they couldn't comply with Jack's request. If someone needed money to pay their mortgage so they could keep the house, Jack would give them half and make a deal with the bank that the person would do work for the nonprofit at a rate of twenty dollar per hour, which was, on the average, above what most people in Troy made per hour. They'd have a time card and would do work either cleaning up the career center, helping tutor the children of those getting an education at the center, babysitting their children while they went through the program or a hundred different jobs they could do to earn their money. They could help hand out flyers on the weekend, instead of just Jack, week in and week out. Jack would hire a volunteer coordinator who'd keep track of what was owed and what was earned back. Anyone who paid up in full would receive a certificate that he'd offer with pride for a job well done.

If Debbie wanted to get her master's degree, Jack would pay the tuition, and she'd earn back half by working on the weekends at the new center. There would be no free rides. Jack also had a plan for a trust to be set up for Maureen, Mark, and Debbie. When Maureen reached age sixty-two, he'd give her one million dollars, tax-free. He felt an obligation because they did spend almost twenty-five years together, for better or worse, as they say. It was now worse, but he'd do it anyway. Each of the kids would get two million dollars on their thirty-fifth birthday, if they paid back their share of their student loans by working off the balance at the center. If they didn't, they'd be penalized. However, if any one of the three decided to sue him for money, all three would lose their trust accounts. He'd put that in writing and back it up with why. Why? Maureen took him to the cleaners and mocked him. Debbie never spoke to him after he was thrown out of the house. Mark couldn't have cared less about him. Jack believed that this would be their just reward.

Jack stopped at Testo's and bought a pizza, wings, and soda to take to Ethel's. He'd ordered it on the way, and it was ready for him when he arrived. He was a regular there but didn't want to start any conversation in the restaurant. He paid for the pizza with his debit card. That was a new feeling. He couldn't spell debit card a few weeks ago, he thought and laughed. He drove over to 6th Avenue from the restaurant and looked around before he went to the front door. It looked like, if anyone had hung around to get a glimpse of him, they'd already left for the day. He had his house key in his right hand, carrying the pizza and wings in his right with the bottle of soda tucked under his left arm.

As he opened the front door, he hollered, "Ethel, it's Jack. I'm back. Are you here?"

"Of course, I'm here. What do you think I'm deaf?"

Of course, she's deaf, he said to himself.

Jack walked into the kitchen where Ethel was sitting at the dinette table. The house looked like it did in 1962. Nothing was changed. Maybe it was a little dirtier since he hadn't been home. Of course, her son never stopped by to help her.

"Hi, Ethel. How the hell are you?"

"Well, if it isn't Mr. Millionaire, himself," she said with a smile.

"That's Mr. Multi-Millionaire," he said, matching her grin from ear to ear. He went over and gave her a big hug. "Has your son been here to see you since I've been gone," he asked.

"What do you think?" she said "Of course not. Maybe once to bring me groceries while he complained the entire time he was here for all of fifteen minutes. Are you leaving me, Jack?"

"I have to for now because of the publicity. If I stayed here, you wouldn't have a minute's peace. So I'm staying at a hotel in Albany. I won't give you my number because I don't want your son to have it, and you can't hear me on the phone anyway."

"I can hear you fine."

"You hear what you want to hear, Ethel." Jack sighed. "Here's what I want to ask you. Are you happy here? If I got you a fulltime housekeeper and a cook, do you want to stay here or go to The Eddy where you'll be waited on hand and foot?"

"This is my home, Jack. I don't want to go anywhere."

"Well, without talking to your son, can we go ahead and hire you some help while I do what I have to do? I promise to stop by twice a week to make sure you're okay. If I can't, I'll ask Mary to drop by. Is that okay?"

"I like Mary. I like her better than you even," she said and laughed.

"Well, let's eat. I'm hungry. I'm sure you are, too. Want pizza and wings?"

"Of course. And don't think because I'm old, I'm not grateful, Jack. I'd tell you that you're like a son to me, but my son happens to be a jerk so I won't tell you that, okay."

Jack smiled. "Fine. Let's eat. I snuck out on my bodyguards but I have to be back soon, or they'll be pissed. Eat up."

They did, and Jack left to drive back to Albany. As he was leaving, the phone rang. He checked Ethel's old phone. It weighed about ten pounds with no caller ID, obviously.

He picked it up. "Hello?"

"Jack? It's Maureen."

Shit. Why did I pick up the phone? he asked himself. *I have to be a moron.*

CHAPTER 17

Yes, Maureen. How are you?"

"I'm great. Congratulations on your winning the lottery. That's great news. The kids are thrilled to death. If you have time, they'd both like to see you."

"Really? Why's that?" he asked factiously.

"Well, they want to congratulate you, of course."

"Of course."

"You don't seem to be pleased, Jack. Why is that?"

"Maureen, do we have to go down this road? You dumped me. You cheated on me with the same guy you're now living with. You divorced me. You took everything I had, including the kids. You wouldn't even talk to me at the bank. You turned your head, when I said hello, and walked away. Debbie hasn't spoken one word to me since the day you threw me out of the house. I spoke to Mark occasionally but never even got invited to his graduation ceremony from college that I helped pay for. Do I need any more reasons not to be pleased with my so-called family?"

"You should be happy now and consider that water under the bridge, Jack. What do you want me to tell the kids?"

"You can tell them that, at ages twenty-two and twenty-one, they could probably call me themselves without their mother's intervention. That's what you could tell them. I'm working on investing all the money into several projects, including my family, if I'm not harassed. You can wait for me to get back to all of you. If you call again, Maureen, whatever I had planned for your future will be discarded, just like I was discarded. Do you understand? I have no financial obligations to any of you, according to the settlement. The kids are both over age twenty-one and no longer my problem or obligation. You can try to sue me, if that's what Chuck recommends, Maureen, but trust me, I can block a lawsuit for the next hundred years and beyond. Now, do you understand me?"

"Yes. You'll call us when you're ready. Is that correct?"

"That's correct, Maureen. Good luck." With that, he hung up the phone. He was more sad than irritated. He knew sooner or later everyone would be hitting him up for something. He wondered if Chuck Falcone had put her up to the phone call or if she called on her own. He wouldn't ask her so he'd never know.

⁊ᴐ⁊ᴐ

Maureen called Debbie first. She told Debbie that when Dad was ready to see her, he'd call and not to call him. She left the same message for Mark at his office in Albany. He'd call them. Jack told Maureen that he'd thrown away his burner phone, and he was not giving out his new number. He also told her not to call Ethel's number at the house because he'd no longer be living there. Of course, Ethel would never hear the phone and wouldn't even know that someone called. Her answering machine would fill up and not receive any more messages. Jack thought that would be fine with Ethel, since she never bothered anyway. He laughed to himself that Ethel's son would try to answer all the calls and put his foot in his mouth, making it worse, but that would be his problem. Jack could get Ethel a new phone, but she could always make calls out with the one she had. She just didn't need, or want, to answer it.

⁊ᴐ⁊ᴐ

Jack headed back to the hotel, and as he got to his room, Fred stuck his head out the door. "Can we talk?"

"Sure. Give me a minute. Come on in."

Fred and John both walked into Jack's room. "Jack, you can't just take off like that. I know you left a message, but why are we here? If you don't need us, just say so. We've got other work we can do. Trust me, we don't need this gig. This was a favor to Tom Matthews and Joe Traynor."

"I'm sorry, guys. I had a few things I had to take care of. I apologize. It won't happen again. Can I buy you a drink downstairs?"

"Sure, but don't screw up again, or we'll be out of here when you really need us. The shit's going to hit the fan when people find out where you're staying. We need to get you out of here to a more remote spot. Downtown Albany at State and North Pearl? Could you be more conspicuous? Why not wear a sign that says, 'Powerball winner—free money for everyone.'"

"The horse is dead. Get off. I hear you loud and clear. Do you have a few ideas? I need to be near the attorney's office as well as close to Troy to see how the plans are developing. Once the building is up, I've got plans to actually live there on the very top floor in an apartment that'll be hidden from view. In fact, I plan on one for me and one for Mary. It'll have a shorter roof line, so no one will actually know there'll be a fourth floor."

"Sounds like a plan. Hope you get there before you get killed," Fred quipped.

Jack smiled. "I get it. I really do. I won't go anywhere without you unless I get lucky, of course. Then you can stand outside the door and listen."

"You needed to hit the Powerball to get lucky, that's for sure," John said with a laugh.

"Touché."

They headed down to the bar at the Albany Hilton. Jack wanted a snack anyway. He loved peanuts and popcorn with a beer. He hoped they had some there.

He called Mary when they got to the bar. She was fine. She said she was a little tired. Her friends were now on board and excited. She told Jack that she didn't tell Jane and Martha that she was given fifteen million dollars to play with, but she told them that she'd take care of them if and when they retired. They believed her. Mary was that way. If she said something, she meant it. Jane was going to Catholic High the next day and would talk to the principal and tell her that Mary was taking a leave of absence for a while. She would say that Mary wasn't feeling well and would call her when she was better. Martha said she'd do the same at Saint Augustine's. They didn't like to lie, but a small fib would be okay. They both knew that something was up between Jack and Mary, but they weren't sure what. They knew that they went away together to Key West and Walt Disney World but also knew that Jack hit the big one. They were sure that Jack would take care of Mary, since they were best friends, and that Mary would share her largesse with them. They'd absolutely freak if they thought Jack had given her fifteen million dollars.

"Mary, can you meet at Kristen's office tomorrow after ten a.m. I'm going to use the gym at the hotel early. I've been out of it since we got back from Florida. I don't want to die of a heart attack by being out of shape, especially now."

"I'll be there. I need to sit with the accountant and Kristen, later on, to start my planning as well. Maybe we can do some joint things, so we don't overlap and waste our time and money."

"I'll see you tomorrow. Say hi to the ladies."

CHAPTER 18

Maureen got home around five-thirty p.m. Chuck was already there and taking a shower. Debbie had just walked in from Siena.

Maureen took off her coat and changed her clothes. She'd start dinner and have Debbie finish it while she took her shower. She'd make chicken and broccoli Alfredo. It never took too long with Debbie making the Alfredo sauce. Maureen hoped they could get through dinner tonight without another fight. It was very obvious that Debbie couldn't stand Chuck.

Maureen had turned Debbie against her father when they divorced. That was why she never called him. Debbie was very surprised when Chuck moved in, only a few weeks after her father left the house. She wondered if her mother had been playing her all this time. Debbie didn't believe that her mother dumped her father and fell immediately in love with this guy, all within a few weeks. She thought that Mom had to be cheating on Dad while he was still around. She was mad at her father but was dealing with her mother's infidelity, if that was what it was, and she believed it was. She'd let her mother talk her into turning her back on her father, and then her mother seemed to turn her back on Debbie.

That was why Debbie called nine-one-one when her mother and Chuck had a long, dragged-out fight a month ago. Maureen threw a bottle at him, and that was enough for Debbie.

Chuck and Maureen had made up, and now Debbie was the bad guy for calling the cops. The problem was that she had no other place to go while she was finishing up at Siena. She couldn't move into the dorm for a few weeks and didn't have enough money to cover room and board for the fall. She was stuck at home. After that, it would take a few more years for her master's degree. She didn't know if she'd make it. She wondered if her father would forgive her and take her in, especially now that he was rich. She needed to do something and soon.

"Well, did you call him, Maureen?" Chuck asked, as he came into the kitchen while she started dinner.

"Yes, I did. Why do you ask?"

"What did he say? Are you going to tell me or not? Do I have to guess?"

"He said not to call him again. He'd call us when he was ready. He was mad at me for calling for the kids instead of them calling him. He said they're old enough to fight their own battles. Happy?"

"What's that mean? Happy?" he hissed. "You should be getting a chunk of that lottery money. You spent almost twenty-five years with him. Did you check your divorce papers or call your attorney to see what you can do about it? It's only been a little over six months since he left. Hell, your divorce only took place a few months ago. There must be something you can do? What're your kids getting? Nothing?"

"He didn't say. He said he'd call. I don't believe he'd cut the kids out, but I'm a different story. You saw how low he got when the divorce went through. I can only imagine how much he hates me and you."

"That's why you have to strike while the fire is hot, Maureen. Call your attorney."

"Is this about you, Chuck, or about us? What's your problem? You think you'll be getting something from kids or from me, if we ever see a dime? Is that what this is about? Huh?" She was getting furious. "He told me, point blank, that if I tried to sue him that he had enough money to stop me for a hundred years. Does that sound like I'm getting something, Chucky?"

Now Chuck was as furious as she was. "Is that what you think of me, Maureen? What, am I your play toy? Is that it? Are you going to dump me now and make a play for the big bucks? Think he'll take you back? Think again. Your only hope is to sue him for whatever you can get," he said.

She looked him in the eye. "What have you contributed to the household since you've been here, Chuck? Have you bought groceries? Paid the taxes or heat and light bill? Thank God, we don't have a mortgage, or we couldn't pay it with what you've contributed to this 'love nest.'"

At that point, Debbie came back into the room. She had the house phone in her hand and said to both of them, "Should I call nine-one-one, *again*?" with the emphasis on 'again.'"

Maureen looked at Chuck. "Go for a walk. Get a drink. Do something. Don't come back if you can't change your attitude. Sorry, Chuck. Debbie's right. This has to stop now."

Chuck grabbed his keys and his jacket and headed for his BMW. He didn't have to take this crap. Debbie started it every time, and Maureen always took her side. If he stayed, would there be some money in it for him? If not, he was history. He could start up again by simply looking into his well-hidden little black book of former lovers. He didn't need this shit. Maureen was mercurial, and he could see why Jack put her in her place. Maybe he was happy to leave her and stick her with Chuck. Maybe giving up everything to get rid of her wasn't such a bad idea, after all. It took him only six months to become a multi-millionaire. Next time, Chuck would think about running a credit report on a woman before he got into bed with her. No matter what, he didn't think this would end well.

"Happy, Debbie? There goes Chuck. Can't you get along with anyone? Christ. What do I have to do, play referee every night?"

"Are you kidding me?" Debby said. "You move this leech into our house. It's our house, not just yours. Then what do you do? Constantly fight. What do you see in him, Mom? Don't you know his reputation? Everyone on the block knows his reputation. Why don't you dump him? At least then you could go back to your ex-husband on hands and knees and beg for forgiveness for your infidelity."

"Infidelity? What're you talking about? I never cheated on your father, ever."

"I see the light, Mom. It's shining in my eyes. It's telling me that you're full of crap, and now you're torn. You finally figured out why Chucky is here. And, you could lose millions of dollars because of it. It's called fate, Mom. Fate. And you stuck me in the same boat. Thank you." With that, Debbie walked down the hall and slammed her door. She put on her coat and walked out of the house.

Maureen was left alone, all alone. Mark didn't even call tonight. She wondered if she brought this on herself or if it really was fate. "What the hell can I do now?" she asked herself.

She had a good fourteen more years before she could even think about taking early retirement at age sixty-two. She had to do something. She blew it, but maybe just maybe, she could fix it. Jack loved her for almost twenty-five years. She knew she could get him back if she apologized and told him that she'd changed and realized she wanted only him. She'd even sign a pre-nup, if they remarried, just to prove to him that she still loved him. At least that's what she'd tell him. She was about to have a chat with Chuck, if and when he came back. If not, his things would be on the front steps by morning.

CHAPTER 19

Jack would meet Mary at Kristen's office. He spent so much time there and across the street at the Hilton that he automatically turned toward 69 State Street when heading out of the hotel. Of course, his Explorer was parked at the bank lot anyway. He wondered how long they'd let him continue to park there, probably as long as he had business with them. He'd stop within a week or so if he had a new place to live. He had no idea where to go. He'd discuss it with Mary and Kristen this morning.

Jack saw Mary in the hallway, and they walked together into Kristen's office.

"Coffee?" Kristen asked.

"Already ate and had coffee. Just water, for now, would be good," he said.

"I'll have coffee, Kristen," Mary said.

"Coming up."

As they settled at her conference table, Kristen said, "Well, all your funds have been transferred from the lottery commission to your account, Jack. We'll need you to sign a check payable to Mary's trust to transfer the funds to her. Our team is working on the taxes, the trusts for both of you, and buying AAA non-taxable municipal bonds for Jack. Mary, we haven't discussed where your funds will wind up."

"Finish Jack's stuff first. It's the most important. Just

don't create a tax event for me until I'm ready to decide. I kind of know what I want to do, but I spoke to Jack, and we want to coordinate our efforts, so we don't fund the same things."

"That's a great idea, Mary," Kristen said.

Jack leaned forward "Kristen, I also have a plan, and I want to hash it out with you two. I'm sure I'm going to be hit up a lot now that everyone knows I have money. I really don't want anyone finding out about Mary's trust until she's prepared to deal with it. However, I may need some additional help from your office to handle financial requests. What I want to do is give people an eight hundred number to call, not affiliated with your law firm to handle requests. I also want an email address and a website, separate from everything we plan to do. I want this to be manned forty hours a week, Monday through Friday, eight a.m. to five p.m. There should also be an emergency number, in case of just that—an emergency. If people call that number constantly as a first choice, then we'll get rid of it.

"What I also want to do, out of the fifty million dollars is to provide matching funds to valid requests by individuals, community members, nonprofits, and other situations that don't fit, like a valid Troy business going under because the banks won't help them, and they provide a valuable service to the inner city of Troy. However, the match isn't a freebie. Anyone getting funding from me because they don't have the cash and it's critical to the community, will provide volunteer hours to our new center or any place else we deem appropriate. If someone needs one thousand dollars, I'll give that person five hundred, and they can earn the rest at twenty dollars per hour by helping us out. They'll sign an agreement for the hours owed. Like all businesses, I'm sure we'll be burned a few times before it sinks into the community that we're trying to help the less fortunate move up and break the cycle of poverty. They can make phone calls, recruit, clean the offices, paint, or even help us build and remodel homes in the neighborhood to be sold as affordable housing below market rate. Am I clear? I'm still hashing this out."

"Let me summarize," Kristen said, with Mary listening intently. "You need at least one full time person to start now —as a volunteer coordinator to keep track of funds given out, volunteer hours owed, and paid for, et cetera. How much do you think you'll hand out and over what time period?"

"About a million dollars over the next few years that we'll give to this venture…or should I say 'adventure'?… maybe several million by the time we're done. Can you two excuse me? I've been meaning to call Joe Traynor's father and brother for a few days now, but I've haven't had the time."

"We met Joe and his wife Julie down in Key West. I'll explain who they are as Jack makes his call," said Mary.

With that, Jack went out into the waiting area and pulled out the card that Joe Traynor gave him a few weeks ago. He dialed the number on the card for Traynor Electrical Construction Company.

"Hello. Traynor Electrical. How may I help you?" said the man's voice on the other end.

It was an older man's voice, so Jack said, "Mr. Traynor? John Traynor?"

"Speaking. How may I help you?"

"Mr. Traynor, my name is Jack Manning. We met your son, Joe and his wife Julie, down in Key West, a few weeks ago."

"Yes, Mr. Manning. Joe called us and told us that you might call. Nice to meet you, at least on the phone." John chuckled. "How can I help you?"

"Well, first, I'd be interested in meeting with you and your other son, Peter, to discuss a business opportunity for both of us. Did Joe tell you that we're going to build a new building in downtown Troy, right next to the Troy Community Council building?"

"Joe told us you were going to do that. Great story. I recognize your name now. I don't think you'll have any trouble paying for it, I gather?"

"None, whatsoever. I also don't want to get screwed over because everyone thinks they can now." He went on to say, "I need an honest contractor like you and your son to tell me whom I should be dealing with in the city of Troy or the capital region. Joe said you've been in business for over thirty years and that's good enough for me. You wouldn't be in business that long if you weren't honorable. I'd certainly give you all the electrical work as well as any other you can handle for helping me. I'll make sure it's in the general contractor's agreement. I've got plans for the building next door that we can discuss as well."

"When do you want to meet? Pete will be here in a while. Where are you staying? I heard you were from the Burgh, but no one can find you lately." John chuckled again.

"I'm at the Albany Hilton. Want some lunch somewhere? How about TGIF in Latham, around one p.m.? We should be done here by then. It's away from Troy but quiet during the day. I eat there a lot, so I know."

"One it is." John gave Jack his cell phone number and his son's. Jack gave him his as well.

"I just connected with John Traynor, Mary. I'm meeting him for lunch at TGIF in Latham. Want to come?"

"Sure. I have to meet with Kristen's partner, Gerald Reynolds, who's in charge of estate planning, trusts, and probate. We're not dead yet, so we don't need probate. Who're you meeting with before lunch?"

"Kristen set me up with Colleen Coleman, the tax law partner. We have to go downstairs to the bank's trust department to meet Cady Hanover, the VP for that department. We'll be selecting about sixty million dollars in triple A tax-free municipals. The rate just hit over three-point-five percent from two-point-eighty-eight percent, which doesn't seem like much, but with no taxes on sixty million dollars, it's three hundred seventy-two dollars extra over the old rate for one year. On your fifteen million dollars, it's only a paltry ninety-three thousand dollars a year." He laughed. "That three hundred seventy-two thousand dollars will pay for almost five full time employees including benefits. Not a bad day's work, huh? I'll see you at twelve-thirty p.m., and we'll head out. I'll drive. I haven't put a hundred miles on the Explorer yet. Time to take it out. Want to go to Lake George for the rest of the day? We can go to Bolton Landing, to the Sagamore, for dinner and then head home."

"I'm not sure what's planned for me here and what I have to sign. Let's get through lunch."

"By the way, Maureen called me last night. I forgot to tell you. She and kids want to meet me and congratulate me on my success. What do you think? Kind of unexpected, huh?"

"Unexpected? Sure, Jack, it's unexpected. What do you plan on doing with your 'family'?"

"I'll tell you on the way to Latham. I think there might be a little trouble in paradise. She didn't say anything, but I'd bet old Chuck isn't as cute as he used to be. You know?"

"Jack, let me warn you. Don't get caught up in a trap. I'm sure she'll drop Mr. Falcone like a bag of garbage if she thought there was a way back into your heart."

"Don't worry about me," he said.

Mary has no idea how I feel about her, does she? Or does she and is giving me a warning? I'll have to think about it. I don't want to ask and ruin the best friendship I've ever had. I don't want her to think I gave her money to get her for myself. I don't want that to happen.

CHAPTER 20

John and Pete were waiting in the small front lobby. They were both dressed in their construction clothes. No pretentions. Just the way Jack liked it. Jack's bodyguards followed them to TGIF and parked right next to Jack. They all walked in to the building together.

"John?" Jack asked.

"Yes," John said as he shook Jack's hand. "This is Peter, my son and Joe's older brother."

"Nice to meet you. This is Mary Evans, my partner. These two gentlemen are ex-FBI agents, John Jefferson and Fred Tucker. Your son, Joe, knows them very well. They handed him his Coast Guard special award a while ago with the Mexican Mafia takedown in Albany."

"Nice to meet you, Mary, John, and Fred. And of course, Jack," said John. Peter nodded and shook their hands as well.

"Partner? Did I just get a promotion," Mary said with a smile. "Nice to meet you, John and Peter. I can see the resemblance to Joe."

"Handsome devil, isn't he?" John said with a smirk.

Peter just smiled and shook his head as to say, "There goes my charming father. Irish to the end."

"Actually, yes but his wife is pretty damn good looking as well," Mary said.

John laughed. "I asked her if she was nuts, and she said she loved him, no matter what. You just can't talk sense into some people."

He asked the waitress if they could have a booth in the back. They sat near the back wall, looking out toward Target. There weren't many people eating at this hour. John and Fred took a table away from them so they could talk quietly.

"Why the FBI?"

"You son recommended that I talk to his friend, Tom Matthews. He said with this new amount of money, I should think about protection until the thrill wears off by those who want something. I took him up on it, and they've been extremely helpful so far. I might not need them long, but you never know."

John told Jack and Mary that Joe had called them right after they'd met and asked them to give Jack a hand if they could. He explained the situation as well as he knew but told them that Jack had very specific plans and Traynor Electrical could be a very big part of those plans. They ordered lunch with ice teas and large ice waters all around with a lot of ice and lemon.

"So you're going to put up a brand new building right next to TCC? As you know, we're Irish as well, and we all think that's great. Joe couldn't stop laughing on the phone. But let me tell you about Traynor Electrical Construction Company, so you know that whatever you tell us goes no further, especially at Joe's request."

John went on to tell Jack and Mary that they'd been in business for over thirty years, started by John in 1986. They were now a New York State Energy Research and Development Authority or NYSERDA Leeds certified for both residential and commercial construction, both new and rehab. He gave Jack a list of pretty impressive projects that they'd worked on over the years. John told him of his recent heart issues and that Peter had taken over and would remain as the head of the company, but John was fully involved. Pete spoke up and continued the conversation.

"Guys, your background and history is quite impressive," Jack said. "I want you involved, and I'd like the name of one or two local large, reliable commercial contractors who can put up our new building in six months with quality construction, without totally worrying about the cost. I'm not a patsy, but I want it done ASAP." He went on, "I'm also planning on purchasing the TCC building, if available, and I believe it will be if I offer incentives to the owner for doing so. I found out from my attorney who did some investigation that the building is owned by a very prominent person in Troy who has been working without a lease to TCC for the last year, after it ran out. They were also behind in their payments. However, he's skeptical about giving a long-term commitment to them. They've been going month to month. If I get that building, I want to fully upgrade it to match the new one as far as energy efficiency, technology, safety, and security. That could cost us a million dollars or so just in retrofits."

John said, "It certainly could, but we'd be glad to assist you in any way you deem appropriate. Right now, we have several large projects, but you won't need us until the shell is up on the new building. That could take three to four months, even if there is a push to get it done."

Jack told Pete and John the name of the owner of the building. John knew the man personally. Pete didn't. The man was a lot older than John and had some health issues. He had a place in Florida and had spent a lot of time there but was staying closer to home now. John thought a good price, a little over fair market value, would get them the building. He thought it was worth somewhere in the neighborhood of a half million dollars because of age, needed repairs, and location in the gut of Troy, surrounded by derelict buildings. John drove by the building almost every day on the way home to the Burgh.

"We'll be purchasing those vacant, derelict buildings,

hopefully," Jack said. "We want the city to give us every-thing they own in the footprint of where we want to build. We believe that they own seven of the ten buildings. For the three buildings that aren't owned by the city but by slum landlords, we'll buy those with an incentive for the owners, or they'll be condemned. The families living in those prop-erties will be offered the option of a cash settlement to move, or we'll move them into up-to-code housing, and then these same families will have first option to rent or rent-to-own new town houses that our youth and contractors will build right in the neighborhood. In no case will they be charged more than they're currently paying for rent.

"There's no income from the property owned by the city, taken over for back taxes. The other three properties don't bring in five thousand dollars a year in total. We plan on making this venture a for-profit building and for-profit training center. I don't want to be accused of being another non-profit, like RPI and all the others, not paying their fair share to help the residence of the city. I believe the property taxes will be almost one hundred thousand dollars a year and the sales tax alone on the building materials could run as high as one hundred-fifty thousand dollars. We'll also employ construction workers and an additional staff of at least ten professionals, once we get started. I'll put in at least a million dollars a year in operating expenses for the business and not charge TCC for the building upgrades. Does all this sound fair and doable when we contact the city?"

"Fair? You're bending over backward to help the resi-dents of the city of Troy. What more could anyone ask?" said Peter.

"Well, when the board and officers of TCC find out what's going on, they may be scared to death and may try to squash this. So, please keep everything to yourself, at least for now. Can you quietly set up an appointment with a few honest, reliable contractors, like yourself, so we can kind of move forward? I'm working on the property through my attorneys, Miller, Reynolds, Coleman, and Straus."

"How did you get them, by the way? They're one of the best in the state."

"Mary is best friends with Kristen Sanderson, one of the up-and-coming partners."

Mary smiled. "Kristen and I were in the convent together, and we both got out. She went on to better things, and I got stuck with Jack."

"Really? That's interesting. One of my closest friends is the bishop, Harold Humphries. We went to school together. Were you a teacher?"

"Yes, right now I still teach part time at Catholic High, and I serve as a teacher's aide at Saint Augustine's. I'll be leaving there once this starts up."

"So, you two aren't…"

Jack sighed. "No. We aren't. We're best friends, and Mary may have some work for you as well. You might know that I was one of the nine-hundred-and-ninety-million-dollar Powerball winners a few weeks ago. I got one third and, after taxes, have about two hundred million dollars left. We split that up into what I wanted to keep, and fifty million dollars went into a trust for this venture. I gave fifteen million dollars to Mary to do what she wants. She may have plans for Saint Augustine's, now that they're closing the school and the gym."

"How do I become your best friend, Jack?" John said with a smile.

Jack and Mary laughed, and Jack said, "You just did. If you help us pull this off, you'll wind up with a very sizeable chunk of change. I'll make sure of it. I can screw this up by a factor of ten and still have enough money to last all our lives and our children's lives."

"Sounds like a plan," Peter said.

John chuckled. "Pete is much quieter than Joe, as you probably observed."

"What would Joe call him, 'The silent assassin'?"

"Probably."

"By the way, would you know of any properties around that are secluded and can be rented for six months to a year until we decide where we really want to live? It needs to be fully furnished. We'll need bedrooms for John and Fred and Mary if she chooses to stay with us, and I hope she does. We'll need several bathrooms if possible. Mary could take a master and bath, and the guys could bunk together if we have to," Jack said.

"I might just have a place for you. A close friend of mine has been trying to retire and move to Florida. It seems that all my friends are trying to retire and move to Florida. But he hasn't sold it, and you might like it. Do you know Toby Jensen? He's a pharmacist that I went to school with. Just retired. He worked at CVS in Latham for years. His house is about a mile and a half up Old Plank Road, off Route One-Forty-Two in Brunswick, on the town line, at the top of the hill coming out of the Burgh. It's just past the bank, up Old Plank. It's on the left hand side. He owns ten acres, and the house is thirty-five-hundred square feet with an un-attached two-car garage. He wants four hundred and fifty thousand dollars for it, but he told me that he'd rent it to someone he could trust for about three thousand dollars a month, plus he'd pay the heat and taxes. I can call him if you want. Maybe we can see him tonight or tomorrow if you're in a hurry. He's leaving in the fall but said he'd leave sooner if he found a renter or buyer."

"Actually, that's not a bad option. We won't be in the Burgh, and it's only ten minutes to downtown Troy and twenty minutes to Albany. I like going to Vermont a lot, and that's on the way as well. I'd love to see it as soon as we can. What do you think, Mary? You could actually move in your friends if you wanted to as well. How many bedrooms, John?"

"I think four bedrooms and three and a half baths. You'll need maintenance. Mowing the lawn is a challenge, but the view of the Hudson Valley from the top is impressive. I'll call you after I make contact. Maybe you can see him tonight."

They finished lunch, shook hands, and Jack took Mary back to the attorneys to finish up her paperwork. Jack hit the Northway south to I-90 East to head back to downtown Albany, followed by John and Fred. As soon as he got there, he got a call from John Traynor.

"Jack, it's John Traynor. I called Toby, and he's around. How about six p.m. tonight? Can you and Mary make it?"

Jack spoke to Mary who nodded her head. "Yes," she said. "Why don't we go to the Rustic Barn for dinner afterward?"

The Rustic Barn was around the corner from Old Plank Road, up Route 40.

"John, we'll meet you there. Is that okay?"

"Sure, by the way, I have a few guys in mind that I can trust to talk to you about your new building and renovations of the old. Are you free this week?"

"Let me know when, and we can plan around it. I need to talk to my real estate attorney, Andy Miller, the Managing Director. He knows the mayor of Troy and wants to speak to him before we do anything. I'm keeping a low profile, and no one—I mean, no one—will know about my plans until the papers are signed, and they can't do anything about it. See you at six p.m. tonight." He hung up and turned to Mary. "I haven't worked this hard in years. I'm going to have to pace myself."

"Getting old, are you, Jack? You better start working out again. You're going to need it."

<h1 style="text-align:center">CHAPTER 21</h1>

Howard and Marvin had a board meeting this morning. They'd hoped that they'd be further along with the transformation to a Medicaid-based non-profit program. They hooked up with both the Albany Medical Center led program as well as the Saint Peter's Health Partners system, which included both Troy hospitals. They were now part of the Medicaid Redesign Team, but it did little to put any funding in their pocket. They were going to provide mental health services from birth through age twenty-one through the school districts and outreach patient programs. They didn't have any primary care facilities for those most in need, which provided the best bang for the buck. Treating kids in school was a lot less than the eighteen hundred dollars per day they'd get if they had their own medical facility to treat mental health issues.

The building they were in was less than adequate and not up to par. They thought they could get several million dollars to build a new medical facility right next to their own but evidently what they submitted to the New York State Health and Mental Health departments didn't fly. New York State enticed everyone with a six-billion-dollar grant program to cut Medicaid waste, but Howard and Marvin weren't getting any of it now.

They never reapplied for funding for their career development program and let many people go, thinking they wouldn't need them. They didn't realize that these were the employees most attuned to the needs of the community.

Losing Jack Manning and Mary Evans didn't seem like much of a loss at the time, but now they had little traffic in and out of their building. Those who used to spread the word about all their programs were the kids getting job training. Now, the center was getting limited word of mouth. They didn't realize how many additional services these youth were getting in other areas of the TCC. They got Medicaid-related health, mental health, family planning, mentoring, parenting education, and other services that were paid for directly by Medicaid. These services were no longer being used by the hundreds of youth who were no longer there.

Now, if Howard and Marvin wanted to collect under Medicaid through the New York State Health Department, they'd have to bill directly instead of subcontracting through Rensselaer County Social Services. That would cost them an additional $100,000 just for the software, or they weren't going to collect anything in the months coming up. They were in a real bind. Their billings weren't only down the amount received for career development but another quarter million dollars in related services. They hadn't paid the rent this month, not until they collected under Medicaid. They didn't think that through either. The career development grant dollars were prepaid while Medicaid made them wait ninety days for payment. That was a three to four month gap in cash flow, and they now had to get a line of credit from a local bank. That was what today's meeting was about.

"Marvin, what're you going to tell the board?"

"I'll give them the same treasurer's report that I always do and tell them that we need to cover the cash flow, but it won't be a problem since we'll get enough in Medicaid payments coming in any day now."

"Is that true?" Howard asked.

"What else am I going to tell them? That the rent's past due? Do you have any suggestions, Howard? After all, you're the president. I'm only the treasurer and vice president of human resources."

Nice, Howard thought, *when the going gets tough Marvin gets going, leaving me to hold the bag.* "I'm going to tell them the truth, Marvin. Be prepared to answer questions. In fact, now we may not qualify for certain foundation grants because our officer salaries have risen against a declining revenue stream. Do you want to recommend everyone take a pay cut for a while? After all, we're a nonprofit here to serve the public."

"No, I'm not taking a pay cut, Howard. Don't pursue that. We'll get through this. Let me talk to the board about a new fundraising idea. We need to tap into their wealth. Our board hasn't given much in the way of annual donations. That'll affect how we're perceived by the foundations that we're applying to as well as to our health partners at the hospitals."

Howard and Marvin went to the meeting, and the only thing the board members wanted to talk about was Jack Manning winning three hundred and thirty million dollars in the Powerball drawing.

"Do you think he'd give us a donation? After all, he worked here for over twelve years," said the chairman.

Neither Marvin nor Howard told them how badly Jack Manning and Mary Evan's firings went. The board had no idea. Marvin covered it up because they never believed there would ever be any ramifications about how Jack and Mary were treated. They never heard from either one of them before or since the Powerball announcement. Howard and Marvin never told the board that Marvin blocked Jack's unemployment insurance payment. He told the state that he left voluntarily, and Jack had no money to fight it. Mary, as an ex-nun, didn't even ask. She went to work for the Catholic schools in the Burgh, never to be heard from again. Both

Howard and Marvin were sure that Jack Manning would be long gone from the city of Troy after hitting the jackpot.

"We haven't heard from Jack Manning since he resigned. I'm sure he's left the area after hitting the lottery. You can't blame him, you know?" Howard said.

He went on to tell them about the state-of-the-state for the TCC. He explained that they'd need a line of credit to support the late Medicaid payments. They blamed the New York State Health Department for holding up their money. It wasn't their fault. Once fully up and running, they'd have more than enough funding to cover all their current needs. Like most nonprofit boards, they believed every word Howard said, backed up by Marvin.

"I think we dodged a bullet today," Howard said to Marvin after the meeting was over. "I'm glad they only meet once every six weeks. By then, we should be okay, don't you think?"

"No, I don't think, but you better come up with some better ideas. You need to get to the bank before we have to file this year's nine-ninety form. It won't be pretty. Get the line of credit based on last year's numbers. That shouldn't be a problem."

"What do you think Jack Manning is doing?" Howard asked.

"I've no idea, and I don't care. He was a jerk and good riddance to him and the nun. They aren't our problem anymore."

CHAPTER 22

Jack and Mary met John and Peter Traynor at Toby's house on Old Plank Road, right at six p.m. They drove up the winding and narrow road and pulled in after seeing three men standing at the far end of a long driveway. They stopped the car, parking next to John's. John Jefferson and Fred Tucker pulled in right behind them. Jack was getting concerned that it would start to look like a wagon train after a while.

As they got out of the car, Mary commented, "Wow, what a view. Jack, look over there. That's Saratoga Springs and to the south is the Helderberg Mountains. See the Capital and the Egg. What a view."

"It's very nice, Mary. It's kind of a trek up that hill though. I wonder how the winter will be?"

She laughed. "I'll buy matching snowmobiles for Christmas, if you're nice."

"Fine." Jack had learned that "fine" meant "not fine" from his ex-wife, Maureen.

John walked over to shake their hands and brought them over to meet Toby Jensen. Toby grew up on a farm right at this location. The farmhouse and outbuildings were long gone, but Toby built this beautiful house many years ago for his wife, Sheila, who had passed away a few years ago. Toby's wife was a close friend of John's wife, Veronica, who also passed away a few years ago from breast cancer.

Toby hated farming and, after high school, went to the Albany College of Pharmacy and started his own pharmacy in the Burgh many years ago. As the chains took over almost every corner in the city, Toby joined CVS after he sold his pharmacy to them. They moved him to Latham, and he'd been there ever since. He wanted to retire and move to Florida but had had difficulty in today's market. He wasn't going to give the place away. He wanted a decent price but wasn't being outrageous about it. John had told Jack that Toby was a good and fair man.

Jack introduced himself and Mary, and both shook Toby's hand. "What a beautiful place you have here, Toby. These two gentlemen are John and Fred. They're keeping an eye on us for a while."

"Thank you. It's a beautiful place, but it's a lot for me to handle now that Sheila is gone. I'm about to retire and move to Florida. Mary, I heard you talk about the view. Wait for an hour and see the sunset. If that doesn't convince you, nothing will. Come on in, and I'll show you the house."

They all walked from room to room. There was a huge living room with a floor to ceiling fireplace built from the rocks taken from the property. The house consisted of ten rooms and a full basement with a large unattached garage. They went from the living room to the dining room and then the kitchen and then to the back of the house where there was a family room with another fireplace. The four bedroom and three baths were to the side, all in a row with the master at the end with its own bath area. There was nothing not to want. The half bath was by the kitchen.

They walked out to the living area and said to Toby, "We love your house, but I can only make a commitment for six months to a year. We're in the middle of a series of projects, and if they hit, I'd love to buy this place, but I need to rent it first, fully furnished. We'll reimburse you for any damage or wear and tear on the furnishings. You can leave here and rest assured that we'll take care of things for you. We'll sign an agreement and pay you in advance if you'd prefer."

"I'm asking four hundred and fifty thousand dollars for the property but would rent it to you with the understanding that I want to sell it first and rent it second."

"We understand. I'm not asking you to give us a deal or a rent-to-buy with the payments coming off the asking price. Trust me, I and Mary both have enough to do the deal. It's just that I can't get into other projects at this time. Mary, you could buy this as well, you know. Especially for your friends to retire."

She laughed. "That's true. Maybe we can move Ethel up her as well."

"No."

"Private joke?" Peter asked.

"Yes, Ethel is my current landlady. I need to take care of her, but babysitting her isn't going to happen. I really like her, and I'll visit her and take care of her, but she has a son, and he needs to be more responsible."

Toby nodded. "To rent, I'm asking for three thousand dollars a month, and I'll pay the heat and light bills and the taxes. If you pay me upfront for six months, that would be even better. It'll help me pay for my move."

"Mary, what do you think?" Jack turned back to Toby. "Does it include the furniture and everything here?"

"Yes it does," Toby answered.

Mary nodded. "Do it, Jack. I think I'll love it here. The family room can be used for our office set up. It's close but far enough out to keep people away, and the view is spectacular."

"Toby, do you mind if I have John and Pete upgrade all your alarm systems at no cost to you, and if we decide to leave, the upgrade is yours, free and clear?"

"That would be great. So, is it a deal?"

"It's a deal," Jack said. "When can we move in?"

"How about you give me ten days from now over the following weekend. I have to get a moving van to take my clothes and personal items. Everything else is yours."

Jack pulled out his checkbook and, on the spot, wrote Toby a check for $18,000 for the next six months. He'd subtract that from his sixty-eight-plus million-dollar balance. *Let the bank take care of that*, he thought.

"Can we keep the utilities in your name? If you do, I'll pay the utility bill as well. Or, you tell me what you spent over these same six months last year, and I'll add twenty percent to cover my tech equipment and give you that check the day you leave. If it's more at the end, I'll pay you the difference.

"That's even better," said Toby.

"Well, we better get packing, Mary. Pick whatever room you want. Probably you'll pick the master at the end?"

"John and Fred might be staying here with us as well. If they are, they can each pick a room. I don't care which one they get."

John Jefferson said, "We'll stay for a month maybe. After that, we'll play it by ear. I don't expect that you'll get hassled up here, but you never know. If you upgrade the alarms, we can have it signal our phones, and we'll be here in fifteen minutes from our homes. Fred is only a few minutes away." John lived in Menands, just two miles north of downtown Albany, and Fred lived in Waterford, right across the Hudson from the Burgh.

"We'll need new bed linens and towels and things," Mary said. "I'll get my friends to help me pack and go on a shopping spree. We'll get groceries from Price Chopper the day we move in. We'll need a lot if we don't plan on going anywhere for a while, at least until we get everything settled."

"Thank you, Toby. This works out great. Thank you, John and Pete. You were a big help. We have to get back. Mary wants to stop at the Rustic Barn for pizza. Do you want to join us?" They knew that John and Fred would be along with them. They might know someone at the restaurant, but they'd eat quickly and get out as soon as they could. Jack had a big day planned for the next day. He'd be meeting some contractors, and he was going with his attorney to meet the mayor of Troy about the property. He needed to be very quiet about this, or it could ruin his plans. He knew how politicians could be. They just couldn't help bragging about what they'd done. They were always campaigning for the next election. Jack knew that some campaign contributions needed to be unleashed, to both parties in town. You never knew who'd be in or out at any election in the city of Troy.

CHAPTER 23

Jack and Mary were back at Kristen's office the next morning. Jack told Kristen about their new home for the next six months. He invited the entire staff out to a cookout after they'd moved in, the weekend after next. Mary would invite Jack's landlady and her two roommates, Jane and Martha.

That should take the chill out of the air for her roomies. They weren't thrilled about her leaving, but Mary said that if they wanted, she'd pay the entire rent bill for them at their house on 7th Avenue in the Burgh. That seemed to placate them for now. They mentioned something about her reputation to uphold as an ex-nun, now living with Jack. She didn't even mention the two ex-FBI agents that would be there 24/7. Both the ladies were with it but still had some of that old provincial Catholic teaching that they couldn't seem to get over. Working at the two Catholic schools didn't help their worldly view one iota. Mary wondered to herself why she held a more worldly view. It was probably because of her time over the last twelve years working with Jack at the TCC. The stories about life, told to her by her students at the center, could have set her roommates' hair on fire.

Andy Miller, the managing director of the firm and Jack's real estate expert, walked into the room. He had his valise with him, and he was set to go. "Ready?"

"Mary do you want to come and meet the mayor?" asked Jack.

"Not really," she said. "I've other things to do this afternoon. Are you meeting with the owner of the building at TCC?"

"Tomorrow morning at ten a.m. at their home in Troy, off Pawling Avenue."

"I want to go to that one," she said.

"I'll see you tomorrow then. Call me tonight, and I'll let you know what's going on."

They were meeting Mayor Timothy Thompson at his office on River Street at the old Cluett Peabody & Company building. The city of Troy offices had been temporarily located there for the last several years after they found out that city hall was about to collapse. Right now, the old city hall site was an empty lot after being bulldozed, and they were looking for buyers for the property. It was something that Jack was considering as well, if he couldn't get the property adjacent to the TCC building. John and Fred followed them once again.

Andy introduced Jack to the mayor. They'd met previously, and Jack told him of his connection to the TCC. John and Fred sat outside the mayor's office and would wait until they came out. They knew that, up to now, nothing was happening so that Jack wouldn't need protection but if his plans went through, as he told them previously, all that could change.

"So, what can I do for you, Mr. Manning? I understand that congratulations are in order."

Jack told him about his plans to build a new four million dollar for-profit career center right next to the TCC building. "I understand that the city of Troy owns seven of the ten parcels that I'm interested in obtaining. The other three are owned by non-resident, out of town landlords, who pay next to nothing in taxes. My plan is to quietly take over all ten properties and place the new center in the middle with expanded parking for the future. I'd like the city to give my new corporation the property, free and clear, and pay for the demolition. It could be an issue if I did it because there could be asbestos and lead in the buildings, and it's better if you make the property shovel ready. I'll sign an agreement to pay one hundred percent of the tax bill for at least the next ten years as a for-profit owner. I'll also run the center as a for-profit operation that'll only rely on my annual donations of at least one million dollars per year. There will be no charge to Troy youth residents for services, education, job training, and placement into new businesses that I'll start using for graduates. I'll also try to place graduates in existing businesses in Troy. All of this will be at no charge to anyone in the city of Troy. I've set up a fifty-million-dollar trust fund for this purpose and for other ventures down the road. I plan on spending the next ten years working at this, and then I'll retire to Florida. That's the plan.

"What happens to the people living in the houses to be demolished?" asked the mayor.

"I'll also guarantee that anyone displaced by these efforts will be placed into a legal, up-to-code apartment, in the nearby area at no additional cost to them. In addition, if they help work on the projects that'll come out of this, including affordable housing, they'll be first in line to own a new townhouse nearby, and I'll donate the down payment and first year's mortgage payment, including taxes. The city will have to guarantee that the taxes will be based on the affordable selling price not the fair market value for at least ten years. We'll be selling the homes for under one hundred thousand dollars, not at the one-hundred-seventy-five-thousand-dollar estimated cost for construction."

The mayor shook his head. "It might cost us up to two hundred fifty thousand dollars to knock over the buildings and even more if there's lead or asbestos. We don't have that kind of money."

"I'll be paying, minimally, one million dollars in taxes over the next ten years if this works out. I also plan on purchasing the TCC building and putting another million dollars into that facility and will pay full taxes on that as well. I understand that they're in arrears on that building and that TCC isn't up-to-date on its rent. That could be another derelict building and an eyesore, close to downtown. It can be seen from the Collar City Bridge. If you can't get the money up front, I'll pay it and deduct it from the taxes owed over the first two years. That way you don't have to do a thing other than run it through your city agency to make everything Kosher. Is that okay?

"That could work even better. Are you planning on writing grants to support your efforts?"

"No, this will be a for-profit venture all the way. In ten years' time, depending on where we stand, we may make the operation non-profit, but I'll always own the buildings through my corporation. I've seen too many nonprofits manipulate people out of officer positions, sell the facility, take the cash, and go out of business. This way that I'm proposing, it will never happen. I also would like you to sign a confidentiality agreement and non-circumvention agreement to ensure that none of this is repeated. If it happens, I'll move my operation to Albany. I hope that's clear. I've enough money to start up anywhere."

"Can I ask you just one question?" asked the mayor.

"Sure."

"Why are you doing this? It's great for the city and the kids living here and their families but what's the benefit to you?"

"The benefit's that I have one hundred ninety-eight million dollars after the cash payment and before taxes. I can either give it to the United Stated government or New York State or I can start a trust and pay little or no taxes and ensure that the money goes directly to projects that benefit where I've lived my entire life." Jack went on, "Mary Evans and I were fired and heaved out of the TCC building six months ago by two individuals who need a lesson in civility, empathy, and morals, and I assure you that before this is done, that'll happen."

"Revenge and payback, huh?"

"No, I plan on killing them with kindness and building the TCC into what it was set up to do originally. It was established to help the poorest of the poor not to support large salaries for people who don't care about the mission. Is this doable or not? I plan on having a new building standing on this property in less than nine months."

"I believe you can have my commitment to move forward. I have to talk to the council quietly, but I'll sign the agreements and not divulge ownership until you say it's okay. I know you want the other building as well before any announcement is made."

"That's correct. Andy will draw up all the agreements in the name of the corporate owner. There will be no disclosure or discussion about my involvement."

With that said, they shook hands, and the mayor walked them out of the building. Jack turned to Andy. "That went okay, but I'm not signing until I've got the TCC building ownership in my hands. Is that understood?"

"Understood. We'll see him in the morning. I think this will be the fastest real estate turnaround in the history of the city of Troy."

They went back to the Albany office to talk to Kristen. Jack would remain at the hotel until they moved, two weekends away. He was also meeting two contractors and John and Peter Traynor at the hotel for dinner to discuss the new and renovated buildings.

On the way back, John Traynor called to reconfirm the meeting for six p.m. Jack was quite grateful for their help, but he knew that he was taking them away from their own projects for Traynor Electrical Construction Company. Jack wrote a check out in the car to the company for $25,000 as a retainer for professional services rendered for helping him along the way. They'd get $250 an hour each, the same as Kristen was getting as the lowest paid partner at her law firm. The morning's four hours just cost Jack $3,000 at $750 per hour for Andy's services. Like anything else,

Andy brought him to the meeting, saved him the cost of purchasing the properties outright, and $250,000 in potential demolition costs. Jack wasn't used to such sizeable figures but knew he had to get used to it if he was going to join the big boys. He thought of this as a Berlitz course in business. All of this was above and beyond the million dollars plus he'd be paying the law firm annually for managing his multimillion dollars in cash. At least the mayor didn't hit him up immediately for a campaign contribution. That would come later. Jack was sure he'd have tons of pictures taken in front of the new building for his administration's accomplishments. If everything went as planned, the mayor could take as many pictures as he wanted. Who cared? Jack couldn't have cared less.

CHAPTER 24

Jack met John and Peter at the bar at the Albany Hilton right before six p.m. They were waiting for the two contractors as well as the president of the Capital Region Builders and Remodelers Association. Jack didn't know why he was coming, but he thought the more, the merrier.

John and Peter were sitting at the bar as Jack walked in. "Hey, Jack. How are you? They should be here shortly."

"Good, I've got something I want to give you before they come. I appreciate everything that you've done for me, and, again, I thank Joe and Julie as well. I'd have never met you without them." With that, Jack handed John a check from the Evangeline Realty Corporation for $25,000, made payable to the Traynor Electrical Construction Company. "Is that the right name?"

"Yes, but why? That's a lot of money," said John as Peter peered over his shoulder and shook his head.

"So far, you've saved me a bundle, served as my eyes and ears, and gotten us settled up on Old Plank Road. I expect to pay you for your time, just like I pay my attorneys or anyone else. There are no free rides," said Jack.

"But for what?"

"This is a retainer payment of twenty-five thousand dollars to your business for your time. I'll pay you at a rate of two hundred fifty dollars per hour each, for your time, the same as my personal attorney. So far, I believe that you've spent at least ten hours of your time, so at five hundred dollars per hour for the two of you together for ten hours is five thousand dollars that's yours out of the retainer." Jack went on, "You had to work me into your schedule, and I appreciate it. I don't want you not getting paid during your upstate New York construction season. God knows it's short enough."

"We won't turn it down. Thank you. This is very honorable. Joe said you were a good, honest guy, so we'll tell him that. Thank you again. We thought we might just get the electrical and tech piece, but this is wonderful."

As John put the check into his wallet, the three gentlemen they were meeting walked in the door and went up to John to shake his hand and then Peter's. John introduced Jack to Don Dunlop, the president and owner of Metro Capital Construction of Albany, Harry Hilton of HBC Corporation, and Luke Curtis, president of the association.

Jack introduced his two ex-FBI bodyguards. "They're shadowing me over the next month or two. The crazies come out when they hear you've got a lot of money."

They took a table in the dining room at the far corner where no one else would be sitting. They had a panoramic view of North Pearl Street, with the hustle and bustle of all the state workers heading for home. John Jefferson and Fred Tucker sat a few tables away as not to disturb the meeting. Jack told them to simply bill everything for both parties to his room.

Don said, "It's amazing to see one hundred fifty thousand people leave the capital, almost at the exact same time, to head back to their bedroom community. This place is a ghost town after six-thirty p.m."

"I believe it," said Jack.

They each ordered a drink and dinner and settled in for a meeting. John began by introducing Jack and what had happened to date. Everyone at the table was aware that Jack hit the Powerball and that they might be speaking to the richest man in Albany, sitting right at the table. After John completed his short introduction, he asked Jack to continue. They waited until dinner was served and they began to dig in. It appeared that everyone was hungry. Jack said to go ahead and wait, and he'd begin when they were done. There was small talk about the state of the Yankees, Siena College basketball, and the Saratoga Springs Thoroughbred Track coming up in August. Jack was unaware that most contractors had reserved box seats for the season for their customer's entertainment. He made a mental note to take Mary and her friends, if offered. They offered immediately, and Jack thought that would be terrific. The waiter cleared the table, and they ordered another round of drinks, and, when delivered, Jack asked the waiter to give them some space for their meeting. He nodded his head as Jack discreetly gave him two twenties. The waiter bowed and left.

Jack went through his plans. He didn't hold back because he trusted John implicitly. He told them that he wanted his new building up in six months and could use both builders and Traynor Electrical to complete the project. He told them that John and Peter would be his direct contact and liaison for the project. He expected a building for around one million dollars per floor and then added in the infrastructure, technology equipment, and office equipment, and he'd be approaching four million in cash. He expected to have the contractors build an energy-efficient green construction, LEEDS-built facility and to tap into rebates from NYSERDA, for energy efficiency; from National Grid, for weatherization and windows; Spectrum, for cable, internet access, and T-1 lines; Verizon for phone service; along with any New York State programs. If they had to double up to get the funding, he told him that was fine. He said he was getting the property from the city of Troy for free in shovel-ready condition after they did the demolition. He said he'd pay for it and subtract the cost from the first two years of tax payments. The agreement from the city took no time at all. They met with the council that afternoon and signed off on the non-disclosure and non-circumvention agreements. Jack also told them that he and Andy Miller, whom they knew, would be meeting with the owner of the Troy Community Council's building owner the next day. He said he'd make the owner an offer he couldn't refuse. He'd add another million dollars to that building only after they had the grand opening for the Evangeline Career Center, expected to be opened no later than January or February of next year. It was now almost June of this year, so they'd have to hustle.

Don Dunlop was quite impressed by Jack's newly acquired acumen in only a short time. He turned to Harry. "Harry, can we do this together with John and Peter to get it done on time."

"We've never had one like this before, but, of course, with cash on the barrel head, we can move quickly. We can file the paperwork for the programs you mentioned, Jack, but we won't have the rebates until well after the completion. Is that all right?"

That's fine. The rebates are going toward the million dollars to put into the TCC building regardless if they're there or not. I can double my training at any time, and I'll have the parking available, which is the biggest hassle."

Jack continued, "I have expectations of you, Don, and Harry, and from you, Luke, as well. My youth will have their high school degrees, they'll have NYSERDA training and certification, and they're going to college on my dime or starting a construction career. I want you to hire these individuals, at least give them a fair shake. They'll be better trained than what you have right now. I also want them to go into the unions, and I need your support for that."

"Tell us why you're doing this, Jack?" asked Luke. "By the way, John told me your intent, and that's why I'm here."

"I was asked that by the mayor of Troy and this is what I told them. I won three hundred and thirty million dollars before the discounted cash payment, which brought it down to one hundred and ninety-eight million dollars. From there,

I can pay almost fifty percent in taxes to the feds or New York State or give it away to charity, closer to home, in my own hometown of Troy. I'm also not all that altruistic because more than anything, I'm really pissed about getting fired by those two jerks running the TCC, and they fired my best friend, Mary Evans, as well. By the way, you might like to be nice to Mary. I gave her fifteen million dollars to play with," he said and laughed.

Harry laughed. "So, is that why you're buying the TCC building? To piss them off? And when do we meet Mary?"

"Partially. It's also because they haven't paid the rent in six months, and I pulled their Federal nine-ninety from last year, and it looks like, since we left, they're down at least two hundred fifty thousand dollars in billing and nonpayment of rent. I want TCC to succeed, like I always did. Mary and I put our heart and soul into the operation going on thirteen years. We gave new life to over four hundred kids who now have jobs, a family, and a hope for the future. Those two jerks running the show pissed it all away because they thought they were smarter than everyone else. Besides, I hate the treasurer, so that's more than enough reason to screw with them. So how's that for a motivational speech?"

"Not bad but I'd leave the 'jerks' remark—even if true—for their ears only."

"Duly noted," said Jack. "Dessert?"

Everyone said no, and Jack signed the bill. They'd discussed next steps, and they'd have a contract for Jack within the week, based on everything he mentioned. When Jack brought up living on the top floor, they discouraged it as too costly. His dinky little two-bedroom apartment on top would cost him a million dollars, just like another floor. It gave him an added incentive to buy the Old Plank Road property so he'd discuss it with Kristen and Mary in a few days. Tomorrow they were meeting with Louis and Addie Freeman at ten a.m. at their home off Pawling Avenue.

CHAPTER 25

Jack and Mary met at Miller, Reynolds, Coleman, and Straus at nine a.m. Mary got there first and was having coffee with Kristen when Jack walked across the street from the hotel, up to the twelfth floor, and into Kristen's office. They treated him like an employee now. Hell, he paid for many of their annual salaries with his million dollars a year fee. Andy walked into Kristen's office with coffee in hand and was reviewing a potential purchase agreement for the TCC property.

"What do you think, Jack? It's standard, but I think we might want to include an incentive or two and definitely put together a note for payment of the past due rent. That way, if the TCC decide to move, they can because they don't have a formal rental agreement anymore, since it expired a while ago, but they can't back out on a signed note for the past due rent. You can buy the note from the Freemans and make it due and payable anytime you want. I put together a demand note that's payable upon request, and we can fill in the amount when we get the exact past due amount."

"What incentives?"

"I'd give the owner a twenty-five thousand dollar deposit toward the full purchase price immediately after your building is completed. That way, we can keep your name out of everything, and no one will know that you're buying the TCC building until it's too late to do anything, like make a higher purchase offer. The deposit locks in the price, and if you buy the demand note, it further locks in the transaction."

"What do you think Mary and Kristen?" asked Jack.

Mary said, "This is your deal, Jack. Whatever you want to do, it's fine with me. I just want to get it over so I can concentrate on doing something with Saint Augustine's school and gymnasium. I don't know what, but I need Andy to explore that for me as well."

"Andy, there's no charge for any of Mary's transactions. Correct?" asked Jack.

"Well, this is different than managing her fifteen million dollar account, but we won't split hairs. We want both of you happy for the long term. So, no charge."

"Great, then, Mary, why don't you take care of your plans while I meet the Freemans with Andy. I don't think you need to be there, and then maybe you can keep your low profile. I also think it's time to split up our bodyguards. I want you to take either John or Fred. It's up to you. We'll be moving in a week or so, and then they'll be back together at our house up on Old Plank."

"All right, if you insist, but only during the day. He can follow me back to the Burgh and then go home or meet back up with you at the hotel. It's up to you. I don't care. If he shows up, my roomies will be very curious as to why an ex-nun now has a bodyguard."

"Good point." Jack went out to the lunchroom where the bodyguards were having coffee and asked them about it. They thought it would be fine, but it would change if there were a problem either way. Fred would stay with Mary during the day.

Andy, John, and Jack decided to go in one SUV. It was getting crazy having multiple cars running around, especially when they were heading back to the attorney's office where Jack would be meeting with his ex-wife and children. Before he, John, and Andy left, Jack asked to speak to Kristen. He wanted her with him in the afternoon as a witness to what was said. He also wanted recorders and a camera set up, unbeknownst to his family. At this point, he knew he couldn't trust Maureen, but he was unsure about his children, especially his daughter Debbie, who seemed to be extremely hostile toward him. She was never overly loving but never belligerent before he left the house. He thought that was Maureen's doing, and he was going to avoid any hostility during the meetings. Jack asked Kristen to download some specific information concerning the Catholic Church, and he wanted her prepared for the meeting. In addition to her specialty of family law for the firm, she also had as a client the Roman Catholic Diocese of Albany for several situations that popped up that she couldn't discuss.

Andy and Jack got out of John's vehicle and went to the front door of Louis and Addie Freeman's home on Pawling Avenue, on the east side of Troy. John stayed with the SUV parked at the curb of this main thoroughfare, heading east out of Troy. The house was a large two-story Victorian home that had to have been built in the early 1900s.

The east side of the city housed many of Troy's rich and famous in the past but was starting to show its age now. Many of the homes have been turned into multi-family houses, funeral homes and many into smaller nursing homes and RPI fraternities. Emma Willard still stood out as a testament to the past. The people who lived here all their lives wanted to stay in the area. They were mostly Troy's attorneys, shopkeepers, business owners and administrators and professors from Rensselaer Polytechnic Institute. RPI still bought up a lot of these houses, and as soon as the older residents passed on, they kept the property for RPI's benefit. It was a rather large sore point for the residents of the city who had to pay increased taxes after these houses were taken off the tax rolls, now owned by RPI.

Jack shook his head about the tax situation whenever he drove this way up to Jack's hamburger stand in Wynantskill. Jack's had been in business for over sixty years and started by an RPI graduate as one of the first to move into the fast food business. The first sign of spring was the smell of Jack's slider burgers with melted fried onions and catsup. People came out in droves as a right of passage to spring. When Jack was at Troy High School many years ago, he and his friends would head out in an old car and buy ten burgers each with a few bottles of chocolate milk and a hundred napkins to catch the grease before it covered their shirts. He smiled every time he thought about it. The burgers were now $2.25 each but still worth every penny. Jack debated heading over there with Andy and John if their meeting went well.

"What're you smiling at?" asked Andy.

"Jack's in Wynantskill. Are you game?"

"Yes. I haven't been there in twenty years. Right after."

Mrs. Freeman opened the door and asked Andy and Jack to come in. She pointed to the living room where Louis Freeman, her husband of sixty years, was now sitting. A carafe of coffee and a plate full of chocolate chip cookies starred them in the face. Jack was a sucker for chocolate chip cookies and, apparently, from the look on Andy's face, so was he.

Louis and Addie Freeman sat next to each other. He was eighty-one, and she just turned seventy-eight. They were high school sweethearts. Unfortunately, they never had any children, but he ran a successful printing operation on the east side for almost fifty years. He sold it a few years ago and had a substantial holding in real estate in the city of Troy. They had a winter place in Sarasota, Florida but were only going for a few months every winter now that they were getting older. He had a bout with cancer but seemed to come through okay. She was the vision of health and would probably live to be a hundred.

Andy knew Mr. Freeman from several real estate dealings where Andy represented a buyer on several occasions. They seemed to have a good rapport, so Andy spoke first. He went through why they were there and asked if they'd entertain selling the building housing the Troy Community

Council. Mr. Freeman knew the facility well and had been their landlord for many years. He said he knew that they were now having difficulty, and it was very clear that they'd stopped paying their rent. They were six months behind but blamed it on slow Medicaid payments, not on their own incompetency.

Jack held nothing back. He explained how he was involved with TCC for almost thirteen years and was proud of their accomplishments of giving over 400 kids a chance at life, a job, and a future. He told them how all that changed when they decided to go the Medicaid route without an understanding of what that meant and how it would be detrimental to the TCC mission. He explained that he lost his job when the move was made, along with their best employees.

"I have come into money," Jack told Mr. and Mrs. Freeman, "and am building a new center right next door to the TCC building. I want that building as well, not to close it but to make it succeed by getting their programs back to meet the mission for which they were set up, which was to help the poor of Troy succeed, not provide hundred-thousand-dollar jobs for a select few. I looked up the facility on the tax rolls, know what the assessment is, and have a fair market evaluation estimated tentatively for this meeting. The property should be worth around five hundred thousand dollars but is only assessed for a little over two hundred fifty thousand dollars, due to its location in the bad section of the city. It is about thirty thousand square feet, and we can rehab it and bring everything up to code eventually. It's surrounded by other derelict properties, which I want to pick up for my new building. I will pay a premium and will pick up the past due rent, but I need it done a certain way for it to work."

Mr. Freeman nodded. "I'm unhappy with the current management of the TCC and was going to put money into the property but didn't once they stopped making their rent payments. They pay ten thousand dollars a month and are behind about sixty thousand dollars at this point."

"I'll pay six hundred thousand dollars for the building, as is, and will also purchase a separate demand note that we'll get from the TCC for past due rent. I don't want to purchase the building until my building is opened in late winter, next year. In the meantime, I'll buy the demand note at full value and give you a twenty-five thousand dollar deposit on the property. At least you'll have eight-five thousand dollars more than you have right now, and then you'll receive payment in full upon transfer of the building to Evangeline Realty, just formed."

Both Mr. and Mrs. Freeman seemed pleased, and they also had to sign a nondisclosure and non-circumvention agreement to close the first part of the deal. They shook hands, and Andy said he'd get the paperwork to them or their attorney and two checks for the deposit and for the demand note.

They left the house and headed for Jack's in Wynantskill. "John, have you ever been to Jack's?" Jack asked.

"No."

"You're in for a real treat but be careful if you have digestion problems."

All three ate with abandon, smiling from ear to ear. Andy had to keep his arms out wide not to spill on his suit coat. Jack didn't care. He was going to go across the street to the hotel to change into more casual wear, when they got back, for the meet with his family in the afternoon. He hoped that went as smoothly as this did, but he doubted it.

Chapter 26

Mark and Debbie, here's what's going to happen. Chuck will bring us to the attorney's office and be our moral support. We're all in this together. If we stick together, we'll win. Your father will back down from what he told me the other day. Just remember, if he doesn't, and I don't get anything, you two will split your shares three ways to include me. After all, I'm your mother, and you came with me after the divorce."

"If he gives any of you a hard time, I'll be there to set the record straight," Chuck said. "I won't hurt him, but I'll put him in his place. He'll back down if I threaten him. You just wait and see,"

Chuck had come home that night after thinking about what Maureen said. He had everything to lose and nothing to gain if he walked out. He knew she'd take him back if he apologized. What else could she do?

She wasn't going anywhere, and her future wouldn't be very promising with a small bank retirement and social security. She'd still be paying the kid's college student loans because she signed off on them. She got everything Jack owned, including the bills at the time. Chuck thought that was about to change. From all the stories Maureen told him about her ex-husband, Jack was a wimp and would fold like a paper cup. Chuck certainly wasn't worried about the peon ex-husband.

"I'll tell your father that I'm sorry for hurting him, and I apologize. I'm sure that'll soften him up. I want both of you to apologize to him as well to get the meeting off on the right foot."

"For what? Why do I have to apologize?" Debbie said.

"Because I said so. That's why," said Maureen.

"It's the smart thing to do, Debbie," Chuck said. "That's why."

"Sure, Chuck. Whatever you say."

"Are you sure about this, Mom," Mark said. "Why are you bringing Chuck? What, to antagonize Dad? Do you think that'll work?"

"Chuck and I discussed it, and that's what we're doing, Mark. If you don't like it, go on your own and see what happens. You were the only one who never stood up to your father. Do you think you can start now? I doubt it," Maureen said. "Did you talk to him for more than two minutes when he called you? Of course not. You didn't know what to say, did you?"

Mark just sat there and steamed. *Let her handle it with Chuck. Who knows? Maybe they're right. So far, we haven't seen a dime.*

Jack went back to the hotel and changed. He decided to wear khakis and a button down striped shirt with casual shoes. He really hadn't shopped much other than when they were in Tampa on the way to Key West. He shaved again, splashing on a light aftershave. He had his hair cut in the hotel the day before. He didn't seem to be missing much, living in the hotel for the last couple of weeks, but he did look forward to moving up to Old Plank Road the following weekend. He didn't have much to move. He'd gone back to Ethel's and packed but left everything there that he didn't need at the hotel. When he said that Maureen took him to the cleaners, he wasn't kidding. She took everything from the house, including the silverware. He walked out with his clothes and hadn't purchased much of anything over those horrible six months.

Maureen, Chuck, Debbie, and Mark appeared at the reception desk at the office. Maureen told the receptionist who they were, and the receptionist said they were expected. She moved the four of them into the large conference room at the end of the hall. Jack saw them walking by Kristen's office window looking out onto the hallway. Mary was there as well.

"Do you have the cameras on and the sound recorder set up?"

Kristen turned to her credenza and rotated the knob on what looked like a Bose stereo. She then turned her computer screen to face Jack and Mary. There were the four of them sitting in the conference room, talking to each other in whispers. The thrust of the conversation was to let Maureen and Chuck speak first to set the tone. Maureen told them to only answer questions with yes or no answers unless something else was required but to keep their answers short.

"You ready Jack?" Kristen asked. "Mary, you can watch in here if you want."

"No offense, but, Jack, this is your business only, not mine. I don't need to know what you're telling them. You're an honest, hard-working, good man, and I believe you'll come to a decision that you believe is right and that you can live with."

She left to go shopping downtown. She'd only met Maureen and the kids a few times over those many years and didn't believe they'd even know who she was, but she didn't want to take a chance.

Jack and Kristen got up and walked to the conference room, opened the door, and walked in. Jack introduced Kristen as his personal attorney who'd be staying for all conversations with his family members.

"Mr. Falcone, you aren't a member of my family, so I'll ask you to leave right now. You can wait downstairs in the bank lobby. There are comfortable chairs and magazines. The receptionist will call ahead, so there's no problem."

"He's not going anywhere," Maureen said. "I want him here for this discussion. So do the kids."

Jack looked at his two children who starred blankly back at him. "I guess this meeting is now over. Any questions, Maureen, Debbie, or Mark, please address them to Mrs. Sanderson at her convenience. Thank you." With that, he walked out of the conference room and closed the door.

They were all stunned, including Kristen.

"Sorry," she said. "It looks like this meeting is over. I don't believe there will be another, knowing Jack Manning the way I do."

Maureen was stunned, and she looked at Chuck as if to say, "What the hell do we do now?"

He shook his head. "What do you have to lose?" he said quietly. "Obviously, he won't be talking with me in the room. So, I'll leave. Big deal. You handle it, Maureen." His look said, "Don't screw it up."

Jack was back in Kristen's office, looking at the video and listening to the conversation. He heard Maureen say to Kristen, "Can you get him back in here? Chuck will leave."

He heard Kristen say, "I'll check, but I can't promise you anything. Sit down, and I'll see if he'll come back." They sat. Kristen went back to her office and smiled at Jack. "Nice family. I can see why you left."

"Where's your compassion? Aren't you an ex-nun? That's my family you're talking about," he said and laughed.

"My compassion went out with my veil, pal. Go back and meet them. This should be interesting. By the way, you got my information on annulments, right?"

"I sure did. I can't wait to see the expression on her face," he added.

"Just a quick question. Does the annulment have anything to do with Mary?"

"None of your business." He smiled. "Let's go, Counselor."

Jack and Kristen walked back into the conference room. He looked around and saw that Chuck was gone. He turned to Maureen. "I'd like to talk to both Mark and Debbie alone. You can wait by the receptionist, and, when we're done, I want to talk to you at length."

Maureen knew she was beaten at this point. When Chuck left, she knew Jack had her. He looked the same, but he was very different from the man whom she divorced last year. *Maybe money does that to you*, she thought. "I'll wait out in the reception area." She got up, left, and closed the door. Kristen stayed right where she was.

"Mark and Debbie, I've got a lot to say to you. You're adults, over the age of twenty-one, and I don't have to do a thing for you, but you're my children. When you each reach the age of thirty-five, you'll receive the proceeds of a trust fund set up at two million dollars each. It will be set up this week, and the annuity will pay three-point-five percent. So, at age thirty-five, you'll receive the entire principal and the interest. However, as of now, your mother's divorce decree stated that she'd pay your student loans and any future student loans. Debbie, if you want a master's degree, ask your mother. Now, in the meantime, if you need spending money or books or transportation or any necessity that your mother doesn't, can't, or won't pay for, I'll allow you to work it off on a volunteer basis at several nonprofits that I'll either run or fund. You'll sign a note, and work off the balance owed at a rate of twenty dollars per hour, which is unheard of for volunteer work. I don't care if you babysit the children for students at my new center, clean the toilets, or anything else required of you by the volunteer manager. You'll get paid monthly minus taxes like anyone else. Hopefully, by age thirty-five, you'll have matured, both of you, into something other than spoiled little brats. Also, you can't tell anybody, even your mom, about this conversation or what you're getting, or the deal is off. Am I understood clearly?"

Debbie was in tears. "Mom said if we were nice, we'd get something."

"I believe two million plus isn't nothing."

"I mean now," she said.

"You'll never starve. You'll just have to work it off like anyone else. Debbie, I'm done with you. Take it or leave it," Jack continued. "Mark, you were never a pain in the ass to me like Debbie, but I believe that's because you didn't give a crap about me and couldn't care less. Does that sum it up? You can have the same deal. I wasn't invited to your graduation, and I don't expect to be invited to the wedding with the girl you're living with. Don't expect a present. Once you sign these nondisclosure statements, you both can leave."

Once they left, Kristen looked like the bird that swallowed the canary. "Nice. Good job. Think they'll come around?"

"They better because I'm closer to my students than I am to either of them. That's now clearly obvious. Please go get Maureen and make sure my kids are parked in the reception area, so they don't overhear anything. Thanks, Kristen. This isn't as much fun as I thought it would be."

"Kidding, right?"

"Yes."

Kristen escorted Maureen back to the conference room. They both took a seat.

Kristen went to the head of the table, and Maureen sat immediately across from Jack on the other side of the large table.

Jack started by saying, "Maureen, this conversation isn't to be discussed with Chuck or with Mark and Debbie. You're also not to ask them what they're getting. Are we clear?"

"Yes." She was now on the verge of tears but, as she looked at Jack, she knew that she hurt him dearly and, no matter what she said, it wouldn't change anything. "I just want you to know that I'm sorry, Jack, for everything that happened. If I could change it, I would."

"Thank you for the apology, but I question your sincerity. Can we get started?"

"Fine."

There was the old "fine" meaning "not fine," but he could live with it now because he just didn't care.

"I have a proposition for you." As he said it, he passed an envelope over to Maureen. "That envelope contains my proposition. These are the grounds for marriage annulment in the Roman Catholic Church. There are twenty very-well-defined canonical grounds for marriage annulment. Once these have been established, marriage annulment can proceed. It's important to understand the grounds for marriage annulment before making application, and if in doubt, you should consult your priest, if you still attend church. Kristen is an expert in canonical law and, of the twenty different grounds, see the five specific ones she's highlighted for your consideration. These include number fifteen, Force; number sixteen, Fear; number seventeen, Error regarding marital unity that determined the will; number eighteen, Error regarding marital indissolubility that determined the will; and number nineteen, Error regarding marital sacramental dignity that determined the will. Read all of them carefully, including the other fifteen.

"If you want a trust set up, I want an annulment started by you, and it must be determined that you were the one who couldn't live up to the canonical rules of marriage—not me. Kristen will help you, and I'll sign any documentation required of me as long as I'm not the one in the wrong. For that, I'll immediately give you five hundred thousand dollars with the taxes paid. In addition at age sixty-two, you'll receive another five hundred thousand that's been earning interest at a rate of three-point-five percent per year on tax-free municipal bonds. That'll grow for fourteen years, ages forty-eight to sixty-two, to eight hundred, nine thousand, three hundred thirty-four dollars and twenty-six cents, tax-free. However, if there's no annulment, you'll get nothing. Maybe when you retire, Debbie and Mark will be willing to share their largesse with you but nothing until then. Also, you aren't to ask them to discuss anything. I made them sign a nondisclosure agreement each. You're to do the same. You also can't tell Chuck about this arrangement so he won't be able to screw it up."

"That's all fine, but if I don't tell Chuck, then he may leave."

"I'd suggest you're better off, but that's your business."

"What if we got together and sued you for more? How would that look that you didn't care about your family?"

"Well, first, I don't care. Second, if you do that, you know I have enough money to start digging up evidence of your unfaithfulness from the beginning of time. I was too weak and too stupid to figure that out, but I'm not now, and there's nothing that you can do. I could hold you off until the end of time. I could move to Florida, and you'll never see a dime."

"What if I don't want an annulment or can't get one?"

"A good attempt in baseball is still a zero batting average if you don't come through. If you don't come through, you get nothing from me but maybe some from the kids when they're thirty-five. If they tell you anything before then, they lose their trust fund. Also, you're to pay Debbie's tuition and student loans. If she needs anything above that, I told her to call my volunteer coordinator, and she'll be paid twenty dollars per hour to work at a designated nonprofit. Mark doesn't seem to care one way or the other."

"That's it. That's what we get when you've been given millions?"

"Timing's a bitch. Isn't it? You really did make your bed, and now you have to lie in it. Don't say a word to Chuck, or all bets are off. Have a nice life. I really mean that. You can retire or at least live very well if you get the annulment. Thank you. That's it." With that, he got up and left the room. Kristen was left there, shuffling her papers until Maureen left the conference room.

They all left together in silence. Jack sat in Kristen's office. He felt empty. He wasn't happy. He could always change his mind and help them out, if push came to shove. He'd have to wait. He had other things on his mind, like a new nonprofit, a new building, the rehab of the TCC and Mary's requests. He wanted Mary to be happy more than anything else. She was truly the only one who really cared about him when he was down and out.

CHAPTER 27

What did he say?" Chuck asked on the way back to the car. "I waited for well over an hour downstairs in the bank lobby reading about the economy. Not a lot of fun. So, what did he say, Maureen?"

"He said I can't tell you anything or discuss anything with anyone, or I'll lose everything that he offered me."

Mark turned around in the parking lot. "Dad told us the same thing. So, Debbie, you aren't to tell anyone anything, not even Mom. You got that, right? I'm not losing everything because you're mad at him. Keep your mouth shut would be my advice. If you say anything at all, I'll lose too, and that's not going to happen."

"Fine, but I'm not happy," Debbie said. "I have to get through college myself, and if I need anything, I have to ask Mom or work."

"Shut the hell up, Debbie. You heard me. Nothing. Say nothing, for God's sake," Mark said.

"You can't say anything to me, you guys? Nothing? He told me the same thing and not to ask, or he'd find out, and we'll lose everything. You have your marching orders, and I've got mine, and that's what's going to happen," Maureen said.

"What about me?" Chuck said. "Where the hell do I stand? What's in it for me? Nothing?"

"We can't say a thing, so you'll have to trust us or make

other plans, Chuck," she remarked. "That's all I can say for now. His directions to me were very specific and probably to the kids as well. I'm not blowing it, and I don't think they want to either. So, it's up to you what you want to do, Chuck. But please don't ask us again."

It was quiet all the way home. Chuck was fuming. "Can I ask you when you'll be getting whatever you're getting, at least?"

"No, you can't, and that goes for Mark and Debbie as well."

Now he was really furious. They were getting something, but it looked like he was the odd man out. He needed to do something. He had to find out what was going on. One of them would slip. Were they getting millions? They wouldn't be so secretive if they were getting nothing. They'd be pissed. Debbie was pissed but kept her mouth shut.

Chuck guessed that her father was very firm on his decision and there was no room for discussion. Perhaps later in the throws of passion, Maureen would let him know what was going on. He'd get it out of her sooner or later.

It was a few days later, and John Traynor called Jack on his cell. He was one of the very few who had the number. John told Jack that right after they met for dinner, the guys discussed this project, and they were all in, including the association president. He wanted to see if the association would provide employment for the certified graduates. It would be a good deal for the companies to get trained help and might even be able to throw some money back to the center to help.

They'd guarantee Jack a move-in ready price of three million dollars for his new building, but that was complete. He could live with it. They'd show Jack all the costs, mark it up twenty percent as their gross profit, and eat any cost overruns out of that figure. It would also include a parking lot for seventy-five cars, which should be more than enough for expansion and for any overlap if he needed it for the

TCC building right next door, which he planned to own upon completion of the new building.

Jack told him to put the paperwork together and the law firm would then review it. He said to send it to Kristen Sanderson and Andy Miller. He thought they'd approve the plan once reviewed. John also told him that the building's exterior would be up in three months after the land was shovel-ready. That would give them three months to do the entire inside including all the wiring and technology required for a green, state-of-the-art facility. John would do all the paperwork for rebates by the multiple state agencies and National Grid, Spectrum, and Verizon. Jack was now thrilled to death.

Mary wasn't around, but at home, so he called her and made a date for dinner at the Dinosaur Bar B Que, in downtown Troy, right at the Green Island Bridge, for six p.m. He was dying for ribs. She said okay, as long as she remembered to bring back dinner for Jane and Martha.

Andy called Jack and told him that all the paperwork for the TCC building was prepared. The Freeman's attorney sent Andy the deed for an update, and the property was free and clear with no back taxes owed. Jack was asked to sign a prepared check for $25,000 as a non-refundable deposit on the sale, and Mr. Freeman was meeting with the president and treasurer of the TCC to convey that he'd turn the past due rent into a demand note, which Andy had already prepared and sent over to Mr. Freeman. Once it was signed by the chairman of the board of directors of the TCC, Jack would purchase the instrument at a face value of $60,000, the amount owed for six months past due. It was no guarantee that the current rent would be paid on time, but that would be up to Mr. Freeman to collect over the next six months. The transfer of the TCC property would take place immediately after the grand opening of the new Evangeline Career Center.

Jack was now very pleased, and, in the late afternoon, he sat down with Gerald Reynolds, the partner for estate planning, trust, and probate, and with Colleen Coleman for taxation law. They'd summarize where he now stood financially.

Nothing had happened with Mary's fifteen million dollars. He only spent a few thousand dollars out of his own estimated sixty-eight million dollars left after taxes. Of the fifty million dollars set up in a non-profit trust, he already allocated about four million dollars for his own new building and about $750,000 for the TCC purchase. He'd set aside, out of his own money, the three trusts for Maureen, Mark, and Debbie, about five million dollars, leaving him with a still nice fat chunk of change at sixty-three million. He'd also allocate ten million dollars to run the facility over the next ten years and another million to rehab the TCC building. He still had at least thirty-four million dollars in the non-profit trust left for other nonprofit projects to help those individuals that he cared about and who gave their all for very little. They'd be shocked when he handed them a large donation that could change the direction of their organization forever. He was pleased with that.

Finally, Jack knew that the AAA municipal bonds already purchased, at a non-taxable rate of three-point-five percent would generate enough income to pay the annual million dollar attorney fee plus another million or two to add back to what he hadn't already spent. By age sixty, when he knew he wanted to retire, he'd still have enough money for many lifetimes, so he never had to worry. He needed protection from those who'd do him harm if they knew what he was worth, and he wondered how long he'd need bodyguards at a few hundred thousand dollars a year. He knew he'd need them for at least the next year but was unsure beyond that.

Jack walked out of the office with his head spinning, followed by John Jefferson, but knew he could probably pay his way out of any problem that existed over the next ten years. He was happy, but he was also lonely. He had Mary as a close friend—best friend, actually. But he wanted more. He knew that he'd never start back up with Maureen. That was just too much to bear. He hoped that, with time, his children would understand what he was trying to do and how he wanted them to stand on their own before becoming trust fund babies.

He hoped that by age thirty-five, they'd be married, have their own families, and start thinking about others beside themselves. He looked back at his life, and he married too young, had children too young, and never really had time to think about life in general. His work became everything, and he knew that was a sore point with Maureen, but he didn't realize that it was too late before it became too late. He now had time to plan, to think, to help, to do things the way he wanted, and maybe make a difference, He hoped that giving back the next ten years of his life, would be rewarding to him and those around him. Then it was his time in the sun.

He sure hoped he'd get that annulment. At age fifty, he still might get married again, and he wanted to be able to do it in the Catholic Church. He was a regular churchgoer and went to Mass every Sunday. It was important to him. He didn't want the divorce hanging over his head. He didn't want it. He didn't plan it, but maybe he wouldn't be stuck with it. Time would tell.

CHAPTER 28

Jack saw Mary getting out of her car in the Dinosaur parking lot. He'd just gotten out of his SUV and waited for her at the front door. The outdoor smoker was going with a man throwing chunks of wood into the pit. The smell was marvelous. Jack's mouth began to water.

"Hi, Mary. I just got here, too."

They walked in together and got a booth overlooking the Hudson River. It was a clear night, and traffic on the Green Island Bridge was heavy with people heading home. Boats were floating by, and the Captain JP Cruise Line was just pulling out onto the river for its moonlight dinner cruise. As usual, the boat was packed, and a band was playing, with people looking over the top rails of the boat, laughing, talking, and having drinks. It was a perfect night out on the river.

Jack ordered the half rack of ribs and Mary had the smoked turkey breast sandwich with fries and a side of fried green tomatoes. The fried green tomatoes were a house specialty, crispy fried and sprinkled with Pecorino Romano cheese, served with a cayenne buttermilk ranch dressing. Jack ordered a beer and Mary had an Arnold Palmer, another specialty, half ice tea and half lemonade served in a jelly jar.

"Jack, I've got to clear something up," she said. "Jane and Martha are all over me to tell them what's going on with us. I haven't even had the heart to tell them that I'm sort of moving, but I'm still keeping my room at the apartment. I have to pay my share, or they're in trouble financially. I can't go on not telling them that I've got fifteen million dollars to spend. I may even need their suggestions on what to spend it on."

"I know it's been a problem and a headache for you, but I don't want them spreading rumors about what they think is going on. Even worse, on what they know we're going to do. You can tell them I gave you fifteen million dollars for yourself and any projects that you wanted to honor. Hell, you can give them some too, if you want. You have to tell them that you're moving up the hill, at least for a while. I don't think it's safe with you at the apartment, even with your bodyguard. Now, he leaves as soon as you get home, and you're vulnerable to God knows what."

Jack looked around, and John Jefferson and Fred Tucker were only two booths away from them.

"Can you come with me tonight and help me tell Jane and Martha what's going on? I need you, Jack. This is too hard for me as it is. I'm not used to this, you know."

"I'll be glad to, and I'm not used to it either. I think it will be easier when we're all at Old Plank Road. Let me tell you what's just happened, what we need to do next, and when that's done, I'll stop doing things, and we'll work together on your projects. I've got a few not-so-small ones of my own, but I think you'll appreciate the gestures that I want to make. I think yours will be in the same vain."

They ate dinner. Jack was covered with barbeque sauce and used up about ten wet naps. He excused himself and headed toward the bathroom to clean up the rest that he missed. Mary turned and waved at John and Fred and pointed to their bill to give it to her. While Jack was in the bathroom, she paid both bills with a nice tip. She was anxious to get back to Jane and Martha to tell them what she couldn't before. Jack got out and was surprised that Mary and the two guys were standing waiting for him. He nodded thanks to Mary for paying the bill. He laughed to himself that she could take it out of the fifteen million dollars. The problem was that she never even opened a checking account yet or had a credit and debit card. She must have paid cash out of her meager salary from the schools. Four cars heading back to the Burgh was quite a waste of time and gasoline.

John and Fred sat in their vehicles while Mary and Jack headed into the 7th Avenue apartment to talk to Jane and Martha. Mary carried in the dinner orders that she got from the takeout window while waiting for Jack. "Come and get it, ladies. Ribs, ribs, and more ribs with chicken, cornbread, fries, and baked beans. Dig in."

Jane went over to the refrigerator and brought out a six-pack of Sam Adams. "When in Rome," she said. She popped open four bottles as they sat at the kitchen table.

"Jack, we haven't seen you in God knows how long. Congratulations by the way. How's it going?"

"It's going, sometimes great and then not so great. Mary asked me to stop by to talk to you two about what's going on. I have to be careful because we've got some plans underway that could be undermined if word got out. Not that you'd say anything on purpose, but it could slip. So, we have to be careful. What I have to say to you goes no further. Is that okay, ladies?"

"Sure," Martha said as she attacked her third rib and piece of cornbread. Mary watched both of them eat with delight. She slowly drank her beer, waiting for Jack to continue. He seemed to be hesitant, but he said he'd tell them what he could.

"As you know, I hit the lottery, split nine hundred and ninety million dollars three ways. The net was one hundred and ninety-eight million after the cash payment was calculated rather than taking it over thirty years. I don't think I have thirty years left. Anyway, I sent up a sizeable trust for several nonprofit ventures, including building a new career development center in downtown right next to our old TCC building. I'm buying that building as soon as the new building opens. Ladies, it's complicated, but Mary and I are going back in business over the next ten years. By the way, I also gave Mary fifteen million dollars to do with what she wants."

"*What*? Fifteen million dollars? No wonder you never said anything, Mary. That's great. What're you going to do with the money?" Jane asked.

"Keep some for yourself, we hope," said both.

"That's why I couldn't say anything. But, when Jack's plans and financing are completed, then I'll be able to concentrate on what I'd also like to do. It's to complement what Jack's doing, just a little differently. By the way, I'm moving this weekend up to Old Plank Road with Jack and two retired FBI agent bodyguards. I'll still keep my room here for now, but it's not safe if it gets out what I'm worth, just like Jack."

"Is that why a large fellow has been around here a lot lately, sitting in a vehicle down the street? There appears to be two in two separate vehicles now."

Jack nodded. "One for me and one for Mary for at least the next two to three months until things settle down a little. Everyone is worried about robbery and kidnapping of lottery winners. It's happened in the past."

"Are you two…" Martha asked point blank.

"No," Jack said. "We're like always. She's my best and, evidently, my only friend."

Mary jumped in to ease the conversation. "I'm going to pay the rent from now on. In addition, after the trust is set up, and I decide what to keep, I'll be setting up a fund for you two that'll give you both thirty thousand dollars a year, tax free, to live on for life. It's not to give away. Do you hear me? Now, if you want to work, you can, and you don't have to get paid. Also, when the center is opened, you'll receive a benefit package for your health plan, free and clear. I'll pay in to that. Right now, none of us have health insurance, and we need to take care of that."

Jack nodded. "Great thinking, Mary. I forgot that we don't have any health insurance. I'll have Kristen set up a program now before construction begins so everyone we hire will receive a health insurance plan who doesn't have one now. It will be in effect from the time they're hired until they go to work at the center. Then, they'll be under a different plan. By the way, ladies, if you ever hear the name, The Evangeline Trust, you'll know that it's us."

"Kristen Sanderson's former Sister of Saint Joseph name, right?" asked Jane.

"Yes, it is. We immediately liked the name, and she thought it was great. It was the easiest decision we made, to date. By the way, we're having a cookout this Sunday. We're moving in starting Friday night and ending on late Saturday afternoon. Come up Saturday if you want to see the place before the party."

"I also need help with groceries and preparation for the cookout. Can you two help?" asked Mary. "The house is beautiful, with a great view, and it's fully furnished. That's why I'm leaving my stuff here, most of it anyway. Jack has packed his one bag, and he's ready. He's been carting it around in his SUV all week, champing at the bit. He's tired of the hotel."

"I don't blame him," said Jane. "Of course, we'll help."

Jack peeled off $700 in cash for groceries and handed it to Martha. "Is that enough? I'll stop and buy the beer and wine and a few bottles of liquor, at the bottom of the hill."

"I'd imagine. How many are coming?"

"Maybe twenty to thirty. No more than that I think. I'll invite my kids, and you two are invited, along with Ethel my old landlady, and our friends at the attorney's office, a few contractors, and an older couple, the Freemans. That's it, I think."

Jane and Martha finished their dinners while Jack and Mary drained their beers. Mary was staying for the night, trying to pack a few things. She imagined after he left they'd have a million questions, including Jack and Mary's non-existent romantic status. Jack said goodbye and hopped into his Explorer. He blew the horn at John and Fred. Jack couldn't wait until the parade ended.

He'd be in the Albany Hilton for only a few more nights, and that was it. He'd settle up his bill. He needed to make sure that Kristen assigned a few helpers for Ethel at her house in the Burgh. Her son never came through as usual. After his questions about Jack's good fortune, he hadn't been back since.

Kristen had told him before he left for the Dinosaur that they've been getting tons of calls from people who wanted to contact Jack Manning. The calls ranged from perfect strangers asking for help and money; to relatives that he hadn't seen in years and didn't even remember existed; to the news media, including all the local newspapers, TV, and radio stations. They all wanted a piece of Jack. He didn't spend more than twenty minutes at lottery headquarters in Schenectady that day, and he knew that it would eventually catch up to him. Kristen said there was a bag full of mail from people across the country, according to the return addresses.

She told Jack that it was time to get the volunteer manager in place and a small team of staff to separate inquiries into different categories, and Jack could decide what responses were appropriate, if any. He didn't want them at the new house on Old Plank Road, but he thought he might rent a small storefront in Troy and staff it. He'd take the burden off the law firm because he needed them for other things, and it was too costly to process responses using the legal staff.

The only reason they contacted the law firm was because Kristen showed up with Jack at the announcement, and several media members knew she was from the law firm of Miller, Reynolds, Coleman, and Straus. Thus, all the calls went directly to their main number and were wreaking havoc on the staff. He needed a volunteer manager, so he might

as well start looking into employees for the new center
since everything was now in place and ready to build.

CHAPTER 29

Toward the end of the week, everyone was getting on edge. Jack couldn't wait to move. He knew that the law firm was moving mountains for him, and they probably needed a break from seeing him every day, along with Mary. Kristen got a few temporary staff from a temp service down the street. She set them up in an empty room that was for rent on the floor below. She made a deal with the building owner to allow five temps to come in and sort mail for a few weeks. She had a shredder ordered and had it placed on the eleventh floor, one below them. The five workers would separate requests—by state, by individual, by nonprofit, by category, then by local requests based on zip code.

They were older workers that seemed to understand when she explained what they were trying to do. Jack would come in for three hours a day, sometimes with Mary, and put requests in two files, one to the dump and one for further review. Since he now had time, he'd concentrate on all requests from the 12180, 12181, and 12182 zip codes, the immediate Troy zip codes. From there, he'd take those area codes immediately next to Troy, including the Town of Brunswick, Cohoes, Watervliet, Green Island, and Waterford. All the others would be placed in a large non-Troy pile for further review. All those requests outside New York State would be dumped. He knew from his vast experience working for nonprofits that you couldn't possibly provide enough resources for everyone. Someone once told him that he couldn't save all the whales. They said pick one. Then move on after that. So, that's what he was doing.

They made a good size dent in the pile. Since he'd be at the new house the following week, he took a ten-inch pile and put it into a plastic bag. He'd keep them in his SUV and read each one when he got a chance, or if he got bored.

Jack took Friday off from all activities, so he could move up to the new house. He had his bag already packed and waiting in the SUV. He stopped at Mary's, and she gave him a few boxes of things she wanted at the new house. She was going to leave a lot at the apartment, but she'd take most of her summer and fall clothes with her. Her winter clothes were packed tightly in the back of the closet along with winter boots, shoes, hats, and gloves. They were going nowhere. Jack took her bicycle as well. It wouldn't fit in her car. Jane and Martha took the afternoon off and went to both Hannaford and Price Chopper in the Burgh and got groceries and staples that they'd need. Toby Jensen had cleaned out the pantry and refrigerator. There wasn't much to keep. Most of the condiments were already expired. Jane took half the list, and Martha took the other and said they'd meet Jack at the house after six p.m. They said they didn't realize or forgot what it was like moving into a new house for the first time.

Mary took the afternoon to vacuum and dust and clean all the windows. She was armed with all her cleaning supplies from the apartment and stopped at the Dollar Store on the way up the hill to get a few plastic buckets and tons of paper towels. Jack would take care of the outside. The lawn was mowed, thank God, because it was about ten acres. He called Toby's maintenance man and told him that he'd take over the bill for the next six months. He wanted to be fair to Toby and make sure he didn't lose money on the deal. Jack took out the hose and reel and put it together. He hosed off the outdoor furniture, the patio and the walls off the deck.

Tons of winter debris that clung to the sides came rolling off. It was a warm day so it would dry quickly. Jack had a ton of keys and started labeling each one as he tried the doors, the garage, and the outside basement entrance. The garage was huge and had Toby's Cub Cadet tractor housed if Jack wanted to use it, along with gardening tools and rakes and shovels. Jack really liked this place. It reminded him of his old house out in Brunswick, just twice the size and ten times the property.

Jane blew her horn as she drove up the long drive to let Mary and Jack know that they were there. She pulled in right by the deck and opened all the doors. The trunk, backseat, and floors were covered with grocery bags with Martha holding half a dozen in her lap. She couldn't even get out of the car. Jack came down the stairs and opened Martha's passenger door, said, "What you bring me?" and laughed.

"What didn't we bring you? The kitchen sink is in the trunk," she said with a smile.

It took a good twenty minutes to bring all the bags inside and placed on the floor. Mary was trying to figure out where everything went. At least they'd separated the dry goods, condiments, and refrigerated and freezer items. "Great job, ladies," she said.

"Anything to eat?" said Jack

All three looked at him as if to say "smartass."

After all the groceries were put away, Jane gave Jack back $400 from the money he gave her.

He looked at her. "Thanks, but keep it."

"No, that's not right. You're our friends, and this isn't about money, so here." She gave it back.

"Do you want me to pick up dinner so Mary can show you around? Spaghetti and meatballs and salad, from Testo's?"

Mary nodded. "That would be great, Jack. Thanks. Did you get the beverages for Sunday?"

"I'm doing that tomorrow, but I'll pick up a case of beer

and a few bottles of wine for dinner tonight down the hill on the way. Ladies, you can stay all weekend or anytime for that matter, whenever you want."

"We'll eat dinner and then head out and leave you alone. We'll come back tomorrow to help Mary make salads and get everything ready for Sunday."

"Thanks," he said and headed out the door to do his errands.

"Jane and Martha, what do you think? Is this one of the nicest homes you've ever seen? We may just buy this place when the lease is up. Who knows? If we last ten years here and do a good job with the center and other things, we may move to Key West. I have to tell you about the trip to Key West. By the way, you could wind up with this house if you're nice to me," she said and laughed out loud. She was thoroughly enjoying herself.

"So fifteen million dollars helps takes away a lot of stress, huh?"

"Sure does," Mary told Martha.

Jack was back within the hour. He unloaded the beer and wine first, giving the case to Mary and the bottles of wine to Jane. Martha grabbed the bag with the salad and bread. Jack had a tub of spaghetti and meatballs. He dropped the stuff on the kitchen table. "Dig in. I'm hungry."

The table was already set with plates, silverware, napkins, shaker cheese, and red pepper flakes—his favorite. He thought that it was nice to have some women around who cared. All he did for six months was take care of his eighty-year-old landlady, which was difficult getting her to eat before he had to go to work for the night at the store. It was nice to sit down to a meal that he didn't have to cook and could pay for it with what was now pocket change to him. He could learn to love this, he thought.

After they ate, they cleaned the dishes, and Jane and Martha left Mary with a wink and a nod and a smirk on their faces. "Have a great night, and we'll see you tomorrow. Around noon, Mary?"

Mary was turning red. "Fine," she said, which everyone knew meant, "Mind your own business girls."

The ladies came on Saturday. Jack made all the calls to make sure that people would come. He spent enough on groceries that would have lasted him two months. Mary finished the cleaning as Jane and Martha made the macaroni, potato, and pasta salads. They said everything would taste better the next day. They had lunch made of leftover meatballs and rolls. He always bought extra meatballs from Testo's.

After lunch, Jack went into the makeshift office that was formerly the family room, overlooking the huge expanse of back lawn, about six acres worth. He called Mark who said he'd be there with his girlfriend, Cara Brooks. Jack had never met Cara, so this would be a nice visit with Mark, without any other influences. He called Debbie, who didn't pick up, and he didn't expect her to, but he left a message. He was sure that Debbie would tell Maureen and Chuck about the party.

Jack didn't need to call John and Peter Traynor. They were already at the house earlier setting up a brand new alarm system and showed Jack and Mary how to set the alarm. They were also there when Time Warner came to set up the internet and cable. Toby didn't bother with cable, so they had to string it in from the road. Jack made sure every bedroom had access to both internet and cable television. Peter told Jack that Tanya Fields, his fiancée, was coming as well. The Freemans were surprised by the invitation but gladly accepted. Jack gave them directions.

He'd already invited the attorneys and staff, and they were coming, including Kristen and her husband, Bill. Andy Miller and Gerry Reynolds were coming stag, along with two of the assistants who were part of Jack and Mary's trust team. Mary took care of calling Ethel Rounds. Jane and Martha would pick her up and bring her home. At least Ethel would be able to talk to the Freemans, someone her own age.

Both John Jefferson and Fred Tucker came on Friday night around eleven p.m. and set up their rooms. They were there for the duration. Jack finally confirmed that the contractors, Don Dunlop and Harry Hilton, would be there with their wives along with Luke Curtis, the association president, and his wife. Altogether, it looked like there would be twenty-five to thirty people at the party, including Mary and Jack.

He finally felt good about it. He hoped they were coming because they liked Mary and him, but it was still okay if they didn't. He wanted them all to know their importance to him and wanted them to feel like a member of his team, because he could never do any of this on his own. But he knew he couldn't buy real friendship—no one could.

CHAPTER 30

Sunday morning, Jack and Mary met Jane and Martha at the nine a.m. Mass at Saint Augustine's. They'd pick up any last minute items that were always forgotten. The party wasn't going to begin until three p.m. By then, everything would be set up and the grill ready for hot dogs and hamburgers. They'd cook steak and chicken and shrimp at five p.m. That would be complemented by all the salads the ladies prepared. Martha said she'd pick up the cake ordered from Bella Napoli after getting Ethel for the party, around two p.m.

Everyone started to arrive around three p.m. Jack manned the grill, cooking hot dogs and hamburgers, set up like a buffet on the deck. Beer and soda sat in a large tub of ice with wine set in a bucket on the table. A bottle each of Scotch and bourbon sat alone at the end of the table with several shot glasses and appropriate cocktail glasses. Introductions were made all the way around. Louis, Addie, and Ethel sat as if they were the patriarch and matriarch for a family gathering. Everyone served them, and they were delighted. Jack ran around until everyone was situated and had something to eat or drink then made his way back, one by one, to introduce Mary. It was a little awkward when he introduced Mary to his son, Mark, and his son's fiancée, Cara. Jack had just met her as well, so they were on a level playing field.

"Nice to meet you, Cara. This is my friend and business partner, Mary Evans."

"Nice to meet both of you, especially you, Mr. Manning," she said quite graciously.

Mark was standing by her side, grinning from ear to ear. Cara was a knockout and appeared to be nobody's fool. She'd just graduated from the University at Albany with Mark with an MBA. She was a little older than Mark, but Jack thought that's what he probably needed. Jack excused himself to greet everyone else, so Mary stayed and chatted up both Mark and Cara.

Mark didn't seem to know what was going on or the reason for the party.

"If you stay around or catch your father by himself," Mary said, "I'm sure he'll tell you what his plans are for the near future."

"That's great because I haven't the foggiest idea," he said.

Cara quietly whispered in his ear, and he smiled. "Okay, I'll go with the flow."

Mary excused herself and went to meet up with Jack who was talking to the Freemans. He was explaining to them why he really wanted the building and what he was planning on doing. The Freemans, childless, fully supported the youth in Troy and gave substantial amounts to the TCC and others who worked with youth. Jack never met them or knew anything about them. All he knew was that they owned the building that he wanted, that housed the TCC. He quietly told them that he'd be glad to go back to their house with Mary and explain more fully about his plans for the career center and his vision for a new concept for the surrounding area.

He explained that he wanted to develop a village within the city. The village would be named North Central Village. It would contain the most improved housing structures in the city, along with a new charter school, pre-K through grade twelve, for all the kids living in the eight-block square radius of the most underserved section of the city of Troy. Every house in this designated area would be re-habbed with Jack's own money at no charge to the residents. Those living in slum landlord buildings would be offered the opportunity to own their own home at the same monthly payment that they were now giving to these absentee landlords for substandard housing. Jack told the Freemans that this would take ten years, start to finish, and only then would he retire at age sixty. He'd still have more than enough money to live quite comfortably for many lifetimes.

Little did Jack know that as he was speaking, he became the center of attention. Mark and Cara came over quietly and listened attentively as Jack revealed his vision for a new North Central Village that would improve the lives of the poorest families in Troy. He was giving them a lifeline and the tools to escape the downward spiral of poverty. As he went on, he explained that his vision included starting new businesses that would rehab the several hundred houses in the area, along with jobs for the future including high technology, EMT as a basis for most medical technical fields, and energy efficiency to work with high tech companies coming out of RPI, only blocks from their stately campus. Those jobs always went to outsiders, but Jack's vision included having such a well-educated and technically trained population that even RPI couldn't overlook the value that was coming from the North Central Village, right down the hill.

Jack was so engrossed in his conversation that he didn't realize that he had the attention of all those at the party. When he finished, everyone clapped and seemed to be enthralled by this. The contractors and association president told him that they'd back him one hundred percent because this was a vision that didn't include government interference or subsidies or higher taxes. They praised him for using his own money. To add to the conversation, Kristen Sanderson told everyone that this wasn't a pie in the sky. It was already set up, and it was going to happen. The money was sitting in a separate trust fund to do exactly what Jack said he was going to do.

Mark patted his father on the back. "I'm very proud of you, Dad. Now I know why you spoke to us and told us what we'd be getting and when. I never knew what you wanted to do. I guess it's better late than never. If you need any help, especially from my accounting point of view or from using Cara's MBA, please don't hesitate to ask us."

"Thank you, Mark. That means a lot to me. It's been a long time since we spoke to each other, and I'd like that to continue. I hope, in the long run, Debbie feels the same. I just don't know about her. Cara, thank you as well. I'm really glad that Mark has someone like you in his life."

"By the way, who or what is Mary? Is that too forward?" asked Mark.

"You met her several times when I worked at the TCC. You probably don't remember. She came to me to work right from leaving the Sister's of Saint Joseph. She's an ex-nun who lives in the Burgh with two other ex-nuns. Mark, she was the only friend I had when I was asked to leave our home. She's my best friend, ever. She and I have the same vision. Hers is more religiously related than mine, but each of us has a social bent that seems to complement each other. I won't lie to you. She now has her own sizable trust fund to do things in Troy or wherever she wants to improve the lives of those who need it most. Or, of course, she can keep it, and I'll run away with her," he said and laughed.

Both Cara and Mark got his meaning. She stood by him when he was down and out, and she meant the world to him and perhaps might take Mark's mother's place someday. Mark was okay with that. He saw how his mother treated his father and was not pleased, but he didn't want to upset her because he needed her to pay his student loans.

He now felt bad. Not about the lottery winnings but because he never knew his father that well and what he wanted out of life. Mark knew he was dedicated to those he served at TCC, but he never understood what they meant to Jack, or Mary, for that matter.

Pete Traynor came over to Jack and handed him his cell phone. "It's Joe for you."

"Hi, Joe, how you doing? How's Julie? I can't thank you enough for getting me together with your father and brother. They've been terrific, and I'm counting on them to help with the construction and other things as well. This is going to be a long relationship. I'm your new much-older brother, Joe," Jack said with a chuckle.

"I heard," Joe said. "All they talked to me about was you handing them a check for twenty-five thousand dollars for doing nothing. They were shocked and called me right away. Well, brother, I guess you wouldn't have hired them if you didn't need them."

"I need them, all right. Do you know how much they saved me already? At least a quarter million dollars. They deserve whatever they get from me, and more. They'll be busy wiring and bringing technology into over two hundred homes in our new North Central Village."

"When are you coming back to the Keys?"

"Mary and I'll be busy for the next month or two, and then we'll be on hold for a few months while the new building goes up. I think we'd like to head back and visit with you and Julie and Skip and Linda Lennon. We might be interested in buying a home in Key West, on the water if possible. If I don't spend the money now, it could go very quickly for other projects and overruns along the way, so this is one thing I know I want to do. It won't take any time to convince Mary, I don't think."

"Are you and Mary…"

Jack moved to the other side of the deck by himself. "Honestly, I don't know you that well, but I trust you," he said quietly. "I've asked my ex-wife for an annulment. I'll wait to see how that goes. As an ex-nun and fervent Catholic, I'm sure if we ever got to feel that way about each other, she'd want to get married in the Catholic Church. You probably know how I feel, but I've never said a word to Mary. I don't want to ruin anything by being too premature. It could upset everything, and I don't want that."

"Sounds like a plan. Let us know when you're coming. I'll meet you at the airport. The Florida Keys Community College, where I'm stationed, is only minutes door-to-door. Julie can come down with Bella, and we can spend the weekend in Key West. We're about seventy miles away in Tavernier. It's a pain driving it every day, but I'm getting used to it. We'll see you when we see you."

They exchanged goodbyes, and Jack hung up and gave Pete back his cell phone.

"He didn't want to talk to you," he said with a smirk.

"Me neither," Peter said as he put his phone in his pocket and grabbed a beer from the ice tub.

The party went well. Everyone pitched in to cook the steaks, chicken, and shrimp. Everyone helped set the picnic tables on the deck. Some ate inside because it was getting cooler. By seven p.m., after cake and coffee, most everyone said his or her goodbyes. Jack told Mark and Cara to come up anytime and to say hi to Debbie. Jane and Martha helped Mary clean up, and then they left to take home Ethel, who seemed to enjoy the day. The Freemans told Jack to call them because they had some plans of their own and would like to help him with his. They said they weren't exactly poor and admired him for doing what they did quietly for years.

They said his plan had enough clout to work. It wasn't just feeding the poor but helping them feed themselves and turn their lives around. The contractors said they'd stay in touch with the Traynors, and they had some ideas about apprenticeships in the various local unions, especially for minority recruitment. Jack thanked them.

All in all, Jack accomplished what he wanted. He wanted to spend more time with Mary, but she was too busy running around. After his little speech, she gave him a kiss on the cheek and told him that she didn't know all that he was planning, and she was surprised and delighted. He was surprised at the kiss because that was only one of a few times it happened in all those years. The first time was when he offered, to her, her very first job coming out of the convent with little or no experience. It was a long time between kisses.

CHAPTER 31

On Monday, Jack checked into the eleventh floor at the bank building where the temps were still separating the envelopes into the various piles for his review. Mary went to Saint Augustine's School to let the principal know that she wouldn't be back, after all. She was just too busy. However, she stopped at the rectory to see if she could set up a meeting with the pastor, Father Jim Brady. She wanted Jack to meet with him as well. She felt more confident with Jack there. She wanted the real facts about the pending closing of the school. If it could be saved, she wouldn't mind giving a $100,000 a year to help the school break even. She'd heard that it was closer to $250,000 deficit last year with the parish and the diocese making up the difference. They weren't going to do it the following year. It was too much of a drain. The average tuition for those who could pay was under $3,000 a year with half of the families paying less, due to their financial circumstances. There was now less than 100 children kindergarten through sixth grade in the school. Even twenty years ago there were over 600 students and more than 1,000 students over forty years ago. The cost per student was now over $10,000 each, comparable to the cost of a private high school, let alone an elementary school.

She was not going to make up that difference because it would be the only project she could fund out of a hundred at least as deserving. She'd run out of money in ten years if that were the case and there were no guarantees from anyone that the school population would rise anywhere near what it was in the past. It was a losing proposition from the start.

Mary wanted to look at the school and gym to see if it could be purchased for a charter school and then use the gymnasium, across the street, as a separate facility for religious education. Charter elementary schools tended to do as well, if not better, than regular school district buildings. The difference was funding. If it was a charter school and those 100 could still attend the next year, they'd pay nothing, since it would be a public school in the state of New York. The charter school would receive eighty percent of what the school district received from the New York State Education Department per pupil cost of $17,534 per student per year. They'd then receive $14,027 per student, almost six times more than they received now. They could cap the student base at 400-500 students and never fear about falling behind financially, especially if she owned the two buildings and they didn't have to pay any rent. It all depended on what they'd sell the facilities for. A few years ago, Saint Patrick's School was sold to a charter school for under $200,000. Unfortunately, that charter school was now closed, due to not meeting the New York State education mandates. It had a lot to do with not getting enough funding to support the most at-risk kids in the north central area of Troy, where Jack wanted to do his work.

The original Lansingburgh Academy was right across the street from Saint Augustine's School, at the north corner of 4th Avenue and 114th Street. On December 24, 1795, a group of prominent residents petitioned the Regents of the State of New York for a charter, for the purpose of establishing the Lansingburgh Academy. They'd erected a wooden building on the west side of the village green. The charter was granted on February 20, 1796, and signed by John Jay. The trustees selected as the first principal, the

Reverend Chauncey Lee, who was a noted educator and author. He invented the dollar sign and first used it in a textbook he'd published in Lansingburgh.

In a new building with its expanded facilities at the same site, the Lansingburgh Academy flourished for the next eighty years. The academy offered such an advanced program of study that students were able to enter college as sophomores after graduating from the secondary school. Many famous people were connected to the academy. Samuel Blatchford, an early president, was later the president of Rensselaer Polytechnic Institute. Ebenezer Maltbie was in charge of the Academy when author Herman Melville graduated with a degree in surveying and engineering. Chester A. Arthur, future president of the United States, taught a course in 'Elements of Law' when he resided at the Academy. Many decades later, in 1975, the Lansingburgh Citizen's Council was given full access to the building by the school district, then owner of the building. The Council soon put together a proposal for the rehabilitation and restoration of the old Lansingburgh Academy so it could be used as an expanded branch of the Troy Public Library and as a neighborhood arts center. Also in 1975, the building was placed on the National Register of Historic Places. In 1976, the Council, under the auspices of the City of Troy, was awarded a $350,000 grant for this project. Work included a new roof, complete interior and exterior painting, new doors, a handicapped access ramp, new heating and air conditioning systems and extensive interior construction work. The project was completed in 1980.

As Mary had noted to herself, Lansingburgh was a well-educated community, and she wanted to use her trust-fund money to continue that tradition if she could. She felt there must be a way to bring it back and thought it would be very rewarding to have a new charter school named The Lansingburgh Academy Charter School. It would be a full circle improvement for a community now suffering from a downward cycle of poverty as older residents passed away with new minority families moving in, the same as the Irish, Italian, Poles, and Danes did a hundred years ago. It was a great place to live and could be again.

Mary met with Father Jim and set up a meeting for Wednesday afternoon so they could continue their discussion once joined by Jack. They exchanged pleasantries. Father had known Mary since she was a child, graduating from Saint Augustine's and then Catholic High and into the convent. Getting her teaching degree from The College of Saint Rose only gave her more credibility that she knew the state of education, particularly Catholic education, and what was required to meet the challenges of a new technology-based curriculum for the twenty-first century.

"Jack, can you meet us at the rectory at two p.m.?" she asked.

"Yes, of course. I've been thinking about the school and how you'd like to take it over as a charter school. That's all fine and well, but there are a few issues that you should be aware of, like asbestos and lead contamination. Most building, constructed prior to 1940, contain both elements. If you buy the building, you take over liability for any contamination since it existed. You might want to entertain the idea of leasing it for ten years, with the option to buy, and prepay the entire ten years, so they know you're serious. However, they'll continue to be responsible for any contamination."

"I never thought of that, Jack. Thank you. That's a great idea. Can you present it to Father Brady tomorrow? By the way, aren't you in the same situation if you buy the TCC building downtown?"

"Yes, and no. Let me explain. I just got off the phone with the Freemans. They'll donate the purchase price to us if we set up a scholarship fund for graduates of the program. On top of that, Louis got an estimate about potential contamination a few years ago. There were a few issues, but at the time, he remedied all the pipes by encapsulating the lead and asbestos. There's no other contamination on the property, so he says. I was going to put a million dollars into the building for upgrades, and before I buy it, I'll have the architect and the Traynors take a look and see if the problem is solved. I thought of that immediately. I want to make a point to their board by buying the building but not if it jeopardizes what we want to do."

"Got it," she said. "See you tomorrow."

They met with Father Brady. The conclusion was that, due to the changing of the face of Lansingburgh, a Catholic school was not going to increase and thrive. However, since the district had such an increase in a minority population, there had been a lot of issues with bringing students up to standard. Lansingburgh was ripe for a charter school, and Mary could fund it properly and increase the number of students, only as an elementary school. After sixth grade, the students would attend Catholic High or the public high schools, from their own district. Students came to a charter school from many districts, but the home district had first option. Mary brought up the issues of lead and asbestos, and Father Brady was very straightforward and said, like many old buildings, in fact, it had those issues. So, immediately, she asked Father Brady if they could discuss a ten-year lease option, prepaid, so there would be no questions about financial security.

She'd get Kristen to investigate obtaining a charter for this building. Father Brady also thought it was very clever to keep the two buildings separate under different corporations for liability issues. She'd propose to lease the school for $100,000 a year and the gymnasium for $20,000 to hold religious education on Wednesday afternoon and on Sundays throughout the year. She'd also allow the charter school students to use the building for school functions, if the potential charter school paid for liability insurance for those purposes.

It was a good meeting, and Father Brady would call the bishop to discuss this opportunity. This year, a high school charter school in Albany moved into a Catholic High School building that was unused because the high school charter school couldn't pay the rent on a ten million dollar facility that was owned by another entity. The rent for the Catholic School was one-tenth of the other.

After the meeting, it was five p.m., so Jack invited Mary and Father Brady to an early dinner at Verdile's on 2nd Avenue, right around the corner from the church. On a Wednesday night, it wouldn't be very crowded at all.

On the way home, Jack brought Mary up to date, starting with having the bodyguards not follow them anymore until after the building was up. Then, they'd be part of the Troy scene and would probably need them. They really didn't need them living on Old Plank Road. It was getting to Jack, and he knew that Mary was uneasy as well. He gave them a two-month bonus payment each, and both said they'd definitely be back. For the payment, they'd be on 24/7 call in case of an emergency only. It was a good deal for everyone.

Jack also explained that an ad was going into the paper for a volunteer manager position with the address and phone number for the attorneys' office. Kristen would screen the individual applicants with their human resources manager and select one as soon as possible. He or she would work at the Albany location until the building was finished. He also mentioned that they needed to start hiring several employees for the career center with a generic description of what they'd be doing without giving away the location or ownership.

CHAPTER 32

The monthly meeting of the board of directors of the Troy Community Council began promptly at nine a.m., led by its president, Howard Singer MSW. Marvin Manville, treasurer and vice president of human resources, gave the monthly treasurer's report, which was not promising. The board was uneasy and started to question exactly what was going on. Howard jumped in and said that the cash flow was suffering because it was taking longer to collect from Medicaid than expected.

The chairman, Craig Livingston, said to Howard Singer, "I thought signing the demand note for the building owner freed up a lot of cash that was owed for past due rent."

Howard nodded. "We still have some issues, and that helped, but we're down about $250,000 this year from lower revenue generation, which also affects cash flow."

"The lower income came from doing away with the career center, didn't it? How can you make that revenue up? The expenses haven't gone down accordingly. Yes, you saved on two or three salaries but transferred a few people over to other departments with no income to cover them. How's that working out?" he said with a not-so-pleasant facial expression.

"It will take time to build up our Medicaid areas, and when that happens, the collections will catch up with what we lost in the transfer."

"Really? I don't believe it," piped in another board member.

Howard looked to Marvin to save him, but the man simply sat there like it wasn't his problem. Howard was now officially peeved. He'd have a word with Marvin after the meeting.

"By the way," Mr. Livingston said, "What's the construction going on all around us? Is there a new building going up and, if there is, what it is? It seemed to happen overnight. A few weeks ago there were quite a few houses surrounding us. They were derelict and city-owned—most of them anyway—but now they're gone. Why?"

"We don't know," Marvin said, finally. "We're looking into it. We've got a call into the city, but it looks like they're stonewalling us for some reason. I was thinking of filing a FOIL or Freedom of Information Law document to see what's happening. We'll let you know at the next meeting."

The chairman stepped in, looking at both Howard and Marvin. "Let us know as soon as you know. Anything could happen in the meantime. Maybe with the construction, we should look at buying this building. If we could get it on the cheap, maybe Mr. Freeman would forgive the demand note and even donate the building to us. It needs work, but I still think it's worth looking into. Don't you?"

"Yes, sir. We'll do that."

"One last thing," said a board member down at the end of the room. "Who knows where Jack Manning is these days? Anybody? You know, if we met with him, maybe he'd let bygones be bygones and help us out financially. What's he worth now, about three hundred million dollars? It's worth a shot. Don't you think?"

"We'll look into that as well, if he's around. We're not sure where he is. We haven't seen him downtown or anywhere else in Troy. For all we know, he took off as soon as he hit. We heard that somewhere."

Marvin looked at Howard with disgust as if to say,

"Lucky bastard. Of all the dumb luck. Now we'll have to kiss his ass and probably apologize as well."

∽∾∽

All the houses were simply gone, and the property leveled for all three acres. The city kept its word and never said a thing to anyone. They sent Jack a bill for $225,000 for the removal and a bill for three houses for $75,000 at $25,000 each, after condemning the properties and paying off the slum landlords. The landlords accepted the payment from the city because all three houses owed back taxes, sewer, and water payments. They took the money and ran. The six families in the three houses that were occupied were given access to small homes up the hill that were owned by the city but vacant. They'd be given an incentive of free rent for a year, and Jack would pay the taxes and power bills as well for the entire year. After that, they'd have first dibs on a reconstructed home formerly owned by the city in the new North Central Village. They signed papers, agreeing to the terms with a nondisclosure clause. If they said anything, they were out on their ears, and they knew it.

It was a good deal so they wouldn't say anything anyway. Jack immediately transferred $300,000 to the city by wire so no one outside a select few would know what was going on. At the end of the year, he'd add $25,000 for the rental costs for the move of the residents.

If and when the city had to divulge the new owners of the property and building, it would simply be The Evangeline Realty Company, Inc., of 69 State Street, Albany, New York, which address was the law offices of Miller, Reynolds, Coleman, and Straus.

There were three layers of corporate ownership even before they ever got to Jack as the owner of the for-profit realty company.

Jack had the firm establish a corporate holding company

that split ownership between several sub-corporations for the nonprofit trust, real estate holdings for projects, and real estate in Florida and on Old Plank Road, if he and Mary were to buy it after six months. He was leaning that way. By the time anyone found out anything, the building would be opened, and Mary and Jack, with city officials standing by, would be cutting the ribbon. There was no gold shovel hitting the ground with group pictures for *The Record* when the first building came tumbling down. It was demolished at dawn and, by noon, three buildings were down. After looking at the remnants, no one could ever believe that families actually lived in these structures. At least the blight was gone, and these families with children were now in free in-code housing, attending the same schools as before. If all went well, they'd attend the new North Central Village Charter School in a few years. Jack needed a discussion with the Freemans before that could happen.

The advertisement for the volunteer manager position went well that weekend with over one hundred responses to the advertisement flowing in by the first of the week. The $60,000 salary and benefits were attractive in this economy in upstate New York. Kristen and the in-house human resources officer would weed out those that didn't match the required position description.

Earlier that day, Jack and Mary sat with Kristen and the HR person and pounded out position descriptions for the new career center as well. Jack and Mary would run the career center from a strategic and planning point of view but would leave the operations to a competent, well paid staff, whom would buy into the project and the concept. They'd serve the hundreds of young people who were put on hold when the TCC program was shut down. They'd train as many as they could as quickly as they could because they wanted these trained individuals working on the North Central Village program building houses, a school, and whatever else that developed.

The ad would go in the following weekend for an executive director, treasurer, human resource professional, two recruiters and three job counselors, three TASC teachers, a construction coordinator and two administrative assistants. They'd be hired two months prior to the completion of the building.

Jack would ask Father Brady if they could use Saint Augustine's School, since it would already be closed down, as potential headquarters before moving into the new facility. None of this would be announced or discussed until after all personnel was hired and offered contracts and a nondisclosure agreement. They'd receive full benefits as soon as they started. As an incentive, Jack would use the old Garden Way Manufacturing of Troy benefit structure, the founder of the Troy Rototiller Company. Each employee would be given four weeks vacation, and they'd receive double pay, while on vacation, so they could actually afford to go somewhere. Garden Way went out of business, but not because of the benefit costs. It actually improved moral, and everyone in the community wanted to work there. It was Wall Street greed where new owners came in, robbed the company blind, and sold off its parts, leaving the company bankrupt and the employees penniless in the process. Another tragedy could have been prevented.

Jack and Mary would also contact graduates of the old TCC career center and see if they'd be interested in working for a few new companies that would be started for the graduates of the program. The old graduates could help jumpstart the businesses and actually rehab several homes right now while the new building was going up. Jack had a lot planned and little time.

CHAPTER 33

Howard called Craig Livingston with the name of the owner of the new building. Marvin had filed a FOIL request, gotten the information, and given it to Howard to make the call. Howard was still upset with Marvin for not backing him up and for sitting at the meeting while saying nothing. Marvin said the city was reluctant to give him anything, but when he said it was for Mr. Livingston, they backed down since Livingston was a well-known local attorney.

"Craig, the property is in the name of The Evangeline Realty Company, Incorporated, with an address of 69 State Street in Albany. It's the Bank of America building on the corner of State and North Pearl in downtown Albany. There are a lot of attorney offices there, so it's probably a cover for the real address. What I do know is that it's a for-profit company. It's not a nonprofit. That might be great news since they'll be our next-door-neighbor. We can ask them for donations once they open. Maybe we can offer one of them a board seat for TCC. At least it's not something to worry about. You know that a for-profit can't compete with us because we're not taxable and they are. Their taxes alone have to be well over $100,000 a year once completed. I think it's going to be some kind of office building. I also think it gives us better exposure since we aren't among a bunch of derelict buildings that were falling down. If anything, our building may be worth more, so I'll contact Mr. Freeman and ask about donating the building to us as a tax write off."

"Call Mr. Freeman as soon as possible. I don't want the demand note and the past due rent hanging over our heads while we're transitioning into Medicaid. Let me know what he says."

"Will do."

☙❧

Jack was driving through the Burgh, heading to the Price Chopper, when he noticed a pickup truck that seemed to be following him since he left Old Plank Road. It was parked off Gypsy Lane and seemed to follow him down the hill once he went past it. He took a few shortcuts and would stop at the Price Chopper later. He went over the bridge to Waterford to go to the post office around the corner. After he stopped, he glanced at the truck as it moved quickly past him. It was an older Dodge Ram, maybe an early 2000 model. He got the first few numbers and letters from the license plate and wrote the numbers down on the back of his bank envelope.

He needed to head to the Bank of America on the corner, in Waterford after he dropped off his letters. He was then heading back to pick up steaks and chicken at the grocery store for dinner. Even though he was now worth millions, he still couldn't resist getting his own groceries. He had a small list for Ethel as well, and he'd pick up her stuff and drop it off on the way home. Going back over the bridge, he noticed the truck, three cars behind him. It made him nervous, so he pulled into the Rite Aid lot right at the Troy end of the bridge. He immediately looked at the truck and got the last three digits of the license.

He called Fred who answered on the third ring. "Hope I'm not disturbing you," Jack said. "I think I'm being followed. Maybe I'm paranoid, but I don't think so. I'm at the Rite Aid at the end of the Burgh by the bridge. It's a Dodge Ram, about fifteen years old." He gave Fred the license plate number and told him he put it together from two separate times he was followed in the last half hour or so.

"Don't go anywhere. I'll call John, and I'll be there in five minutes." Fred only lived at the top of the hill in Waterford. Being retired, he didn't take any other job other than guarding Jack because he paid so well and he liked him. He didn't need anything else. He pulled up in less than five minutes.

Fred rolled down his window. "I'm on the line with Tom Matthews. He'll get me the registration, shortly."

Jack waited in his Explorer while Fred was talking on the phone. John Jefferson pulled up right beside him and waved. He got out of his vehicle and opened the passenger door to Fred's vehicle. Jack got out and hopped into the back seat.

"The owner's name is Marty Sizemore. He lives in South Troy. I don't know what the connection is to you or anyone else. Tom is checking right now. He's forty years old and basically unemployed. He's a part-time bartender at Nick's Tavern in South Troy. He has two DWI convictions and a misdemeanor conviction, which was plea-bargained down from a felony possession for drugs. He used to work at UPS in Menands. He was a driver until he got his second DWI conviction."

Jack had a light bulb go off. "Can you find out if he ever worked with Chuck Falcone, who's still there? He's my ex-wife's live-in boyfriend at my old house. He showed up at the attorney's office when I met with Mark, Debbie, and Maureen a while back. I made him wait in the lobby downstairs at the bank."

"We'll check, but until this Sizemore character actually does something or talks to you, we can do nothing. Do you carry a recorder with you just in case?"

"The phone they gave me from the attorney's probably has one, but I don't know how to use it."

John shook his head. "Amateur." Then he smiled. He looked at Jack's iPhone and showed him how to record a conversation. Then he made Jack record something as he spoke to Fred. It was recorded. Jack finally got it and smiled. He would still buy a small recorder that would be easy to use.

"Thanks. You're a full service provider, aren't you guys?"

"Yep. That's us, boss," said Fred. "Is there anything else we can do for you?"

"I'd like more information on Mr. Sizemore if that's possible."

"We're going to stop downtown at the Troy Police Department and talk to one of our buddies to see if they can follow him around for a while. If it's obvious that he's trying to intimidate you, then we can get him held and maybe, with his convictions, we can scare him into giving up Chuck Falcone. Just maybe."

"Should I talk to Maureen, alone?"

"It can't hurt," they both said.

Jack finished his chores, dropped off Ethel's order, and went back to the house. He put the groceries away and dialed Maureen's cell number. "Maureen? It's Jack. Can I see you for a minute? It's important. I wouldn't call you if I didn't think so…No, it's nothing to do with the annulment but since you mentioned it, how is it going?…You filed the paperwork after discussing it with Kristen? Good. I'll see you down at the bank downtown in a half hour."

He parked along Broadway in downtown and walked through the bank's side entrance. He nodded to Maureen who was just finishing up with a customer. She held up five fingers and pointed to the door. She meant in five minutes outside. After almost twenty-five years of marriage, he knew her sign language pretty well.

She finished up, put on her coat, and told her assistant she'd be back in twenty minutes. She met Jack on Broadway, and they started walking toward the Uncle Sam Mall. They sat on a bench right outside the entrance door. "What's up?" she asked.

"I just wanted to give you a heads up. I hope I'm doing the right thing. It's nothing to do with the annulment or your trust fund, but it could affect it if you were part of this."

"What thing? What're you accusing me of, Jack? I've done nothing. I'm doing what you asked me to do. I don't want to jeopardize anything."

"I'm going to tell you something in confidence, and I hope you keep it that way, for your sake and the kids, especially for Debbie."

"You're scaring me, Jack. What's the problem?"

"Your boyfriend, Chuck, is having me followed by a known felon. His name is Marty Sizemore. He used to work with Chuck. He's now a part time bartender down in South Troy. Maureen, he has two convictions for DWI and a misdemeanor, which started as a felony and was plea-bargained. He's not a nice guy. He's been following me today, and God knows when else. I only spotted him today, and I got the license number and gave it to my ex-FBI guys. I think he knew that I called off the guards this week and then he started up. I believe he worked with Chuck at the UPS facility in Menands. I don't know what Chuck wants, but it can't be good."

"How do you know Chuck has anything to do with this?"

"I don't, but I'm going to find out everything. I've got the resources, the people, and the time, and it won't go well for Chuck if this Sizemore guy accosts me, and he gives up Chuck. My bodyguards are now back on the clock, Maureen. The Troy Police will also be involved now. I'm not telling you what to do, Maureen, but if Chuck is thinking about doing me harm to get more money, he's sadly mistaken. If the annulment goes through, over time, you'll be worth at least a million dollars. If you want to share that with him, go ahead, but it'll never be enough. You're just asking for trouble. You can tell him to stop, but I don't know what good it will do."

"I'll take it under advisement. I haven't told him a thing about what Mark, Debbie, or I are getting. You said we'd lose it if we did. I can't stop him from doing anything, but I'll talk to him."

"If you're afraid of him, we can do something about it, Maureen. I can get you a full time bodyguard anytime you want, twenty-four/seven, only if he leaves and threatens you. I never wanted anything to happen to you, Maureen. I never wished you harm."

"Thank you for telling me. I've no idea what to do. If I have a problem, can I call you? What if Debbie doesn't want to stay at the house anymore? What can I do?"

"I'll pay for a car and room and board at Siena for her. However, she or you will work it off at my new nonprofit like everyone else. She needs discipline, Maureen. She has none and thinks the world owes her a living. It doesn't, and she needs to learn. The money she gets at age thirty-five won't help her unless she changes her attitude. The way it is now, she'll plow through that in a few years and be penniless and then blame the world just like she's doing now. She needs a kick in the ass, Maureen—from you."

With that, he got up from the bench and handed her his card with his new numbers. "Guard this with your life, Maureen, or it could cost you." He walked back to his car and then home. How could Mary and Maureen be so different?

CHAPTER 34

Chuck? I need to talk to you for a minute."

Maureen had just gotten home from work. Her meeting with Jack shook her up. She wasn't sure what she was going to say to Chuck about having her ex-husband tailed. Why was he doing it? Did he think he'd get something out of it? What if Jack was hurt or even killed by this Marty Sizemore. There was nothing in writing about what she was getting for the annulment. For that matter, Jack never put into writing what he was going to do for the kids either. She knew that if she pissed him off, she'd get nothing. Holding off on the annulment to get more money wouldn't work. She saw that in his eyes when they met at the attorney's office.

Her meeting today kind of proved that he didn't want anything or anyone to hurt her or the kids. She knew that in her heart. She also knew that any chance of getting back together with him wasn't going to happen. Maybe time would heal the wounds that she caused him. At least he was going to be generous and make sure she could retire with enough money to last her entire retirement. She wasn't sure if Chuck fit into her plans now, let alone fourteen years from now when she hit sixty-two. If he got his hands on the $500,000 she was promised if she got the annulment, he'd go through it like water. What would she do then? She had to find out what was going on in that head of his. Following Jack was just plain stupid and could get somebody hurt.

"What? What do you want?" he asked her. "I'm going out in a while to meet the guys."

"Okay, fine. I just have one question. Why are you having a friend of yours tail Jack around? What do you plan on doing?"

"Follow him around? What're you talking about? I'm not following anyone," he said.

"Who's Marty Sizemore and what's he to you?"

"I don't know any Marty. Oh, wait, I do. I used to work with him at UPS in Menands before he got fired. I forgot. He's following your ex?"

"Yes, he is, and he won't be happy when the shit hits the fan. You won't be either if you're caught up in anything he's planned. I thought when you came back after our big fight that you were sorry. I said I was sorry. Then you drove us to the attorney's office. I thought you were happy. If you're not, please let me know. We can make other arrangements, Chuck," she said with a dagger in her eyes.

"I'm happy. I don't know anything. I haven't seen him in forever. Tell your ex that I've nothing to do with this."

"I will. I hope you're right, Chuck, because I don't think you'll like the end result."

Chuck left to see his friends at the bar. Before he went downtown, he went to Nick's in South Troy to warn Marty. How could Marty be so stupid? He said he knew how to shadow someone without being spotted. *Yeah, that worked*, Chuck thought. He'd wanted Marty to beat the crap out of Jack, not get caught. Then, after the beating, he'd whisper in his ear that it would continue until he did right by his ex-wife. Chuck promised Marty a big payday if it happened. Chuck wasn't going to get his hands dirty if he could help it. There were million of dollars just waiting to be taken. He needed a better plan. Then, he could dump Maureen and head south where no one would ever find him. Maybe he could have Jack kidnapped and that could get him a few million dollars for his trouble. It wouldn't make a dent in Jack's winnings. Chuck had to put his foot down with Maureen. Leaving her now with nothing wasn't in the plan.

☙❧

Jack and Mary started to review the job applicants for the positions that they advertised in the Times Union. They kept the ads out of *The Record* so local Troy people wouldn't figure out what the new building on the hill would become. The Albany paper had better coverage, and most people in the Capital Region got the *Times Union*. There had to be 500 applicants for each position. Many of those came from out of the region. Jack wanted to give the positions to qualified people who lived in Troy. That was the point of trying to build Troy back up again with the new concept of the North Central Village. He also asked Mary to gather all the names of the graduates and wanted to hold a meeting at Saint Augustine's gymnasium in a few weeks to discuss potential new business opportunities for recent TCC graduates who were now out in the cold. He didn't want that meeting in the paper but placed on telephone polls and word of mouth. He'd call a few and spread the word. He'd start up his Saturday visits and walk the blocks where he once recruited. He'd hand out flyers like before.

"Jack, it's Fred. John and I stopped at the Troy Police Station and talked to a detective friend of ours about this Marty Sizemore character. They think he might be a person of interest in a few local break-ins and rip-offs. We told him all about you and your plans for the city, and he thought that was great. He said they'd all keep an eye out for you as you run around the city getting stuff done. Here's his number." Fred read off the number to him with the extension. "Call him anytime you're around, and they'll have a squad car meander by wherever you're going. As an ex-fed, we're better liked than when we were on duty."

"That's great. Thanks, Fred."

"By the way, Jack, our friend and his partner stopped at the bar, took Sizemore out back, and read him the riot act. They told him that they knew he was working for Chuck Falcone, and if he wanted to go to jail for a long time as a three-time felon, they could make that happen. He bitched and said he had no felonies, but they told him they begged to differ. They told him that, by the end of the week, he'd be working on his third. They told him to let Chuck know that they had him in their sights. Anything happens to you, will happen even worse to him. He got the message, they believe."

"I can't thank you enough, but you guys were right. I need you back here at the house to follow us, but can you make it as invisible as possible or even hire a few more guys to lag behind? We're getting kind of paranoid, at least I am," Jack said.

"I'll call Tom Matthews and see that it happens. Do we send the bill to the attorney's office?"

"Yes, exactly the same. Come tonight. I'll be cooking steaks on the grill with a few cold ones."

"No drinking on the job for us if we're there. Make it iced tea, Jack."

"I hear you. See you later."

Jack called Mary. "Fred and John will be back at the house tonight. We had an incident that I'll tell you about when I get there."

"Are you okay? You don't sound okay."

"I'm a little shook up, but I'll be fine. We need to take more precaution, not less, as our plans come out to the public. You never know what could happen. I'll see you later."

Jack and Mary would be meeting with the new volunteer manager, Kristen, and the HR director for the law office. They'd look for a small office in downtown Troy, only after everyone was hired. The eleventh floor at 69 State Street was working out, and they rented a few more offices to hold interviews for the advertised positions and a conference room for meetings. Jack hated going to Albany every day, but it was necessary until everyone was hired and in place. He'd also make his calls to former graduates from there but then meet them on their own turf in Troy and hold a bigger meeting at Saint Augustine's gymnasium in a few weeks. He needed to develop the chain of command, the organizational chart, and fine tune the job descriptions as the project went from just a career development center to a full blown village strategic plan. He was good at strategy but needed to put in the seat time instead of running around for everything. He needed an executive director for the career center, and then he could work on the village infrastructure concept. He needed to ask Andy to set up another meeting with Mayor Timothy Thompson of Troy to show him the white paper he was working on that included the mission, vision statement, and timeline for his full-blown plan.

CHAPTER 35

J ack, I'd like you to meet your new Volunteer Manager, Ann Cushing," said Kristen.

"It's a pleasure to meet you. This is Mary Evans, my partner in this venture."

"Nice to meet you, and you as well, Mary," Ann said.

"So, where do we begin?" Jack said. "It's been a while since we've had a staff or anyone other than our favorite attorney, Kristen, and her entire law office at our disposal."

Kristen turned to Ann. "Please bring Jack and Mary up to date on your background and education and how you fit the job description."

Ann did exactly that. She was thirty-two years old. She had an MBA from Siena, was just recently married, and lived in Clifton Park. She worked for nine years, after getting her MBA, at two places—the first in Schenectady at a major nonprofit and the second in Clifton Park, where she was now employed. She had given her two-week notice and was now ready to start.

"Why did you take the job?" Mary asked.

"To be perfectly honest, I'm scared to death over whether I did the right thing or not. I was doing fine at my current position, but most of the staff were older, and the organization was stagnant and going nowhere. I just couldn't see myself sitting there for the next twenty years or so, doing nothing. Mrs. Sanderson explained what you were trying to do and that you hit the Powerball and were making plans to bring back the city of Troy. I thought that was wonderful, and I wanted to be part of it, even a small part. You're starting from the ground up, and I think that's exciting. She also told me about you and Mary and what you've accomplished and what more you wanted to do to make it even better. I applaud you. I'm not a brownnoser, by any means, and you'll see that once you get to know me," she said.

"I like you already," said Jack. "You remind me of two ladies I already know well."

"Who did you have in mind?" Kristen said, looking at Mary. She laughed. Mary and Ann laughed as well.

"I also, in the short time I've been here, looked at several resumes and applications for the positions you advertised, other than mine," Ann went on, " I think you might like to see these two applications. Both of these just came in. One is for executive director, and the other is for the treasurer position. Do you know a Howard K. Singer, MSW, and a Marvin Manville? They applied for the two positions. Evidently, they're both employed by the Troy Community Council, which is a nonprofit in Troy. There are several applications from people who work at the TCC. I know the organization well since I interviewed there several years ago for a position. Both of you worked there, didn't you? At the TCC?"

Mary and Jack burst out laughing. Kristen joined them. Ann looked confused. "Did I say something wrong?" she asked, turning red.

"No, No. Not at all," Mary said. "Those two fired both Jack and me close to a year ago. That's why we're doing this. Have you heard about the new building going up in Troy, right next to the TCC?

"Yes, it's been in the papers, but nobody seems to know what it is."

It's ours. It's the new career center we're building to continue our work after those two idiots shut us down. We now have Jack's fifty million dollars to play with in a trust fund and my fifteen million dollars if needed. Hope that helps," Mary said, still laughing.

"Oh my God," Ann said. "I can't believe this. I knew you were doing something in Troy, but Kristen and the HR director didn't say what, exactly. That's beyond belief. I think that's great. You took your winnings and are putting it back into the city? That's great," she repeated.

"Well, thank you, but it's not all altruistic. I'm keeping sixty-eight million dollars after taxes for myself and other projects down the road. Mary can do what she wants. And if you're guessing, we're best friends, and that's it."

By this time, Ann's head was spinning. She laughed about the applications but still wanted to be taken seriously. It was her first full week on the job, and she wanted to make a good impression. "I did pick out a few applications for each of the jobs, and I think you'd be impressed by the quality of the people who answered your ad. I must say, the ads were very well written, to the point, and the salaries and benefits are more than competitive in this market. If you can afford it, you'll get the cream of the Capital Region crop for those jobs."

Jack told her about his benefits package that included double pay for four weeks while the person was on vacation and that made her day. Ann was so excited that she couldn't contain herself. "I can't believe this. Thank you to whoever approved my hiring. I'm thrilled to death."

"Just remember, you'll be working for a couple of people who got fired and two ex-nuns, so how good could it be?" he said, laughing.

"Are you kidding me? I went to Siena. I can handle ex-nuns, not Franciscan Friars, like at Siena. They're a whole different breed of people."

"Trust us. We know," said Kristen.

Andy popped his head into the eleventh floor offices. "I've got Tim Thompson on the phone. Can you make tomorrow at two p.m. at his office?"

"Sure."

Mary and Jack gathered up a bunch of applications and resumes, and Jack gave Ann his card with all their numbers on it. He invited her up to their new house on Old Plank Road to show her where the real action was taking place, and she accepted. He also asked her if she'd like to meet the mayor with them, and she was shocked. She said that would be wonderful and that today was the best she'd had in a long time and thanked them both. Andy had plans for the next day through noon and would meet them at Tim's office at the Cluett building on River Street at two p.m.

The next day, Andy once again introduced Jack and then Mary, Kristen, and Ann Cushing to the mayor. They went into the conference room, and there was coffee and snacks waiting for them. After making themselves comfortable, the mayor invited his deputy to join them.

"What can we do for you? So far, so good. We're very excited about your new building going up. Thank you for promptly sending us the check for reimbursement for the demolition and property acquisition for the three properties we didn't own."

"To be clear, the check is actually our payment of taxes for the first two years so you wouldn't have to come up with the cash."

"Yes, of course. That's clear and correct. Sorry about that. So, what can we do for you?"

"The building will be up in a few months, and the parking lot will be ready before winter so we can use it when we open in February. What I'm about to tell you shouldn't leave this room and, hopefully, it will benefit the entire city of Troy. As you know, I hit the lottery for a lot of money. I think you know that Mary and I were fired by TCC when they closed the career center. That's what we're building brand new and better than ever. As soon as our new career center opens, I made a deal with the Freemans, whom you know, to buy the TCC building and their demand note. I'm planning on putting in a million dollars into the TCC facility, in spite of their losing business plan. I plan on giving them enough business from my students' families that they'll break even. However, it will be without their current administrative team, or there will be no TCC. What I want to talk to you about is our plans for the next ten years at that location in the north central section of Troy."

Ann Cussing sat there, mesmerized, along with Andy, Kristen, the mayor, and his deputy. All eyes were on Jack as he pulled out a rendering of his vision. It was completed a few days earlier, and the only one privy to it was Mary.

"I've allocated fifty million dollars to this project if I can get agreement from the city of Troy and any other government agency that I need help from. What I don't need is red tape and government money. If I need more than fifty million dollars, I have it already. So, there will be no discussion on that topic."

They all shook their heads but Mary. They'd never heard of such a proposal. Jack pulled out the architectural drawing that he had John and Pete Traynor draw up with the help of his two other contractors and the association president.

"What I envision is called The North Central Village' It consists of the properties from Hoosick Street to Federal Street to the south and from Fifth Avenue to the east to River Street at the west end. It's about an eight square block area that might just be the worst section in the Capital Region. I want to create a community and a village that everyone will be proud of and who'll want to live there because they'll have a chance to own a completely rehabbed house, at no additional cost to them. The village will have a park in the exact center, and the street will be paved with cobblestones or brick and closed to traffic on the weekend. The new career center will be at the heart of the community along with the TCC building. A new North Central Village Charter School, grades pre-K through high school, if approved, will be built at the heart of the village. Those graduates will be given scholarships to Hudson Valley Community College, a full ride and then tuition assistance to any four-year college. We're looking into submitting an application as soon as the center is opened. We'll add funding to the school as an incentive, and we've other financial backers to make it work.

"I looked, and there are over two hundred substandard houses sitting in that eight-block radius. Half are owned by the city, some by individuals, and the rest by slum landlords. I want the city to donate their properties to the Evangeline Trust to rehab at no cost to the owners. They'll receive reduced taxes for the first five years and graduate to full assessment after ten. For new owners, the buildings will be sold as affordable housing and the monthly rent will be no higher than what they now pay in rent for substandard housing. The slum landlords will be foreclosed on by the city, and I'll buy the property to be used for new townhouses if they can't be rehabbed. By the way, the rehabs and construction will be done by career center graduates, both current and future, and they'll be hired by contractors already selected to provide jobs for these residents or by companies started by these graduates or by myself once we get rolling.

"Schoolteachers who teach at the charter school will be given free housing that they'll own if they stay ten years. The new owners will fully own the houses after ten years. If they up and move and sell the property, they'll have to pay us back for the work. I expect that the city of Troy will put in new LED old-fashioned gaslight style streetlights and provide a police sub station right next to the school, which I'll fully pay for. This project will take five to ten years but not because of lack of funding. I'd also like a gate-like structure put up at the entrances of each road that's embossed, "North Central Village." It should look just like the wrought iron entrance to Russell Sage College on their third street entrance.

"By year three, I want to see if we can pick up the old church and lyceum down the street to be used as a tech incubator program, just like RPI's incubator program. RPI also has its own technology center in the old chapel right on campus across from the library. So, having a tech center in an old church isn't a new idea. If approved, we'll offer space to new emerging tech companies coming out of the local colleges, including RPI, Russell Sage, Siena, Hudson Valley and the University at Albany, or any other institution. In lieu of rent, heat, light, and electric, those companies, who occupy space at the tech center, will offer training and internships to our career center students. We don't just want construction training with all these resources around us. We want high tech, EMT, and health-related certifications all leading to jobs right in the new village or nearby. This may be the only opportunity for kids living here to see what can be possible. For many years, RPI sent student volunteers and professors to mentor students in Troy's public housing projects. They can do the same here but receive the benefit of our minority students' cutting-edge education and certifications.

"I know that's a mouthful. Any questions?"

"Wow," said Tim. The deputy mayor was speechless. Everyone was completely focused on Jack.

The deputy simply asked, "Why would you do this? You'll spend fifty million dollars and more if needed? Why?"

"Do you have any idea what having two hundred million dollars is like? Well, I didn't either. I don't need it to be happy, but I'm certainly not sad that I have it. I'm keeping sixty million plus for myself. I think that's enough. I couldn't spend that in several lifetimes. This vision came to fruition after I hit the lottery, but it began a long time ago. How many of you wrote down what you'd do if you hit the lottery for a million, ten million, or even a hundred million? Do you know how much three hundred million is? After the cash discount by forty percent, it still leaves almost two hundred million. Then, if I keep it, it's taxed at almost fifty percent. So, why not give it to the residents of Troy instead of to the federal government and New York State where it will wind up being pissed away by someone who wants to get elected? No offense, guys," Jack said, as he studied the mayor and his deputy.

"I'm not naïve. If you guys help, I'll help you get reelected. I really don't care what side of the aisle you're on, quite frankly. This is one hundred percent nonpolitical. But I believe that this is the right thing to do. We can take back Troy, one village at a time. Next is the area north of this, then the Burgh and South Troy. The hill areas are all owned by RPI anyway so who cares? I want this to be a model for a small city, not New York or Chicago but for the Troy's of the world. This shouldn't be done with government money except to fix the sidewalks, the roads, the lighting, and infrastructure that's owned by everyone.

"Every rich person who has one hundred million dollars or more should pick a spot in the city where he or she lives and fix it with their own money. They don't need a handout. If we do this, we could be the envy of the world. By the way, Mary and I'll do this for no more than ten years. I'll be sixty, and I'm moving to Key West for most of the year, but I'll keep a place here. We just wanted to help. So, in finishing, what turned out to be revenge and me being pissed off at the administration of TCC for firing Mary and me might just turn out to be something exceptional. This isn't the urban renewal of the 1960s and '70s. This is minority homeownership, job security for a tech world, and a hand up to those who never got a break in life. This is community renewal, not a catch phrase."

"What do you want us to do right now?" asked the mayor.

"As soon as we have the grand opening, we'll purchase the TCC and start the rehab. That'll be late February into March next year. Construction starts in April, and for every block we rehab, I want the streets done with new lighting. We want the entrance signs placed at each main street, so everyone knows what's happening. If anyone complains, I'll buy him or her off, and I'm not kidding. I'd like to prove that, with enough money, done correctly, without red tape and government interference, we'd succeed in bringing our cities back, one village at a time."

"Got it," said the mayor. "We'll keep it as quiet as we can until we can't. I have to speak to the city council but since they're 'us,' I think they'll go along with a fifty-plus million dollar investment into the community with no catches. This is almost like getting a fifty-million-dollar grant," he said.

"That's it, exactly," said Jack.

On the way out, he said to everyone, "I think that went well."

Ann said, "I've never been a part of anything like this. What you just said is an understatement. They're ecstatic."

Andy and Kristen said the same thing. Mary just smiled. She thought back to the small team they had at the TCC and what they were able to accomplish with next to nothing for a budget.

This had opened up a whole new world. She still had her ideas, and some would be part of Jack's vision. However, as a teacher, she wanted to make sure that education came first. Without that, everything else went away. There were no jobs for the undereducated in the twenty-first century. A high school degree didn't mean anything. College alone didn't mean anything. People needed on-the-job training and certifications in the new tech world, and she wanted to be part of the solution. She was still thinking about the Lansingburgh Academy.

She'd talk to Jack to remind him of her plans as well. She was so proud of Jack. In six months he'd come light years ahead of where he was. He wasn't really management back then but more of a hands-on teacher. Now, she could see him leading a vision and the charge for a change in thinking about how communities evolved.

Chapter 36

D ad? It's Debbie," she said and then silence.

"Hi, Debbie. How are you? What's up?"

"Can I see you? I need to talk to you. I know it's been a while, and I know I've been difficult but I really need to talk to you."

"Sure. When?"

"How about tonight? Can I meet you at the Notty Pine Tavern tonight around six p.m., alone?"

"Sure, I'll meet you in the back by the family entrance. I'll be there at six p.m.," he said. He laughed to himself that the Notty Pine Tavern had been in business for seventy years and never replaced the original K in its name. So, everyone knew it as the Notty Pine or just the Pine.

Jack finished up what he was doing and headed out from home. He took Oakwood to the end where it hit Hoosick Street and then across for a block and up the hill, which was a one-way street. If you didn't live in Troy, you wouldn't have the foggiest idea how the streets ran. You'd have to go four blocks out of your way to park near the tavern. The Pine had the best pizza in town by far. There's absolutely nothing better than a Pine pizza, hot and right from the oven. They had the Cob specialty, which had the cheese on the bottom and the sauce on the top. You ordered it plain with no toppings to get the full effect. You've never had a pizza that tasted like this. Jack's mouth started watering as he pulled up to the curb, taking the last spot open by the tavern. He spotted Maureen's car parked in the back lot. Debbie didn't have a car and shared Maureen's whenever she could. He met her inside the door.

Debbie said hi and smiled at him. There was no hugging or kissing. Jack felt awkward at best and simply asked the waitress for a booth. He, Maureen, and the kids had come here forever, so he knew all the staff. They said hi to Jack and Debbie by name as they took a booth near the back TV.

"Eight-cut Cob, Jack?" said the waitress.

"Yes, but on the way out, can I get another two to take home? I promised I wouldn't forget this time." He didn't think that she knew that he was divorced from Maureen and this was a very awkward meeting with his daughter. He ordered a beer and Debbie got a coke.

The waitress came back with the red pepper flakes, shaker cheese, extra napkins, plates, forks, and knives. She dropped everything in the middle of the table. "Be just a few minutes, Jack."

He nodded and looked at Debbie as if to say "Well, I'm here, start talking."

She took the cue. "Dad, I can't live at home anymore. I can't stand Chuck living there, and Mom isn't herself. All they do is fight. I've another year at Siena and then two more for my masters, and I won't make it, if I stay there another minute."

"Well, Debbie, you're twenty-one going on twenty-two and a grown woman. Quite clearly, you're an adult, and you took sides when your mother threw me out of the house. You ignored me, and you treated me like crap and never returned a call. Now you need help, and you think I'm going to solve your problem? You hurt me more than you'll ever know." He looked at her and was never more serious in his life. The pizza was delivered, and Jack thanked the waitress. He took his knife and cut the pieces so he could slide the slices onto their plates. He put cheese and red pepper flakes on his and took a bite. He honestly believed it was the best thing he'd ever eaten, bar none. Now, he felt a little better and looked at Debbie. She started to cry when he told her what he thought of her actions.

"Debbie, I won't hold a grudge against you. As a matter of fact, I believe I set up a trust for you starting at age thirty-five, for a few million dollars that you don't deserve. I could think of a hundred people who deserve it more than you. Here's what I'll do for you. The trust stays as is. I'll pay for you to stay at the Siena dorm until you graduate, and then I'll pay for your master's and for a car and insurance. However, there are no free rides. I'll add it all up and pay for everything as needed, but you'll be required to pay one-half of every dollar you need.

"You'll start tomorrow paying it back, at the same volunteer rate required by everyone else, who needs support. You'll get a better deal because you're my daughter, my ungrateful daughter at best, but still my daughter. As an example, if next year's tuition, room and board, car and insurance, and your masters add up to fifty thousand dollars, which it certainly might, you owe back twenty-five thousand at the volunteer rate of twenty dollars per hour, or one thousand, two hundred fifty hours. You'll check in with Ann Cushing, our new volunteer manager, and you work on whatever project she decides. It's out of my hands. I'll call her and tell her so. Here is her information for you to call her and set up an appointment. She's at Sixty-Nine State Street in downtown Albany, the eleventh floor, for now.

"I think you'll be sorting requests for money into several categories, not unlike your own request. You'll sign and date a notarized legal contract that you'll honor. If you fail, I'll sue you. Is all of this clear? This is a business transaction. If you'd like to once again become family, I'll be more than happy to welcome you back with open arms. Debbie, I love you, but your selfishness and lack of loyalty hasn't been lost on me."

"I guess saying I'm sorry doesn't cut it, huh?"

"No. Actions speak louder than words. In fact, I'll make a deal with you. If you have any friends who need help and want to work off a loan at twenty dollars an hour, contact Ann, and we'll set up a meeting. They can work at a number of new programs that'll be rolled out very shortly."

"Thank you. I'll do that. Are you going to tell me what you're working on? I understand that you and Mary Evans are partners in some big projects that you'll be funding. Mark told me to call you by the way, not Mom."

"I'll tell you if you become part of our venture. Otherwise, you've no reason to know what we're planning or doing. That's business, Debbie, not family matters."

They ate their pizza. Debbie thanked him for his help, and she said she'd call him as often as she could, and she'd like to see him more often if he wanted her to. He said he did and gave her his new unlisted cell number to only be used for father-daughter activities, not business. From now on, if she had a monetary request, she was to write it up and give it to Ann Cushing who'd take care of the pending issue at that time. The waitress came out and gave Jack the extra pizzas to go. He left the tip, paid the bill, and they headed out.

He said, "I have time next week if you want to look at cars. I'll tell Ann that you'll need insurance and registration. You can learn to take care of those items yourself. It's grownup time, Debbie."

"I know. I'll try not to let you down," she said.

"There's no trying. You won't let me down, Debbie. You have everything to gain. And, I do love you. I've never stopped loving you. I was hurt, but I'll get over it. Your mother is another issue all together. For that, I've moved on. I don't want to move on from you and Mark."

She went up to him and gave him a kiss and a hug. "Thank you, Dad. I appreciate it. I'll do better, and I do love you. I hated you, but that's on me."

Jack headed back to Old Plank Road as quickly as possible. There was nothing better than a hot pizza right out of the oven but nothing worse than a cold one. He kicked the door to the house because his hands were full and John Jefferson opened it. They were back as bodyguards after the incident in Waterford. Fred's eyes picked up, and he looked at the pizza boxes, hungrily.

"Get back, guys," said Mary. "I'm first. I ordered the Cobb, and you're second so get in line. Open me a beer-please," she added as she grabbed several slices onto a plate. The guys dug in. It didn't take ten minutes before all of one pizza was gone and half the other. They looked like they were in ecstasy.

"How'd it go with Debbie, Jack?"

"Much better than I expected. I think Maureen's love life has taken a toll on our daughter's mental health. I'll pay for her to move to the dorm and get her a car but she's to report to Ann tomorrow to get her volunteer-slash-not-so-volunteer assignments. I think she'll learn. She said she hated me but not now. I hope it's not the money talking because that won't save the day. I guess we'll have to play it by ear."

"You're a good guy, Jack," said Fred.

"Thanks."

"How did dinner go with your dad?" Debbie's mom asked.

"It went better than expected. He said he'll help me, but I have to earn it. He'll pay everything up front, but I'll have to volunteer at twenty dollars an hour and report in to someone named Ann Cushing. Do you know her?"

"No, who's she?"

"Dad said it was their volunteer manager."

Who's 'their'?"

"I believe he means Mary and he and whoever else is working on his projects."

"I don't know anything about his projects. Do you?"

"No. I'm simply to report to Ann Cushing tomorrow and take it from there. I called Siena. They said they have an open dorm room, a single. The girl left school because of a death in the family and I can have the room for the rest of the semester and then a room for all of next year, if I get my bid in early. By the way, he's taking me car shopping next week. Knowing Dad, it'll be a used car, but that's better than what I have now."

"Who's moving? You, Debbie? Where?" Chuck said as he came into the living room.

"I have a dorm room at Siena. I'm moving in this weekend," Debbie said.

"Who's paying for that?" he asked.

"Not you," Maureen said. She then turned back to Debbie. "That's great. I'll help you move. If you need a car or ride just take mine, and I'll help you all day Saturday and Sunday if needed."

"Thanks, Mom."

With that, she looked at Chuck and went to her room. She'd pack as quickly as possible. She finally realized that only her mother brought on her mother's problems. Debbie started to think about how quickly she took sides with her mother because she thought that was natural for a girl. Now, after all these months, she realized that her mother started the ball rolling by hooking up with Chuck long before her father even knew about it. Debbie also realized that her mother taking her father to the cleaners only made her realize even more how wrong her mother was and how wrong this Chuck was for her. Debbie knew she had to get out. She just hoped that her mother would come to her senses and throw him out.

CHAPTER 37

J ack, when you get a chance, I want you to catch up on how the annulment is going," Kristen said. "Do you have time to come down this afternoon? I've been working with Maureen, and we filed all the papers, but I want to go through the process with you and the timing. It's easier than before but definitely not easy."

"Can I meet you for lunch? I have to meet with the Freemans this morning, and we should be finished by twelve-thirty p.m. or so."

"Sure. Let's grab a sandwich down the street. Call me when you hit the parking lot, and I'll meet you by the back-door. We can head to the Greenhouse Restaurant at Fifty North Pearl. Is that okay?"

"It'll be closer to one p.m."

"Just call me. Thanks," Kristen said.

Jack headed up to see the Freeman's in the Albia section of Troy. He was there a while ago when he asked them if he could purchase the TCC building. He and the Freemans hit it off very well. When he invited them to the cookout on Old Plank, it went even better. Louis even suggested that the purchase price could be turned into scholarships for the new center's graduates. Jack wanted to give them his ex-panded vision on how a North Central Village would be put together in a timely manner. The Freemans were toward the end of their lives, and Jack wanted to spend the next ten years, maximum, toward this project. This would be a perfect time to put their heads together to discuss a new charter school for the planned village. He pulled up in front of their house on Pawling Avenue and parked. It was a busy street heading toward downtown. He'd have loved to make another run to Jack's Hamburgers in Wynantskill, but he had to meet Kristen by one p.m. He got out of his SUV, walked up the steps, and rang the bell. Mrs. Freeman met him at the front door.

"Hello, Mr. Manning. How are you?" Addie said.

"Please, call me Jack."

"Please come in, Jack. Louis is on the phone and will be in shortly." They headed to the living room where Mrs. Freeman had already placed a pot of coffee and pastries. "Please take a seat and have some coffee and Danish."

"Thank you, Mrs. Freeman."

"If it's Jack, then I'm Addie," she said and smiled.

"Thank you, Addie. Here comes Louis. Hi, Louis. How are you?" he said.

"Alive. Not bad for eighty-one, you know? Addie's not bad for seventy-eight either, but we're starting to feel the ruminations of old age."

"Well, I hope I make it to eighty-one, Louis or even seventy-eight, Addie," said Jack. "I wanted to tell you the entire story of what I want to do in North Central Troy. Do you have time so I can tell you everything to date? I have to be in Albany at one p.m. to meet Kristen, my attorney."

"All we have is time, Jack," said Addie. "Please go ahead. We'll let you know when it's twelve-thirty p.m. so you can head out. We're very appreciative of your time. Most people come to ask us for money. This is a new phenomenon. By the way, we just got a call from Howard Singer, who wants to meet us this week. Do you have any idea why?"

"I'd assume that he sees the new building going up next door and that it might be an opportunity to obtain your TCC building because it would be more valuable with an upscale street coming to fruition. That's my guess. I also guess that since they can't pay the rent and you have a demand note from them that they'd like you two to donate the building to them. That's what I foresee, but I could be wrong."

"I don't think you're wrong," said Addie. "Not at all."

Jack went into a long discussion and told them exactly how much he was going to spend on this project. He went step by step with them so they'd understand his vision of what fifty million dollars should and could buy. He went through the grand opening of the new building and how he'd allocated a million dollars a year to its support for at least ten years. He told him that if the TCC building was free from contamination, that he'd upgrade the building for another million and subcontract various services to TCC to keep them afloat, only if Howard and Marvin were gone and new management put into place. He then told them about the rehabbing of over 200 substandard houses in the eight-block area, a new tech center at the old church, and a park in the middle of the village with a bandstand for concerts. He then told them that he wanted to build a charter school, grades pre-K through high school with those students also receiving career training at his new center, followed by a free college education.

"How much do you think the charter school will cost to build?" Louis asked.

"First, it has to be built for the student population. I believe that we should have a school to support up to seven hundred students, or fifty per class size. So, fifty times twelve grades plus fifty in pre-K and Kindergarten would be seven hundred students at the end of ten years. We'd start with pre-K through grade six for now and then add a grade, each year, as the students moved up. I've already checked and a school that size would cost around eight million dollars up to ten million dollars but no more. The problem that I have is that ten million dollars would rehab two hundred homes in the area. I'll do it, but I don't want to spend all my money on just a school without the necessary family-oriented neighborhood, with family owned homes, to support it."

"What, if in addition to the proceeds from the sale of the TCC building going into scholarships, Addie and I donate half of the cost of the building? Would that get you over the hump?"

"I'd sign the papers immediately. The reason charter schools fail is that the cost of the facility causes large deficits so they can't hire the proper teachers or staff to be successful. I'd only have them pay for heat, light, electric, and general maintenance. A trust could be set up for ownership of the facility with a long-term lease included. That would work great," Jack said.

"Can we think it over, Jack?" Louis asked. "It's a lot of money. Don't get me wrong, we have it, and we have no children to leave it to. We want to give the money to the best organization who deserves it, and so far, you seem to be it and fully committed with your own money."

"We can wait, Louis and Addie," said Jack. "There's no rush. However, it takes a year to get a charter, and we need to have a full commitment upfront if it's to be approved by the New York State Education Department. By the way, a charter school in New York State receives eighty percent of what student aid is for any particular district. That would be about fourteen thousand dollars per student or nine million, eight hundred thousand dollars when at full capacity of seven hundred students. That would more than cover the expenses and leave a nice pot at the end for field trips, college visits, and sports programs."

"You've certainly thought a lot about this haven't you, Jack?"

"It's not just winning the money that made me think of this. I've been thinking about it for the last ten years. What does this poor community really need to succeed? They need safe, affordable housing that they own and to have pride in their neighborhood, a good local education, leading to an affordable college degree with job training and certifications that lead to twenty-first century, real, good-paying jobs. Then they can support a family and have benefits, including affordable health care as well. Single mothers working three or four jobs at minimum wage, with no benefits, only adds to the downward spiral of poverty. If I can do all that with my money for an eight-block area, then I'll be happy. Now I'll get off my soapbox."

"I'll take your soapbox anytime, Jack. We're in," said Addie. "Aren't we, Louis?"

"Of course. Let us know what's needed and when. In case something happens to us, we'll instruct our attorney to redraw our wills to include those exact provisions as they happen."

"I don't know what to say. You're very honorable people, and I'm glad to have met you when I did. I want to call on you as my personal adviser. I don't know everything, and neither do the people I've relied on. I need your age, wisdom, and experience, and I'm not flattering you. You made it on your own. I need you to tell that to the kids who come through our program. Thank you from the bottom of my heart."

With that, Jack headed out to Albany after Addie pointed out the time to him.

He met Kristen at the Greenhouse Restaurant at exactly one p.m. after parking in the bank lot. It was a block away. Kristen was already there. He'd called her instead of meeting in the lot. She ordered for both of them, and his meal was already at the table. Kristen had a full day still left and only had a half hour to give to Jack.

"Thanks for meeting me, Kristen. So, how are the annulment wars?"

"Don't laugh," she said. "You've no idea how lucky you are if you really want this annulment. If it weren't for Pope Francis, we wouldn't have a shot after you being married almost twenty-five years. Remember, you asked me to work with Maureen on an annulment because I know canon law and I do work for the Diocese. I've also done several annulments, not for the law firm, but as a volunteer to the church and the bishop. I really know what I'm doing when it comes to this," she said.

"I know, and I appreciate it," Jack said.

She continued. "The reforms the pope announced last year remove the requirement for a second judgment on annulment decisions, a process that would lengthen the process by many months. They also reduced the first tribunal to one member of the clergy and allow local bishops to fast track the annulment process in certain cases—for example, petitions not contested by a spouse. I don't believe that in your case and Maureen's, either of you will contest it."

"That certainly true in my case."

"The pope's announcement sent a clear message that the church is sympathetic to those with flawed marriages," she said. "The church wants you to do this. There's been a lot of misunderstanding, and the paradox is it's kind of hard to get the word out to people who feel that they've been banished. So, your timing couldn't be better. In order to obtain a declaration of nullity, Maureen had to approach the diocesan tribunal. Most applications for nullity that are heard by the tribunal are granted because one or both parties are judged to have given invalid consent. She stipulated that was the case. It used to take forever with different layers of consent, and now you can get your annulment in twelve to eighteen months, and we're hoping for twelve. How's that sound?"

"Are you kidding? That sounds great. Thank you."

"Can I ask a personal question, Jack?"

"Sure," he said.

"Are you doing this for Mary? Is she even aware that you're asking for an annulment?"

"I've never said anything to Mary. I'm a Catholic, and whatever I did to Maureen so that she'd cheat on me and get an immediate divorce, I didn't deserve. I never cheated on her. I want the annulment because if I ever decide to get married again, I want to be married in the church. And yes, it's also because of Mary. I'd never pursue a relationship with her if it didn't include marriage in the church because of her background and beliefs."

"I thought so," said Kristen. "I'd never say anything, but I think this is certainly the right approach. You're best friends, and that could lead to something else. It'd certainly be good to build on a friendship first. Liking each other certainly improves the situation. Besides, she knows what you went through, and she's been at your side since you left your house."

"Thrown out of my house," he said and laughed.

"I stand corrected," said Kristen. "That's where we are, and I think everything is moving ahead quiet smoothly. By the way, I know about the million dollars for Maureen, and I'm not really pleased but I understand the situation, and I can live with it. It might not be the first annulment received that way," she surmised.

"I'd never get it, otherwise, Kristen."

Jack walked back with her to the bank building. He needed some cash from his checking account. She waited for him, and they went upstairs. Kristen told him that Ann told her that his daughter Debbie would be there that afternoon, and he might want to say hello. He thanked her and got off on the eleventh floor before Kristen's twelfth-floor exit.

He walked into the office, and the ladies were still busy sorting the requests into various piles. He went over to Ann's office, knocked on the door, and waved to Ann and Debbie. They were just finishing up their introductory meeting.

"Sorry to interrupt. I just wanted to say hello to my daughter and welcome her to the never ending request unit," he said with a laugh.

"I can see that," said Debbie and she smiled at her father. Ann walked out to give them a few moments to speak to each other. Debbie told him that she was very surprised at the organization he'd assembled in such a short time. He'd called Ann earlier and told her that she could tell Debbie anything she deemed appropriate but to make her sign a confidentiality agreement, especially concerning her mother knowing what they were doing. She'd signed just before he arrived.

Debbie thanked him for allowing her to move into the dorms and for the car that they'd be picking out. He told her he was pleased to have her and it seemed to continue to break the ice in what was a considerable stalemate of wills. As she left, she gave him a kiss on the cheek and a hug, a rather big deal in Jack's eyes. Maybe there was hope for their future.

After she left, Jack and Ann sat down, and she told him what she thought about his daughter's potential, working not just in the "mail room," but also in her long-term ambitions in the nonprofit world. She said with a master's degree she could fit in quite nicely into a number of positions at the new career center.

Jack really liked Ann because she didn't pull any punches and told him exactly what she thought. She also proved her commitment to what they planned to do. He told her that he wanted her fully involved in all aspects of the new operation for the career center, for the TCC, and for the new village and school. She said that it was a remarkable opportunity for her at such a young age, and she thanked him again.

She asked him when they'd move to Troy and he said, "What're you waiting for? Pick an office close to the new building and move. Sign whatever you need to sign, and it's yours."

She was in shock. When he left, she called Kristen and then Mary and told them what he said and they both said, "He's the boss so do what he told you. He obviously trusts you. He doesn't trust a lot of people after what's happened to him, so count your blessings. He obviously likes you a lot." It made her day.

Jack was meeting with several prior TCC graduates at the Ale House in Troy at six p.m. He wanted them on board even before some of the new employees were hired. He knew their talents and wanted to present them an opportunity before he hired others who may not have had the same commitment. It was around three-thirty p.m. so he headed back to Old Plank Road to meet Mary and bring her to the meeting. They hadn't even seen each other but in passing since they moved into the ranch house on the hill. She was still deciding on what to do with Saint Augustine's school and gymnasium, and he wanted to update her on everything he was doing. That was, everything except the annulment. That wouldn't be divulged until he was ready.

CHAPTER 38

They arrived at the Ale House on River Street in Troy just as Tara Wilson and Brandon Moore came across the street from the parking lot. They exchanged hellos and hugs, and Jack asked if the rest were coming. Brandon said as far as he knew all five would be there. Jack wanted this meeting before any big meeting at Saint Augustine's gymnasium. Brandon said he was surprised that Jack called him but was glad to hear him from him. He congratulated Jack on hitting the lottery but wasn't boisterous about it. These kids were cool to the nth degree. They had so much crap thrown at them at such a young age, they didn't expect much from anyone because that's what they got. They felt that way about most everyone, everyone that was except for Jack and Mary. They never lied to them, and they kept their promises. The young people knew that Jack and Mary had been fired but wanted to see what was up.

They walked through the bar area, saying hello to friends. Jack hadn't seen his old pals in a long time, ever since he left home. This was his hangout, and no matter how long you've been away, it didn't matter—it was like yesterday. No one said a word about the lottery. They went to the back and saw Imani Wilson, Cameron Mitchell, and Jayden Anderson sitting at the back table by the overhead TV. It was like homecoming week. They weren't strangers to the Ale House since Jack always held birthdays and success days there, and then they started to come on their own after graduating from the TCC. They had the best chicken wings on the planet. It was a dive, but it was their dive.

"Hey, guys," Jack said to the three already seated. They gave hugs all the way around. They'd already ordered wings, beer, and soda by the pitcher.

"Our treat," said Cameron. "Wasn't always that way, but it is now," he said.

"Thanks, guys," said Mary. "How are you all?"

They told her. Tara Robinson at twenty-three was the second oldest. She had arrived at the old TCC career center as a hapless dropout at eighteen, with two children and no husband. She'd struggled for her then GED—now TASC— and passed with flying colors. She went to HVCC for one year for the EMT training and passed the certification test from the state. She now worked—this her second year—for Tri-City Ambulance, right around the corner from her home and the Ale House. She walked to work after putting her oldest on the bus and the youngest with the babysitter.

Imani Wilson hadn't fared as well. At nineteen, she was from the last graduating class. After graduation, TCC closed down the department, and there was no follow up for jobs or additional training. She'd been on the dole since early last year and was very depressed, to say the least. Brandon Moore was in the same boat at twenty-one—no job, no follow up, and no prospects.

Cameron Mitchell, along with Tara became the two most successful to date. Cameron, age twenty-five, graduated from the program and went on to SUNY Poly in Albany for training in cleanroom maintenance. It might not seem like much, but cleanroom specialists pulled down $70,000 a year, plus benefits. He was set for life and could go on at SUNY Poly to get an engineering degree if he so chose.

Jayden Anderson went the college route. He was in the previous TCC class before closing and made out fine. He was twenty-two and graduated from Hudson Valley Community College with an AAB in business and was now a junior at Oneonta State College, studying to be an accountant. These five represented the kids in the area that traveled many routes to get here. Some had to get off drugs before entering the program, and, to them, that was the hardest choice. The program was a piece of cake compared to where they came from.

Their orders came, and they began to eat. As they did, Jack relayed the story of what had transpired since the day he and Mary were fired by the Troy Community Council as they closed up the career center. He went on as to what happened to him, not unlike what happened to them. Poverty was a killer of individuals, the family, and the community.

He went through what happened to him after he hit the Powerball and explained what he received versus what everyone at large believed. He told them of his and Mary's plans for a new career center, fully funded, and the concept of the North Central Village. Tara Robinson asked if that meant she could be a homeowner of a completely rehabbed house, and Jack said she was the first one he had in mind. That pleased her and the entire table.

Jack explained what he needed from all his graduates and, in particular, from these five sitting at the table. He needed Tara, Cameron, and Jayden to be examples of success, and he turned to Imani and Brandon. "As of tomorrow, if you want a job, you're my first line recruiters for the kids in the eight-block area. You'll be given a full-time salary and benefits, and if you do well, you'll be promoted and have a job for a minimum of ten years. That's the best I can promise. If you don't perform, it's on you."

Imani looked at Jack with tears in her eyes. "Really? No shit?"

"No shit," Jack said.

Brendon and Imani hugged Jack and Mary and wouldn't let go. They both wanted to know, "How much?"

"To start, you'll be given six hundred dollars a week and benefits to go on the street recruiting and anything else we need. You'll report to our volunteer manager, Ann Cushing, who'll be opening an office a few blocks away within the next week or two. Just call her, and you'll go on the payroll immediately." He handed all of them his card. "You'll love Ann, trust me."

"Jack, what do you want from us?" Jayden said.

"If you want a full-time job, it's yours. I'll match whatever you're now being paid plus ten percent, and you'll like my double pay vacation plan and benefits. However, Tara and Cameron, I like you right where you are, but I want you to sit on my new board for the career center. By the way, it's a for-profit not a nonprofit, so you'll never have to worry about fund raising. I got it covered. I'll pay you both ten thousand dollars, each, for your board duties. If you need anything else, just ask Ann, Mary, or me. Okay?

Mary sat in amazement. She'd never seen Jack in this light before. He made excellent quick decisions. He could because it was his money. But there was something different about him. He had grown tremendously. It was like the singers on the *Voice* that went from just being thankful for being picked to knowing they belonged in the top ten. It was a growing process that confirmed their own internal self-worth and self-esteem.

"When did you think of all this, Jack?" she asked him on the way out the door.

"On the way over here," he said. "Why?"

"Because you were right on the money," she said.

"Money is a motivator, but belief in someone's abilities is even a bigger motivator. Giving them a leg up isn't the same as handing them an advantage." These guys earned it, and it was obvious. Just being dealt a bad hand for Brandon and Imani slowed them down, but would never interfere with their advancement if he had anything to do with it.

Before leaving, he discussed exactly what he wanted from each of them and then said he'd send to them written instructions, meeting dates, and times, and deliverables that he needed done before the grand opening. They were to produce 100 kids at the front door ready to start learning, to get their high school degrees, certifications, and a job, starting from the first day. That was their charge. Eventually, he'd assign several more graduates the task of working with the Traynors and other construction companies in the early stages of rehabbing 200-plus homes, the TCC building, and the old church into a high tech center. They headed home, exhausted, and fell asleep as soon as their heads hit the pillow, in separate rooms, of course. Jack remarked that even though their two bodyguards were around, they'd started to go unnoticed. Perhaps that was because Mary and Jack had started to relax with others or Fred and John got better at hiding in plain sight.

This was a big day for Jack, and he needed Mary's help. All the accumulated mail requests for money had dwindled over the last few weeks and then were separated into piles for approval or non-approval. The ladies working on the files, Mary, Kristen, Ann, or even his daughter didn't know what his plans would be for the funding. He allocated funding every year to give to other charitable causes that would be hand selected. Little did the women know that Jack was going to let them vote on the funding for half a million dollars. He thought that they'd been working diligently on the project that they were as entitled as he was to decide. Who the hell knew what one would be better than the other. The obvious cancer patients or those in extreme poverty would never have to provide matching funds or work off their half by volunteering at the new center or at any other facility that needed the help.

They hopped in the car and headed to Albany for the ten a.m. meeting. He and Mary went directly to the eleventh floor and walked in. He gathered the five women who'd been there for months—along with Kristen, his daughter, as well as Mary and Ann—and began by telling them that they all had a vote for up to a half million dollars. They need not explain their reasons unless a tiebreaker was needed. They'd vote again after explanations, and if still tied, he'd simply toss a coin for heads or tails. He also told them that no one was to say a word about the voting or where the money came from. A simple check from the Evangeline Trust would be mailed to the lucky party. Of course, there would a full accounting by the law firms CPAs to make sure of the proper tax benefits.

Everyone in the room was shocked. There were over fifty appropriate requests out of three thousand that seemed to have stood out and far outweighed all the rest. Those applications also came using Jack's geographic criteria. As he explained before starting, "You can't save all the whales—pick one and put your name on it. Own it."

There were a few that didn't meet the geographic specific criteria, but a few of the women wanted to discuss the situation with Jack. He said fine. The process took all day and they had a luncheon brought in for the ten of them. By the end of the day, the half million dollars was spent on thirty different requests that added up to the total allocated. Of the thirty, twenty were for individuals who'd be unable to pay back anything. The other ten would be required to match funds, either a cash match or the hours would be added up and multiplied by the twenty dollars an hour volunteer rate. Every two weeks, that half payment check would go out only as the matching hours grew and the balance was paid off. Everyone thought that was an appropriate system if they wanted to be funded. So, overall the method was appropriate and worked. If the ten didn't like the results, they'd pick another ten at a later date.

After the last request was funded, Jack told Kristen, Ann, Mary, and Debbie that he wanted to meet with them right after for a different discussion. The ladies who worked on the project were then handed a bonus check, thanked, and said they'd be called if they'd any future requests. All of them were pleased, and Jack made a few new friends. They all said they'd be at the new center's grand opening. Jack told them that if they needed work and could make it to Troy to call him and he'd find something for them that would be appropriate for their skills. They thanked him profusely and then left, all smiling.

After they left, Jack said he had another idea for the second half million dollars. He explained to Mary, Kristen, Ann, and Debbie that he wanted to fund several nonprofits that already served the people who lived in the newly proposed North Central Village area. He'd like letters to go out from the attorney's office that a funder would be interested in supporting their programs, if they provided valid services to the neighborhood. He'd personally picked three food pantries, two veterans' centers, a family counseling center, two homeless shelters, and two drug and alcohol rehab centers. There would be ten in all. In the letter, it would state that a charitable organization would match one hundred percent their last three months expenses for direct services to clients living in the designated area.

The charitable organization would require a valid accounting firm's statement that what would be presented to them that was true with a supporting statement from an accounting firm. They'd match up to $50,000 worth of expenses over these three months, and if the nonprofit didn't have an accounting firm, doing their taxes or 990 forms, the charitable organization would pay up to $1,000 for the preparation for the request. The funds would be wired to the organization, one month from the date they received the application. He'd spend $50,000 times ten organizations equaling $500,000, every year, based on their value to the village. It was a win-win for the area, for the non-profits, and, eventually, everyone would know that the funding came from the newly created Evangeline Trust, but still wouldn't know who owned it. The Troy Community Council would never receive any funding from this trust until their administration had changed significantly to the liking of Jack.

"That's great, Jack," said Kristen. "I'll start working on it right now."

"You're full of surprises, Jack," said Mary. "First, you hired the graduates and now this? You're on a roll, aren't you? Will you have any money left?"

"More than I'll ever need. I'll still have my sixty-eight million plus your fifteen million and at least twenty to twenty-five million more after everything is added up, including a new charter school. This is really a lot of fun, isn't it? Just making it happen gives me the chills," he said.

Debbie was looking at him in a whole new light. She was smiling and looked proud. Maybe hooking up with her dad wasn't such a bad idea, after all. She could learn about social services, funding, psychology and everything else, right on this job. It could add valuable experience to her classroom education. She thought that she really needed to reexamine her own feelings and start thinking about what really went down with her mom and dad. It was like she was brainwashed and was now coming out of it, slowly but surely. These people that he surrounded himself with were women who were well educated and thoughtful and thought the world of her dad. There had to be a reason. He couldn't have done all this if he was inexperienced and in over his head. The money was fine but what he was doing with it, setting everything up strategically not to fail, was remarkable. She needed to sit down with him to discuss what his thought process was in developing all this. Maybe when he took her car shopping soon, she'd try to ask him why he was doing what he was doing. It wasn't natural to give away millions of dollars to perfect strangers—or was it?

She had no idea.

CHAPTER 39

It was a beautiful Saturday morning. Debbie was coming over to see her father's new home on Old Plank Road. A few weeks ago, Mary and Jack decided to buy the place from the previous owner for the price they agreed on, six months ago. Their lease was coming due, and it was time. They loved the place. It was in great shape and a good deal for both parties. Mary never owned anything before, so they decided to split ownership to make her feel more comfortable. He'd simply leave it to her in his will, and she'd leave it to her two friends, Jane and Martha, upon her death. They'd called Kristen to advise them of the purchase and to close on the house and make adjustments to their wills.

Debbie drove her mother's car over to Jack's house, and they'd go to the local Honda dealership in Jack's SUV. Debbie had her heart set on a Honda even though Jack preferred Fords. Mary would stay back and, afterward, Jack's son, Mark, and his girlfriend, Cara, would come over for a cookout later in the afternoon. Debbie soon arrived, and Mary showed her around while Jack finished up mowing part of the front lawn. Even though they had a lawn care service, he wanted to try out the riding mower that Toby left him.

Debbie especially liked the ten acres of lawn and all the extra room inside the house. She loved the expansive deck overlooking the Hudson Valley. She now lived in a tiny dorm room, but it was better than living back at the old house with her mother and Chuck. She was getting to know Mary because of her duties that intersected. Debbie was also assigned by Ann to help Mary down at St. Augustine's. They were going to make macaroni and potato salad and then put the containers into the refrigerator to stay cold for later.

Jack hopped off the mower. "I'll be there in ten minutes. I need a shower."

The dealer was only three miles away. They had a wide array of cars and SUVs but Debbie, and he'd talked about it during the week. All she needed was decent transportation for the next three years. They walked through the aisles of used cars and saw a silver Honda Civic. It was in very good shape, not a scratch on the body, and the interior looked clean. The window invoice stated that it was a 2012 Civic with 62,000 miles, which wasn't bad for a Honda, even though Jack preferred buying American. The sticker said it was an automatic with air conditioning, Bluetooth, a moon roof, MP3 player, keyless entry, and alloy wheels. It also got thirty-nine miles to a gallon on the highway, which impressed him. His Ford Explorer got only twenty-three on the highway. When they first got there, there were salesmen falling all over themselves trying to help them. Jack asked where the used cars were and told them if they were interested, he'd then see about a test drive. They'd gone out on the lot alone. After seeing the 2012 Civic, they went back inside the showroom and asked the salesman for a test drive. It took a few minutes to get the car ready, but it suddenly appeared outside the front door. The salesman gave Jack the key and he, in turn, handed it to Debbie. They went out onto Route 7, took a right, and drove to Pittstown and back. Then, they went to a side street, off Hoosick, to see if she could park it on the street. She did fine, and they went back to the dealer.

"What do you think?" asked Jack.

"Are you kidding? It's exactly what I need to get around for school and work. It's terrific. How much is it?"

"They want twelve thousand, five hundred dollars, but a cash deal today could get it down by one thousand at least. Let's see if they want to sell cars today. Remember, you have to put in volunteer time. This is a loan, not a gift."

"Got it, and I appreciate it."

After a half hour of haggling, Jack said, "I'll give you eleven thousand dollars for the car, right now in cash."

"How about eleven thousand, five hundred dollars?" the salesman said.

"Split the difference. Throw in floor mats, and you got a deal."

"Done." With that, Jack pulled out $11,250 in cash from his pocket.

Debbie looked astounded. "Really? Cash?" she said.

"We want the car registered in her name, and I'll get you the insurance information on Monday. Can we pick it up, late Monday afternoon?"

"Of course. Do you need a vehicle, Mr. Manning? That was the quickest sale I think I ever made. Thanks. Actually, you made the sale. I had nothing to do with it," the salesman said with a laugh.

"No, I'm fine. I like Fords. She likes Hondas. That's what makes the world go round."

They hopped back into Jacks SUV and headed to his place. Before starting the vehicle, Debbie reached over and gave him a hug of appreciation. First time that happened since she was a kid at Christmas. Maybe he was wrong. Maybe she didn't inherit her mother's genes. Maybe she only borrowed them for a while, he thought.

"Back at the ranch," he liked to say to himself. He really liked this place—a lot. So did Mary and, evidently, everyone else. As they pulled into the driveway, he noticed that Mark's car was there. He and Cara must have come a little early. *That's a good sign*, Jack thought. It was now around two-thirty p.m., so he showed Mark all his new toys in the pole barn garage. Mark was impressed. Jack started the mower and let Mark drive it around the property, showing him how to change gears and drop the mower into the various heights, depending on how high the grass was. He wanted to keep it a few inches high to combat drying out the lawn too quickly.

Cara didn't really know Debbie very well. They'd only met a few times before Mark moved out of the house. Mary left them alone while she went about her business. She invited Jane and Martha up for dinner. All they had to do was go up the hill and turn left onto Old Plank Road from the Burgh. They showed up on time, around four-thirty p.m.

Jack got the grill going for the burgers and hot dogs. He bought ribs and steaks for Jane and Martha. He knew how much they loved the Dinosaur Bar-B-Que ribs, so he picked up a few racks on the way back from the car dealer. All he had to do was heat them up, and they were ready to go. After dinner, Mary had plenty of help. Debbie told her earlier that she and Mark would like to talk to their father alone after dinner if they could. She said of course. Mary, Cara, Jane, and Martha all went into the house to clean up. Jack looked around and only saw his two children. He wondered what was going on.

"What's up?" he said.

"Mary was nice enough to leave us alone so we could talk to you, just Debbie and me," Mark said.

"What about?"

"It's not about the money," Debbie began. "We just wanted to let you know that. We're grateful for what you've done for us. After the way we acted, we didn't think we'd ever see you again, and, for that, we're grateful."

Mark nodded. "Dad, we panicked when Mom threw you out of the house. We thought you did something very wrong. We couldn't have been more wrong, and we want to apologize and ask you for your forgiveness. We didn't know what to do. Believe me when I say, we've grown up a lot in the last year. We now understand what Mom did to you. We can understand why you'd never forgive her, but we want a continued relationship with you. We don't want to lose both our parents. We know we're losing Mom every time we see Chuck, but we hope that'll change when she realizes the mistakes she's made."

"I totally agree, Dad," Debbie said.

"You know the saying, 'Forgive and forget'? Well, I'm Irish, and I've been told that the Irish never forgive or forget. I made a deal with your mother so that she'll be taken care of in a short while and, later, when she retires, only if she does what I asked her to do. I won't tell you what that is, but it's all on her. It has nothing to do with Chuck. This is her issue only," Jack continued. "However, in your cases, I'll try to forgive and forget. I won't kid you or change what my thinking is, especially about the volunteering to pay off your debts, especially you, Debbie. It may take time, but I do love both of you, and I want to continue loving you. As my father said to me, many times, 'Stop screwing up and everything will be fine,'" he said and smiled.

They smiled too, and both said, "No more screw-ups, promise."

"I don't believe that's possible, since you're a Manning, through and through, but before you do something that you're not sure of, ask me."

"I will," said Mark.

"I will, too," said Debbie.

Jack hugged them both, and they went back to the porch where everyone else was starting on dessert.

"By the way, the building will be up in a few months. In the meantime, we're trying to get everything in order, the best we can. We can't do everything because that's impossible but we can try right up until the grand opening. However, Mary and I are taking a month off and heading back to Key West. We made some good friends down there when we first left after winning the lottery. We've decided that's where we'll head when we're done with our project over the next few years. Hopefully, it will be less than expected.

We'll keep this place and stay in Key West for as long as the weather allows, probably from November through April at least. During the next ten years, if everything goes well, we'll take a month off every few months to head south. We can be back at a minute's notice. If there're real problems, we'll simply charter our own plane to get back. All you guys know we're rich, right?"

"Don't rub it in," said Mark, and everyone laughed.

It was true, though, and Jack had just vocalized what everyone was thinking, *WE"RE RICH!!! FILTHY RICH!!! AND WE'RE GOING TO HAVE SOME FUN, TOO!!! STARTING NOW!!!*

CHAPTER 40

"Jack? Hi. It's Skip Lennon, down in sunny old Key West. How are you?"

"Doing great, Skip. Were your ears ringing? We were thinking about heading south for a few weeks. Are you booked up?"

"Yes, we're fully booked, but that's not why I called. We live on Allamanda Terrace, just west of the airport on our own little Key. The neighborhood is great, and one of our oldest friends has to give up his house, right on the water. He's in his mid-eighties, and his wife died two years ago. He can't keep the house up. So, I was wondering if you'd be interested in being our neighbor? We live two doors down, right on the water, and I park by boat right here."

"Sounds great, Skip. We were thinking about getting a place down there. How much is it going for?"

"Well, we bought ours in 1995 at around three hundred fifty thousand dollars, but Key West has been very popular at this point. He wants to list it at a million one and change. That's about the market. He's going to list it in a few weeks. It needs some minor repairs but nothing to be worried about. Also, the nice things is, our son, Tom, and our daughter, Jamie, run a side business taking care of houses for people like you when you're away."

"Tell him we're interested, and maybe we can come to an agreement and save the realtor fee. Is it seven percent down there? That's what it is here."

"I'm not sure, but it's something like that. It would save you about seventy thousand dollars and change, not that I'm suggesting anything. Joe and Julie told us what you're doing up there, and that's great. They also said that Joe's father and brother will be pretty busy for quite some time."

"Yes, they'll be the electrical contractors for two building and over two hundred rehabs in the central part of Troy. Should be busy for the next four or five years."

"That's great. Keep it in the family, as we like to say. So, can you make it down? If so, I'll tell Jerry to hold off until you get here."

"How about if we come down the end of next week? I've got a lot to do in a short time frame, and then we're off for the next month. The grand opening of our new building will be coming up shortly, so we'll have to be back for that and restart the business of training kids for jobs."

"Call us with your flight plans. We'll pick you up. It's about ten minutes to the airport. You can stay with us while you look at the place and then go on your merry way if you want. If you like it, Jerry Titus, our neighbor, can hand you the keys lock, stock, and barrel, and you can move in. He can take his time moving out, it sounds like.

"That'll work for us. I'll call you and email you our itinerary. Thanks, Skip."

Jack turned to Mary. "Mary, we're heading to Key West next Friday, if you want. We need to book a flight, and we're staying with the Lennons. There's a house for sale two doors from them, and they want us to look at it. We can certainly afford it."

"I'd like that," she said.

Linda had just emailed him the real estate data sheet, and he read it off to Mary. "Ten Allamanda Terrace has four bedrooms, two and a half baths, and almost three thousand square feet. It sits on a nine-thousand-square-foot lot, which is about a quarter acre. We've got ten acres here, but that house is on the water. The property taxes are about twelve thousand a year, and the owner, Jerry Titus, is asking about a million one. Without the real estate commission, it would be right around a million dollars. It's far cheaper than anything else we looked at in the real estate guide," he said.

They'd been looking for a while, but most of those they liked were in the four or five million-dollar range. No matter how much money Jack had at his disposal, he'd never spend that much, regardless. A million dollars was still an eye opener for him, but he'd have to pay it if they wanted to be in Key West, owning property, right on the ocean. Having someone like the Lennon's son and daughter watch out for the property while they were away would be a Godsend as well. Whatever they charged, and he doubted it would be a lot, considering, it would be well worth it.

Mary ordered the tickets to Key West, this time flying from Albany to Washington, DC and then directly to the Key West airport. They'd be there around four p.m. on Friday. Skip and Linda were picking them up and heading back to their house for a cookout. Tom and Jamie would be doing the cooking along with Tom's girlfriend and Jamie's boyfriend. They invited Jerry Titus over to meet Jack and Mary as well. They thought that after dinner, they could mosey over to see the property. If they weren't interested, then they'd head to the Southernmost Resort once again. The Lennon's boat was fully booked for the month so they'd only stay a week in Key West to walk around and perhaps look at other properties if they felt like it. Jack and Mary decided that when they headed south, they'd leave all the planning behind and simply enjoy themselves. In any case, they'd rent a car because they wanted to take a day trip up to see Joe and Julie and their daughter Bella.

Debbie took her father and Mary to the airport for their flight. He told her if she wanted to that she could stay at the house on Old Plank if she got tired of her dorm room. He added, like any father, bring a few friends, but no big parties. John and Fred would stay there while they were away. They didn't believe that anyone would bother them in Key West, while they were with a retired Coast Guard officer, in a place loaded with the Coast Guard. They'd be safe for a while. Jack and Mary gave Debbie a hug and thanked her. She said to call her, and she'd pick them up. There was no reason to leave a car at the airport when they weren't sure how long they'd be away.

They landed right on schedule. All they had was their carry-on bags. Mary knew that if she ran out of anything, she'd pick the item up in Key West. They could always ship stuff back if necessary. It wasn't worth carrying a large suitcase all the way to Key West. She learned her lesson, she told Jack after lugging that huge suitcase around that she bought in Tampa when they first headed south. They walked through the airport's main entrance and were greeted by Skip and Linda with hugs all around. He was parked right at the entrance since this airport was rather small. They put their carry-ons in the trunk and headed to the Lennon for dinner and to meet Jerry Titus.

After arriving, Tom introduced his girlfriend to Jack and Mary and Jamie did the same with her boyfriend. They were such independent young people that Jack admired them. Not only did they work on the boat but started their own business with a service that a lot of snowbirds needed. Someone to keep an eye on the house, keep it clean, and ready for occupancy when the owner got there was not just a convenience, but also a necessity. Key West was not crime free by anyone's imagination. It housed some of the most diverse people that anyone could ever meet. It also attracted those who had no place else to go, starting over as waitresses, bartenders, and other service providers. Theft was a big issue.

The cookout was terrific. They had a few beers and met Jerry Titus, a wonderful older man who just couldn't keep up with maintenance on his place. Tom and Jamie helped him out but the writing was on the wall. It was time for him to move on and into a minimum care facility where he'd receive quality care. He'd have plenty of money from the sale of his house, which was free and clear. The senior facility was only a few blocks away so the neighbors could drop by to see him now and then.

After dinner, they walked down the street with Mr. Titus as they looked at the setting sun. To see the sun set in Key West, every night, was a gift from God. There wasn't a more scenic spot in the entire world. As they looked through the house, they noticed that it was built to last to withstand tropical storms and severe weather. It had a new roof, and the house was about thirty years old. If not, it would have sold for two times the amount. The kitchen and bathrooms were dated, but the rest of the house had been recently painted, and the furniture was older but in perfect shape. You could tell the care that went into this home. It had a one-car garage, four bedrooms, two and a half baths, and everything was in working order.

Before leaving for the Keys, Jack called Kristen and asked her to be ready to wire transfer about a million dollars to a bank in Key West. He told her about the deal, and she cleared it with Andy who thought it was a very good deal and a good investment. The house would be paid for with his own after-tax millions, in the name of Evangeline Realty, Inc., a for-profit corporation, he owned one hundred percent. That would limit his personal liability. When you were worth a lot of money, people would go after you for everything and anything. At least now he had the ability to hide behind the corporate shield. It cost more in taxes but the limited liability more than made up for the increased expenses.

"Mr. Titus, we love your place. However, I don't want to have to pay a commission to a real estate broker if I don't have to. If you haven't hired a broker yet, we'd be interested in buying it for cash as soon as your lawyer is ready to close. I can have the money transferred to any account you deem appropriate. How much are you willing to sell it for?"

"I'm asking a million one, but without the commission, I was thinking about a million dollars."

Jack considered. "Looking around, I figure there's probably about fifty thousand dollars' worth of upgrades and repairs necessary along with some new furnishings. How about nine hundred fifty thousand dollars in cash, right now?"

"How about nine hundred seventy-five thousand dollars in cash right now and it's a deal?"

"Sold," Jack said.

Mary smiled. "Yes."

She couldn't believe where they started, where they were headed, and what had already happened along the way. This was the cherry on top, she thought.

"We're here until next Thursday, flying out Friday morning," Jack said. "If we can close by then, I'll have your money in hand by the time we leave. We also need to make sure that Tom and Jamie agree to take care of this place for us while we're away. We still have a lot to do up north before we can even think about settling in Key West."

"Where are you staying?" Jerry asked.

'We're staying with Skip and Linda tonight and moving into a hotel tomorrow."

"Don't be silly. You can have this place. I'll go visit my daughter up in Key Largo for a week and then meet you back here for the closing. Sound like a plan?"

"Sure does," said Jack. "Mary, we'll need to rent a car to get around this week. We'll ask Skip to drop us off at Enterprise tomorrow morning. Are you happy?"

"I'm thrilled, but I'm not sure how I fit in here, Jack. Can we talk about where this is leading?"

"Mary, I'm really sorry. I just thought this is what you wanted. I can put it in your name if you want. I only want what's best for you, you know?"

"I know, but I'm not sure what's best for me. I never planned any of this, and it looks like I went along for the ride. Jack, we're best friends, but I don't know how that works when you have millions of dollars at stake. I really don't. Can we talk about it?"

"Of course. I don't mean to push you into anything. I hope I haven't. And, I hope you're happy. That's all I really want. The money doesn't mean anything to me, Mary, if I can't share it with you."

"I know. I'm just on edge. That's all. Let's talk about it this week when we've got time and we're by ourselves. Okay?"

"Mary, I'll never, ever, take you for granted. I hope you believe me?"

"I do," she said.

Jack thought that "I do" might be the response he'd be looking for if and when his annulment came through. He'd recheck with Kristen when he got back. She'd updated him and said it was going fine, but it would take about a year at best. He was wondering if he could ever hold off telling Mary how he felt about her. She knew they were best friends, but he wondered if she really knew how he felt about her. He hoped the money didn't get in the way.

CHAPTER 41

On the flight back to Albany from Key West, Jack and Mary had plenty of time to talk. They'd also have a layover in Washington, DC, for an hour. As soon as they got in the air, heading home, Jack asked, "Can we talk?"

"Sure," she said.

"So, what's wrong? Are you unhappy?"

Mary looked a little forlorn or even a little overwhelmed. "It's not that, Jack. My life was pretty set until the day we got fired, or quit, or whatever you call it. I went from high school to the convent, got my degree, got out of the convent, and then went to work directly for you at the Troy Community Council. That's it. That's what my total life was in a nutshell. Now, I'm worth fifteen million dollars, living with a guy, buying a house with a guy, and flying down to Key West to buy a house on the ocean. The real problem might be that I'm doing all this by the seat of my pants, Jack. We're not married. We're best friends, but at this point, I don't even know what that means. Do you understand how overwhelming this is to me? I simply moved out of my apartment with my two friends who were ex-nuns and moved in with you. I've no idea what that really means."

Jack became a little flustered himself. He wasn't sure that he wanted to tell Mary about getting an annulment and eventually asking her to marry him. He wasn't even sure if that was in the cards. He simply wanted to be with her every day and counted on her to be there. That probably wasn't fair, he thought.

"Mary, I never intended for you to feel uneasy around me but that's the vibe I'm getting. I hope that isn't it. I've been so caught up in what we're trying to do that I never thought that you weren't along for the ride. For that, I apologize. Maybe that's why Maureen left me. I think I took advantage of you without even trying. For that I'm sorry."

"Jack, I'm with you one hundred percent, but I'm unsure of what I want for the future. I don't just want to be your partner in this venture. I want to do my own thing as well. However, I can't picture not being a part of your life every day. That means more to me than anything. I know we've grown closer than ever, but I don't know what that means to you."

"I didn't want to say anything, but here it is. I asked Maureen for an annulment. She's working on it with Kristen who promised to never say a word to anyone. I'll tell you now that I'm not proud of this, but I didn't know what else to do. I promised Maureen a certain amount of money for her future if we got an annulment. Just remember she left me and threw me out of the house. I was taken by complete surprise. At this point, there will never be reconciliation. She chose her path, with or without Chuck, the minute she did this to me. I'm certain that I was responsible for her behavior, but I never got a chance to correct it. Like you, I'm Catholic and someday I may want to remarry in the church. She's just getting a little more than most for her efforts.

"Mary, I wake up every day thinking of you, and I look forward to every minute I spend with you. I think both Debbie and Mark know this but haven't said anything. They both told me how much they like and respect you, especially for having my back. I know I'm beating around the bush, here. Mary. If I get an annulment, will you take a chance on me, to see how it might work out for the long run? I'm no good at this, but I know more about you than anyone else in the world, and I'd like to spend the rest of my life with you whatever the circumstances. There I said it," he said with a wince.

"Didn't see that coming, but I should have. I've never been married and never had more than a few prom dates and one boyfriend in all my years. I've thought about it but didn't think it would happen to me, especially this late in life. I too want to spend my time with you, and I can see your reluctance to date me, if you will, knowing that I'm an ex-nun and probably will always be a Catholic. So, knowing that, if I was to marry, it would be in the Catholic Church. So, you went ahead to pursue an annulment, thinking this was so?"

"Yes, it's true. I did," he said. "I never wanted to force myself on you, especially since you mean so much to me."

"Jack, you don't need an annulment to ask me out, you know? I'm perfectly fine with this. I've thought long and hard about it but I never pursued it because you were married, but now you're not. An annulment would be nice, but I don't think you know that both of you don't have to seek an annulment now for it to happen. Under Pope Francis, you can do it yourself, without the other party's involvement. I know you want to do it right, though. So, where does that leave us?"

"First, I want to make it crystal clear. Mary, I love you. I have for a long time, but I thought I'd be stuck until the day I died. Hitting the lottery didn't change anything. Getting fired changed everything and the way you stuck up for me, meant the world to me. Whatever you want, I'll go along with it."

"Can we take it slowly, Jack? It's not that I'm unsure of you, I'm unsure of myself, and I don't want to jump into anything that would hurt our relationship, which I cherish. You know that, right?"

"I feel the same. But, are you willing to move forward quietly without telling the world. Not that I'm concerned, but I don't want everyone to know that we're an item now and living together too. It would kill your friends, don't you think?"

"Jane and Martha aren't dumb, Jack. They knew that, when I moved up the hill with you, it wasn't just about business. They may be ex-nuns, but they're certainly women. They know, even if you think the world doesn't. How many people have said, and I quote, 'Are you two…' without finishing the sentence?"

"A lot, including Debbie."

"Where do we go from here? Do we have a 'date night'?"

"That would work if you know I'm picking you up for a date and maybe, just maybe, expect a good night kiss, even if we walk through the same door to the same house. I wouldn't expect anything more unless you want to, Mary."

"That'll work for now," she said. She smiled, took his arm, and folded hers into his. She put her head on his shoulder and closed her eyes.

God that was hard, he thought.

They landed in Albany early that night. Debbie was waiting for them right at the front door. Albany might be labeled an "International Airport" but you could park 100 feet from the front door in a free half hour space. Debbie gave them both a hug and noticed a difference in both of them. She thought maybe they were just happy to be home and had a nice time. Some day she'd look back and see that this was the day that everything changed in her father's life, all for the better.

The few weeks after they got back were hectic, to say the least. His recruiters got a hold of the last graduating class, and those who didn't have jobs said they'd be glad to come back for retraining and to work on rehabbing houses. They met them at Saint Augustine's gymnasium to tell them about the project. Of the thirty-eight graduating from the last class, twenty would be available for the grand opening. Those twenty, like the twelve apostles, were charged with recruiting two others who could benefit from the training and a job. The two contractors agreed to help rehab the first five houses with the twenty grads, supervising the complete reconstruction of those homes. It wasn't the cost as much as the slack they'd pick up to ensure that everything was done in a timely manner.

Jack and Mary reviewed the applications for the most important jobs including an executive director and controller. They found two people whom they both knew and respected. Both were in their late fifties and said they'd stay until they retired at sixty-five or until they found someone that they could train to take their place. Jack ultimately wanted program graduates to run the nonprofit and the programs for the North Central Village. They'd graduate from the career center, go to HVCC, get their degree and move on to a four-year college. Those individuals would be paid a stipend or salary to stay on and work holidays, during the summer and spend time on an internship at one of the many non-profits located in the Village.

Jack and Mary, together, started to look at the paperwork involved in getting a charter school approved by the New York State Education Department. They thought it might just succeed if they both applied at the same time, using the same concepts of a free facility that would save a school thousands of dollars needed, not for a facility but pay for the quality teachers necessary to have children succeed in the classroom. Most failed because the funding went to the building instead.

The concept would work because the Lansingburgh Academy Charter School was in the Lansingburgh Central School District while the North Central Village Charter School was in the Enlarged City School District of Troy. These were two separate school districts within the city of Troy. Only a handful of cities in the state of New York had two separate school districts within the city itself. It was a unique setup.

Everything seemed to be moving ahead and aligned, except the actual purchase of the TCC building owned by the Freemans. Jack wanted to wait before taking over the property, but once the grand opening took place, it would be harder to do what he wanted to do with the facility and the programs under the TCC umbrella. Instead, since the property was now certified as being free and clear of any contamination, Jack bought the building and held a closing on the property on the quiet. He didn't want anyone to know about it until he met with the TCC administration or board, a week prior to the grand opening of the new Evangeline Career Center. The Freemans took the proceeds and had their attorney set up a scholarship fund for graduates to attend HVCC. If there were enough funds, they'd also allow individuals to move on to four-year degrees if they came back and did community service within the Village.

❦

It was about a week and a half before the grand opening in early March. The weather was clearing up, and it was a very mild winter. The new building was getting its finishing touches, and people were running around trying to complete all the tasks necessary for the grand opening. It was Wednesday morning around eleven a.m. Jack had held a meeting a few days prior with his law firm and all the new employees. He told them that he'd simply show up at the TCC building and invite the administration, the board, staff, and clients to attend the grand opening.

He was anticipating that as soon as he got to the front door that someone would block his path into the building. He just wanted to see what they'd do if he showed up. If accosted, he wouldn't tell them anything or invite them to the grand opening. He wanted to see for himself if they were vindictive toward him and Mary. He asked Mary if she wanted to go with him, but she thought she might be a distraction, and if they actually insulted her, she knew about Jack's unknown temper. She'd seen it before but not often. No one else seemed to know about this character flaw of his. It was a flaw, but it also made him stronger when his back was against the wall. She told him point blank that if it happened, simply smile and walk away. Then the crap would hit the fan with an eviction notice and a presentation for payment of the demand note. Both knew TCC couldn't handle either one.

Jack dressed nicely for the day. He'd gotten new clothes for the grand opening but would make this day special by wearing his new very expensive custom-tailored suit, expensive tie, and shirt with a pair of very expensive shoes. Mary made him spend almost $3,000 on his custom-fitted clothes and get a very expensive salon haircut. She laughed and told him that he looked like a million bucks, and he said, "Is that all?" He laughed. He could look like a $100 million if he wanted.

Jack pulled up in front of the Troy Community Council building. He parked his FBI-style Ford Explorer, right by the front door. He'd already cleared it with the local cops whom he knew very well and who knew what he intended to do. They were parked in a squad car around the corner in case there was an issue. The Traynors made sure that everyone knew from the mayor to the local cops that this was Jack's moment. He'd waited for this for almost a year and a half, and if he'd never hit the Powerball, this moment would have never arrived. He walked to the front door and pushed it in. He went to the receptionist to the right and asked to speak to Howard Singer and Marvin Manville. He gave his name. She rang up stairs. Immediately, he could hear scurrying from room to room coming from up the stairs on the second floor. He kind of chuckled to himself, "Wonder what's happening?" He knew what was coming.

Marvin Manville came down first with a head of steam, followed by Mr. Singer.

"What the hell do you want? You can't come in here. Get out and stay out. You're not wanted here. You were fired a year ago. Hit the lottery? Big deal. Get out of this building before I call the cops."

Jack smiled. "Howard, do you feel the same about me, after all this time?" He wasn't sure because time had passed, but deep down inside, he was kind of hoping that what had just transpired actually would. He had thought he was going to feel bad about asking the board for their resignations, but now all he could feel was a deep sense of gratitude for what happened to him over the last year. He'd grown. Before, he'd kick the living crap out of Marvin after a confrontation like this. Now, he finally understood what it was like to feel a little 'presidential.'

"Jack, it's better if you just leave now before Marvin calls the cops. You're really not wanted here, and there's no need for you to be here," he said.

"Okay, fine. I'll leave. I just wanted to stop by and say hello, but I take it that you're not interested in burying the hatchet. So, it seems. It's been nice seeing you again. Good luck to both of you."

"Get out and stay out," Marvin said as he held the door open to make sure Jack would leave.

With that, Jack smiled a smile he just found. It was a smile of satisfaction that he never had before. He knew that on the day of the grand opening, he'd be celebrating a life-changing event. He also knew that they'd be feeling the effects of a life-changing event as well. The minute that he began to speak to the audience at the grand opening, Mr. Singer and Mr. Manville be served eviction papers and a demand for payment for past due rent. Screw them, he thought, walked to his SUV, got in, and drove away. He was very proud of himself for not crushing Marvin's skull into tiny little pieces. Mary would be proud. No one else would even guess how he felt, at least not many. He couldn't wait to go home and tell Mary exactly what just transpired. He was almost giddy with anticipation for the grand opening, but now, he couldn't wait to get a call from Howard, Marvin, or the board chairman as to what his intentions were concerning the TCC facility. He might just tell them that he was tearing down the building for a parking lot. He best not do a thing until he was calmer, if that day would ever come. He couldn't help but laugh and say to himself, "Well, Jack, you did it. You confronted your worst fears, and you survived. It wasn't that bad. In fact, it was almost a little like fun." He'd sleep on what he'd do. However, before heading home, he stopped at the liquor store at the bottom of the hill and bought their best bottle of champagne. They'd have fun tonight. Of that, he was sure.

CHAPTER 42

The grand opening of the Evangeline Career Center was to begin at noon. All the guests had been invited. Politician included the mayor of Troy, the city council members, and local New York State assembly members and senators. One of the New York State senators was coming from Washington as well. Dignitaries from the local colleges and school districts were also invited along with local residents and church pastors and other nonprofits, not including the TCC.

Jack's recruiting team did a remarkable job in signing up students for the first class in the new facility. Twenty previous graduates, who needed additional services, would be joined by eighty others, split equally between young men and women, ages eighteen to twenty-four. The team was in place, including a new administrative team as well as TASC teachers and counselors. The two builders, with help from John and Pete Traynor and the local builders' association, had already completed four houses, completely rehabbed, all on one block. These were city-owned houses that would eventually have been demolished but now would be sold as affordable housing units to families who'd pay no more than they did before in rent. The property taxes would be paid on a graduated basis, so after ten years, these homes would be fully assessed and pay their full share of the tax burden.

The new facility was completed on time and under budget at $3,800,000, including all the furniture, fixtures and technology included. It contained three floors with 10,000 square feet per floor. Offices were scattered around the building so that the administration and staff always had a presence on each floor. The new technology center, although smaller than what would eventually be built at the church site, was state-of-the-art with full WIFI and hookups to Spectrum and Verizon, with distance learning capabilities. It would connect to various colleges so their students wouldn't have to travel to classes. They could virtually get their associates degree at this facility. The on-the-job training was already taking place in the rehabbed homes with NYSERDA curriculum for energy efficiency. The new building was considered LEEDS certified and green. Jack knew that this would be held up as a model for replication for the rest of the state of New York, if not the nation.

Doing it all with private funds was what separated it from all other projects. Maybe after ten years, Jack would reconsider and make it a nonprofit but, as of now, he and his trust and realty companies didn't have to answer to any government agency to prove that grant funds were spent as contracted. He didn't take any, and this sped up the process a hundred-fold.

Before the noon celebration, Jack asked Kristen and Andy to hand deliver the eviction notice and demand note for payment directly to Howard Singer and Marvin Manville and get a receipt that they received the documents. Having two high-powered attorneys deliver the documents was expensive but worth every dime to Jack. At the bottom of each document, Jack signed his name as the owner of the building and as president of the realty company. There would be no misunderstanding as to ownership after this.

୧ରେ୨

Kristen and Andy parked in the new lot and would join

Jack at the celebration. It was now eleven a.m., and they wanted to make sure that they delivered the materials before noon. Andy Miller as the head of the law firm called Howard Singer the day before to make sure that both he and Mr. Manville would be there to accept the material. He never explained why he was coming other than it was important that they be there. He might have even suggested that it might be financially rewarding to them. Andy had chuckled to himself and then told Kristen that he couldn't wait to see the expression on their faces as he handed over the package.

Kristen and Andy walked through the front door of the TCC building and asked for Mr. Singer and Mr. Manville. They took a seat in the lobby and waited until they were paged.

"Hello. I'm Howard Singer, president of the Troy Community Council, and this is Marvin Manville, vice president and treasurer. How may we help you?"

Andy introduced himself as the managing director of the law offices of Miller, Reynolds, Coleman, and Straus with Kristen Sanderson as a partner.

"We're here to give you the following documents," he said. "First, this is an eviction notice for the Troy Community Council to vacate the premises within thirty days. The second document is the request for payment in full for your demand note of sixty thousand dollars. The owner of your property is now Evangeline Realty, Incorporated, who purchased both your property and the note from Louis and Addie Freeman. All these papers are in order, notarized, and signed by the owner and president of the Evangeline Realty, Incorporated. You'll see the signature below. The demand is simply that. It is a demand for full payment immediately. You'll have two days to pay the note and thirty days to vacate the premises."

Howard and Marvin both looked at Andy and Kristen with the most incredulous look they'd ever seen. "The Freemans own the property and the note. What's this?" Marvin asked.

"Not anymore," Andy said. "All the papers are in order."

Howard and Marvin looked at the documentation again, and their eyes went to the bottom of the page where it was signed by the owner and president of the corporation. "Why did Jack Manning sign these documents? What's he got to do with this?" Howard asked.

"He owns Evangeline Realty, Incorporated and Evangeline Trust, which is having a grand opening next door to you in less than an hour. Jack tried to bury the hatchet with you two just last week, but you simply treated him badly and threw him out of his own building. He only came here to invite you and your staff and board members to the grand opening, but you never gave him a chance. It's amazing how you two act when you don't think anyone is watching. You didn't realize that everyone is watching you now. Please sign this sheet that you've received your documents."

Kristen whipped out her phone and took a picture of the signing and of Howard holding the documents in his hands.

They turned around and left immediately. "See you around," Andy said as he looked back.

⌬⌬⌬

"Holy shit," Howard said. "Are you kidding me? What do we do now? We never called the Freemans, and all this time, they were selling our building and note to Manning. What a prick. We better call Craig Livingston and tell him what just transpired."

"We better cover our asses as well. We just tell Craig we don't know what they're talking about. Jack never came here, and we never met him. Get that straight, Howard. We have to stonewall, or it's our jobs on the line. Who the hell would ever think Jack Manning would spend all his money right here just to get even?"

"Hello, Craig? It's Howard at TCC. Do you have a minute? We've got a pretty big problem. The Freemans sold our building and the note to Evangeline Realty and Evangeline Trust. They gave us an eviction notice and immediate demand for payment on the note. The owner is none other than Jack Manning. His attorneys handed us the documents, and we had to accept. They even took a picture of us accepting the package. They said that Manning came here to talk to us, and we treated him badly. I swear to God we don't know what he's talking about, Craig. Can you get to the bottom of this?"

"Send me the information for the law firm. I'll set up a meeting for early next week at the TCC. Hell, if he owns the building and the note, there's not much we can do about it, but at least maybe we can talk to them and fix this. Did you ever call the Freemans like I asked you to? We could have avoided this entirely if they donated the building to us."

"I tried and Marvin tried, but they said they weren't interested and everything was fine as it was as far as they were concerned. So, we felt that everything was fine. Evidently, Manning made them an offer they couldn't refuse. I think this is just to get back at us for shutting down the department. It's sour grapes, Craig, that's all."

"Sour or not, you better make this right, Howard, or you and Marvin can kiss your jobs goodbye." Craig hung up and called Miller, Reynolds, Coleman, and Straus.

The secretary said she'd contact Mr. Miller to set up an appointment if they were agreeable. Craig hoped they were agreeable.

⌘

Kristen and Andy made it back to the grand opening just in time. Jack and Mary didn't want to be part of the ceremony. They weren't program speakers either. Everyone in the know knew what this was all about. They didn't need the publicity, personally. All the big shots meandered back to shake Jack and Mary's hands to congratulate them and praise them for this facility and for what it would mean to the city of Troy. Eventually, after the publicity calmed down, he'd sit down and formulate his strategic plan and share it with the economic development council for Troy and the state of New York. He didn't want to explain anything today. This was about the kids and the opportunity to improve their lives and their community.

Karen Steele delivered the presentation for the grand opening. She was the new executive director for the Evangeline Career Center. It was a feather in Jack's cap for getting her to join up. Mary did quite a lobbying effort along with their politically astute attorneys. Karen was fifty-five years old and just retired as the deputy director of the New York State Labor Department, headquartered in Albany. On top of that, she was a crackerjack labor attorney. She'd be extremely helpful in getting their graduates placed in jobs once they were certified. Jack didn't want her for her lobbying efforts or for grants. He guaranteed her a ten-year contract, and she could retire anytime she wanted with a large bonus. She, too, was swayed by the generous vacation and benefit plan. She was married with two grown children and had the patience, experience, and education to do an even better job than Jack could. Being rich didn't mean he knew everything. Jack was very clear about that, and it impressed her. She asked Jack quite clearly if she was offered the job because she was African-American. He said no, it didn't enter his mind but it certainly didn't hurt he said. Half his students were minorities, and this would give them hope. She didn't seem to mind at all because, as she said, "Jack, you put your money where your mouth is, and I like that. I'll take the job."

Following her was Sam Ryan, the new controller and vice president. He was actually a year younger than Karen and a professor at U Albany. Jack's son, Mark, studied under him and had introduced him to his father. Jack reached out just at the right time.

He too was retiring from the university and was looking for a second career. He said this would be a terrific option. He told the crowd just that. That this career center was for second chances and even thirds if the students worked hard enough, they'd succeed.

Jack couldn't stand the political backslapping, but he had to hand it to the mayor. He did exactly what Jack asked him to do. Both were rewarded for their perseverance. Quietly, Jack told him to call him if he was running again. The mayor knew what that meant. The publicity alone for the new North Central Village concept would carry the election.

The party went well. The 100 students were dressed appropriately with Evangeline T-shirts and slacks with work shoes appropriate for what was coming. The ones who came back hugged Jack and Mary for what was happening. They couldn't believe it. They thought they were lost again back to the black hole of poverty. It gave them hope. Not one person asked how much Jack was worth. He already demonstrated that it didn't mean anything if he didn't share it.

As Jack and Mary were leaving the building, after everyone else had left, Jack looked over at the TCC building. There were people milling around the front of the building. He recognized many of the individuals who waved to him and Mary. Most of them applied for jobs at the new career center without even knowing what it was about. It wasn't just Howard and Marvin who applied, probably a third of the staff put in applications. That told Jack and Mary a lot about the future of the TCC. They'd have to act fast to save it, but it would be without Howard and Marvin and a few of the others who treated the former students like crap. That would never happen again. That was a promise he made to himself, the day he decided to do this and share it with

Mary. If wasn't for Mary, none of this would have happened. He smiled at her and simply said, "Thanks."

She looked at him on the steps. "I guess this is happening for real."

"It is," he said.

CHAPTER 43

Grand opening week was wildly successful. Now the entire Capital Region knew that Jack Manning, Powerball winner, had started the Evangeline Trust to fund a new career center in Troy. Word got out that he used to work at the Troy Community Council as the director for workforce development but was let go when they closed that department over a year earlier. The press had been calling the new number for the career center trying to get an interview with Mr. Manning, to no avail. The message on the machine stated that all requests for interviews were to be placed in writing to the law firm of Miller, Reynolds, Coleman, and Straus, 69 State Street, Albany, New York, care of Kristen Sanderson, partner. The message then went on to the various departments and administration.

Calls were steadily going in to the TCC as well. Howard and Marvin were hunkering down not wanting to speak to the media. None of the fallout from this was good for them, so they thought. Craig Livingston called Howard and told him that he'd set up a meeting with Jack Manning for Tuesday at ten a.m. He told them to be prepared and to help and not hinder the situation. Craig said they only took his call because he was a member of the bar in good standing. He said they wouldn't even talk to him if he wasn't a lawyer and would let the eviction and demand note stand.

Jack and Mary finally got a few hours to sit with Karen Steele and Sam Ryan. They went through the entire timeline of when they were fired right up to today. Jack told him that he went to TCC to invite everyone to the grand opening and they threw him out of the building.

Karen smiled and turned to Jack. "Wasn't that kind of what you wanted, anyway?"

"Probably," he said with a laugh. "I have to meet with them and the board on Tuesday at ten a.m. I prefer to go alone, in case it became embarrassing. I really don't want to drag anyone into my issues, or now Mary's as well."

"Yes, those are now my issues as well," she said and smiled. "Thanks."

"If they do what I want them to do, I'd like it if all three of you came with me the next time and we can make suggestions to help them."

"What do you want them to do, Jack?" Sam asked.

"Fire Howard Singer and Marvin Manville and yell at a few more of their staff for being uncaring to their clients. If they do that, I'm more than willing to bring TCC back into the black. In the long run, without those two, we're better off with TCC than without. They have great family services and counseling that, quite frankly, I don't think we have their expertise or experience in those areas. They gave a lot of that up when they went full blown Medicaid, and it hurt them. They're showing losses from which they won't recover without help. Karen, it's one hundred percent your call, not mine. I'll financially back whatever you say or for whatever you need. That's my promise and Mary's. By the way, she's worth fifteen million all by herself, in case you need to hit her up as well," he said with a laugh.

"Really? Mary, my new best friend," Karen said. "Lets talk about some things, woman to woman. Jack probably doesn't have a clue what I'm talking about. We need mentors and counselors to give the young ladies some self-esteem. The young guys don't seem to have that problem. They're just broke," she said.

Mary laughed, "Yes, broke and horny with no job and no money. That doesn't seem to work out too well with the ladies."

"We've our work cut out then," Jack said. "I'll let you know how I make out at the meeting. If I don't get back in a timely manner, please send some of our ex-Troy High football players to come get me."

Jack walked over from the career center to the TCC building right at ten a.m. on Tuesday. The receptionist showed him to the boardroom where he was met by Craig Livingston, chairman, the full board, and both Howard Singer and Marvin Manville.

"Thank you for coming today, Mr. Manning. It's appreciated," Craig said.

Both Howard and Marvin were squirming in their seats, ready to pounce.

"Can you please tell us why you had your attorneys give Howard and Marvin the eviction notice and request for immediate payment of the demand note for sixty thousand dollars for the past due rent."

"Be glad to," Jack said. "I stopped by the week before our grand opening to invite the administration, staff, and board to our grand opening. Mr. Singer and Mr. Manville treated me with disrespect. As you now know, I purchased the building and the demand note from the Freemans. I had plans to assist you and update your building for at least a million dollars. That's what the Freemans said it needed to bring it up to full code compliance. By the way, the Freemans are setting up a scholarship fund with the proceeds of the sale for our graduating students to continue their college education. So, now, after being insulted, and after you're evicted, I plan on knocking the building down and paving the space for a parking lot or place our new charter school right on your footprint rather than somewhere else. I haven't decided."

He looked directly at each member of the board as he was speaking.

Craig looked at Jack. "Evidently there's a difference of opinion about the situation, Mr. Manning. Mr. Singer told me that you were never here, and he never spoke to you, or he'd have been glad to be at the grand opening. Do you care to clarify your position? I know it won't matter to you because you're obviously going to do what you want anyway. We'll probably have to fight you, even though it would be an expense that we can't afford to incur."

Jack looked at both Howard and Marvin. "Are you going to stick with that absurd story, guys?"

"We've no idea what you're talking about, Mr. Manning," Howard said.

Jack pulled out his recorder and turned to Mr. Livingston. "If I may?"

"What's that?" Marvin said.

"It's funny how my perspective on life has changed, Marvin. Before, I was sucked in to every story ever told to me. I believed that everyone was telling the truth, and guess what? I paid dearly for that. I even got fired because of it."

With that, he hit the 'play' button, and the boardroom had a sudden hush over it.

You could hear Marvin's voice clear as day. "What the hell do you want? You can't come in here. Get out and stay out. You're not wanted here. You were fired a year ago. Hit the lottery? Big deal. Get out of this building before I call the cops."

Then Jack's voice came on. "Howard, do you feel the same about me, after all this time?"

Then you could hear Howard clearly say, "Jack, it's better if you just leave now before Marvin calls the cops. You're really not wanted here, and there's no need for you to be here."

Jack then said, "Okay, fine. I'll leave. I just wanted to stop by and say hello, but I take it that you're not interested in burying the hatchet. It's been nice seeing you again. Good luck to both of you."

And, finally, Marvin said, "Get out and stay out."

Jack turned off the recorder and looked at Craig Living-ston and the entire board.

"You can't use that recording. We're unaware of it," Marvin said. "We'll sue you for this."

Craig looked at both of them with absolute disgust. "What recording? Howard, you said Mr. Manning was never here, and you didn't know what he was talking about. I think we'll leave it at that, Mr. Manning. Thank you for clarifying your position in all of this. It's greatly appreciated and thank you for your valuable time."

Jack nodded. "I'm leaving now. I think you have some soul searching to do. I have the capability of bringing the Troy Community Council back to the black once again and giving it a long future as a partner with the Evangeline Career Center, right next door. You need new management to accomplish that. Call your neighboring nonprofits, right around the corner, and ask them what we've already done for them and what my total plans are for this area. You can be a parking lot or a valued partner. It's up to you." With that, he gave Craig the names of five employees, who had treated the clients unfairly, along with his card with his private cell number. "When you're ready to call me, we can start a new relationship built on trust."

Then he got up and walked out.

CHAPTER 44

It wasn't an hour later that Jack received the call from the TCC chairman of the board. "Will you come back and speak with the board again."

"Are Howard and Marvin still there?" Jack had asked. "If they are, I'm not coming."

"Mr. Singer and Mr. Manville were released from their duties approximately fifteen minutes after you left. They were escorted directly out of the building under great protest. They were not allowed to pack their things. We told them that whatever we thought was their property, we'd ship to their home. All the rest would stay. In addition, we immediately spoke to the five individual employees of TCC whom you told us treated our clients with disdain. They now have a letter of reprimand in their files. There will be no next time, and they believe it. It seems that the firing of Howard and Marvin have shaken our little nonprofit to the core. Of course, in hindsight, that's exactly what we needed to do but failed."

"I'm never happy when someone loses their job, but in this case, they deserved it beyond question. Thank you for speaking to the others."

"We more than spoke to them, Mr. Manning. They're on notice."

"What time do you want us there, Craig?"

"As soon as possible, but us?"

"Yes, us. I'm not in charge. Karen Steele and Sam Ryan are the administrators at our center. Mary and I are in charge of other neighborhood opportunities and strategic planning, along with simply being their bank. We'll be right over," he said.

Jack gathered Mary, Karen, and Sam and walked down the street and into the building. All TCC eyes were now on them with trepidation. They walked through the door and up the stairs to the boardroom without asking. Jack reintroduced Mary Evans and then formally introduced Ms. Steele and Mr. Ryan. Craig started with an apology on behalf of the board, the administration, and on behalf of all those clients that Jack and Mary had faithfully served for over a decade.

Without holding anything back, Jack went over everything that had happened from that terrible day over a year ago until today. He went over the strategic plans for the Evangeline Career Center and for his vision of the North Central Village. He also discussed how he'd get the TCC back from pending closure. He'd subcontract all family services to them that the career center needed for its participants. He was not going to cover all their sins at once, but it would be well over a half a million dollars a year with a built in profit of $200,000, which would bring them back to profitability in less than two years. For that, the TCC board was not only thankful but also extremely grateful. Jack didn't need to point out that they had a fiduciary responsibility as a board member and could be sued personally for malfeasance. The TCC had canceled their officer's liability policy due to lack of funding. They also discussed potential replacements for Howard and Marvin.

"We received over two hundred applications for those two positions from many solid individuals," Jack said. "None were even close to Karen and Sam, but they were capable, and we could pass along an opportunity at TCC to these individuals if your board approves."

"That's a tremendous offer and appreciated." Craig

looked at all four of them and then handed Jack a check for $60,000 to cover the demand note. "Every board member, within the last hour, chipped in to cover the debt as a good faith measure. I know it doesn't make up for the past, but I hope it gets us to the future."

Jack was very surprised and took the check. "I'll have our attorneys send you the paid demand note once the check clears. As I said, I learned a lot in the last year, and this is one of those life lessons." He smiled. The TCC board and Jack's people all laughed and smiled for the first time together. "By the way, I'll prepay TCC for the services we need over the next six months. I'll wire transfer two hundred fifty thousand dollars to your TCC corporate account, after the contracts for services are approved by Karen and Sam, and by our attorneys. That should keep you whole for a while," he said.

"Thank you, Jack, and thank you to your new team. We're very pleased," said Craig.

"I'll take this check and add it to the proceeds of the building from the Freemans for scholarships for our graduates. My father always told me to take the check because you could always return it but I'm not returning this," he said and shook Craig's hand.

Mary, Karen, Sam, and Jack went around to all the board members and shook their hands. Jack added, "Once we get rolling with our subcontracts, I want to revisit fixing up your building, bringing it back to full code compliance."

"Anytime you want, we'll be glad to talk. Who's on your board by the way?"

"You're looking at them," he said. "We're for-profit and don't need to comply with nonprofit rules and regulations. We aren't applying for funding. Everything is paid for through the trust, and for any added expenses, by me."

"Glad to know. You know what a pain it is moving through the system," Craig said.

"We do, and that's why we're doing everything ourselves. At least until the fund is used up," Jack said. "By the way, the timing on this is pretty important. You might not know that both Howard and Marvin applied for jobs, but a lot of your staff did as well. Hopefully, we can change that with a good partnership and cooperation."

Everyone nodded their approval and then Jack and his team left the building.

Karen turned to Jack. "Jack, why were you never considered for president of the TCC? They missed one hell of an opportunity with you, and Mary as well."

Mary turned and looked at Karen and Jack. "This is a new version of Jack. The old version of Jack was that of a nice guy, caring and considerate, but no administrator or head for business. I personally don't want to deal with the new Jack if he ever got mad at me. The new Jack has his stuff together and is ten steps ahead."

"We can see that now," said Sam. "I'm glad you're on our side," he continued as they walked up the stairs and were greeted by 100 young adults running around from class to class.

A brand new staff of eager, well-paid, well-educated, and dedicated professionals followed the students.

Time would tell.

ぐ୬ぐ୬

Sitting at the Recovery Room bar at the Hilton Garden Inn up the hill on Hoosick Street, Marvin and Howard were bitching, moaning, and complaining to each other as they waited for rides from their wives. They both had to hand back the keys to their nicely appointed company cars, a very nice perk with their jobs. They knew they wouldn't be getting any positive references anytime soon from the TCC board. That bastard, Jack Manning, maneuvered them perfectly into a bold-faced lie that they couldn't have gotten out of.

"You know, Marvin, you played one too many hands. I told you to own up, but you stonewalled, and I listened to you. We'll be lucky to get a job anywhere around here. We'll both have to leave the area. We so underestimated that son-of-a-bitch. Who'd have thought he recorded us, especially you?" Howard said.

"My fault? If it weren't for me, you'd have been out of a job years ago. What decisions did you ever make on your own, Howard? You wimp. I'm suing Manning, the TCC, and that new stupid Evangeline business. What kind of name is that, anyway? What'd they name it after, that TV nun, Sister Evangeline? What a crock. I already have a call in to my attorney."

⋅⋅⋅

Jack knew, that if they were fired, for which he was hoping, Howard and Marvin could sue him. So, a few weeks earlier, Jack sat with his attorney and put together an unfair labor practice lawsuit against the TCC and both Howard and Marvin as the top two administrators. He'd turned fifty just before he was fired and was then in a protected age class as a senior—as viewed by both the federal and New York State Labor Department.

No one ever pursued such a lawsuit because it was too costly and too cumbersome, and you usually spent more money than you ever received in any potential settlement. Jack didn't care. He knew this day would come if the TCC board were smart. He called his attorney and told them to hand deliver the notice of suit to both Howard and Marvin the night they were fired. If they had plans to sue him, this would hit them like a sledgehammer, and they might think twice before proceeding. He'd hold off on the TCC lawsuit because he probably wouldn't sue them anyway since he wanted this to work out.

The lawyers had two process servers go to Howard and Marvin's home to serve both with the lawsuit for one million dollars each. The servers were to call Howard and Marvin's houses, while outside in their vehicles, to make sure they were home, before ringing their front doorbell. When they called, both wives picked up their respective phones. The servers asked for the two men, and when they got there and asked whom it was, the servers hung up, knowing they'd be home to receive the lawsuit papers. They'd rung the doorbells and asked for the individuals by name. As they got to the door, Howard and Marvin were each handed the lawsuit. They couldn't believe that this was happening to them after just getting fired. It would certainly hold up any thoughts of suing Jack, but as he said, "Bring it on, I welcome the challenge. At least I have the dough to back it up." They each called their respective attorneys to call Jack's to see what was going to happen. Jack doubted that Marvin and Howard would remain friends in the future.

Jack smiled. He never hurt a fly before. He wondered if they knew what getting fired and thrown out of their houses, ending in divorce, felt like. It was time to move on. He was getting better at handling trauma and anxiety, he thought.

CHAPTER 45

M aureen? Are you going to tell me what's going on?"

"What do mean, Chuck?" she answered.

"You know exactly what I mean. You shut down after your meeting with your ex-husband, and then you've been running around in secrecy, and I want to know what's going on. I have a right."

"I can't tell you anything, Chuck. I signed a confidentiality agreement, and I can't say anything, but it's all good," she said.

"He can't expect you not to tell me what's going on. I live with you, for God's sake. Your kids are grown and gone. It's just us two now. I've got a right to know." He knew he was finally getting to her.

"If you promise not to say anything, I'll tell you. You have to keep it a secret," she said.

"I promise, I promise. Tell me."

"At the meeting, Jack handed me paperwork to fill out to send into the Roman Catholic Diocese of Albany. He wanted me to seek an annulment of our marriage. If I do that, I'll get a half million dollars when the annulment goes through and another half million when I turn sixty-two."

"What're you getting now? It seems that the burden is on you and none on him. You were married almost twenty-five years. How can you get an annulment? I'm not really Catholic anymore, so I don't know anything about it."

"He said that since I divorced him and was cheating on him with you well before I threw him out, that it's my fault, and I'm the one who has to seek out the annulment, or I won't get a dime."

"That's bullshit. You were only divorced for a few months before he hit the lottery. I'm sure your entitled to half of his millions. Now, he's going to only give you a million out of the hundreds of millions, and you have to do the work? Bullshit. Why don't you get the million up front and then apply for the annulment? Isn't that a good faith effort?"

"He said he didn't care. He said no annulment, no money. I can see his point. I was with you, cheating on him, threw him out of the house, and took everything he had. I'm sure he thinks he has a good reason for being mad."

"It doesn't matter. You know he's screwing you, and he knows it. Call him and tell him that you'll stop the annulment proceedings unless you get the million up front. At least that's something. Then you'll have enough to pay a lawyer to get your half that you deserve. Nobody cares about divorce anymore."

"He does, but maybe you're right. I really don't think I've got anything to lose by asking him for the money up-front. He won't cut me out. I'm the mother of his children, regardless of how he feels. He's been a pushover his whole life. That's one of the reasons I got tired of him. He could never say no to anyone. You're right. I'm calling him."

Finally, maybe we're getting some place. That million can get us half of his lottery winnings. She can reopen the divorce proceedings and get more. Then, I won't mind staying here with good old pain in the ass, Maureen.

"Jack? Hi, it's Maureen. I want to talk to you about the annulment."

"What about it?" he said. He knew that, eventually, something would go wrong. It always did with Maureen. She never got this or that, or this was a problem, or…

He didn't care. He was over her and her self-serving requests.

"I've been thinking about it, and it's not fair that I don't get any money unless the annulment goes through. That could take well over a year and almost two, according to your attorney. Jack, if you want the annulment, I want the million dollars upfront. I'm not waiting while you sit on millions. It's not fair."

"When did you decide this, Maureen?"

"Chuck and I discussed it, and we both feel that this is a fair resolution. No money upfront, no annulment."

"Maureen, you may not know or didn't pay attention that for every call I receive, there's a disclaimer on the phone that this message is being recorded. It doesn't matter if you leave a recorded message or not. It records live conversations as well."

"So, what do I care?"

"You just told me that you violated the confidentiality agreement that you signed. It stated that you were to tell no one, and we emphasized that it included Chuck Falcone."

"You can't be serious. We live together, for God's sake."

"Maureen, I tried to be fair with you because we spent close to twenty-five years together. You gave me no chance and spotted the opportunity to dump me and keep everything we owned. You signed off that you got everything I owned on the day that the divorce was finalized. I didn't even have the money to pay my attorney's final bill. You left me destitute. Did you forget everything?"

"That's water under the bridge, Jack. No million dollars upfront, no annulment, and that's final."

"Fine by me. I'll have my attorney, Kristen Sanderson, send you a notice that the agreement is null and void. She'll also be sending you and Chuck notice of a restraining order not to come within one hundred feet of me anytime, anywhere. Goodbye, Maureen. I really can't believe that you'd call my bluff on this. You just gambled and lost. Good luck." With that, he hung up and called Kristen. "Kristen?"

"Hi, Jack. What's up?"

"Please cancel Maureen's agreement for payment on the annulment. She violated the non-disclosure clause and told Chuck everything. She's going to go ahead and cancel the annulment proceedings. She wanted a million dollars upfront, and it's not happening. I also want a restraining order against both her and Chuck Falcone. Please make it happen."

"Jack, I know you're pissed, but listen to me. I'm actually glad this happened because I was seriously opposed to you paying a million dollars for an annulment. I know everyone thinks you can easily buy an annulment, but as a Catholic in good standing as well as you, I was uncomfortable. I also represent the diocese for canon law issues. However, did you know that under the new rules, you don't need both parties to sign off? You can apply yourself for an annulment without Maureen's consent. I'm afraid it'll cost you one thousand dollars but you'll have to bear the pain of that," she said.

"Are you making fun of me?" he asked with a chuckle. *A thousand dollars. Good one.*

"Yes, I'm making fun of you. Let's do this right, shall we?"

"Sounds like a plan."

"We can use all the same paperwork since I wrote up everything and had her sign the documents. We can choose a new category for annulment that you can live with. However, don't get caught up with who's fault it was. Let's just get it done and get your annulment. You can think about the rest later. From where I sit, you were the aggrieved one, not her."

"Thank you for that. I still would like an annulment, but I can tell you now, I spoke to Mary when we were coming back from Florida, and she didn't seem to care one way or the other. Even as an ex-nun, she seems more up to date than I'll ever be," he said.

"Give me the dirt. I need to know. Are you two an item now? Tell me."

"We're talking about it, but nothing has happened. It's me. I don't want to screw anything up. She means the world to me, and Maureen made me very leery of marriage."

"I know. Keep your chin up. It'll be a few days before I hear that she canceled the annulment request, and then we'll go ahead with yours."

A few days later, Kristen called Jack to let him know that Maureen went through with dropping the request. Maureen must have been very sure that he'd fold, like usual, and give in. She hadn't really been a party to the new Jack and how he now handled various touchy situations. He now handled situations head on without hesitation. There seemed to be a growing respect for his abilities that had carried over to his business plans and personal life.

CHAPTER 46

I haven't gotten any calls back from Jack yet," Maureen
said.

"Just wait. He'll give you what you want if he wants an
annulment. You have leverage, Maureen. Just play your
cards out. He'll fold, like always. Then you can thank me.
You'll have a million dollars in cash to go after him for
your half."

"Don't say anything to Mark or Debbie, please," she
asked.

"They haven't even been around at all for the last month.
Did you get any calls from them? You didn't tell me what
they were getting. Do you know?"

"I've no idea. I begged them to tell me, but they said
they weren't going to go against their father's wishes. They
also signed a non-disclosure agreement. You didn't tell
anyone, did you?"

"You think I'm that stupid, Maureen?" he said. "There's
a million dollars on the line here."

"Well, I certainly hope not. I don't want to piss him off
any more than I already have. We took a chance, but you're
right. As they say, 'a bird in the hand is worth two in the
bush.'"

"I told you. This will turn out very well for us." *Us, you
got that, Maureen? Us.*

The doorbell rang, and there was a deliveryman at the

door. He asked for Maureen Manning, and she nodded that she was Maureen. She signed for a package and brought it back into the house.

"What's that?" asked Chuck.

"It's from the law offices of Miller, Reynolds, Coleman, and Straus. Do you think it's for a check for a million dollars?" she asked.

They were both excited, and she carefully opened the envelope so she wouldn't tear any of the paperwork inside. She went through the pages, looking for a check. "I'll be a son-of-a-bitch. There's no check. Here is a letter canceling the agreement for payment once the annulment went through. There's also a restraining order against you and me, ordering us to stay at least one hundred feet away from Jack at all times. Son-of-a-bitch!"

"Let me see that envelope." He went through everything himself and saw the same letter canceling her agreement and initiating a restraining order. "I'll fix his ass. He's not getting away with this. He can't do this. We'll get an attorney. We'll fight this," he said.

"We? I just lost a million dollars. We? Who's we?" She was beside herself. Not for one second did she ever imagine that Jack would have the nerve to do this, but he did.

Chuck looked on in great disbelief then grabbed his jacket. "I'll be back in a little while."

"Where you going?"

"Out."

∽∽∽

Jack was just getting back from a meeting at city hall. The city was going to utilize community development block grant funds to repave the streets in the area now known as North Central Village. The cost of the sidewalks would have to be spread over several years. As Jack had the crews rehab the derelict houses, as soon as one side of a street was completed, the new sidewalks and lighting would go up immediately. The project would be paid for out of the taxes coming from the TCC building, the new career center, and from the rehab houses, even though the taxes were at a reduced rate for the early years of occupancy. Up until now, they received nothing from city owned abandoned properties.

As he was walking toward the front of the building, from the parking lot, he heard a familiar voice calling his name. He turned and saw Chuck Falcone coming at him with a full head of steam. Jack remained calm and didn't want any problems, especially in front of the career center and next to the TCC building.

Chuck caught up to Jack and grabbed his arm. "I want to talk to you," he said.

"What do you want, Chuck? I've got a restraining order against you. You know that, right?"

"Who cares? What do you think you're doing? Do you think you'll get away with screwing Maureen over? I won't let you do it. You owe her a million dollars, and I want a check in her name, right now!" he demanded.

"Not going to happen, Chuck. We had an agreement, but you had to interfere. Is this about Maureen or about you getting something for nothing, Chuck? Why she told you anything is beyond me. She canceled the annulment, expecting me to roll over. Or was that your doing, Chuck? Sounds more like you."

Chuck was infuriated. He shoved Jack to the ground and started to kick him in the side. "How's that feel, asshole. Have enough? You better pay up, or I'll kill you."

Just as he was about to kick Jack again, Fred came running out of his vehicle and John from the other one. No one had seen them over the last several weeks since Jack asked them to become invisible. Fred grabbed Chuck and punched him right in the face, breaking his nose. He hit him twice more, knocking him out cold.

Several students came running out of the career center when they heard the commotion. Two giant ex-football players asked Jack if he was all right. Jack had a hard time getting up. He thought he might have a fractured rib from the second kick. The first thing Jack did, as soon as he was able to get up, was to check his pocket recorder. As soon as Chuck had started yelling at him, Jack had hit the on-button and recorded the entire conversation. He was also sure that the cameras at the front of the building would have recorded Chuck pushing and kicking Jack while on he was on the ground.

John Jefferson called the Troy Police, who arrived within minutes. Chuck was just coming out of it when the officer slapped the cuffs on him. They threw him into the backseat of the police car and asked Jack, John, and Fred to come to the station and file a complaint to press charges.

Mary came running out of the building. She was in a meeting with Karen Steele and Sam Ryan. They followed her and looked at Jack.

"Are you all right, Jack?" asked Mary.

Karen and Sam had no idea what was going on. Mary told them she'd explain later.

The Troy Police would have to wait. John brought Jack to the Samaritan Hospital emergency room. It was now hard to find the emergency door entrance with all the construction going on. Finally, they parked off of Peoples Avenue and went to the emergency room the back way. After several minutes, he was brought in to see the doctor. Jack was a crime victim at this point, but when John and Fred showed them their retired-FBI credentials, the hospital staff became very attentive to Jack. Within minutes, the chief of police and head of the detective unit arrived as well.

"You're lucky, Mr. Manning," the doctor said. "You don't have any fractures, but you have two very large contusions on your side. In some cases, you'd wish you had a fracture. It's like some sprained ankles that hurt worse than a hairline fracture. We don't tape up your sides anymore because it sometimes causes pneumonia with the restriction around your chest. It makes it hard to breathe." The doctor gave him a prescription for pain medicine and told him to rest for at least a week if not two.

As the doctor was leaving, Mary came into the emergency room. "I drove your SUV in case you needed a ride home. I don't think my little Focus would help any." She'd gotten the keys from John before he took Jack to the hospital. She left her car in the career center parking lot.

Mary drove Jack home and helped him through the door and into his bed. She helped him get out of his clothes as best she could.

"Hey, what're doing? Are you trying to take advantage of me in my condition? The nerve of you," he said with a grimace and a smile.

"Don't you wish?" she said and laughed. "Take it easy, stud-muffin."

"Stud muffin? Thanks. You made my day. But how hard could that be after getting the crap kicked out of me?"

"Go to sleep now, and we'll talk when you wake up."

John and Fred filed the complaint to press charges for a felony to cause bodily harm to Mr. Jack Manning against Mr. Chuck Falcone. Jack had handed them the recorder and told them about the restraining order just sent out against his ex-wife and Falcone. He told them that Chuck didn't take it very well and came after him. He had both their voices recorded. He believed that the camera at the front of the building would have picked up the incident.

The complaint was filed, and Mr. Falcone was formally charged with misdemeanor assault and violating a court restraining order. It could appear to be a felonious assault, which required the actual infliction of serious bodily injury or death to another person, or the threat of serious bodily injury or death. Jack's injuries could be construed as felony related. A misdemeanor assault was generally something like minor touching of another person when the victim didn't welcome or invite the touching. A misdemeanor assault might include a slap in the face, pushing, or shoving. The shoving happened to Jack, and the kicking was a lot more, but it would probably be plea-bargained down from a felony.

However, it could probably be held over Chuck's head if he didn't plead guilty to the misdemeanor charge. Typically, punishment for a misdemeanor assault included incarceration in a city or county jail for anywhere from six to eighteen months, with fines ranging from $500 to $2,000, while punishments for felonious assaults usually ranged from two years to life in prison, depending on the type and severity of the assault.

Jack had a chip to play to keep Chuck out of his life forever. He didn't believe that Maureen approved of this beforehand, but nevertheless, she was responsible for Chuck's behavior.

Unless he was permanently gone, she'd never receive a dime, even when she retired. He had been thinking about that before, but certainly not now.

❧❧❧

Chuck called Maureen from jail. "Maureen, can you come get me and bring your checkbook?"

"Where are you, Chuck?"

"I'm in the Troy City Jail. I've been arrested for assault. I need you to come bail me out—now, Maureen."

"How much is bail?"

"It's twenty-five thousand dollars or a bail bond at ten percent, which is twenty-five hundred dollars. Can you swing that?"

"Why are you there again?"

"I was accused of assault."

"Of whom?" she asked.

I guess there's no stalling her now, he thought. "Jack Manning."

"My ex-husband, Jack Manning? You assaulted him? Why?"

"He pissed me off."

"Any witnesses?"

"Evidently, yes. Can you come get me?"

"Where's *your* checkbook, Chuck?"

"I don't have twenty-five hundred dollars, Maureen. You know that."

"Don't you have overdraft privileges?"

"Yes," he said.

"Then use it and take a taxi home." And she hung up.

Maureen called Jack's cell number but got no answer.

His phone was on the dresser and Mary grabbed it to see who called. She checked the last number and hit "call back."

"Hello?" Maureen asked. "Who's this?"

"Mary Evans, Maureen. Why are you calling Jack?"

"To see if he's all right."

"He's not, and you've no reason to contact him." Jack had told Mary everything that happened about the annulment and restraining order on the way back from the hospital. "He has a restraining order against you and Chuck. Not that it meant anything to Chuck. Don't ever call here again. Do you hear me?"

With that, Mary hung up and called both Mark and Debbie to let them know what was going on. They both said they'd be right over to the house. She told them to take their time because their father wasn't going anywhere for a while. Of course, neither was Chuck Falcone.

Mary then called Karen and Sam. She also called Kristen to tell the attorneys to get ready for Chuck's trial. Kristen said she'd be right over. Karen and Sam did as well. It looked like a party was coming together. This was just what she needed at the moment. No matter how much money you had, it didn't mean a thing, if you had health issues or you were in danger.

She'd have a long conversation with Fred and John. Instead of covering Mary and Jack, they should spend their time covering Maureen and Chuck Falcone. She was officially pissed at the world and would let everyone know it. She now realized how much Jack really meant to her and she to him. This was going on way too long, and she was about to fix it. Ex-nun? What a crock. She was more than that and would step up big time. This would never happen again.

CHAPTER 47

The Troy Police came by that night to get Jack's signature on the complaint form. Jack also mentioned to the officers that Chuck had Marty Sizemore following him around a while ago. Two detectives had already written up that incident, met with Mr. Sizemore, and told him what would happen to him if he continued. Evidently, Mr. Sizemore stopped, but it didn't stop Chuck. By evening, it was clear that Chuck would plead down to a low-level misdemeanor as per his attorney. Chuck's attorney, asking for the favor, had already contacted Kristen's team. Chuck would spend three months in the Rensselaer County Jail with three years' probation and a fine. He'd probably lose his job, making him a burden to Maureen.

That suited Jack just fine, as long as the restraining order was still in place against Chuck and Maureen. Jack was still shaking his head over the entire incident.

Debbie and Mark were dumbfounded by what happened. They couldn't believe that their mother would be with someone like Chuck. They both knew that she was being led around by the nose, but they couldn't do anything about it. Mark had already moved out when Chuck moved in, and Debbie practically begged her father to let her live in the dorm. It was now apparent that she'd need a place to stay during the summer before her senior year. She could stay with Mark, but she was working off her hours at the career center in Troy and would prefer to live with her father, his place being more convenient to Troy.

Jack would have to free up a bedroom for her to stay. He'd probably only need one of his bodyguards now since the biggest threat, Chuck Falcone, seemed to be removed. Jack would ask if they could go down to one man and split the time. He didn't think it would be an issue for either one. There were four bedrooms, but it would be very crowded with two women living there. They each needed their own bathroom attached to their bedroom. There were only two like that so that would mean something would have to happen. He thought that they wouldn't need any protection during the day since they were mainly at the career center. However, Chuck did attack him during the daytime. But at least that was resolved. It was the nighttime that concerned Jack. He'd check with them during the week.

Jack and Mary sat with Karen and Sam to tell them the entire story of how they ended up with today's event. Karen and Sam loved the house on Old Plank Road but were concerned for Mary and Jack's safety. They talked it through and came up with a decision to hire security at the career center during the day, and since Fred Tucker lived in Waterford, only five minutes from them, he'd spend the nights on Old Plank Road, when necessary.

Kristen was still shaken up by the entire incident. She was only slightly aware of the situation with Chuck, only because she was handling the annulment with Maureen. She was there when Jack asked Chuck to leave the attorney's office because he wasn't family, but it had never alarmed her. It did now.

It became clear to everyone that multimillionaires weren't like everyone else and never could be. There was too much attention paid to their wealth, which brought out the animosity in a lot of people. Those who asked for money and were rejected were the worst. They actually hated Jack because of this. Others immediately assumed he was difficult or that he thought he was better than everyone else.

He never once let on to anyone what he was doing with his money—giving it away to improve the lives of others. Just the fact that he handled requests by giving the person a card to contact the volunteer manager immediately angered people. They had no idea how many requests he received daily. They had no idea how much money he had already given away. He wanted to remain anonymous, but it was impossible when he continued to reside in the same town where he grew up. It would have been so much easier to have packed up and left for Florida, or he could have purchased some island where he'd never be bothered. It was wearing on him, but he had a plan, and he'd see it to the end. He just hoped that it *would* end.

❧

Maureen wouldn't take no for an answer. She continued to call Jack's phone until he finally picked up. She wanted him to drop all the charges against Chuck and said she'd make sure he never bothered Jack again. She never understood that it was she who was the annoying one. Chuck was very easy to read. He came head on. That was his downfall. Maureen kept apologizing, hoping that she'd get her million dollars back, but it was to no avail. She said she'd reinstitute the annulment, but Jack told her not to bother, that he'd taken care of it himself.

She called both Mark and Debbie and asked them to speak with their father on her behalf, but they both declined, telling her that she was a disgrace and until she got rid of Chuck, neither of them wanted anything to do with her. She'd hit a brick wall. She'd always relied on her feminine wiles to get her way. It wasn't working with Jack or her children. It also appeared to not be working with Chuck.

Her own children could have told her that. He was only after her money, and he couldn't have cared less about her. Debbie told her about the other women in the neighborhood, but Maureen wouldn't believe it. Now she was on her own.

✧✧✧

Jane and Martha stopped by to see Mary and knew nothing about what happened. They also wanted to get any new gossip about her and Jack. Mary let it slip that she and Jack talked about a relationship beyond their decade-long friendship.

They wanted to know everything. Unfortunately, Jack and Mary had been so busy that nothing had happened, yet. They had a few short conversations, but they were too tired at the end of the day or simply postponed the discussion until after the grand opening.

This attack on Jack really opened Mary's eyes, and she knew it was time to begin the new relationship. She just didn't know how. Neither did her two friends. She wanted to sit with Kristen who got over the hump, married, and now had three teenage children. She was much younger at the time than Mary was now, but circumstances were similar. When Kristen was leaving to heads home for the night, Mary asked her if she could stay for a few minutes to talk to her privately. Jack took his pain medicine and was out like a light. It was around nine p.m. so everyone was leaving after a very long day.

Mary opened a bottle of wine, and she and Kristen sat on the porch overlooking the expansive lawn with the view of downtown Albany, from fifteen miles away. The lights from the Egg and state offices were twinkling. You could see the planes landing at the Albany International Airport. You could see the cars starting to thin out on 787, I-90 and Alternate Route 7, going up the hill to Latham where it hit the Northway. The view was stunning.

"Kristen, I need some advice. I'm forty-seven and Jack's fifty. When he told me about the annulment, I knew what that meant. I've been in love with him for years but obviously never said a thing. His divorce hit him hard. It may have been partially his fault, but the way Maureen treated him, I wouldn't treat a snake. I want to move forward but, trust me, I'm in a quandary. I had one boyfriend when I was eighteen before going into the convent. It was my first love, but it didn't go far. When I got out of the convent, I dated a few guys, but it never amounted to much. Yes, I've had sex, but that's not what I meant. How do we get to the next level? I really want it to happen, annulment or no annulment."

"You're asking me?" Kristen laughed. "I knew early on that the convent wasn't for me, but I too was unworldly, to say the least. I met Bill at a concert at SPAC, believe it nor not. We're both the same age. He didn't know I was an ex-nun. I went with two friends, and they knew Bill from his days at The College of Saint Rose. He played baseball there with one of my friend's boyfriends. He introduced Bill to me, and he was with a few guy friends. He sat with us for a while on the lawn and then came over later, during the concert, to ask me for my phone number. I was shocked. I guess what I'm saying is, Mary, if it's meant to be, then it's meant to be. Just relax and enjoy the ride. You're very fortunate to have someone in your life who appears to adore you and wants nothing but the best for you. If someone gave me fifteen million dollars, I'd be attracted to him as well."

"Thanks. Keep it up, and I'll get a new attorney," Mary quipped. "So, go with the flow and see what happens? Hell, we already own this place together. That seemed to work out. As you may well imagine, Jane and Martha are living vicariously through me at this point and want to know everything. What do I tell them?"

"Nothing. It will drive them crazy, and they'll deserve it. They aren't that old and could enjoy the same opportunities if they left themselves open to change. They won't. So, don't worry about them. They'll come around. Can I be a bridesmaid?"

"Sure, but the dresses will be five thousand dollars each. I'll lend you the money if you can't afford it, smartass."

"Sounds like a plan," said Kristen.

CHAPTER 48

Over the next several months, Jack and Mary had a full schedule. After that, they'd once again head to Key West to stay at their newly purchased home, down the street from the Lennons. Skip; Linda's son, Tom; and daughter, Jamie had been keeping the outside lawns, hedges, bushes, and flowers in good shape. They were also overseeing the painters recommended by Skip. They were repainting the entire inside of the house. Jack didn't care, but Mary and Linda had been back and forth with Jamie, picking colors and using FaceTime to go from room to room to see how it looked. So far, so good.

The furniture that came with the house was in good shape but dated as well as the kitchen and the bathrooms. Mary wanted to get down there to select a contractor to redo both the kitchen and baths. It was funny that, up in Troy spending $20,000 on a kitchen was a big deal when the entire house cost $150,000. Down in the Keys, it didn't make a dent in the million-dollar price tag home. Since they had a garage, they both thought it would be a good idea to purchase a car to keep at the house.

When they weren't there, they'd offer the house to Jack's children, to Kristen, and to Jane and Martha, if they'd ever leave Troy. Jack wanted a convertible and Mary wanted an SUV so she could pick up the groceries, stop at Home Depot for plants and flowers, and whatever else they'd need after the house was brought up to date. They'd decide when they got there. Jack knew who'd win.

Jack promised Mary an entire week dedicated to the items on her list. She'd set up a meeting at the New York State Education Department to discuss potential charter schools, one for Lansingburgh and the other for the North Central Village. The governor had been very clear that he was in favor of charter schools, but several had failed recently, both educationally and financially. Both Jack and Mary believed that the educational failure was due to lack of proper funding for those children most at-risk who flocked to the charter schools for a better opportunity. Now, however, with Saint Augustine's School closing, there would be both those who attended the Catholic school previously and those who were failing in the local public school. There was no doubt that money played a very important role in both situations. Mary and Jack would take care of the building expenses, which was the major contributor to financial failure.

As planned, Jack and Mary picked up the Freemans at their house in Albia for a full tour of both the new career center and the TCC building, as well as for a discussion on the funding and application for the charter school for the village. Mary hadn't been to their house before so it was a nice chance to chat and thank them both for their generosity. Mary felt is was time to start taking a more active role, not only with her own funds, but with Jack's projects for the entire village concept.

They'd set up a small luncheon for the Freemans to meet Karen and Sam and the rest of the new team. From there, they'd all walk over to the TCC building, if Louis and Addie were able, and discuss potential upgrades to the building. After all, the Freemans donated the proceeds of the sale of the TCC building to the career center graduates for college scholarships. Jack wanted to surprise them both by naming the upgraded TCC building and the new technology center, at the career center, after both of them. He wanted to hear their ideas about both buildings to incorporate their thoughts into the plans. After all, the Freemans were also splitting the cost of the charter school building, once the charter was approved. That alone was well over four million dollars each for Jack and the Freemans.

The day went very well, but it was clear that it wore on the Freemans, he being eighty-one and she in her late seventies. Jack and Mary brought them home and, after assisting them to their front door, Jack said, "I hope everything was to your liking today. We couldn't have done it without you, Louis and Addie."

"Yes, you could have but thanks for making us feel like we're part of your plans."

Mary said, "Mr. and Mrs. Freeman, you're an integral part of our plans, and we've one more thing to show you. Can we come in for a minute?" She was holding a long cardboard tube that appeared to be holding some poster materials.

"Of course, you're always welcome in our home. Can I get you coffee or anything?"

"No that's fine, but we need to ask your permission for something." With that, she rolled out two posters. The first was a rendering of the upgraded TCC building with a new facade that was clearly labeled "The Louis and Addie Freeman Center." She then pulled out the career center technology center blue prints with the new facade that was labeled "The Louis and Addie Freeman Technology Center" at the North Central Village. "What do you think?" Mary asked. "If we get the church property, we'll move the sign over to that after it's completed."

Addie had tears coming down her face, dand Louis was just shaking his head in appreciation.

"In all our years, no one has ever done anything like this for us," Louis said. "Sure, they asked for donations and gave us a plaque but not clearly out of love and kindness. Thank you."

"Thank you," Addie agreed. "That's very generous."

Jack then added, "I'd put your name on the career center and the new charter school, but I don't want to make it look like it was bought and paid for by you. Legally, I have to keep the center, as 'The Evangeline Career Center' and I most definitely want the new charter school to connote it as being the center of the North Central Village. That's the name that's going in on the application, The North Central Village Charter School, and we don't want to confuse the issue. That's clearly our attorneys' point of view."

Addie sighed. "Jack, you never needed us, and we thank you for allowing two old people to once again feel respected and appreciated in the community."

Jack grinned. "By the way, if you're up to it, both of you, and please let me know if you aren't, we want you on our board at the Evangeline Career Center. If you've time and want to be on the TCC board, that can be arranged as well."

"Looks like we hit the jackpot, Addie. Right after Jack," Louis said, laughing. "And I may add Mary's name to the list as well."

"You know that Mary received some proceeds from the lottery winnings, but she has other plans for Lansingburgh. I promised her that, this week, I'd drop everything, and we'd start the ball rolling with her ideas and initiatives."

"We were aware of your generosity with Mary, and it's well deserved from everything we've heard. We're old but not out of the loop yet," said Louis, who smiled at Addie.

Jack looked at the two of them. They were married for two lifetimes and still loved each other just as they had the day they were married. You could just see it in their eyes. Maybe they never had children but their love for each other more than made up for it. Jack hoped that his life would be filled with joy someday, just like theirs, and he'd be able to forget the past and concentrate on a happy future.

It was past five p.m. when they finally left the Freemans. They ordered two take-out dinners from Verdile's and picked up a bottle of wine at the foot of the hill before heading home to Old Plank Road. It seemed like a long time ago that it had just been the two of them for the evening. Jack wanted to delve into the conversation that they had on the plane back from Key West. It seemed like forever.

Since returning, they'd been nonstop trying to get everything in place and settled. Every day they reviewed their plans. Jack had his strategy all laid out in print with check marks when they hit certain goals. Mary's might as well have been on the back of an envelope compared to Jack's.

She wanted to start her projects that began with The Lansingburgh Academy Charter School, and the Saint Augustine's gymnasium that would become the heart of religious education for the community after the Catholic school closed. She also wanted to make sure that the Lansingburgh Boys and Girls Club had proper funding after years of downward donations. Burgh citizens always funded the club, but as the residents aged and died, funding dried up, and they were now on the cusp of closing. The community now had changing demographics with more renters than homeowners, with less disposable income but far more social services needed. The club couldn't keep up, and Mary wanted to see how she could supplement several of the programs that were special to her.

They used to serve almost 20,000 lunches and dinners annually to kids in the community who counted on the club for their only meal of the day in many cases. They closed the program for lack of funding, even though they received grants for new equipment. Someone had to run the program. They badly needed a mentoring program for middle and high school kids who appeared to be directionless, more and more every day. Crime in the Burgh was climbing, and graduation levels in the district were falling. Changing demographics and economics went hand in hand, and Mary wanted to help.

They sat down for dinner. Jack uncorked the bottle of wine and Mary brought out plates. They both asked John and Fred to give them a few weeks to themselves, especially at night. Karen had added security to the career center, and that seemed to be going well, especially with the extra cameras, added to both their building and the TCC, and several others added to the poles going down the street and into the parking lot. It seemed to be working. Even their students, at times, needed to know that they were under scrutiny while participating in all the programs. Not everyone succeeded, and not everyone failed, but there were always a few that, no matter what you did, just didn't get it. It was better to pick up those few individuals and their activities as soon as possible. There was too much time and money riding on the success of the whole North Central Village project.

Jack and Mary finished their meals and had another glass of wine while doing the dishes. They both understood the significance of time alone to make sure that, if their friendship turned into more, like they planned, they needed to have alone time together.

It was now well past ten p.m. when they leisurely wiped the last dish. Mary looked at Jack. "Jack, I haven't properly thanked you for everything that you've done for me. It's not the money, and it's not the annulment. It's just how much you care for me that I appreciate. I just wanted you to know that I care about you, just as much."

With that, she took Jack's hand in hers and walked him to her bedroom. They were finally all alone for the first time in over nine months. "Let me properly thank you," she said with a smile on her face." She put her arms around him and gently kissed him on the lips. To say he was elated was an understatement.

"Are you sure, Mary?"

"I've never been so sure of anything in my life." She gently pushed him onto the bed and kissed him harder with a yearning that he hadn't seen from her. "Love me, Jack," she said.

He did. They looked into each other's eyes and knew that this was the moment that they both had been waiting for. Jack didn't know that Mary had been waiting for years.

The eleven p.m. news came on, and Mary was sleeping gently in Jack's arms. He didn't want to move. He'd never been so happy. He couldn't believe how life changed from minute to minute. He was a firm believer that, if you worked hard and did the right thing, good things would happen to you. He almost lost everything and started to believe that his life was over. Lying here with Mary in his arms was a dream come true. He kind of laughed to himself that if it was up to him, he'd probably still be doing the dishes, trying to figure out what to do. At age twenty or fifty, most men hadn't a clue. Mary made this happen, and he thanked God she did.

They got up early around seven a.m. Mary had a complete schedule planned for Jack for the week. It was her turn now. She had her plans, but in the back of her mind, she wanted to do something different, something exciting. She'd never been any place until Jack took her to Florida. She loved it. She loved every minute of it. However, for many years, she'd a dream about going to Cuba. She read that the Catholic Church was the only institution allowed in Cuba other than the government. With Pope Francis leading the charge, and with the U.S. embargo lifted, she knew that Cuba was changing and there would be many opportunities. Cuba was still, after all those years of communism, over fifty percent Catholic but not many practicing. She learned about the Catholic Diocese of Albany's plans to send a goodwill team to Cuba to see how the church really was functioning there and to see if there was a chance to reinstitute Catholic schools on the island. Mary thought that might be a dream come true for her and Jack to go with a team to see what possibilities could evolve. She'd ask him about it after breakfast.

Chapter 49

Mary had set up appointments for the week. One was to meet with officials from the New York State Education Department to discuss two applications for charter schools in the city of Troy, New York. It was also possible to become approved through the State University of New York higher education system, but State Ed seemed to be the first choice. They'd speak to State Ed first to seek out feelers about their respective applications. Another meeting was with the superintendent of the Albany Catholic Diocesan schools to seek approval for a long-term lease for Saint Augustine's school and gymnasium in the Lansingburgh section of Troy.

The school would be used as a charter school and the gymnasium as a focal point for the parish's religious education program. Mary also wanted information on the Diocese's goodwill tour of Havana, Cuba. The inside scoop from Kristen Sanderson was that this superintendent was a key member of the committee that would go to Cuba within the next two years and Mary wanted to be on that committee. They'd be discussing potential Catholic schools in Havana. Currently, the only entity in Cuba other than the government was the Roman Catholic Church. However, all Catholic and private schools were disbanded after the revolution. Everyone in Cuba received a public education that didn't include any religious education.

The superintendent was housed on North Main Avenue in Albany, right around the corner from Mary's Alma Mater, The College of Saint Rose. Mary hadn't been there in years and wanted to walk around the campus, after the meeting, to see what had changed. What had changed dramatically in the last year were the reduction of their premier teacher education program and the firing of tenured professors. There have been protests, newspaper articles, and TV interviews, all giving St. Rose a very bad black eye. There had been a substantial decrease in the student population in the teacher education area with limited explanations as to why. The answers pouring out of the administration had been weak at best, making students and parents question attendance at the college. They'd been in crisis mode for sometime. As Jack had pointed out in regard to charter schools, overpayment for rent or ownership of large facilities dealt a deathblow to a number of Capital Region and New York City charter schools. Overpayment for facilities cut into the quality of the teaching staff, which made the burden not just financial but academically challenging. St. Rose was a prime example of overbuilding and overspending for unnecessary facilities in the wake of a decreasing student population for the teaching profession.

Evidently, the superintendent had done his research on both Jack and Mary. Father Jim Brady, the pastor at St. Augustine's, had called him and given his personal approval and recommendation for the project proposed by Mary Evans. He told the superintendent of Mary's ex-nun status and continued status as a teacher and teacher aid at both Catholic High and St. Augustine's school. He also told him that she'd taken a leave of absence and was given fifteen million dollars from Jack Manning's winnings. He was well aware that Jack Manning was the Powerball winner and was made aware of his projects by Kristen Sanderson, who still pulled a lot of weight as the attorney for canon law for the Diocese.

In the superintendent's office, Mary spoke first since it was her project that brought them to this meeting. Jack would speak first to the state education people the following day for his massive project with the charter school as a focal point within the new village.

She explained her ideas of converting St. Augustine's into The Lansingburgh Academy Charter School, whose historical significance across the street, was well known. She also explained that St. Augustine's was both their parish and they wanted to assist the parish in keeping religious education alive. She mentioned that a favorable letter from the Diocese would go a long way in aiding her cause for this charter school application. She was willing to sign a ten-year lease for the school, with all the money up front, if the charter was approved. They also needed a plan to include the one hundred students, who attended St. Augustine's, into the new charter school. This was an issue because there would be a student lottery drawing for seats at the academy. She mentioned that if the school could serve at least 500 students from the Lansingburgh community, there would be a very good chance that the 100 St. Augustine's students would be included. The charter school would serve the same pre-K through sixth grade classes. Both Jack and Mary promised, in writing, that they'd give $100,000 per year to St. Augustine's parish to keep the gymnasium and religious education program alive, if the charter school was approved. If not approved, they'd still support Catholic education in a different manner.

The superintendent was very appreciative of their commitment to the Diocese and was in agreement with their plans. The Diocese had just assisted an Albany charter school that moved from a brand new building that they couldn't afford to a closed Catholic high school at much less than what they were paying previously. Again, this made their charter school viable and now successful and in the black. Everyone was a winner as he told Jack and Mary. This could prove successful as well.

As an aside, Mary mentioned that she was very interested in being part of the Albany Diocese team that would be going to Cuba. She was in full support of starting a Catholic school, whatever grades, in Havana. The superintendent understood her passion for education and for Catholic education in particular. He said that he'd be meeting with the bishop at the end of the week and he'd mention her request for inclusion in the trip. She thanked him.

The meeting ended on a positive note, and they believed that they were moving in the right direction. It might take one to three years to implement their plans, but they were on the right path. Jack left his SUV in the Diocesan parking lot on North Main Avenue, and they walked over to the college where they grabbed lunch in the student cafeteria. After their brief tour, Mary told Jack that she felt ancient compared to the faces running around campus. Jack smiled at her. "You aren't getting older, Mary. You're getting better."

"Thank you for that," she said. "I still feel old. It'll be my twenty-fifth reunion from St. Rose coming up this year. Boy does time fly," she added.

The next day was just as important. They had to meet with the New York State Education Department deputy commissioner to discuss both charter school applications. They also invited Kristen and her partners at the law firm as evidence that they were serious applicants. They'd also drawn up a proposed financial funding document that would outline Jack and the Freemans' financial commitment to build a North Central Village Charter School. It also didn't take long to receive an email from the superintendent of the Catholic schools approving their plans for St. Augustine's School. The printout from the Diocese was included in Mary's financial commitment. They deliberately left off any reference to religious education or the gymnasium's usage so as not to confuse the issue of a charter school application.

The best part of living in the Capital Region was that Albany was the state capital. Several hundred thousand people worked for the state, all located in the greater Capital Region. It was the financial backbone of the area. Unemployment was always much less than the rest of the state and nation because the government still needed workers, regardless of the economy. Hopping into the car from their house in Brunswick to the State Education Department on upper State Street took less than half an hour, including finding a parking spot. Jack used to kid everyone that if you had a roll of quarters, you could own Albany. The meters only had two hours' parking, and their meeting would be less than that. They parked in front of the massive building and walked in the front door. Kristen Sanderson and the rest of the team met them at the front door as they checked in at the guard station and meandered down the hall to the deputy commissioner's office.

Having your lawyers located in downtown Albany didn't hurt any. Some of their staff performed lobbying duties to state government just like Kristen did with the Albany Catholic Diocese. Having them there was a Godsend since they knew many of the state education people already assembled for the meeting.

Gerald Reynolds, head of Estate Planning, Trust, and Probate for the firm, also conducted lobbying on behalf of several unions and organizations that had business with state education. He began the meeting with introductions, and the deputy commissioner did as well. Gerry turned the meeting over to Jack and Mary, with Jack speaking first. He handed out briefs to everyone at the meeting. He was very well prepared. He went through the entire process about hitting the Powerball lottery and how they came to this day, introducing his concepts of a village within a small city. Then he talked about his commitment to a charter school in the village. He apologized that Mr. and Mrs. Freeman couldn't make the meeting. Mrs. Freeman was not feeling well. However, Mr. Freeman's attorney was sent instead, and he handed their financial commitment letter to the assembled staff. Jack gave his and Mary's background. He then asked Mary to speak.

She spoke about the history of Lansingburgh and what St. Augustine's meant to the community and the history of The Lansingburgh Academy, introducing famous teachers and graduates including Chester A. Arthur, Herman Melville and the connection to RPI. She finished with her financial commitment letter as well.

They were told that Troy had two current charter schools in South Troy but none in North Central or Lansingburgh. They said they'd review the documentation and would let them know how they should proceed. Again, they could go through state education or through the SUNY system of universities and colleges. Overall, those assembled thought very favorably about their presentations and commitment of resources to the city of Troy and its youth. The meeting took less than an hour and a half, and they were promised to hear from the commissioner by the end of the month. The next round for approval for charter schools was in six months, with a one-year approval time period.

As Jack said when they were walking down the stairs from the building, "We have a ten year commitment to do everything we wanted. We've already far exceeded all our goals, and this is just another step in providing everything we can to those residing in the village and in Lansingburgh."

Kristen said, "Mary and Jack, I don't think anyone could have done any more than you've done already. You both deserve a medal, or a peace prize, or something." She laughed.

Kristen took Mary and Jack for a late lunch down the hill at Jack's Oyster House, right across the street from their offices, at the foot of State Street. Jack followed Kristen down the hill in his SUV.

It was a very good week and critical to their overall plans. They could now rest for a while. Everything they wanted to do and planned to due was already started. By the end of the year, the people, the construction, the schools, and the tech centers would be well on their way to fruition. Jack and Mary were smart enough to make sure that each project had its own team of professionals to do the daily work and operations needed to be successful. They'd never be in charge of the day-to-day activities. They did that before at the old TCC, and all it got them was fired. They'd have no input into the daily operating plans of the organization. Now, they sat at the top of the holding company and could move the chess pieces where they wanted to, knowing they had the right people in charge. At least they hoped that was true.

Chapter 50

It seemed like forever since they'd gotten back down to Key West. Mary wanted to see all the changes to their house. She'd supervised at a distance, but it wasn't the same as being there in person. It was like watching a baseball game on television versus being at Yankee Stadium. It just wasn't the same. All the painting was done, and the kitchen had been ripped out, with most of it now back together. One of the two full bathrooms was completed. The bathroom far exceeded her expectations. Jamie and Linda did a great job, making sure everything they talked about was put into place. Jamie's job went from caretaker with her brother to almost fulltime status supervising and helping out. As soon as Mary got there, she made Jamie add up all her hours, and they paid her $3,500. Jamie was delighted but overwhelmed. After all, she was still driving around in Mary's SUV, which was also a bonus.

Mary wasn't worried about the kitchen. They'd eat out most of their meals, and, for breakfast, they made it simple with coffee and cereal. They'd be there for about two weeks and then needed to head back for their big meeting. Every quarter, everyone who worked with them in every capacity, had a chance to listen to Jack and Mary's vision and had input into everything they were working on. It was Jack and Mary's style to let the people working in their positions make important decisions in their own areas. That gave them power over their job, and they bought into doing their very best every day. Money was still no problem as long as what they wanted to do, and needed, fit into the overall strategy that informed all decision-making.

They both made a vow that, when they landed at Key West, there would be no discussion about issues back home. They were there to relax and unwind and continue to get to know each other as a couple. They planned their days around each other's likes, and, then on some days they'd simply hop into Mary's SUV and drive around to see everything they could, to get to know the area better. Jack was kind of a history buff and wanted to know everything about the area. He went online and read all about the history of the Florida Keys. They'd drive, not only around Key West but also up to Islamorada and Key Largo. Once they took a day and drove up to Miami to see Biscayne Bay. They stayed overnight and were amazed that the town didn't start hopping until well after eleven p.m. Everyone seemed to be on Latin American time. They had dinner at an exclusive restaurant at seven p.m. the first night, and there was no one else in the restaurant. After dinner, they walked the promenade and simply enjoyed life. They did feel much better as soon as they crossed over and landed on the Keys side of Florida. It was a long ride on a very narrow road, one lane going both ways. The 150 miles from Miami to Key West seemed to take forever. Getting behind camper vans heading south simply meant that you either pulled over and enjoyed the ambiance or learned patience.

They were into their second week and wanted to stay for another, but it simply wasn't possible with everything going on. Jack was negotiating for the church and the lyceum across the street. It was still owned by the Diocese, who wasn't quite sure of what they were going to do with it. The church had been shut down for a few years, and the parking lot was leased out to another organization, but that was from month to month. Jack offered to share it with them so as to not create any hostility toward the big bad corporation taking over the world. At least he and Mary had the upper hand with Kristin doing their bidding for them on the St. Augustine's properties, the trip to Cuba, and for this closed church, that would be only a block from the new charter school once approved.

They decided not to have a landline in the house in Key West since they both had their own smart phones. The Lennons were only down the street, and they all had access to cell numbers and email addresses in case of a problem. They had Comcast for both cable and Internet service. They left a new iMac at the house in case Jamie needed to download any information or to look up where to buy things requested by Jack or Mary. Tom, Jamie's brother, was a wiz at technology so as soon as Comcast wired the home, Tom did his work and had all the rooms wired for sound, cable television, and internet access points throughout the house. The former owner, Jerry Titus, was in his early eighties and had no need for cable and didn't even own a computer. His daughter took care of anything that he needed.

Jack's cell phone started ringing, so he picked it up off the dresser. "Hello?"

"Hi, Jack. It's Kristen. Having fun?"

"What's not to enjoy, looking out at the ocean from our front window."

"Well, I just wanted to call you and give you some even better news. Which do you want to hear first?"

"If it's all good, just go ahead and tell me. Do you want me to put it on speaker so Mary can hear? She's in the shower."

"Not yet."

"Okay," he said reluctantly.

"First, I want to tell you something, so if you want to tell Mary, you can, but I'm giving you a choice. Okay?"

"Now you got my attention. Go ahead."

"Jack, your annulment just came through. I have the papers in front of me declaring your marriage to Maureen null and void. You can remarry in the Catholic Church as if you'd never been married before."

"Really? You're not kidding, right? You wouldn't kid about that, right?"

"Never," Kristen said. "Congratulations. You can now do what I think you've been planning to do for sometime. You know that Mary and I are very close friends, right? She's been hinting about you two for sometime."

"Yes, I know that you, Jane, and Martha are thicker than thieves or nuns or whatever."

"Thieves or nuns, huh? Thanks a lot." She laughed.

"That's great news. Mary is in the bathroom. Shall I get her for the other news?"

"Yes. I won't say a thing about the annulment. Go ahead and get her."

Jack knocked on the bathroom door and asked Mary if she wanted to get some good news from Kristen. She said she'd be a minute. She was drying herself off.

"Hurry up," said Jack.

"What's your hurry?" she asked. She looked a little quizzical.

"Go ahead, Kristen. Give us the news," said Jack.

"Hi, Mary. Are you both listening?" Both said yes.

"The bishop approved your lease for St. Augustine's School if your charter school is approved. The one hundred thousand dollars a year is fine if you take care of maintenance, heat, light, electric, and any major issues with the building over the ten years. And, you can rent the gym for twenty thousand dollars a year as well."

"That's great news. Now, all we have to do is get approved for the charters."

"Gerry Reynolds also heard back from the deputy commissioner's office. They like both your plans for charter schools for Troy. They can't approve anything or promise anything now. You still have to submit the applications when they're due. However, the weight of the deputy commissioner will go a long way toward the approval. Congrat-ulations to both of you. You're well on your way."

"What about the church for the technology center and the lyceum?" Jack asked.

"Geez, Jack. Give me a break here. I was just getting to that. They want to sell that property and not lease it, but I think they want too much now and you may have to negoti-ate the price when you get back. The people renting the lot aren't thrilled by the offer. They want to keep the lot for themselves, so you might have to deal with them as well. As you said before, it would be nice to use, but you have more than enough room at the career center right now. Isn't it the idea that you want these building brought up to code, so it doesn't matter if you own it or not, just that it fits into the village concept?"

"That's true, but I'd still like to own it to entice RPI to bring down their emerging businesses, so our students can get internships. I don't have room for that, but I guess I could build a much smaller building next to the career cen-ter to accomplish that. At least we're moving forward, and we can address that when we get back."

"Sounds like a plan. I'll let you two go and congratula-tions. I'll catch up with you when you get back."

They both hung up, and Jack looked at Mary with a smile.

"What else did she tell you other than what she said just now? I wasn't privy to your earlier conversation while I was in the shower."

"God, nothing gets by you, does it?" he said, laughing.

"Well? Are you going to tell me?"

"Mary, my annulment just came through. It's signed, sealed, and delivered. I'm very pleased about that. Even more so than anything else."

"That's great news, Jack. But I told you. I didn't need that to love you. I do love you very much."

"Mary Evans—I wish I had a ring right, now but I've been holding off until I got the news." He got to his knee, looked into her eyes. "Mary, will you marry me? I love you very much, and I want to spend the rest of my life with you. You mean everything to me."

Mary had a tear in her eye, and then tears began to flow steadily down her cheeks. "I've been waiting for this moment for a very long time, Jack. Yes, I'll marry you. I love you very much, and I couldn't think of a better way to spend the rest of my life."

He got up and wrapped his arms around her. They kissed and then kissed again and again.

"What do you say we go looking for rings tonight? I don't even know where we should go."

"Why do you think women are always ahead of you, Jack? You're such a guy. When we were first down here and met Joe and Julie at Sloppy Joe's, I told her I loved her engagement and wedding rings. She said that she kept putting it off because they were so expensive and that she wanted a house before a ring but Joe insisted. Joe made her come down and look at rings in the stores on Duval. They stopped in at Diamonds International, and she loved the ring but it was so expensive. The owner gave Joe a very big discount because he was in the Coast Guard. A while later, he got a bonus from his boss, and it covered both their wedding rings and the engagement ring. So let's head to Duval tonight."

"Sounds like a plan."

"Can I call Kristen back and then Jane and Martha? I should call my mother too."

"Tell them not to say anything before I talk to Debbie and Mark. I want to tell them in person, especially because of the situation with their mother. Is that all right?"

"Sure, give me an hour, and then we'll head out."

Mary's friends were elated for her, especially Kristen who traveled the same path many years ago. Jane and Martha said they knew it would happen sooner or later. Mary didn't call her mother because she was getting on in years, and Jack was right, she'd see her in person and tell her when she got back. Mary told her friends not to say anything until they gave the okay.

They were both excited, and as they left the house, they saw Jamie watering the lawn. They asked if her parents were home, and she said yes. They walked down to their house and knocked on the door. Linda opened it and saw the look on Mary's face. "Well? Did he ask you?"

"Yes. We're going to look at rings down on Duval."

"How the hell did you know it? I didn't know it," Jack said.

Linda just smiled at him as if to say, "Fool, of course, I knew."

Skip came to the door, kissed Mary on the cheek, and shook Jack's hand.

Jamie hugged Mary so hard she couldn't breathe. "Congratulations. That's great."

It took about a half hour to remove themselves from the front door, hop in Mary's SUV, and head to Duval. Jack thought that this day couldn't get any better. He was thrilled and hoped that Mary was too.

CHAPTER 51

Jack took Mary to Diamonds International on Duval Street. They were able to park in a lot close enough on Simonton Street, right around the corner. They walked in and were greeted by the manager. Jack mentioned that their friends, Joe and Julie Traynor, had purchased Julie's engagement ring and both their wedding rings from him. The manager knew both of them well. They'd been back several times before making a decision. He remembered that Joe was a lieutenant in the Coast Guard and he gave him a sizeable discount. He mentioned to Mary that whatever she liked in the store, he'd do the same for them.

Jack never let on his about his financial status. He simply nodded and thanked him for the courtesy. Mary went through an array of styles and then came across a mounting that she really liked. It was a solitaire, a single stone. The head secured the diamond. The prongs allowed the diamond to catch the most light. The four-prong-setting showed more of the diamond, but she wanted a six-prong setting which was considered more secure. The diamond was of the finest cut and clarity and was two carats in weight in a traditional round shape. She asked to see the ring, and he took it out of the case. She told Jack that she loved the setting and the stone, but she wanted a six-prong setting. Jack looked at the owner and nodded. The man went back to his books and pulled up the exact setting she wanted. He'd remove the stone and then place it in the setting she preferred. He said that was necessary anyway to separate the stone from the ring to obtain a GIA diamond grading report. Mary would receive a GIA diamond grading report, and the diamond itself would be laser inscribed with a GIA report number and a personal message, symbol, and date. GIA only graded un-mounted diamonds and that would take up to the three weeks delivery time. Jack told them that they'd be leaving for New York shortly and asked about shipping arrangements, sizing, and insurance.

Jack asked Mary if she wanted to be in on the negotiations for the ring and she said yes. She knew it was not about the money but in the back of their minds, neither was a showy person. The ring Mary selected was of uncommon beauty, style, and grace and reflected a certain dignity. It wasn't flashy, and while you might notice the size of the diamond, it certainly was not ostentatious. The manager gave Jack a very nice discount but said he had to order the special 6-pronged setting and it would take three weeks before he could have it ready because of the GIA.

Mary appeared to be thrilled to death and hugged Jack. "This is real, isn't it?"

"Yes. Boy, it didn't take you long to pick something out. I love you to death for that reason alone."

"How hard is it to pick out a two-carat diamond ring? I already knew what I wanted, forever. Remember what you said about knowing how you'd divide up the winnings if you ever hit the lottery? Well, women know what kind of engagement ring they'd want if money were no object."

"Nice to know. Do you want to pick out wedding rings tonight?"

"Let's come back tomorrow and look. I'm way too excited to make any more decisions tonight."

Jack gave the store manager his credit card. The manager said he could give him a bigger break if he paid by check.

"The credit card fees on a purchase like this are a killer," he said.

"Sure," Jack said and pulled out his checkbook. He never had to look at the balance because Kristen told him that his account was set up so he could make large purchases and she'd be notified to cover it. "Kristen's going to know what I paid for this now. Is that okay?"

"Yes. I'm going to call her later tonight anyway and remind her not to say a thing to anyone, especially about the ring price. She's our attorney anyway. She'd never say anything, but I'd certainly take a ribbing from her anyway. Isn't that what friends do? I've never been in this position before, you know."

"You think I have?" He laughed.

They were promised that the ring would be shipped directly to the law firm that would hand deliver it to their house on Old Plank Road at their convenience when they got back.

They went back the following morning and picked out two matching wedding rings. The rings had to be sized correctly and would be included with the shipment of the engagement ring.

They packed and headed to the airport. They really didn't want to leave but they'd too much to do in a very short time. They'd discuss wedding plans on the plane. It seemed that on every return trip they had to make big decisions.

As soon as they got back from Key West, Jack wanted to speak to both his children about his asking Mary to marry him. He wanted to explain to them about the annulment. It didn't mean they weren't legitimate. It simply meant that both children were legitimate in the eyes of the church and of God, but the marriage was invalid from the beginning. They'd either understand or they wouldn't. They were both of an age to make up their own minds.

While Jack would meet with his children, Mary would take her mother to dinner to let her know that she was getting married. Never having married by age forty-seven, going on forty-eight, was a big step, and she thought her mother would understand. It had nothing to do with the money. Her mother already knew about that and was being well taken care by Mary since the day she received the money from Jack.

Jack invited Debbie and Mark to dinner at Reel Seafood on Wolf Road for six-thirty p.m. the following night after they got back. He wanted to talk to them, especially before Mary's engagement ring was delivered and, by then, everyone would know their new status. They'd stop asking, "Are you two…"

At dinner, Jack was very polite but very clear when he spoke to both Debbie and Mark. Mark seemed to take it much better. He knew what happened to his father, and he wanted him to be happy. He knew how his father felt about Mary, and Mark liked Mary very much. He was surprised about the annulment, but, like most guys, he didn't think it was a big deal. Of course, young adult Catholics always seem to lose their faith while out on their own for the first time but seemed to gain it back after they got married and had children. However, today's Catholics weren't so much hung up on what was right and what was wrong, according to the church. They seemed to go with the flow. That was Mark's attitude as well as his girlfriend, Cara's.

Debbie's attitude was slightly different. In the back of her mind, she thought that her father and mother would get back together once her mother dumped that loser, Chuck. That didn't happen, and she couldn't understand why. She was a little hung up about the annulment, and it appeared to affect her. She didn't want to be an illegitimate, unloved child. He told her that would never happen and then went back to tell her what he went through to get her back and be her father once again. At that point, she started to listen and understand.

Toward the end of dinner, he also mentioned that their inheritance, that he'd give them from the winnings, might be given to them earlier if they got married, bought a house, or made decisions that were in their best interest. He then handed both of them a check for $50,000 to use wisely and to pay their bills and put the rest in a savings account for a rainy day. He told Debbie that she still needed to work off her hours at the career center, and she agreed. She said she really like working there and was proud of what he'd done so far.

He studied her. "Upon your graduation, if you need or want a job working in the village, I make no promises but we'll see how your education, skills, and desires fit in with our plans. You'll get no special treatment."

She nodded. "I understand."

❧❧❧

Mary took her mother to dinner at Verdile's and told her about her engagement to Jack. She knew the wedding would be within the next year, depending on how all their plans unfolded. She told her mother that her engagement ring was being sized and then shipped, and she'd show it to her when it arrived. Her mother was very happy for her. Mary thought that it had to be easier telling her mother than what Jack had to do with Mark and Debbie. She wondered how long it would take to get back to Maureen. She hoped there wouldn't be any ramifications over this. That ship had hopefully sailed.

Right on the dot, three weeks later, Jack got a call from the manager at Diamonds International in Key West. "I shipped the package overnight, last night, and it should arrive tonight no later than five p.m.," he said. "It was shipped to the law firm at the address you approved."

"Thanks," Jack said and called Mary, who was out on errands, and Kristen to let them know that it would be at the law firm by five p.m.

Kristen said that she'd stay to accept the package and would hand deliver it that evening. "Buy ribs from Dinosaur and a bottle of champagne. I'll be there with bells on."

Like clockwork, Kristen pulled up their driveway by five forty-five p.m. She got out of her car and waved to Jack and Mary, who were looking out the window. She raised her hand and pointed at the package. She looked like a kid getting a new bicycle.

"Hi, guys. Here it is. Open it, Mary. I want to see your ring."

Mary laughed. "Fine. Thank you. How are you? Doing well? Great."

"Open the damn thing."

Mary carefully opened the bubble-wrapped package and pulled out two velvet-covered boxes, with Diamonds International emblazed on the top. She opened the smaller of the two boxes, which obviously held her engagement ring. She opened it and couldn't speak. She simply stared at it, and Kristen yelled, "It's gorgeous. Oh my God, it's gorgeous. Try it on, Mary. Please."

She did and held her hand up to show both Jack and Kristen. Jack grinned. Kristen was in tears. Mary didn't know what to say.

"Open up the wedding rings, but you can't try them on. That's bad luck," Kristen said.

She did, and Jack looked a little in awe. "Those are both beautiful, Mary. What do you think? Do you like your rings? I like mine."

"Like them? I love them? There absolutely beautiful, Jack. I don't know what to say," she said.

"Well, you're not going to eat ribs with that ring on are you?" asked Kristen kiddingly. "You're not, right? Jack, you bought ribs and champagne?"

"Let's go eat. I'm starved," said Jack.

The following day, Mary and Jack walked into the career center around ten a.m. They had a big night and slept in. They took a little grief from everyone until they noticed Mary's engagement ring. It was like time had stopped completely. Not only did the staff come over to them but also it seemed that every student had to give Mary a kiss and a hug. Karen and Sam were greatly surprised by the commotion and went down the stairs to see what was happening. Karen noticed right away from the expression on Mary's face and the glazed look on Jack's. Sam didn't have a clue. Debbie was at her desk and came over and gave Mary a big hug and a kiss. That meant more to Mary than everything else. Being accepted by Jack's children was very important to her. She never wanted them to think she was an interloper in their lives.

Debbie said, "Mary, that's wonderful. Thank you for marrying my father. He loves you very much, and Mark and I are very happy for both of you. Welcome to the family. You may be nuts but welcome anyway." She laughed and hugged her again.

CHAPTER 52

Jack and Mary had a lot to do in the next several months. The wedding was exactly four months away, on a Saturday at noon, at Saint Augustine's Church in late fall. Father Brady told them that they had to participate in Pre-Cana counseling. However, because of their age and background, Mary being an ex-nun, they were allowed to take the nine Pre-Cana assignments online. The cost was only $199 for couples and could be completed in three to six weeks for a total of twenty hours of online courses. They'd receive a certificate stating that they met all their obligations and could be married in a Catholic Church by a priest.

They both had to decide on who would be in the wedding. Jack was very careful about asking Mark to be his best man, and Mary was reluctant to ask Debbie to be a bridesmaid so as not to offend Maureen at this point.

"Mary, I was thinking of asking Mark, but that's out. How about if I ask Louis Freeman to be my best man? Do you think he'll accept? I really respect the guy, and he's done more for me than anyone, other than you, of course."

"I think he'd be thrilled if you asked him, and Addie would be pleased."

"I'll do that, and I want to see if John and Peter Traynor will be ushers. That's it. No more."

"Actually, that would be perfect. I had to think hard and long about maid or matron of honor. So as not to offend either Jane or Martha, by asking one or the other, I'll ask Kristen to be my matron of honor. Both Jane and Martha will understand, and they can be bridesmaids. Is that okay?"

"That sounds perfect. Then, there'll be three on each side. You can buy the dresses so there's no expense for them, and I'll buy tuxes for the three men and myself. Have you looked into wedding dresses?"

"Not yet but after I ask them, we can go to Latham to check out dresses next weekend. The dresses don't have to be extravagant and the less costly, the better. I just hope that there aren't too many alterations. That takes time. I'll help my mother find a dress by myself."

"Whom do think we should invite to the wedding? The reception will be at the career center as we discussed. Can I throw something out to you?"

"Sure."

"Can we invite all our current students and their families and the former graduates who're working on the construction crews? We can order two buses to pick them up in front of the Center at eleven a.m. and then bring them back to the reception after the ceremony."

"That's a great idea. I plan on inviting some teachers and staff from St. Augustine's and Catholic High and a few neighbors. You can invite Ethel Rounds, your ex-landlady. Is there anyone else?

"Other than Addie, who can sit with Mark and Debbie, the only ones I can think of are some of the partners and staff at the law firm and, of course, Tanya Fields, Pete's fiancée, and of course John Jefferson and Fred Tucker."

Mary said, "I think we'll have enough room and we can also put a large tent in the parking lot, heated of course, for any overflow. We should get the Old Daley to cater it. Maybe we should plan on a few hundred. It's not the money. I don't want it to turn into a circus. There shouldn't be any alcohol for the masses. I don't want to get into that. We can have some for our wedding party in our offices. We'll ask Karen and Sam before doing anything, of course."

"Sounds like a plan," said Jack.

And that's the way it went. There would be a small gathering for the rehearsal and a small dinner afterwards on Friday night.

"We can book the rehearsal dinner at the Century House in Latham for after seven-thirty p.m.," Jack said. "Maybe there'll be twenty all together. If more, we can always use the house on Old Plank. We can play that by ear and have the Old Daley cater it."

"You know you're not staying at the house Friday night, right? You can't see the bride before the wedding. Maybe I'm not overly traditional, but that goes without saying. I'll see you after the dinner Friday night when I walk down the aisle at noon, and not a minute before." She smiled.

"Got it. Maybe I'll bunk at John and Pete's house near the church. We'll figure it out."

"You'll figure it out. That's about all you have to do, mister."

"Yes, ma'am."

Jack was amazed how reasonable Mary was when it came to planning anything. She wasn't laid back, but she was very thoughtful about everything she did. Jack thought that came from her being an ex-nun, but it seemed to be a special grace she had. When Jack was panicking about the annulment, she said she didn't care. That surprised him but not really. That was the way she'd been since the first day he met her when he hired her at the old TCC, close to fifteen years ago.

Before the wedding, Jack and Mary wanted to make sure that all their plans were put into motion at least for the very near future. Long-range goals could wait but certain projects that were started needed to be completed. Jack was in the middle of negotiations to bring a few businesses into the village that would be critical to those living there. Before the rehabbing and construction began, the North Central area was considered derelict at best and a slum at worse. No national chain or even local businesses would bother to build their businesses in this area because of the blight and crime. Now that it was evident that the area was changing dramatically due to Jack's vision, the business community was starting to notice. But noticing and doing anything about it were two different things. Jack put out a questionnaire to the community to see what services they needed the most. They were right next to downtown with access to retail stores and doctor's offices, but they greatly needed a grocery store, a bank that would lend to the community and cash checks, and as simple as it sounded, a mini-mart, for those items that were needed at the last minute when everything else was closed.

To that end, Jack reached out to Aldi Food Market, a national chain from Germany, that specialized in reasonably prices groceries, fresh fruits, meat, and vegetables for communities that were left underserved. Aldi stores were half the size of large supermarkets and would fit in well in the community. Jack had property on River Street that consisted of derelict, falling down houses that could serve as the footprint for a small shopping center, right in the village. He contacted a local bank and the local mini-mart to offer them a plan that they couldn't refuse.

Jack would build all the structures needed through Evangeline Realty, Inc. and charge no rent to these businesses for the first five years. Then, the rent would be implemented on a sliding scale over the next five years until it hit market rate. The businesses would only have to pay for heat, light, and electric. Jack would also pay property taxes on the buildings because they'd eventually, be paying the taxes as a for-profit business. The businesses would have to sign an agreement to offer quality food at the lowest rate in the region for Aldi Food Markets. The mini-mart would offer gas at the lowest rate in the city, and the bank would have to guarantee that they'd not redline but would offer loans for businesses, mortgages for new homes and rehabs, and other accommodations. All the businesses would, in writing, hire local qualified individual graduates from the Evangeline Career Center programs.

In order to entice the commercial entities, Jack sat down with Mary, Karen, and Sam, and the staff to discuss their accomplishments to date. They were now beginning the third year of operation for the Evangeline Career Center. The center had served one hundred and fifty students in the first two years. One hundred and thirty received their high school equivalency, and one hundred went on to Hudson Valley Community College. It was unfortunate, but twenty dropped out of the program before graduating. It was just the way it was.

Fifty just graduated with an associate's degree, and half of those were going on to a four-year college. All the students received one hundred percent tuition scholarships, free and clear. Twenty of the twenty-five, not going to a four-year college were now graduates of the HVCC EMT program and working for the City of Troy's police and fire departments and the local ambulance service. All were making over $35,000 a year to start, with full benefits. Jack and the team were very proud. They also had fifty new students starting this fall, and they expected the same results.

As far as the community was concerned, the construction crews made up of students and contractors, working together, had rehabbed 100 homes in two years at a cost of over five million dollars, at no cost to the homeowners. Jack allocated an additional 150 houses for seven-point-five million dollars. Five of the twelve streets had been repaved, new sidewalks put in, and new LED lights on lampposts dotted the streets, making them much safer. The city took economic development monies for the street program. The city wouldn't charge full assessments on the upgrades to the homes for ten years.

The charter schools applications went in. They wouldn't hear for a while, but it looked favorable. The TCC building was in the middle of a major upgrade at a cost of almost a million dollars. The Troy Community Council, needless to say, was thrilled. The Diocese was holding out for more money for the church and lyceum to serve as a technology incubator training center, but Jack gave them an ultimatum that he'd start building his own tech center next spring. The career center program cost Jack over a million dollars a year as planned for the operation and over $500,000 was given in scholarships to graduates already. A million dollars had already been donated to the local non-profits, located in the village.

Adding up the cost of what Jack had spent or allocated already was staggering. He spent four million dollars for the career center; two million for the TCC when completed—after buying the building; ten million per year for ten years allocated to run the center; four million for the new mini-shopping mall on River Street—allocated; and two million allocated for a tech center. The charter school would cost eight million with half each from Jack and the Freemans, and another million dollars for the local non-profits, and, of course, the millions spent on all the rehabs.

So, in the report, Jack had invested or allocated forty million—out of the original fifty million dollars set up for the Evangeline Trust—over the next seven years, completing the ten-year program. There was still ten million left for other projects and continued scholarships for graduates of the center.

Jack also would have a little over sixty million dollars left of his own funds after gifting monies to his children, buying the houses on Old Plank Road and in Key West, two SUVS, and an annual donation to St. Augustine's for religious education, along with Mary. He knew that he'd eventually be dipping into that as well to make sure all of the projects were successful.

As he told everyone at the meeting, he still had enough money for many lifetimes. Mary still had her fifteen million, and she was prepared to start The Lansingburgh Academy Charter School, pay for religious education at St. Augustine's, a donation to the Lansingburgh Boys and Girls Club, and perhaps down the road, look into her lifelong dream of going to Cuba and maybe restarting Catholic schools on the island. She was sure that the ball was rolling that way after fifty years of an embargo.

The report was generated. It would be used for filing the federal 990 forms for the trust and federal taxes for the realty company and as a marketing tool to attract even more small business to the village. He also needed to pay the law firm almost one-point-three million dollars per year for its work, which was exceptional. That money would come from the tax-free interest generated from the AAA Municipal Bonds that were carefully selected the day Jack won the Powerball lottery. This generated almost three million dollars a year.

The last thing Jack wanted to do before heading for Key West to retire with Mary was to help his graduates start their own businesses, so they'd never have to rely on anyone else. This would stop the downward spiral of poverty—a hand up, a good education, self-esteem, and pride in their community. After paying the annual fee to the law firm, there would still be sufficient earnings to cover starting several new businesses.

CHAPTER 53

The wedding day—it was almost an afterthought but could have proved fatal. They forgot about getting their marriage license with all the confusion. Jack called the mayor, during the week before the wedding, and he told him to come right down with Mary. They did and immediately got their license. Mary dropped it off at St. Augustine's just to make sure. Father Brady put the license in the wedding folder as a precaution. Jack was nervous all week. Mary would hand her ring to Louis Freeman when he got to the church, and not until. She kept Jack's wedding ring close at hand. There would be no problems, she said.

The rehearsal and dinner at the Century House went well. Father Brady went through the ceremony at the church and answered all the questions they had. After the rehearsal dinner, Jack had said goodbye and headed out to drop off the Freemans and then to have a quick drink with the Traynors at the Burgh Grill, right around the corner from their house. It had been almost twenty-five years since Jack had done the same thing on the night before the wedding. It was a hell of a lot calmer when you were fifty and not twenty-five. He almost didn't make it to the church the first time.

It was Saturday morning, and Kristen, Jane, and Martha showed up around nine a.m. at the house on Old Plank Road. Debbie came by to help, and Mary thought that it was very sweet of her. She appreciated the gesture and the help.

Mary's mother came back with her after the wedding rehearsal dinner and stayed over. Just as a precaution, John Jefferson stayed at the house and would follow the limousine down to the church the next morning. Fred Tucker would be bunking with Jack to ensure the same thing.

The photographer showed up at ten a.m. She took group photos and photos of Mary and her mother, alone. They were set around eleven-fifteen a.m. All the pictures were taken, and Mary was ready to leave. She was nervous. You could tell.

Kristen smiled at her. "You waited a long time, and it'll be worth it. Trust me, Mary."

"I will, or is it I do? Oh, that's later. Let's get out of here," Mary said.

They left a few minutes later. It was only a ten-minute trip down the hill to the church. Mary would enter the front of the church around eleven forty-five a.m. They'd have pictures taken of her and the bridal party upon entering the church. After that, the photographer would go to where Jack and Louis were standing. She'd take pictures from there of the ushers and bridesmaids, and Mary and her mother, coming down the aisle.

At noon, Mary and her bridal party started down the aisle. The wedding guests were already seated. Father Brady and two altar servers were waiting at the foot of the altar. Jack and his best man, Louis, were waiting on the right side of the altar. "The Wedding March, Canon in D," started.

Leading the procession were the two bridesmaids, Jane and Martha, arm-in-arm with John and Peter Traynor, followed by Kristen as matron of honor, and then Mary and her mother. Mary's mother would then hand her to Jack at the altar.

Mary was stunning, to say the least. She'd chosen a classic gown design with the empire waist cinched just below the bust line. It was a timeless dress and featured a straight skirt for a streamlined silhouette. Mary's mother bowed to the clergy and then gave Mary to Jack. They both turned to face the altar, hand in hand.

A traditional Catholic wedding consisted of biblical readings, a sermon, the exchange of vows and rings and the Prayer of the Faithful followed by additional prayers. After the processional, the official ceremony began with a greeting by Father Brady. He gave a sermon, which contained personal references to Mary and Jack and hinted at Mary's former profession of faith as a nun. He also commented on how lucky Jack was to be marrying such a beautiful woman. The photographer was well placed to capture all of these moments.

Finally, Jack and Mary turned to each other. Father Brady said, "Mary Evans and Jack Manning have you come here freely and without reservation to give yourselves to each other in marriage?"

They both answered together, "Yes."

"Will you honor each other as man and wife for the rest of your lives?"

"Yes."

"Since it is your intention to enter into marriage, join your right hands, and declare your consent before God and his Church."

"I, Jack Manning, take you, Mary Evans, to be my wife. I promise to be true to you in good times and in bad, in sickness and in health. I will love you and honor you all the days of my life."

"I, Mary Evans, take you, Jack Manning, to be my husband. I promise to be true to you in good times and in bad, in sickness and in health. I will love you and honor you all the days of my life."

Father Brady blessed their rings and then Jack and Mary declared their consent.

After taking the ring from Louis, Jack placed the wedding ring on Mary's ring finger. "Mary, take this ring as a sign of my love and fidelity. In the name of the Father, and of the Son, and of the Holy Spirit."

Mary followed, taking Jack's ring from Kristen, placing the wedding ring on Jack's ring finger. She said, "Jack, take this ring as a sign of my love and fidelity. In the name of the Father, and of the Son, and of the Holy Spirit."

After Holy Communion, to conclude the Mass, Father Brady issued a final blessing and then said, "Jack, you may kiss the bride."

Jack did to the applause of those present.

With that, the Mass was ended. Father Brady then said, "Go in peace."

The assembled congregation said, "Thanks be to God."

The recessional started and "Ode to Joy" began. Together, arm-in-arm, they walked down the aisle as man and wife, out of the church. There wasn't a dry eye. Debbie and Mark looked very pleased. Jack and Mary, and the bridal party, formed a line at the front steps of the church. They kissed, hugged, and thanked everyone coming through the line. After everyone had been greeted, they went back into the church for formal pictures.

At that point, the two buses were refilled with those attending from the Evangeline Career Center and headed for the reception. The rest headed out of the parking lot to their cars and then down 5th Avenue to the reception. Mary and Jack would catch up with them in about forty-five minutes after all the pictures were taken. Jack asked Mark and Debbie to stay behind with them so they could get a picture of the four of them and then just Jack with his two children.

It was beautiful late fall day with a crisp chill in the air and blue skies. Perfect for picture taking, he thought. Jack got a very special picture with Louis and Addie Freeman. He'd have it framed and give it to them and hang another in their own living room. They hopped into the limousine with Mary's mother, the Freemans, Jane, Martha, John, Peter, and Tanya. They'd pick up their cars later.

Jack popped open a magnum of champagne. "Drink up folks. There won't be any alcohol for a while, other than the toast. Not until we can sneak into the offices later and have a few." He kissed Mary and downed his first glass of champagne.

They made it to the career center right before two p.m. Appetizers were already being handed out to the guests. The Old Daley team was moving quickly to serve all those attending. The buffet dinner would be held at three p.m. with dancing until seven p.m. After that, guests would be moved slowly toward the door. After everyone left, except the wedding party and a few close friends, they'd toast Jack and Mary on their special day.

Jack and Mary walked through the front door to the cheers and tinkling of glasses. The band played "Here Comes the Bride" as they settled into the head table in the front of the room. The adults would be served one glass of champagne each for the traditional toast by the best man. Many people were unaware of the friendship between Jack and Louis. There couldn't be two more dissimilar individuals in appearance, but they were kindred spirits in everything else.

Louis stood up, took the microphone, and asked for quiet. He then spoke. "Jack and Mary, you've made an old man and his bride of sixty years very happy. To find such friendship in the later years of your life is a true blessing. May you be as happy and in love as we are. Thank you, Addie. Thank you, Jack and Mary, and to the rest of you, from the old Irish proverb, 'May you be in heaven for one hour before the devil knows you're dead.' Cheers."

Everyone clapped and cheered, and Mary smiled at Addie and Louis as he joined her at the head table. She turned to Jack. "That was beautiful. You made a great choice in Louis Freeman, Jack."

The buffet was served. The waitress for the wedding party had set up a smaller version for them so they wouldn't have to stand in a big line. Most couples never got a bite to eat at their own reception. This was a great idea. As soon as plates were cleared, the band came back on, and the master of ceremonies asked for Mary and Jack to come to the center of the room for their first dance as a married couple. They played Jim Brickman's song, "Destiny," a wedding favorite for years. After Jack "dipped her" and the song ended, Jack went over and took his daughter's hand, and the band played Tug McGraw's, "My Little Girl."

The song meant a lot to Jack, and Debbie started to cry. He turned and gave her a kiss on the cheek. "I love you more than anything, Debbie. I hope you know that. Thanks for being here for Mary and me. It means the world to us."

She simply nodded, kissed his cheek, and laid her head on his shoulder. "Me too," she said.

Mary went over and took Mark's hand, and he followed her to the dance floor, halfway through the song. She said, "Mark, thank you and Cara for being here. Your father and I are very thankful. Your father loves you very much. I hope you know that."

"I do," he said, and they danced to the end of the song.

It was around seven p.m. when most everyone cleared out, except for the wedding party and a few close friends. Karen and Sam went to their offices and brought down a cooler filled with beer and wine and a few bottles of champagne. They toasted and drank until after eight p.m. when they locked up, and everyone headed out. The limousine was parked out front, and as Jack and Mary got in to head back home, Addie came over to them and handed them a brightly wrapped package and a card.

Addie said, "You've no idea what this means to us. You've added ten years to our lives and thank you. Please open my small gift when you get home, and the card is a simple donation in your honor."

Karen came over and handed Jack a small cooler with ice and a bottle of champagne. Little did Mary and Jack know that they'd be using the gift to toast their wedding at home, by themselves.

They made it back to Old Plank Road. John and Fred followed them home and then beeped and waved to say they were leaving them alone on their wedding night. As soon as they got through the door, Mary had to open the gift from Addie. Jack put the cooler on the counter and watched her as she carefully unwrapped the present. As she opened it, her eyes lit up.

Jack looked at her. "What's in the box?"

Mary gently took out two antique champagne flutes from the box. The note read, "'To Mary and Jack: These were our wedding flutes in which we drank our first sip of champagne together at our reception. Louise was twenty-one, and I was eighteen. The flutes are now sixty years old. This is our sixtieth wedding anniversary this year. Congratulations for a wonderful future together for two wonderful people. Love, Louis and Addie.'"

Mary sat down, just shook her head, and handed the card to Jack. "I can't believe this gift. It meant everything to them, and they gave this gift to us."

"Shall we toast them with their own flutes, Mary?"

With that, Jack uncorked the bottle of champagne and poured the two glasses half way. "To Louis and Addie and to you and me, forever."

"Forever," she said, and they drank their champagne, arm-in-arm and finished with a kiss. They headed toward their bedroom. They were exhausted, but the gift gave them new life as they headed toward the bedroom, arm-in-arm.

☙❧

On Sunday, they went to the ten-thirty a.m. Mass at Saint Augustine's. They sat in the back, so they didn't have to see too many people that they knew. As soon as the Mass ended, they headed back to the house after picking up a few sub sandwiches for lunch. They'd pack all day and then head to the airport on Monday for the two p.m. flight from Albany to Key West to start their honeymoon.

Jack finally broke out into a grin. "I have a surprise for you. I had Kristen book a private jet to fly us directly from the Albany airport to Key West International. I looked it up, and the flight is one thousand, one hundred and sixteen nautical miles and takes three and a half hours to get there. We'll do the same thing on the way home. If I never do another extravagant thing in my life, this would be the topper."

"A private jet?"

"Yes, with a full staff, lunch of lobster salad, champagne, and dessert and we'll be there no later than six p.m."

"How much did this set you back? I know you don't care, because we have it, but I'm just curious."

"Round trip, direct flight, private jet with full staff and lunch is thirty thousand dollars, okay?"

"I can't believe you did this."

"Neither can I, but I did so let's enjoy it. It'll never happen again," he said and laughed.

On Monday around one p.m., they got a ride and headed to the airport for their two p.m. takeoff. On the flight, they were treated like a king and queen. Mary brought her unopened wedding cards to look at during the flight. Most of the cards included a statement of a donation to a nonprofit in their honor. Those came from the law firm guests, the Traynors, the contractors, Mary's mother and one that meant more than all the rest was a donation from all their students, current and graduates, for $1,000 to buy books and work clothes for current members.

They were filled with pride. People understood what they'd undertaking and what it meant to them. They were surprised by the donation of $10,000 to Saint Augustine's Church's religious education program by Addie and Louis. This meant so much to Mary.

Epilogue

When Mary and Jack arrived at the Key West International Airport, Skip Lennon picked them up and then surprised them. After dropping off their luggage at their house, Skip told them that Linda wanted to see them right away. They walked up to Skip's house and opened the front door. Linda smiled and hugged them both as they walked into a small wedding reception in their honor.

Tom and Jamie arranged the entire event including a lobster bake. Tom's girlfriend and Jamie's boyfriend ran around and did all the little things, while the Lennons' house was decorated, the backyard was set up for the intimate wedding reception with a three-piece band playing everything from Jimmy Buffet to classic rock and roll. The neighbors were also invited to meet the newlyweds.

Joe and Julie Traynor showed up with the surprise of the day. Both Joe's father and brother, who were in the wedding, and his fiancée, Tanya Fields, came down for the party as well as to visit Joe and Julie. Evidently, John, Peter, and Tanya hopped on a plane early Sunday morning after the wedding to arrive the day before Jack and Mary arrived.

They knew that Jack had hired a private jet to fly down on Monday to avoid all the hassles and delays of changing planes. Jack let it slip during the previous week. Jack told them that they'd leave at two p.m. on Monday afternoon and be in Key West no later than six p.m. Evidently, Skip had previously told Joe and Julie about Linda's plans for a small reception at their house when they arrived. John, Peter, and Tanya had immediately booked their flights to Key West allowing them to arrive a day earlier after Jack let it leak.

Joe and Julie's daughter, Bella, was the hit of the party. They'd booked rooms right down the street, so when Bella became tired, Papa Traynor took her back to the hotel and put her to bed so the others could stay later. Pete and John Traynor wanted to help out with the cost of the party because Jack and Mary had been so good to them. The Lennons wouldn't hear of it. They were glad that Jack and Mary's hometown friends thought enough of them to come down to the Key West celebration.

During the party, Mary took Julie and Tanya to their home, up the street, to show them how their house turned out. It was simply beautiful. Jamie and Linda did a tremendous job helping Mary get everything done while she was up in Troy. FaceTime was a Godsend. New decorating technology also showed Mary exactly what the rooms would look like, not just the finished colors, but the actual kitchen and two-bath renovation in three-D. The place looked great. During the party, Jack brought Joe, Pete, and John over to the house to see what they thought of the construction. John said that they couldn't have done it better themselves for the price. John laughed and turned to Jack. "Not that it makes much of a difference."

"To this day, I still hate to pay more for something regardless of how much we have. It must be in my genes."

"I hear you," said Joe. "My father has the first nickel he's ever earned. He held it so tight, the buffalo's face vanished."

"Thanks, Joe. I love you too. At least you still have your work boots from the old days."

"That I do, Dad. That I do."

The Traynors were down for only a week. They still had over a hundred and fifty homes to help rehab before the village was completed. Jack told everyone at the party what the Traynors had done to help them along the way. Bringing in the contractors, watching their backs, setting up apprenticeships for the graduates and staying on top of the project, meant more to Jack than they'd ever know. Showing up for this party simply solidified their friendship.

The next day, after checking out of the hotel, John, Pete, and Tanya headed up to Joe and Julie's for the rest of the week before they flew back to Albany. Jack and Mary had been to their house before so they drove up for a cookout on the Saturday before they flew out. Joe and Julie's close friends, Mark and Louise Silva, were there for the weekend with their two kids, Jennifer and MJ. They brought camping gear so the kids could sleep in the backyard, freeing up room for the rest. Jack and Mary had a great time and told John and Pete that they'd be back in Troy in two weeks.

Jack said they liked to fly during the week when it was less crowded. Pete asked if they had a ride from the airport when they got back, and Jack said that his daughter, Debbie, would be picking them up. After graduation from Siena College, Debbie was staying at their Old Plank Road home for a while as she was completing her masters at U Albany. Mark and Cara and Debbie were already making plans to head to Key West for Christmas. Jack and Mary would head back to Key West after the holidays because they still had a lot to do with the village projects.

Jack though a lot about his ex-wife, Maureen. He'd heard that she and Chuck were still together, but just barely. Evidently, Chuck's short jail stint put a serious damper on their relationship. Jack had neither heard from nor seen Maureen since Chuck's arrest, well over a year and a half earlier. Maureen's quest for millions finally waned with the realization that none were coming. Jack never said anything to anyone, but when Maureen reached retirement age, he'd make sure that she didn't have major financial issues. After all, in spite of everything, she was still the mother of his children, and he had to give her that. They turned out great, probably in spite of both of them. He thanked his lucky stars that both his children came around and re-embraced him as their father. The father-daughter dance at the wedding reception was something he'd always remember.

When a lot of years had passed, he might bring the subject up to Mary. She was the nicest person he'd ever met, and he was sure, that when push came to shove, she'd give her okay. He was surprised when Debbie told him that the night he was brought home from the hospital that Mary had intercepted Maureen's call and told her never to call him again or there would be hell to pay. He'd never seen that side of her. Of course, she didn't have anyone to protect before, and for that he was grateful.

"Mary? Do you want to go to dinner?" asked Jack. They'd been there almost three weeks, and they'd be leaving in a few days and wanted to get as much Key West ambiance as he could to hold him over until the next time. He was getting used to the idea of spending more time in paradise. Who could blame him? he thought.

"I need to get gas in the SUV and buy my lottery tickets," she said.

"I forgot that you still buy tickets for Powerball. What's the payout this time?"

"Right now it's at four hundred twenty-nine-point-six million dollars. How do they know that to the dollar?"

"It's a guess, but they know pretty closely what it'll pay out. It's been building for about ten weeks now from what I've heard," he said.

"You still pay attention? Do you buy tickets?"

"Once in a while if it's big, like this one," he said. "As they say, 'You never know. A dollar and a dream.' How do you pick numbers? I still use the old numbers that I won on the birthdays of everyone who hated me at the time," he said, laughing. "I also get a few quick picks."

"Here's what I do," she said. "I follow the lottery site www.powerball.com and look for the numbers that have been picked the most. I pick the numbers selected the most and then I buy a ticket for the second numbers selected the most, all chosen since last year. It's all on the site. So, for this Powerball, for the first ticket I picked number twelve, the highest at ten times picked; then thirty-two, picked eleven times; forty, picked ten times; sixty-four, picked ten times; and sixty-nine, picked nine times. Otherwise, you're guessing from one to sixty-nine with no plan. For the Powerball, you have twenty-six numbers, and the most selected was six, picked five times. The second ticket with the second most picks will be the numbers five, twenty-five, twenty-six, forty-four, and sixty-six and the Powerball number five. I haven't won a thing so far, but I'm sticking with this."

"Sounds like a plan," he said.

They hopped into Mary's SUV. Yes, the SUV that she selected over Jack's choice of a convertible. They had room for one car or SUV, and she won. They bought a Toyota Highlander from Key West Toyota, less than a mile from their house. They'd purchased it the last time they came down to approve the renovations on the house. Mary handed the keys to Jamie and told her to drive it around and keep it maintained. She was thrilled and did exactly that. It was like getting a new luxury SUV for free.

They were headed to Duval Street for dinner, so they stopped at Dion's Quik Mart, right near Duval Street and Truman Avenue. Jack filled her tank and Mary went in and bought her tickets. Jack finished filling up the SUV, went in, paid for the gas, and bought his old ticket numbers and a few quick picks. He hopped back into the SUV. "Hey, this is your vehicle. Do I have to pay for the gas, too?" He smiled at her. "Good luck on your numbers."

"Being married is great," she said. "Thanks for filling up my tank, sweetheart. You have more money than me anyway."

"Yes, but I'm down to my last sixty million or so. We better start cutting back, or we won't make it."

"Please," she said.

They got back late, after midnight, knowing that this was their last dinner out in Key West. They'd be heading out in two days so they had to pack and make sure everything was set and the Key West bills were caught up until the next trip. Jamie would come over before they left for her next To Do List. She was thrilled to still be working for them since they'd been coming down more and more. She also loved driving around in the new Highlander.

It was the next morning. They slept in and had breakfast on the deck. They'd go out one last time for a moonlight boat ride with the Lennons that night as a farewell gesture from them.

Mary had her iPad in her hand and went to the Powerball site. They went to bed last night as soon as they got home and had already missed the ten fifty-nine p.m. broadcast. Ever since they'd moved into the house on Old Plank Road, Jack and Mary watched the Wednesday and Saturday drawing, at the beginning of the late news, for the Powerball numbers. It was tradition, but they missed last night's drawing.

"Jack, can you read me the Powerball numbers from last night? Here's my iPad."

He went to the site and read the news. "Evidently, there's been a winner, and only one winner, from last night's drawing. That's weird, Mary. The winner's from Florida." He read on. "Evidently, the winner was from right here in Key West."

"Can you read me the numbers? Please?"

"Sure. The numbers are five, twenty-five, twenty-six, forty-four, sixty-six, and the Powerball number is five. It's for a little over the announced four hundred twenty-nine-point-six million dollars, and there's only one winner."

Mary started to shake. "Jack, can lightning strike twice?"

"What do you mean?" he said.

"Here," she said, handing him the ticket.

"Oh my God," was all he could say.

The End

About the Author

Daniel J. Barrett was born in Rutland, Vermont and has lived his entire life in Troy, New York, ten miles north of Albany. He is a graduate of both Siena College in Loudonville, N.Y. with a BS in Finance, and from Rensselaer Polytechnic Institute in Troy, NY, with an MBA in Management. He has had a varied career, first as a commercial banker, then as the chief accountant and manager of financial and strategic planning for a large division of a major international corporation. He has extensive international experience, traveling worldwide.

Barrett has also served as the first executive director for economic development for a county in New York State, and as the first lay director for a Catholic shrine in Massachusetts. For the last twenty years, he has served as a financial, strategic planning, and educational consultant to corporations, non-profit organizations, colleges and universities, and government agencies.

Currently, he serves as a grant writing and development and strategic planning consultant for a major non-profit organization in the Capital Region of New York State. Barrett continues to live in Troy and has been married to his wife, Sandy, for 43 years. They have three children, Sean, Eileen, and Ryan, and four grandchildren, Shannon, Caden, Megan, and Declan.

An avid reader, and inspired by numerous authors, Barrett has read over 1,300 books in the last five years in preparation to write his first novel, *Conch Town Girl*. He continues to work, as a consultant, serving those most at risk in the Capital Region.